ZERO REGRET

(LOST KINGS MC #13)

AUTUMN JONES LAKE

ZERO REGRET

AUTUMN JONES LAKE

Zero Regret (Lost Kings MC #13)
Copyright 2019 All Rights Reserved.
Autumn Jones Lake
Digital ISBN # 978-1-943950-36-2
Paperback ISBN #:978-1-943950-37-9
Edited by: Kerri Boehm
Proofread by: Rosa Sharon

Cover Models: Justin Cox and Megan Napolitan
Photographer: Wander Aguiar
Cover Designed by: RBA Designs

ABOUT ZERO REGRET

Love happens when you least expect it. So does heartbreak.

I thought we were finally done with the lies.

Secrets? Sure, Lilly's still holding on to plenty of those.

My perfect woman is secrets buried under beautiful layers of deception.

She's the seductive siren bent on destroying my heart.

It doesn't make me want her any less.

Just like before, she's an addiction I can't break.

I'll never learn my lesson when it comes to her.

But I refuse to ever let her go.

One by one I'll unlock all her secrets.

I love a challenge. And I've never followed the rules.

Now that she's back in my life, she's mine forever.

And anyone who hurts or threatens her better prepare to die.

ACKNOWLEDGMENTS

The ladies in my "Lounge" on Facebook. Thank you so much for showing up with your love and kindness every day! Not only for me and for the Lost Kings but for each other as well!

Rosa, Jezzie, Liz, Dani, thank you for helping find those last minute things!

Thank you to Justin Cox for your enthusiasm and helping me promote Z's books!

Big thank you to Mr. Lake who continues to encourage all of my most evil ideas!

ULTIMATE SERIES READING ORDER

DEDICATION

The ultimate measure of a man is not where he stands in moments of comfort and convenience, but where he stands at times of challenge and controversy.

Martin Luther King, Jr.

CHAPTER ONE

ZERO

I THOUGHT WE WERE DONE WITH THE LIES.

How much deception am I supposed to take from the woman I love until I lose it and give up?

Lilly lied to me.

Again.

Ted's words won't stop echoing in my head. *I'm her fiancé.*

That can't be right. I asked her to marry *me* a couple hours ago.

She said yes.

But she'd already said yes to this guy.

This guy? Really?

He's still standing on the porch, awkwardly shifting from foot to foot.

He ain't gettin' an invitation inside from me.

"Dammit, Ted," Lilly snaps. "That's not true. We're not engaged."

"Seems like an odd thing to be confused about." My voice comes out laced with acid. I want nothing more than to jump on my bike and spray gravel all over Ted's shiny rental car. Fifteen, twenty years ago, I probably would've done exactly that the second this clown showed up and opened his mouth.

Today, I have a son. I need to be here *for him*. No matter what.

"Z, it's not true." Her fingers lightly brush against my bare chest, chasing the chill away.

I drag my gaze from Ted to Lilly. An hour ago, she was wrapped around me, whispering declarations of love in my ear while clawing at my back.

Was she doing the same out in California with this guy?

Her hand's still pressed to my chest and as I glance down, the loose sleeve of the robe she threw on when Ted came knocking slips down. The fine edge of the scar I asked about earlier peeks out and somehow, I just *know* it's connected to Ted. To everything.

It's painful. Personal. And she was about to let me in. Finally.

Before *Ted* interrupted.

I grip the doorknob tighter. "You got an engagement ring?" I ask Lilly.

Too stunned by my change in attitude, Lilly shakes her head. "What?"

Ted's such a swell guy, he pipes up and answers for Lilly. "It's back in California."

That's all I need to know.

"You can talk to her tomorrow, Ted," I say. "Thanks for stopping by." With that dismissal, I shove the door closed, slamming it in Ted's face with a satisfying *bang*.

Outside, he mumbles something, but a minute later, a car starts up and speeds down the driveway.

I turn and face Lilly, who's already backing away from me. "Start talking."

"Ted's just a friend."

"I don't give a fuck about *Ted*."

Like a snake, I strike, grabbing both of her wrists in one hand and turning them over. Ruthlessly, I shove both her sleeves out of my way. "What happened?"

She jerks back, but I hold on tighter.

"An accident."

"Bullshit. What accident leaves identical scars like this? Try again."

"Z," she pleads.

"And I know damn well you didn't have them before, so don't even try."

"I can't." She's pleading with everything in her to let this go. Her big brown eyes brimming with tears, her beautiful face, her body that she's desperately trying to pull out of my grip. "Z, I can't."

"You can and you will. I think I've been more than patient. I asked you to *marry me* before. You said yes. Then a few hours later, some clown I've never even heard of shows up claiming he's your fiancé? I'm out of patience with you, woman."

"You're hurting me."

The high, thin whine to her voice jars me enough to release her. She retreats but I'm not done with her. No way.

Step for step, I track her into the living room.

Lilly's a strong woman. Almost nothing seems to make her flinch. Guilt lashes at me for the way she's unraveling because of my questions.

"Who hurt you?" I ask.

She jerks her head up. "What?"

Gentler this time, I reach out and trace my finger over the soft inside of her arm. "Who did this?"

Tears I didn't want to cause roll down her cheeks. She opens her mouth and slicks her tongue over her lips a few times before finally giving me the answer I never expected.

"I did."

CHAPTER TWO

Lilly

A CLOUD OF PAIN WRAPS AROUND MY THROAT, THREATENING TO SUFFOCATE me.

What a nightmare.

I almost wish Z hadn't chased Ted away, because I'd like to strangle him.

My own fault. Weeks ago, I should've yanked up my big girl panties and told Ted our marriage–of *his* convenience–couldn't happen.

That I could have handled with a simple phone call.

Z standing in front of me demanding answers, I can't deal with that. I should have told him about Ted, even if I can't tell him the whole story. But my lies have become a part of me to protect myself. It's my story. The story of two Lillys. The one before. And the one after. Both of them are full of pain and regret. Regrets I can't erase. Pain I don't want to share with anyone. Especially Z.

There's a reason I keep my arms covered as much as possible.

I don't care what anyone *else* thinks.

It's me. I can't stand the reminder of my own weakness. And the events that led me to the darkest time of my life. To attempt something I never thought I was capable of.

"Tell me why," Z persists in a much gentler tone than he used a few seconds ago. "What happened?"

Unable to force out the words, I shake my head and more tears burn my eyelids.

"Here," he says, pushing a glass of water into my hands.

He's quiet while I take a long sip, but then he sits on the couch next to me and pulls my hands into his lap. "Talk to me. You used to say you never wanted kids. Did...you...did this happen when you found out you were pregnant?"

His struggle to understand is clear in his voice so the question doesn't offend me. Besides, he's right. I didn't know how much I wanted to be a mother until Ted pressed that tiny sonogram picture in my hand.

"No." My voice comes out more than a harsh whisper. "I found out I was pregnant *because* of this." I trace my finger down the line on my left arm. It's straighter than the one on my right. It's deeper too. I'm right-handed. "Chance saved me," I whisper.

Maybe that sounds ridiculous. But it's true in so many ways.

"Well, technically Ted saved me," I add.

"How?"

"He was the doctor on-call at the hospital."

What words can explain it to a man like Z? Everything about him radiates strength and bravery. Qualities that appeal to me more than ever. With Z, I always feel safe and protected.

He seems invincible and I've never wanted to drag him into anything that could bring him harm.

"Lilly, talk to me. Why does he think you're engaged?"

Ah, that one weakness of Z's—his caveman mentality—might actually allow me to escape this conversation with a shred of dignity. He wants to know about my relationship with Ted. *Not* the intimate, painful details that led to us meeting in the first place. *That* I can handle.

"It'll sound silly to you."

"It was important enough for him to fly across the country."

"Well, we're friends, too." Although, after he showed up without warning and told Z we were engaged, I may have to rethink our friends status.

"Do you live with him?"

"No," I answer with more force than intended. "He did ask me to move in with him before I came home."

His jaw tightens. "You and my son?"

6

"Yes."

"And what did you say?"

I swallow hard. Z's not going to like this answer. "That I'd think about it."

"So, I didn't even know my kid existed, but you were going to *think about* moving in with another man?"

"It's not like that."

"Then tell me what it's like," he insists. By the tightness of his jaw, I can tell his patience is about to snap. "I never asked," he says. "But you sort of implied you hadn't been dating anyone."

"We weren't dating. We're friends." My gaze skips to the front door. "Although, I'm not so sure about that anymore."

Z doesn't see the humor in my gripe. "Friends don't usually ask friends to marry them."

Do I share Ted's secret? After the bomb he tried to drop on my life, I should. It still feels wrong, but it feels worse to keep any more secrets from Z. "Ted has a...complicated relationship with his family."

"What's that got to do with anything?"

I should've known an answer that vague wouldn't satisfy Z.

My teeth sink into my bottom lip until it stings. I swipe my tongue over the spot and catch Z's eyes following the movement. I don't even have it in me to try and distract him with sex. Not when he's been so patient and deserves some answers.

"Lilly?" he prompts.

"His family's politically connected and he has certain obligations he's supposed to fulfill."

"Don't tell me." Z lets out a dark chuckle. "He's gay and needs a wife for cover."

When I don't laugh, he cuts a look my way. "You're kidding. Who still does that?"

"You'd be surprised."

He snorts. "I thought California was so progressive."

"Maybe. But his family isn't. There's an inheritance and he needs to be married...to a woman to collect it. When enough time had passed, we would've gotten divorced."

"Why would you even consider something like that?"

I sigh and almost regret admitting this. "I know what it's like to be scorned by your family for things that are out of your control. He helped me when I needed it and I wanted to do the same."

By the way Z's jaw keeps flexing, he's having a hard time objecting to my reasoning.

"That's it?"

"Well, I have a lot of…medical debt. From…before…and from when I had Chance and he was going to help me with that."

"Lilly, that's *my* responsibility. Not some guy who's too spineless to tell his family to fuck off."

Once again, in his own crude way, Z proves he's so damn honorable I have no business being with him.

"Mommy?" Chance calls.

I breathe a sigh of relief.

"We're not done," Z says in a low voice, right before Chance shuffles into the living room.

Our son stands there, rubbing his eyes and pouting. "It was loud. And someone yelled." He looks around the room, his gaze finally landing on Z. He scowls as if he blames Z for every new nocturnal noise in his life.

I'd laugh except there's nothing funny about tonight. Instead, I hold out my hands and Chance eagerly runs over and lets me scoop him up. He puts his little arms around my neck and rests his cheek on my shoulder so he's facing Z.

"Did you yell at Mommy?" The accusatory tone of the question might be downright hilarious under other circumstances.

Z reaches over and runs his hand over Chance's back. "No, buddy. Sorry if we woke you. Your mom and I were having an interesting talk. That's all."

Interesting. I snort. That's one way to put it.

Chance places his hands against my shoulders and pushes backwards to stare at me as if he needs confirmation.

"That's all it was," I say. "I'm sorry if we scared you."

"Not scared," he insists. "Of nothin'."

"That's my boy." Z chuckles and it seems to put Chance at ease.

Z

There isn't a sight in this world more beautiful than my woman with our son in her arms.

Even if I do want to strangle her at the moment.

She frustrates the fuck out of me.

Lilly has to be the tightest bundle of secrets and contradictions I've ever encountered. Still, there isn't another person in this world I want to unlock as much as her.

I don't like that we woke Chance, though. I spent years hiding in my room while my parents fought when I was a kid. It's not what I want for my son. Not ever.

The urge to leave and get away from them before I do some damage rises up and I barely hold it together.

"Can I have a doggie?" Chance asks, breaking up the tightness in my chest.

Lilly gives him a soft smile and taps his chest. "You have two doggies. Remember? Ziggy and Zipper?"

Something about the easy way she reminds him of my dogs reassures me everything's going to be okay. Whatever this fuckery is between us right now will get resolved. And when it does, all this turmoil and confusion will have been worth it.

"Yes!" Chance grins and looks to me to make sure it's true.

"Yeah, buddy. They're going to come stay with us at the new house. They'll look after you and Mommy while I'm at work."

He lets out a big yawn and Lilly scoots to the edge of the couch. "Let's put you back to bed."

"Nooooo." Chance's little cheeks turn red and tears well up in his eyes. "I wanna sleep with you."

Lilly hesitates, a troubled expression wrinkles her forehead. "Why, baby?"

He squeezes his arms around her neck even tighter. "Because."

Her gaze slides my way and I shrug, unsure of what she expects me to say. Does she think I'm an asshole who's going to tell my kid to 'man up' or something? He's two-and-a-half years old, we woke him up in the middle of the night, and now he wants his mom. I'm not stupid. I get it.

All my concerns turn into a puddle of mush when he reaches one little hand toward me. "Daddy, too."

"Yup," Lilly reassures him. "Daddy's coming too."

When I find my voice, I answer, "Right behind you."

A few minutes later, Chance is snuggled down smack in the middle of the mattress. Lilly sighs and shakes her head. "He hasn't wanted to sleep with me in a long time."

Ten thousand pounds of guilt threatens to crush me. I had to be a big man, slamming the door in Ted's face tonight instead of acting like a responsible father. "I shouldn't have—"

"No," she cuts me off. "Stuff happens. He'll be okay." She tosses her robe on the chest at the foot of the bed and slides under the covers.

Careful not to disturb Chance, I get in on my side and reach over to shut the lamp off. "Think we should leave it on?" I ask.

"No. As long as we're here when he wakes up, he'll be fine."

"I'm not going anywhere."

I can't see her expression, but she reaches over our son and rests her hand on my arm. "I know you're not."

Twisting my arm, I capture her hand and bring it up to my mouth, slowly brushing my lips against her knuckles. "We still need to talk, Lilly."

"I know," she whispers.

I turn her hand, kissing her open palm down to her wrist. She laughs softly. "That tickles."

"Shh...don't wake him again."

We're both quiet for a few minutes, but it doesn't sound like she's asleep yet.

"I meant what I said earlier."

"You said a lot of things," she whispers.

"That I love you."

The bed shifts and her warmth spreads over my skin. She presses her forehead against my chin for a second before reaching up to kiss my jaw. "I love you too," she whispers. "Don't ever doubt it."

It's not our love I doubt.

It's everything else.

CHAPTER THREE

Lilly

THE NEXT MORNING, WE'RE JARRED FROM SLEEP BY CHANCE JUMPING ON the bed and finally flopping down next to Z.

"Sleep okay, buddy?" Z rasps, barely opening his eyes.

"Yup!" Chance seems to have forgotten all about last night. Even asks why he's in my room, which is a relief.

The weight of Z's stare follows me as I lead Chance out of the bedroom. It takes Z a few minutes, but eventually he finds me. "We still need to talk."

"I'm not marrying anyone but you, Z," I say without turning around.

His warm, solid body presses up against my back and he wraps his big hands around my wrists, forcing me to drop my spatula on the counter. He uses his chin to push my hair out of his way and slides his lips against my neck. "Say that again."

I can't form a coherent thought, let alone remember what I said five seconds ago with him wrapped around me like a wall of warmth, desire, and safety. "You're the only man I've ever wanted to marry."

"Yeah?" He kisses right below my ear. "Remember Rock and Hope's wedding?"

"How could I forget?"

"I couldn't stop thinking about what kind of bride you'd be," he says matter-of-factly.

A tear slips down my cheek, but I can't brush it away without escaping his hold—something I don't want to do. "Really?"

I wish my voice didn't come out so damn wobbly. He notices and leans in closer, kissing my tear-tracked cheek. "That bother you?"

"Not at all." I sniffle and laugh at the same time. "I might have questioned whether you'd slip on a suit or tux for your wedding."

"*Our* wedding," he corrects. "You're trying to distract me again. We need to talk."

Ice-cold fear spreads through my chest. I can't have the conversation he wants to have with Chance around. It doesn't matter how old he is, I don't want any of it poisoning his young mind.

"My brother's been asking about taking Chance for an afternoon."

"Okay," he answers, the *what does that have to do with anything* question clear from his tone.

"Chance...He can't be here for the talk you want to have."

By the way he staggers backwards, Z didn't expect that answer.

"What more do you need to know, Z?"

He recovers from the shock quickly. "Nothing less than everything."

His phone buzzes on the counter and he snatches it up. "Fuck."

"Do you have to go?"

"Club stuff." He frowns and some of the anger I remember from last night bleeds into his expression. "We're not done with this, Lilly." He closes his eyes. "I'm still...pissed."

"I know."

"But I love you and we'll get through it." As hard as he sounds, warmth and conviction still shine through easing some of my skittishness. "Rooster should have some house listings for me. I'm going to check them out with Murphy and Teller later. Unless you want me to wait for you?"

"No, don't delay anything. I trust you." My mouth turns down. "Although, I don't think Teller likes me all that much."

"Fuck." He bites his lip, but I don't think he's upset with me.

Why did I even bother saying anything right now? Because the move is making me anxious? Or something else?

"It's got nothing to do with you, Lilly. He's going through some stuff. If he really gives you attitude, tell me."

"No, I shouldn't have said anything at all. I was joking."

His phone pings again and he groans. Glancing down, he types out a quick response to whoever's looking for him. After sending it, he gives me a crooked smile. "You better be here when I get back. I *will* chase your gorgeous ass down this time."

It's the worst kind of joke for either of us to make, but I laugh anyway. "You're coming back?"

"You're goddamned right I am. You can have a thousand more guys out there waiting for you to answer their marriage proposal. You're mine."

It's absurd, funny, and awful all at the same time. Yet, still somehow sweet. I twist my fingers into his cut and yank him closer. "Get back here soon."

CHAPTER FOUR

Z

The ride downstate helps clear my head, but not much. All the pieces floating around in my brain usually seem to sort themselves out when I'm on my bike. This time, it's harder.

I have my suspicions, but she wouldn't confirm or deny anything with Chance in the house. Lilly wasn't being dramatic. She wants to protect our son and I respect that, no matter how frustrating.

I don't have lots of time before I need to be downstate, but I can't help stopping at the upstate clubhouse.

It feels weird to ride through the gates wearing another charter's bottom rocker. No one treats me differently, but it still doesn't sit right.

Rock greets me out front with a happy, welcoming hug. "Fuck, Prez, look at the smile on your face. You need me to go away more often?"

"No, fuckface. Just glad to see you. What're you doing?"

"Headed back, but it didn't feel right riding by without stopping in."

"Good choice. Soon you won't be riding by at all, right?"

"Planning to look at a place today."

"Murphy said they found a nice area. Safe for the kids."

I glance around at the clubhouse and the woods surrounding us. This has been my home for a long time and I'm not okay with leaving it. It's where I want to raise my son. "It's still not home."

"Yeah, this is some fucked-up shit." He glances at the woods towards his house. "We all know it's a possibility in this life. Doesn't take much. But fuck, shooting him in his own clubhouse's driveway?"

"That's the part that keeps sticking with me."

"How do you feel about the brothers down there? Anyone strike you as especially power-hungry?"

"If they are, they're playing a long game. No one's complained about me taking Sway's place."

"That right there should make you worry."

"Right?" I laugh even though it's not funny. "Jesus, Sway's been trying to stay off of Priest's radar since National."

"Instead, someone made sure he stayed on it."

"Makes you wonder if it was intentional or someone fucked up. Or..." I stare at him for a minute, contemplating my next words. I can trust Rock with anything, but even kicking this idea around is dangerous. "Priest ordered it."

Rock's slow to answer. "Yeah, that crossed my mind, too."

"I hate saying it, but Sway pushed him pretty far and who knows what he's fucked up since then. He wouldn't have had any confidence in Shadow after that arrest."

"Even before that he hinted at us taking over down there."

"Fuck, I'm surprised they're not more suspicious of me."

"Why do you think I sent Murphy and Teller with you? Fuck, I'd be right there with you if I could, brother."

"Thanks, Rock."

He takes a more serious look at me. "Everything okay?"

I run my hand through my hair while I think about where to start. "Did Hope talk to you about the subpoena Lilly got?"

"A little. She didn't have a lot of details."

"Yeah, neither do I."

Rock's one of the smartest people I know, so it doesn't surprise me terribly when he asks, "You think it's connected to why she left?"

"Sort of. I can't put my finger on it exactly." I hesitate, unsure about sharing this. If what Lilly suggested, that she hurt herself, is true, trying to take the easy way out isn't exactly a decision that's respected in our world. A brother trying to take his own life better pray he succeeds, otherwise his club might finish the job.

But Rock's never been one to judge and won't run his mouth to anyone else about it. "She has these marks down her arms." I trace a line down to my wrist, but I have to force the words out. "Like she might have hurt herself."

"Jesus. What'd she tell you?"

"Says that's how she found out about Chance. That he saved her."

His expression softens. "Did you ask why?"

"Some other stuff came up." I don't want to tell Rock about Ted's visit. I can only imagine what he already thinks of Lilly. No need to make it worse. In my mind, Ted's already a non-issue. I'm not nearly as pissed about it as I was last night. "She's a goddamn fortress."

He snorts. "Why do you think that is?"

"She's embarrassed?"

"Maybe."

"She thinks I'll get mad?"

"At her or someone else?"

"Fuck. I don't know. I feel in my gut that the two things are related."

"You think she left to protect you or herself?"

I frown at the question. "Why me?"

His expression hardens and he crosses his arms over his chest. "What would you have done if you found out someone hurt or threatened her?"

That's easy. "Kill the motherfucker."

"Right. We both know that corruption investigation didn't happen overnight."

"You think one of those senators hurt her to keep her quiet?"

He shrugs. "You'll have to ask her."

"It's not a conversation she wants to have with Chance around."

"Even more reason you need to have it." He tilts his head in the direction of his house. "Chance can always stay with us."

"Thanks, brother."

He pulls me in for a quick hug.

"I'm supposed to sit down with everyone in a couple hours."

"Word of advice—"

"Oh, Christ." I smirk and wave my hands at him. "Lay it on me, Prez."

Rock doesn't smile. "You can't have this weighing on your mind and handle business downstate. So, I'd get those answers from her sooner rather than later."

CHAPTER FIVE

Lilly

Alex seems to be over his snit about Z paying off Dad's debt. At least when I call and ask if he can watch Chance for a couple of hours, he doesn't mention it. When I actually arrive at his house, it's a different story.

"Aleth! Aleth!" Chance yells as soon as we pull into the driveway and Alex steps outside.

"You're going to hang out with Uncle Alex for a couple hours. That okay with you?"

"Yup!" He's wiggling and eager to get out of his car seat, so thankfully Alex pops open the back door.

"How's my boy?" he asks, swinging Chance up into his arms. "You been good for Mommy?"

Chance sneaks a quick look at me before answering my brother. "Yup."

Inside, he sets Chance down and points out some new toys gathered by the couch, which my son is all too eager to check out.

"You don't have to buy him stuff all the time, Alex."

"Why not? I want him to have his toys and stuff here so he's comfortable. I'm so happy you're home now so I can see him more."

Here's where I should probably mention I'm moving downstate with Z. "Thank you."

"What's going on? You seemed agitated on the phone. Have a fight with—"

"Watch what you say," I warn.

He stares at me with a smirk forming on his lips. "You ask him about Dad and the money?"

"Yes, I did. And I think the words Dad and you should be looking for are *thank you*. Z didn't have to bail him out."

"Why aren't you more upset your son's father associates with criminals?"

I shrug because the question's absurd given the circumstances. "Why aren't *you* more concerned our father's borrowing money from mobsters?"

He snorts and shakes his head. "I guess you got me there, sis." His face turns more serious. "I worry about you."

"I'm safer with Z than anyone I've ever been with."

"You honestly believe that? Because I've known guys like him, Lilly. They don't think twice about passing their women around. I don't want that—"

I snort, cutting him off. "You haven't spent any time around Z or his brothers. Trust me, that's not a thing in Z's club."

"All right." He holds up his hands. "So, what was so important today?"

"I have some errands to run."

"And where's baby daddy?"

I shoot a glare at him. "Work."

"Shaking down more people for money?"

"You really need to stop that." I cock my head. "Did it occur to your judgmental ass that it's a good thing Z stepped in?"

"Why's that?"

"You really think Dad had the money to pay back the debt?"

"What are you trying to say? He paid it back for Dad?"

I continue staring him down, which isn't easy since my brother's almost a foot taller than me.

"Why would he do that?" He sneers.

My temper flares. "Well, he already has an all-access pass into my panties," I hiss, low enough that Chance can't hear us. "So that's not the reason."

"Thanks for that nightmare-inducing image."

I shrug. "It's my father and his son's grandfather. That's why he did it."

For once my know-it-all brother has nothing to say.

"It's a one-time thing, Alex. If Dad screws up again, he'll have to figure it out on his own."

Still, he's quiet.

"What's wrong? No witty comebacks?"

"All right, all right. I'm sorry. If he really did that for Dad, then yeah, I guess I owe him."

"Knocking off the thug and baby daddy jokes will be thanks enough."

An almost guilty expression crosses his face. "We've always teased each other, Lilly."

"This is different, and you know it."

"Why? Are you gonna marry him?"

I stare at my brother. "Yes."

He blows out a breath. "Is that what you want?"

It doesn't feel awkward to admit it out loud. "It is."

"Good. All right." Slowly, he holds out his arms. "Come here." He envelops me in the kind of brotherly hug I remember from when I was younger and pats my hair. "I really do worry about you. And Chance. Whatever Z's involved with, I don't want it to ever hurt you."

I heave out a deep breath. Nothing could hurt me more than I've already been hurt. "Z's very good to me. He's a good father to Chance. That's all that matters."

"I hope so."

Once I've dealt with my brother, it's time to deal with Ted. After I track him down at his hotel, I push my way in the door, slamming it behind me.

"How could you, Ted?" I'm still fuming. We've only been friends for a few years, but he's been there for me through some of my darkest moments. Apparently, I didn't know him as well as I thought.

"I didn't mean for it to come out like that." The palpable disappointment in his voice might be the only thing that stops me from kicking him in the shins. "I knew when I saw him. You're not coming back to California, are you?"

"That's your excuse for coming to my house in the middle of the night and trying to blow up my life?"

"I wasn't trying to—"

"I told you things were complicated, and I needed to sort things out with Chance's father before I could give you an answer."

"Yeah, and I guess I was selfishly hoping he wouldn't care."

Of course, he was. "That's not who he is at all."

He nods and shoves his hands in his pockets. "How'd he take it? Must've been rough."

Tears prick my eyelids as shame washes over me. Z's been nothing but forgiving and all I've done is lie. "Rocky at first, but he's been more understanding than I would've been."

"Yeah, I got the impression he cares for you deeply." He sighs. "Chance is happy?"

An image of Chance hugging Z and calling him Daddy springs into my mind and I smile. "We told him a while ago and he accepted it pretty quick." I wobble my hand back and forth. "A little jealousy here and there if Z and I get too close."

Ted throws his head back and laughs. "Well, he's had your undivided attention his whole life so that makes sense." He stops laughing and holds my gaze again. "Your parents?"

"Same. Judgmental and critical."

"I'm sorry. Lots of lousy parents somehow come through for their grandchildren. I was hoping that'd be the case for you. That meeting their grandson would warm them up."

"Not so much." I snort and shake my head. "I tried bringing Z over and that didn't go over well either."

Ted actually huffs out a laugh. "He didn't seem like the type to tolerate anyone treating you unkindly."

I snort, because boy is that an understatement. "You would be correct."

He reaches out and squeezes my shoulder. "Good. You need someone to stand up for you with them. I understand why it's difficult for your brother. Even so, someone should've done it a long time ago."

"Thank you. For understanding. I'm sorry—"

"Don't be. I just want you to be well. I want you and Chance to be happy."

"We are."

"That's all I want." He glances at the clock. "Have you had lunch? I'm starving. Show me someplace good around here."

I'm still upset he flew across the country to get an answer from me—not that he can't afford it. Maybe my irritation shows on my face.

He settles his hand on my shoulder. "I'm always here for you. If you change your mind or anything."

"I appreciate that. Everything you've done for us. But I won't change my mind about Z."

CHAPTER SIX

Z

Rock's right. I can't wait much longer to extract some answers from my girl. I also can't leave the club I've taken over in the lurch.

Everyone's waiting for me inside Sway's clubhouse. I may be president now, but this place will always feel like "Sway's clubhouse" to me. Rooster greets me as soon as I step inside and loudly asks to speak to me in private. "Got some of those house listings you asked about."

I glance around at the brothers waiting outside the chapel. "Give us a minute."

"Take your time, brother," Jigsaw calls out. He's a brother around my age. Spent a lot of time on the road before taking over as Sway's Road Captain. Obviously, he isn't sure how he feels about me taking over as president. Since I'm not sure how I feel about it myself, I don't take it too personally.

Rooster shuts the door to Sway's office behind us.

"A bit dramatic to go over some house listings, brother." I nod to the closed door.

Rooster shakes his head and steps aside so I can move behind the desk and shuffle through the few papers that piled up while I was away.

The first stack on top is indeed the house listings. "This right in the same neighborhood Teller and Murphy are moving into?"

He taps the top sheet. "Right next door to their place."

"Perfect." I'm not sure how they'll feel about having me up their asses, but too bad. I want Lilly to have familiar people around her and when Heidi visits, it'll be nice for the kids to play together. "I'll take a look at it later."

"The agent said you can drop by this afternoon. Give her a call and she'll meet you there."

"Thanks." I set the folder to the side and raise an eyebrow at Rooster, who's still blocking the door.

"That's not the only reason I wanted to talk to you." He glances over his shoulder.

"You worried someone's gonna bust in or something?"

"No." He squares his shoulders and faces me. "I've shared a patch with these guys for a long time."

Not liking the tone this conversation's taken, I stand and place my hands on the desk. "Yeah?" I gesture for him to turn around. "Your top rocker say something different than mine?"

He shakes off my sarcasm and keeps his feet planted where they are. "I want you to understand, I'm not a snitch or a kiss-ass. I don't give a fuck about getting on your good side. All I want is what's best for this club. Always."

"I've never doubted that, Rooster. You about to give me a reason I should?"

"No." He glances at the door again. "Shadow's been making noise about pushing into New Jersey territory."

"What? Why?" The Vipers MC run most of New Jersey and, up until two years ago, ran a small portion of New York. Until my charter put them down and took over their territory. Vipers are all the bad stereotypes about MCs rolled into one club and I'm not eager to tangle with them again unless it's absolutely necessary.

"He thinks we should dominate more territory. He's been talking about going to DeLova to back us up."

Jesus Christ, just what we need. Owing DeLova more favors. Sway's an idiot sometimes, but I can't believe he'd approve. "Where did Sway land on this issue?"

"He wanted no part of it. As long as Vipers stayed out of our territory, he wasn't going to push into theirs."

Well, thank fuck for that. "Good. So, what's the problem?"

I already sense what's coming.

"With Sway down, Shadow's been starting this call to take over at least upper New Jersey."

Funny how that happened. "That's still an hour from here. We don't have the numbers to hold that territory down."

"Well, he's been rumbling about it and I'm pretty sure he's trying to pull support from some of the newer members who don't know any better."

Sure, newer members might not understand all the nuances or things involved with dominating a territory. Especially if they didn't prospect long enough. Things like which politicians and law enforcement are receptive to bribes, what other crews might work in the area, and business potential. A whole host of things that don't sound as fun as 'kill rival bikers' and 'blow shit up' to a newer member who doesn't remember the days of serious anarchy, bloodshed, and chaos.

"Where's Steer?"

"He's a hard fuck no. Jigsaw, Hustle, Grip, Suds, they're all full-stop against expansion."

"All right. Good." I give him a pointed look. "I assume you're also a hard no?"

"Damn right. Using Sway's shooting as a way to get around his orders ain't right. Besides that, we don't need the hassle. I know the shit you guys went through getting rid of the Vipers up in your area. No need to swat at that wasp's nest unless it comes at us first."

"Good. Who *do* I need to worry about?"

"Smoke. Old fuck misses the 'glory days' of being able to shoot people in broad daylight and plant car bombs."

"He miss prison too?"

"Apparently."

Pinching the bridge of my nose, I sit and stare at the papers on the desk, not really seeing anything. "I'll address it today."

Rooster shifts and meets my eyes. "Cut him off at the knees before he gathers more support."

That's exactly what I plan to do.

CHAPTER SEVEN

Z

"Settle down." I slam the gavel against the table and everyone shuts up. I'm guessing Sway bangs this thing a lot around here.

Not to be a dick, but Sway's club is into a lot of things Rock, Wrath, and I decided our charter wouldn't touch a long time ago. Petty bullshit that causes a lot of stress, risks arrest, and doesn't bring in enough cash to be worth the trouble.

Sparky set Sway up with a small pot farm for personal use a while back. I haven't floated the idea of expanding into a business yet for three reasons. One, I don't want to introduce too much change into this club too soon. Two, I don't want it to seem like I'm trying to turn their club into a copycat of upstate. Three, while lucrative, growing marijuana for sale and profit isn't easy. Sparky is a one-of-a-kind individual. I haven't decided if anyone here is smart or dedicated enough to make it work.

So, for now, I listen to a report from Suds on the coin-operated laundry the club runs. It's the perfect cash business to launder the money they make from running guns out to Stump's club and beyond. Can't say I'm thrilled to now be overseeing this since gun-running's another thing my charter extracted itself from years ago. Call me a pussy, but doing hard time isn't how this biker wants to spend his days.

Honestly, there are plenty of enterprises I'd rather not dirty my hands with. I enjoy my freedom way too much.

Next up, the pawn shop downtown. It's really a front to move stolen goods. More petty bullshit and scrutiny from law enforcement. No wonder this charter has been struggling lately.

To say I'm unimpressed now that I've gotten a peek behind downstate's curtain is an understatement. I've had my suspicions—we all have. But for the most part, each club is allowed to operate the way the members choose. As long as it doesn't reflect badly on the whole organization. Human trafficking is the only way to earn that's completely off the table for all charters. As it should be. Anyone earning that way deserves a bullet to the head.

Where Sway's been hoping to turn a legitimate profit is his porn production company. My ex, Stella, is a big part of that plan, obviously. Turns out with Sway in the hospital, no one has a lot of information to share.

"He keeps details about her to himself," Shadow explains with a dirty eyebrow wiggle.

Hustler raises his hand. "I have some monthly membership figures."

Well, at least the treasurer has something useful.

"Good. What are we looking at?"

"Membership keeps growing every day. There was a slight increase in cancellations over the last two weeks, but I think that's because no new content has been added."

Fucking great. "What do we do about that?"

"That's always been between Stella and Sway," Steer explains. "We take our cut, but creative control is all hers. She reports to Sway and runs new ideas by him. No one else."

Kill me now. The last damn thing I feel like doing is begging Stella for any updates on what sexual positions she's filming herself in lately. Or worse, collaborating on projects.

Frustrated, I motion for Hustler to hand me the papers he's holding. "I thought he was bankrolling some of her friends too. How are those doing?"

"We are. I got those reports too. None of them have the fan base she does, but they're also on an upswing."

"All right, well at least that's good news." I turn to Rooster. "Where we at with Sway's shooting?"

"I'm at a dead end." He scratches his hand over his beard and flicks his gaze down the table, but no one speaks up. "I've combed through every piece of video footage and got nothing."

Shadow stands without being recognized, something I don't care for. I won't make an issue out of it now, but it'll definitely be addressed at some point. Bikers or not, we have a certain protocol at meetings that *will* be followed.

"We all know Vipers were probably behind this attack." He turns and points down the table. "How many times they come after your club? Almost fucking killed you, right brother?"

Teller sits up, surprised, I think, to be brought into the conversation. "Yeah, but the ones who ran me off the road are," he cough-smirks, "long gone."

"Z knows more about this than I do," Murphy says. "But we never had any indication that the Jersey charter condoned what New York was doing. So why they'd start fucking with us now makes no sense."

"Bullshit." Smoke jumps out of his chair. "We know one club doesn't make a move without the rest of 'em knowing about it. They came after our prez and we need to retaliate before they think we're a bunch of pussies who can't handle our biz."

Christ, that escalated quickly.

"Whoa." I hold my hands up in the air but otherwise remain calm, like none of this ruffles me even though I'm dying to plant my fist in Shadow's face for sharing this conspiracy theory without discussing it with me first. "What are you basing that opinion on?"

"Thirty-five years of gut instinct," Smoke shoots back, slapping his meaty paw over his protruding gut. "I been in the game since you were in diapers, Z."

Rooster sighs and rolls his eyes my way. Further down the table, Jigsaw snorts and shakes his head.

"Rooster knows explosives." Smoke jabs his finger in Rooster's direction. "We should have him wire up their vehicles and hit them at *their* clubhouse, hard and fast. See how they like it."

Hustler stands and leans over the table, catching Smoke's eye. "This ain't your golden oldie days, brother. Thinking before acting will save us all a lot of grief."

"I'm *thinking* the Vipers tried to off our prez and we need to *act* in a way that shows them we won't tolerate it and end it for good," Smoke fires back.

"Bro, cool it." I motion for everyone to take their seats again. "What interaction have you guys had with the Vipers to think they're behind this? Sway's never mentioned an issue."

"I have good intel they've been moving into the south of our territory," Smoke says too quickly to sound believable.

"Z," Teller calls. "Uh, Prez. If you remember, that's how they started with us."

I turn my *don't encourage this* stare his way and he gives me a half-smirk in return.

"See?" Shadow points at Teller. "T knows what's up."

While his brain-to-mouth function leaves a lot to be desired sometimes, Teller's smarter than Shadow, Smoke, and half this club combined. He wouldn't have opened his mouth without a good reason. Even so, I ignore him for now.

"They did shoot at me and Heidi," Murphy reminds us. "Fucking sniper shot from a distance."

I send my glare his way, but he's focused on Shadow.

"Bring me hard proof they're behind it and we'll move," I promise. I go in for the pity strings next. "I've known Sway since I was a teenager. Car-bombing their clubhouse will bring too much heat, but no one wants this fucker caught more than I do."

"Amen, brother," several of the guys mutter and nod their heads at me.

Crisis averted, I adjourn the meeting. Shadow storms out with Smoke right behind him. Rooster catches my eye and nods before leaving.

I want to order Teller and Murphy to park their asses, but I don't want to look like I'm holding separate meetings with the guys from my club. Not when things are still so precarious.

Still, Teller's smart enough not to wander far. I find him and Murphy in the hallway outside my room.

"Look who it is. Tweedle-dee and Tweedle-pain-in-my-ass," I greet as I open the door and shove push both of them inside.

"Which one am I?" Teller snarks.

"You're definitely a *pain in my ass*."

Murphy snort-laughs and drops down on the edge of my bed.

"Get your ass off my bed. I sleep there."

"Not like I'm gonna wipe my ballsack on your pillow. What's your problem?" he bitches but moves to one of the chairs in the corner.

"Why you two gotta feed into Shadow's bullshit? We can't afford to go to war with the Vipers. Not in the state this charter's in."

Teller shrugs. "Will you be disappointed if I don't have a better answer than *keep your enemies close?*"

Murphy taps the side of his head like he's about to Jedi-mind trick me. "Sometimes you win the war by subduing the enemy without fighting."

I stare at him for a second. "You've been living with Rock for too long."

Clearly accepting that as a compliment, he grins at me. "Seriously, Shadow knows I got no love for him. If I take his side against you, he'll trust me more."

"Or know he's being played."

"He ain't *that* smart, bro," Teller says. "Besides, he brought up some good points. Vipers are cowards. Trying to take out Sway the way it went down is right in their wheelhouse."

"I get that, but Rooster says Shadow's been pushing to go after the Vipers since way before this. He's using this as an excuse to call up support to take over Jersey territory."

"Ah, all right." Teller frowns. "Talk to Rock about it, but I think Priest was pretty clear at National that he didn't want any charter starting a war for territory they couldn't finish without big losses or bringing the attention of law enforcement."

"Yeah, I got that vibe from Niner too. Even though National keeps riding our asses to grow membership."

"Growing membership and dominating more territory are two separate things."

"Thank you for the semantics lecture, professor Whelan."

Murphy's still grinning at both of us. "Rock will be so proud of you, Z."

"Shut up, ginger." I pinch the bridge of my nose and take a breath. "Shit, I don't know how the fuck he's put up with all of us for so long."

"Come on." Teller snorts. "Our club's not nearly as obnoxious."

Murphy wobbles his hand back and forth. "Debatable where you're concerned."

Teller glances around the room. "You sweep this for bugs?"

"Every night."

Satisfied the room's clean, Teller continues. "I'm gonna sit down with Hustler and go over the books. Their reports are so sloppy, it made me twitch. I'll see if I can get them set up better while I'm down here."

"Appreciate that." I glance at Murphy. "I got a lead on a house right next to yours. Want to come look at it with me?"

"No shit?" He smiles and stands. "Yeah, let's go. Actually. I need to make a call. Meet you out front?"

"You're really moving Lilly down here?" Teller asks after Murphy leaves.

"Yeah, I miss the shit out of her and Chance. Hate having such a long drive to see them."

"She can't meet you halfway or something?" he asks with a little too much sarcastic jackass in his voice for me to let it slide.

I press a hand against Teller's chest, pushing him back a step. "Are we good here? I need to know I can trust you to watch out for Lilly when I'm not around."

His jaw flexes. "You can always trust me, brother. You trust her, though?"

Shit. Been waitin' for this moment.

I swore I wouldn't divulge the information Rock shared about his newly-discovered paternal relationship to Teller. It's a promise I won't break. I'm sure the news has been an emotional clusterfuck for Teller, something this move downstate hasn't helped. While I'm sympathetic, I can't afford to have him be a dick to Lilly.

"Listen," I say a lot calmer than I'm feeling, "I appreciate the concern, but whatever's in our past is between her and me."

"Real talk, Z?"

Apparently, my warning wasn't clear enough.

"This is as real as it gets, brother." I spread my arms and motion for him to hit me with whatever he wants to say.

"Known you a long time. Almost as long as Rock and Wrath."

"Yeah?"

He shrugs and looks away. "I hate that she did that to you." In a lower voice, he adds, "That's a lot of time you missed with your son."

I should punch him for getting me choked up now. "I appreciate that more than you know."

"How can you accept that kind of betrayal so easily?"

Have I accepted it? *Accept* probably isn't the right word. It's more like I don't see the point in dwelling on things that can't be changed.

"She even tell you why?" he persists.

No, she hasn't. But that's not Teller's business.

"All you need to know is she's my old lady and she's a good mother to my son."

That last part was a bit of a dick thing to say. Teller's own mother was a neglectful bitch who left him in charge of his baby sister when he was only ten years old so she could whore around. Eventually, she abandoned both of them at their grandmother's.

He swallows hard and works his jaw from side to side. "Man, Alexa isn't even my kid and I hated those couple *months* she was living up in Alaska. Think about all the things you missed with him. You're really okay with her keeping Chance from you for more than two *years?*"

Only his genuine concern about the situation stops me from punching him. "No, I'm not okay with it, but that's *our* issue to work out. Not yours."

"A problem of my brother's is a problem of mine…" He gives me a cheeky smirk to go with the familiar biker saying.

I stare him down and speak slowly so my message sinks in this time. "My only problem this second is you're not hearing me."

"I hear you."

I continue as if he hadn't spoken. "I need you to help her feel comfortable and safe down here. There's no one in this clubhouse I trust more than you and Murphy to look after her so please, I'm asking as your friend and your brother, don't be a dick."

He drops the attitude but stares at me for a few seconds before speaking. "You got it." He hesitates. "Wait, did she tell you I gave her a hard time?"

"No, but I know how sensitive you are," I say to throw him off.

"Yeah, about as sensitive as a brick wall." He laughs and shakes his head, then turns serious. "You stuck up for Charlotte from the jump. Even when Wrath kept questioning her loyalty, you had my back."

"So show me the same respect. That's all I'm asking."

He shoves his hands in his pockets and nods. "You got it, brother."

"You two need more time alone?" Murphy asks, poking his head inside the room. "I thought we were meeting out front."

"Yeah, Teller and I needed to straighten out a few things."

"We're good," Teller assures me.

I hope he's right and this is the last time I have to defend my relationship. To any of my brothers.

CHAPTER EIGHT

Z

THREE BIKERS ROARING INTO THE GATED COMMUNITY MAKES AN impression. The poor rental agent pulls a face like she's regretting her life choices when we pull up.

I flash what Lilly says is a panty-dropping smile and the agent blushes. "I'll open it up for you. Take your time."

Murphy and Teller watch her go with matching smirks.

"What do you think?" I ask.

Murphy nods to the house on the left. "It's literally next door."

"I wasn't kidding."

Teller and Murphy follow me up the driveway. We stop on the porch "You're not mad I'll be right next door checking up on you two?"

"Fuck no." Murphy answers. "Safer to have us close together."

Teller shakes his head. "I can't believe I'm sharing a house with you two again. I have enough nightmares about you violating my baby sister as it is."

Murphy jerks his thumb at Teller. "He doesn't want anyone to know all the kinky shit he lets Charlotte do to him," he whispers loud enough for Teller to hear.

Teller plants his hands on Murphy's chest and shoves him. Laughing, Murphy stumbles backwards and flashes a grin.

I yank them in closer to me and slap both of them on the back. "Fuck, I'm glad you two are here. Now, focus."

The house is enormous. Maybe a little much, but as president of downstate, temporary or not, I may have to entertain certain people. I'd rather do it here, in this gated McMansion neighborhood than at the clubhouse. I also want to be able to spend time with my family away from the club.

Perfectly matte white walls everywhere. The kitchen could fit Lilly's whole house. I can perfectly picture her blending up plenty of green smoothies for Chance in it every morning. The living room's furnished and after running my gaze over the beige fabric couch and thick white carpet, I'd say there's a good chance I won't ever see my security deposit.

Outside is the best part. A yard for the dogs to romp in. A semi-indoor pool. The patio surrounding is enclosed in brick and glass, but the ceiling rolls back with the push of a button to give an unobstructed view of the sky.

"Gonna need to keep the kids out or teach them to swim," Murphy points out.

"Yeah, no kidding."

"It's a real high-end area. I'm sure you can find someone to come to the house and give them swim lessons," Teller says. He glances around and shrugs. "Might want to see if you can find a nanny for the kids." He lifts his chin Murphy's way, then mine. "You're gonna need to have the girls with you for club events. Can't ask Hope to drive all the way down here and watch 'em."

Murphy runs his hand over his beard. "I don't want some stranger around my kid." He slides his gaze Teller's way. "You think Carter will mind visiting?"

Teller laughs. "I think he was looking forward to having my house to himself on the weekends."

"Murphy has a good point about not bringing in more strangers than necessary," I say. "And I actually trust Carter. Chance loves him."

"Charlotte and I were talking about buying him a truck." Teller shrugs. "Maybe that's how I'll sell it to him, so he doesn't complain it's charity."

"A nanny-mobile." Murphy snickers into his hand.

The agent's been waiting outside, as if she's afraid to be alone in the house with us. But she pops up now. "I can recommend a cleaning company for you and a nanny service if you need it."

I shrug and glance at Teller. "Perfect. Then Carter won't have to play maid too."

Teller rolls his eyes. "This is *my* future-brother-in-law we're talking about. I'm the only one allowed to exploit him."

"No exploitation necessary. I'll pay him whatever the going nanny-rate is around here."

"You might want to work out his schedule with Rock. Carter's been working in the shop a lot lately."

"All right."

"So, you're gonna take the house?" Murphy asks.

"Yup. Wanna get them moved down here as soon as possible."

Out front, Teller glances down the street. "I'm not thrilled about having so many neighbors, but at least it's quiet."

Murphy clasps his hands behind his back and winks at the agent. "Not for long."

The next morning, I ask Murphy and Teller to stick around the clubhouse and keep an eye on things while I head to the hospital to visit Sway.

Most of our out-of-town brothers have gone back to their charters. Can't fault them. Everyone has their own problems and needed to get back to their own lives. They showed their respect and helped where they could. The rest is up to us.

The number of brothers staying at the hospital around the clock has gone down, but Stitch, the prospect Priest left up here, is hanging out in Sway's room, flipping through a magazine, when I walk in the door.

He jumps up as soon as he sees me.

"How's it going, kid?" I ask.

"Not too bad. Sway's new nurse is so hot, I'm about to go code 143 on her."

I'm too old to decipher that, but Sway laughs, which is good to hear. "I knew you weren't sticking around just to keep me company, you little shit."

Stitch shrugs. "You need me to get anything for you?"

Sway gives him a list that should keep Stitch occupied for a fair amount of time. On his way out, I stop and hand him some cash for his shopping spree.

"How's it going, brother?" Sway asks.

"Not bad. How you feeling today?"

"I'm alive."

I huff out a laugh. "That's promising. You up for a chat?"

"Gee, let me think about it. My afternoon's so busy." He points to a chair. "Have a seat. Entertain me."

I hate bringing up club business when he's supposed to be recovering but with Shadow pushing to go after the Vipers, I'm backed into a corner.

"Was wondering when you were going to ask me for some advice on how to run a club." The nerve damage only allows him to half-grin, and it makes him look even more evil than usual.

"Not exactly advice."

"Gettin' all your pointers from Rock?" He doesn't say it in an angry way, more like he's disappointed I picked old Dad over new Dad.

"It's not a contest, Sway. You gonna let me ask or not? I wanna get you while you're still lucid." Yeah, that was a dick comment, but he pissed me off. Besides, he can take it.

He's not insulted. "Shit, brother. I look forward to your visits. Everyone else whispers, fake smiles, and tiptoes around me. Or cries. Like I'm halfway to my grave."

"You did get shot in the head."

"And I'm still breathing, ain't I?"

"And running your mouth," I add.

He laughs and struggles to sit up. I stay in my seat because, half-dead or not, he'd probably jam the stubby pencil on his nightstand into my neck if I tried to help him.

"All right. What's on your mind?"

"First, have any details of the night you were shot come back to you yet?"

He goes completely still and closes his eyes for a few seconds before answering. "Nothing, brother. It's all black."

"What's the last thing you *do* remember?"

"You think I didn't go over this with the doctor, the cops, Priest, Steer, and everyone else?"

"Humor me."

He closes his eyes again and sits back. "Talking to Tawny on the phone."

"So, you *have* talked to her. People say she's been missing for a while."

"She's *not* missing. At least, she wasn't."

As far as I know, she still hasn't been by to see Sway. I need to find

Janice later and ask if she's heard from her mother. "What does that mean?"

He gestures to the bandage engulfing half his skull. "I've been preoccupied."

"But you talked to her? That night?"

"We talked." He shifts his gaze away. "Or fought. I can't remember."

"Don't get mad, but is there any chance *she* shot you?"

His face darkens. Whatever their issues are, Sway's protective of Tawny. Always has been. Or maybe he feels guilty for all the times he's cheated on her. "You drop that line of thinking right now, Z. I'm not fucking around. Breathe a word of that to anyone, and I'll fucking kill you."

"Easy. This conversation is between you and me. But I need you to be honest. And I need you to seriously consider the question. Is it possible?"

This time, he seems to really weigh the odds of his wife of over twenty years pulling the trigger. "Nah, Tawny woulda shot me in the dick for sure. She always said that's where my brains were, anyway."

"Can't blame her there, brother."

We both have a laugh, which helps to smooth over the awkwardness of accusing his wife of trying to murder him.

I shift forward, indicating the first uncomfortable part of our conversation is over with. Not that this next part will be any easier. "All right. Club business talk. Have you had any indication Vipers have been moving in on your territory?"

His eyes turn cold. "Who said that? Shadow? He trying to stir that bullshit up again while I'm down?"

"Is that a *no*?"

"I don't know. He never brought me enough proof. After National, I wasn't about to start trouble anywhere without a damn good reason. I wanted off Priest's radar."

"And now you're on it."

"Tell me about it."

I can't get the conversation I had with Rock out of my head. "Anyone you can think of who'd want to make a play for your patch?"

He stares at me too long for my liking.

"I can think of one or two people who might benefit."

I meet his gaze head-on, daring him to say it out loud.

"But I just can't see it," he finally finishes.

Sway trusting me is a relief. Although, it still leaves me looking for the shooter too close to home.

"Was Shadow pissed Priest put me in charge?"

"He hasn't said so, but how would you feel?"

Not too good. Which is why I've been firm but cautious with Sway's crew. Taking over downstate has been all sorts of tricky.

"Is there any chance he shot you?"

It's a rough question. Sway helped Shadow patch-in to the club. Promoted him to Vice President. They've worked side-by-side for a long time. But one thing I've learned over the years is that power and greed can corrupt even the best of relationships.

"Before National, I would've said no. But the trouble he got into down there and the way he handled himself..." He looks me straight in the eye. "I honestly don't know."

CHAPTER NINE

Lilly

"You're sure you don't mind?" I ask Z for the third time.

"Is it how I want to spend my evening with you? Not really, but fuck knows I ask you to spend an awful lot of time with my friends and family."

Not exactly reassuring. "Ted's leaving tomorrow morning."

"So, you said."

"Z."

"Lilly, it's fine. You sure Alex doesn't mind watching Chance?"

"No, we talked. Sorted some things out."

"Tell me about it later? I need to run."

"Sure."

I've barely said goodbye before the phone rings again. It's Mara, and eager to find out what she knows about the subpoena I received, I scoop up the phone.

"Hey."

"Good news!" she practically shouts into the phone.

"Thank God. Tell me."

"Damon got the subpoena quashed."

"Oh, thank God! That's great. Thank you."

"Don't thank me yet. He had it thrown out on a technicality. They're supposed to get you to sign something for that kind of subpoena. So, there's a good possibility they're going to try and serve you again."

"Fuck."

"You have somewhere you can hide out? That sexy beast of a man of yours lives in a pretty remote area."

Unsure of how much I can tell my friend about Z taking over the downstate charter, I choose my words carefully. "Actually, he's working a little farther south for a couple of months, but he rented a house for us. Chance and I are supposed to move in this week."

"Oh, that's perfect! Where? No, wait, don't tell me. Oh, I'm so happy for you guys!" she gushes like an enthusiastic teenager.

Her excitement brings a smile to my face. "I miss you, Mara."

"I miss you too, Lilly. When things settle down, let's get together."

"I'd like that."

"Okay, so don't answer the door and beware of process servers hiding in the bushes. Call me if you get another subpoena or anything else hinky."

"Hinky, huh?"

"What? It's a word."

"I'll talk to you soon, Mara."

How much longer before Z arrives?

That's a new feeling. I never thought I'd find myself waiting on any man. It's hard to deny the butterflies dancing in my stomach and the way my mouth keeps tugging up at the corners at the thought of seeing Z again.

"Mommy?" Chance calls. "See the ducks?"

"Sure. You want to ride your tractor to the lake?"

"Yes!" He raises his hands in the air like a miniature boxing champ and runs to the door. Laughing, I follow.

A few hours later, my boots and jeans are splattered with mud. Chance is even filthier. Somehow, he managed to get mud in his hair.

"Let's head back so you can take a bath before we go to Uncle Alex's."

"Don't wanna."

"You want to go all gross and muddy?"

He glances down at his shirt and shrugs.

"Come on." I hold out my hand and wiggle my fingers. After a brief hesitation, he presses the little accelerator on the tractor down and steers toward home.

Z's pulling into the driveway as we come around the side of the house.

"Daddy!" Chance yelps and points.

"He's home." That same excited fluttering starts up in my stomach again.

In his eagerness to see his dad, Chance throws himself off the tractor, tripping and falling. He lands with a soft *oof* in the grass, but jumps up, brushes himself off, and runs. I can't help it. The whole scene's so funny, I end up standing there laughing.

Z scoops Chance into his arms. "Missed you. Have you been good for your mom?"

Too eager to tell Z about all the things he's been up to, Chance barely answers the question. Z's eyes lock with mine as he slowly makes his way over.

"Missed you too, pretty girl," he says, leaning in to give me a kiss.

"Daddy!" Chance huffs. He squirms and wiggles for Z to set him down and then yanks him toward the house.

"Hang on, Chance. Let's put the tractor away. You're not leaving it out for your mom to do."

Chance squints up at him and I have to hold in my laughter. "Otay."

After they secure the tractor in the shed, Chance captures Z's hand again, dragging him up the front stairs. "Where were you?" he demands.

Z chuckles as he opens the door. "Well, I had a meeting. And then I visited a friend in the hospital."

"Like Grandpa?"

"Not quite."

Z looks at me and I shrug. It's up to him how much he wants to tell his son.

Chance doesn't want to let Z out of his sight. Even insisting he help with bath time. I don't think Z knows what to do with that.

"I'm sorry," he apologizes.

"Why? I'm more than happy to hand over bath duties to you." I pass him some towels, a bath bomb, some toys, and wish him luck.

Singing and splashing noises follow me into the kitchen while I prepare a snack for Chance. Eventually they emerge—Z's drenched, but wearing a proud grin and Chance wrapped in his favorite bear-shaped towel.

"Hungry?"

"Yes," they both answer.

While they sit down to eat, I hurry to grab an uninterrupted shower. Something I haven't been able to do in years. Z and Chance should be fine together for a few minutes. Heck, I bet Chance falls asleep right after lunch.

"You know I wanted to soap you up, right?" Z's low, raspy voice startles me and I drop the bottle of conditioner in my hand, narrowly missing my foot.

"Did he pass out?" I ask.

"Practically in his plate. Was that your plan? To tire him out?"

"That's *always* my plan."

There's a thud, followed by another a few seconds later. A clink and rustle of clothing. I peek my head out of the shower. "Joining me?"

"He's in his bed. Still dressed in the bear towel but out cold."

I chuckle and wait. My shower isn't small, but Z definitely takes up a lot of room in it. "Where were you?" he asks.

"About to condition my hair."

He motions for me to give him the bottle and I have to bend over to grab it.

"Jesus, woman. What are you trying to do to me?"

I hand over the bottle and he turns me around, pulling all of my hair into his big hands. "How much of this do I need to use?"

"A lot. I have a lot of hair."

He tugs gently. "Don't ever cut it."

"I thought about it when Chance was smaller because he was always pulling on it and I really didn't have the time or inclination to worry about what I looked like."

"Hmm."

Without turning around, I can't tell if it's a sound of acknowledgment or if he's annoyed I brought up a time he wasn't a part of.

"Will you tell me more?" he asks as he gently kneads his fingers into my scalp.

"About?"

"When you were pregnant. What he was like as a baby."

Tears burn my eyes and I stick my face under the spray of the shower. "Anything you want to know. I have a ton of pictures..." I can't finish the sentence, but I gesture wildly toward the living room.

"Hey." He sets his hands on my shoulder and turns me to face him. Except, I can't face him, so I press my forehead to his wet, slippery chest instead.

His chest rises and falls. He runs his hands up and down my back, offering comfort without saying a word.

After a few minutes, he says in a low voice, "I put the deposit on the house this morning."

"Thank you."

He leans down and tips my head back. "Thank *you*."

"I mean for doing everything. Finding the place. Looking at it—"

"It's the least I could do when I'm asking you to uproot your life for the club."

"You're not...I want...I want to be where you are."

He answers with a kiss, pressing his warm, soft lips against mine while the water pours down over us. Nothing more than a kiss and a little of his hands roaming.

The water gradually cools and he reaches past me to shut it off.

"I didn't get to wash your hair," I protest.

His mouth kicks into a devilish smile. "I came in here to get dirty, not clean."

My gaze strays in the direction of Chance's room and Z chuckles. "Parents still do that, right? I mean, otherwise everyone would be an only child."

I don't have an answer other than to laugh.

He steps out of the shower first and scoops me up.

"We're all slippery." I dig my nails into his shoulder. "You're going to drop me."

"You've always been hard to hold onto." He sets me down on the counter. "But I've got you for good this time."

No point in searching for the double-meaning there.

He steps back and reaches out to lock the bathroom door. "Just in case."

"What do you think is happening in here?"

I'm kidding, of course. The answer's written on his face. In the way his eyes blaze a trail over my body as he prowls closer. And if those things didn't clue me in, his thick erection is a statement all its own.

"I missed you." He braces his hands on my knees, gently pushing them apart and stepping between them. "A lot."

"I'm all wet."

"Good."

No more talking. He traces a line up my leg with his fingers, stopping to settle his thumb in the crease of my thigh, then crushes his mouth against mine. I'm so caught up in his kiss, I gasp in surprise when he slips his arms under my knees, lifting and tilting me.

"Hang on," he rasps. "This'll be quick and furious." One corner of his mouth lifts. "And quiet."

I open my mouth with a sassy comeback. Something like, "I'll do my best." Instead, I end up moaning as he pushes against me.

"Open," he orders, lifting me higher.

I wrap my arms around his neck, holding on tighter. "Oh."

"Shh," he reminds me.

"You feel so good," I whisper. Good god, how did I survive the last couple days without him? Suddenly sex with Z is as necessary as air and water.

He fucks with slow movements, leaning back to stare down at where we're joined. His thumb finds my clit and he rubs in time with his thrusts.

Delicious pleasure builds, everything inside me feels tight, urgent, ready to explode.

Finally, I break, shattering like pieces of glass showering down around us. I'm panting with the effort of swallowing down my cries of ecstasy.

"Fuuuck," Z grits out in a low rasp. His eyes clench shut and he groans against my mouth. "My siren," he whispers as his movements still. "You're going to kill me."

"I love you too much to kill you."

His eyes open and he stares at me with lazy, loving, satisfaction, slowly kissing my cheek and forehead.

"I think you made more noise than I did."

He chuckles as he pulls back. "Maybe."

Slowly, I release my stranglehold on him. He glances over his shoulder and swipes his hand over a spot on his back. Blood's smeared on his fingers. "You ripped me open, Siren."

"I'm so sorry. You had me hanging on for dear life."

He swoops in and kisses my forehead. "Don't be sorry. It's hot."

After we both clean up again, Z follows me into my bedroom, watching me get dressed.

"Are you planning to go to dinner in a towel tonight?"

He glances down. "If you want me to strip, just say so, pretty girl."

"Oh, I'd have you walking around naked all day if I could. Only for me, though." I wink at him.

Z seems to glow from the compliment, something I find endearing. As soon as we're both dressed, he pulls me into the living room.

"Come here, I have something for you."

Still weak-kneed and wearing a love-drunk smile, I follow him. "You already gave me plenty."

His dimples are on full display. "I'll give you that anytime you want." He leans over, plucking his leather cut off the couch and pulls a small, flat white box out of an inside pocket. "This is something special I saw and thought of you."

"Oh." My breath catches.

Z's always been thoughtful. Several times in the few years we've known each other, he's surprised me with small things he knows I'll like. This doesn't feel small, though.

It feels profound.

I slip the lid off the box and gasp at the pendant nestled on a pad of black velvet. It's more than a pendant. A solid white gold chain with a 3D mermaid suspended in the middle. The exquisite detail highlights her struggle to free herself from an anchor embedded in her tail.

"She's strong. Determined. A fighter. Like you." Z's low voice slides over me like honey, making the moment even sweeter. "My beautiful siren."

"It's gorgeous. I've never seen anything like it."

"You'll wear it?"

"Yes. I love it." I turn and lift up my hair. "Will you put it on for me?"

He takes his time, tracing one warm, rough finger over my collar bones. The sensation shoots straight to my nipples and he chuckles low and sensual against my neck.

The pendant rests cool and heavy against my skin. I press my hand over it. "Thank you so much."

There's a thump and a stirring from Chance's room. Z leans down to kiss me again. "I'll get him."

"Thank you," I whisper, still reeling from how well Z knows me.

Z

"You don't have to come inside with me," Lilly says as I pull into her brother's driveway.

I glance over at her but don't respond. She should know me better than that.

Alex opens his front door with a less smug than usual expression. His face brightens when he sees Chance, which helps me dislike the dude less. He might be an ass in general, but at least he's good to my son. And Chance seems to love him, so that's something.

"Hi, Z." He holds out his hand and I shake it.

"Thanks for watching him tonight," Lilly says, ushering Chance inside.

"No problem." Alex glances at me, then Lilly. "You're going to see Ted?"

So, he knows Ted? Does he know the guy proposed to his sister too? Bet Alex would rather have a doctor for a brother-in-law than a biker. Too bad.

"Yes." Her eyes dart my way. "He's heading home tomorrow."

"Tell him I said hi."

"I will."

"Mom?" Chance tugs on Lilly's hand, pulling her further into the house.

"I'll be right back." Lilly turns my way and raises an eyebrow. Silently asking me not to kill Alex? Probably.

I watch Alex for a few seconds without saying anything.

"Lilly tells me you're getting married," he finally says.

Surprised she told her brother, I just nod.

"Don't see a ring on her finger yet."

Now that makes me laugh. "It's coming."

He crosses his arms over his chest.

If he's waiting for more information, he's about to be disappointed. "Would you mind keeping Chance tonight?"

"Not at all. Why?"

"Not sure how late we'll be out." I flick my gaze down the hallway. "Don't mention it to her, though."

"I probably don't want to know. Do I?"

One corner of my mouth twitches up, but it's not a dirty night of pleasure on my mind. No, I want to have a certain discussion with Lilly. And since she made it clear that's not happening with Chance in the house, this seems like my best opportunity before I have to go downstate again.

A lick of guilt brushes against my conscience. It feels like I'm orchestrating an ambush on the woman I love. But I need those answers.

"I'm off all day tomorrow. Let me know when you want to pick him up. Or I can drop him off."

"Thanks."

Chance races around the corner, stops and grins up at both of us.

"You going to be good for Uncle Alex?" I ask in a dad voice I didn't even know I had.

"Yup."

As attached as Chance is to Lilly, he doesn't get upset when we leave, which is a relief.

"Was Alex okay?" Lilly asks after I start the car.

"Did you see me punch him?"

"Not funny. I'm serious."

"That was the least dickish he's ever been."

I don't have to glance over to know she's rolling her eyes. "What did you talk about?"

"Chance." Not a lie. "Oh, and I guess you told him we're getting married?"

"Oh." She hesitates. "I'm sorry. Did you not—"

"You tell everyone and anyone you want, Siren. He wanted to know where your ring was."

"Oh, for fuck's sake. I hope you told him it's not the 1930's?"

I snort but her answer bugs me. "You'll have a ring."

"Oh thank God," she says, mocking me. "I was worried you were going to tattoo 'Property of Z' on my forehead."

"We can do that too." I glance at the upcoming ramp for the Northway. "Which way am I going?"

"South. He's meeting us at the Tipsy Owl."

"The what?"

"It's a restaurant. A good one. Promise."

Doesn't sound like a biker bar. Otherwise, it would be called the Drunk Beaver or Sloshed Sloth. "Am I under-dressed?"

She reaches over and rests her hand on my leg. "You're fine."

I glance over and take in the red skirt of her dress covering her long legs. "Did I mention that you look hot tonight?"

"Once or twice."

"Should've said it a hundred times."

She laughs softly and squeezes my leg. "Tell me. How's it going downstate. Are the guys still okay having you there?"

Whether I plan to marry Lilly or not, there's only so much club business I should share with her. "One of the brothers in particular is being a pain in my ass."

"The VP?"

"What makes you say that?"

"I figured he would've been next in line to take over. I've been wondering if he's upset you landed in what he might have assumed was his spot."

Huh. I've been too busy trying to run downstate to spend a lot of time worrying about Shadow's feelings. I took him at face value when he said he was happy I was there, which probably wasn't my smartest move. The fact that he didn't bother to mention this Viper issue when I initially sat down with him doesn't help either.

"Well, I'm not gonna stroke his ego to make him feel better."

"I didn't think you would." She reaches over and gently touches my arm. "Are you happier being president instead of VP?"

She seems to be asking because she genuinely wants me to be happy. Not because she thinks being with an officer of the club will give her some power, like most women who associate with MCs.

"Not really. I don't mind the responsibility. Trust me, Rock keeps me plenty busy. Downstate are my brothers too, but it's not the same."

"So, Upstate is your immediate family—brothers and sisters. Downstate is more like the cousins you only visit on Thanksgiving and Christmas?"

The comparison draws a chuckle out of me. "Yeah, something like that."

"But Rock doesn't seem like he'll ever retire. There's no chance for you to move up if you stay at your club, right?"

Again, there's nothing in her voice to suggest her question is about anything other than concern for me. "It's not about that. There is no "moving up" as far as I'm concerned. We're each in the role that serves the club best."

"Oh." She's quiet and seems to be thinking that over. "Murphy's your Road Captain, right? What's his specialty?"

"Well, he supervises the maintenance of club vehicles."

"Ahhh...I remember Hope saying something about Murphy taking care of her car and I didn't understand why. Now I get it."

"That's not all. He plans our travel routes when we go on a run. He's the enforcer of the road rules on a run. Executes the commands when we ride in a larger pack."

"So, he's good at that stuff."

"The best."

"Wrath, I understand why he's in his position. No explanation needed."

"It's more than just scaring the shit out of everyone. He helps steer our meetings, enforces the club bylaws—"

"You have bylaws?"

I grin at her. "Yeah, sweetheart."

"What else?"

"Our jobs overlap in places, so we work together a lot. He hands out punishments when a member breaks a rule—"

"Punishments?"

"Can be anything from a fine for missing a meeting without a good excuse or a beating for showing another member disrespect."

"Wow. You actually beat each other up?"

"Why do you sound so surprised?"

"I don't know. It seems a little barbaric."

"All those caveman jokes have a grain of truth, Lilly."

"I guess so," she mutters. "So, what else can you get your ass kicked for? Is that something you can tell me?"

"Lots of different things. Dishonoring the club. Repeatedly showing up late for meetings. Hitting on another member's old lady."

"Really?"

"Hell yes. That's not taken lightly. The property patches the girls have? That's so when we're with other charters, they know who's off-limits."

"Oh."

I sense the confusion. "They'll know you're off-limits because I've made that clear." Of course, I plan to patch Lilly. I just don't know which club I'm going to ask to vote on her yet.

"Hope says it's like an engagement ring?"

"More than that."

"Oh."

I glance over. "I want you to have my patch, Lilly. There's a certain ceremony to it, though, and things have been…"

"Up in the air?"

"Yes." That and I'm not sure my brothers trust her enough yet to vote her in. And Downstate doesn't even know her let alone trust her, so their votes wouldn't be as meaningful if they'd even give 'em. From what I've heard, Steer can be just a big of a dick as Wrath when it comes to accepting an old lady into the club.

"Most offenses…seem related to behavior."

"Respect is everything." How do I explain in a way that she

understands, but doesn't scare her? "While I enjoy your quick wit and sharp tongue, be careful when you're speaking to any patch member."

"Of your club?"

"Any club."

"Would they beat me up?" Her voice holds a hint of lightness, but I answer her seriously anyway.

"It depends. I'd handle it, but I'd rather not be in that situation if I don't need to be."

"Z," she says with an edge to her voice that makes my skin prickle. "Do you think I'm a bitch to everyone I meet?"

"That's not what I was trying to say."

"Are you worried I'll embarrass you now that you're in this new position?"

"Embarrass me? No."

She huffs and fiddles with her dress. "Have you ever received a beating from Wrath?" she asks.

Thank fuck we're veering to another subject. "In the early days, yeah. We kicked the shit out of each other for fun, though. Our SAA, Grinder, was the one who kept us in line."

"Have I met him?"

"No, he's been in prison for years." The fun I'm having explaining these things to Lilly dies at the mention of Grinder's name. "He should've been out a couple years ago. Hopefully soon. He's a good guy. Never should've been inside."

She squeezes my leg. "I'm sorry."

"Haven't visited him in forever. I really need to do that."

"You still visit him?"

"We all do from time to time. Make sure he's taken care of."

"You do?"

"Fuck yeah. He's still a brother. When he's out, we'll help him get set up again too." What I don't say is we'll transition him back into the club slowly. Prison can put you under the influence of a lot of different elements. Out of desperation to survive, inmates can end up aligning with people you'd never do business with on the outside. Sometimes those ties are hard to break, even after they've been released. We'll take care of Grinder, but it will be a while before he's allowed back at the table for sensitive club business.

It'll be awkward as fuck since he went in as an officer of the club. And hell, I might not even be there to help him adjust if I'm still taking care of

Sway's charter. Sway's managed to fuck up my life in so many ways I can't keep track.

"Go straight on nine," Lilly prompts, pulling me out of my thoughts.

The Tipsy Owl looks more like a house than a restaurant. The parking lot's so damn small, I'm glad we took Lilly's car instead of my truck.

Ted's waiting for us on the back porch. His face brightens when he sees Lilly, making me want to punch him again.

The kiss on the cheek and, "Hey, babe," he greets her with has me ready to throat-punch him.

Should be a fun evening.

There isn't enough wine in The Thirsty Owl to make me forget this dude tried to marry my woman.

I don't care why he asked. For Lilly's sake, I try to behave. Mostly I listen to them talk about stuff throughout dinner, only adding comments or grunts to the conversation as necessary.

"Not quite how I thought we'd spend our night together," I say against her ear after the waitress clears our table.

"Well, I appreciate it," she whispers back. In a louder voice, she says to her friend, "Ted, you're headed home tomorrow?"

"First thing in the morning."

The waitress returns and sets the check in the middle of the table. Ted reaches for it, but I snatch it up first. "You're our guest, Ted."

He sits back and gives me a quick smirk. "Next time, I'll buy."

My smile's so tight, my jaw aches. "That's cute you think there'll be a next time."

Lilly glares at me, and I wink at her.

Ted's not offended. His mouth twitches in amusement. Maybe he's not so bad. "When you come out to pack up her place, I'll take you guys out."

"Can't wait." That's not a lie. I can't wait until she's back here permanently.

"If you two will excuse me..." Lilly stands and tosses her napkin on the table. She turns her pleading *please behave* eyes on me once before leaving.

Ted leans over the table. "I'm glad you guys worked things out."

I raise an eyebrow. "Are you?"

"Does it hinder my plans a little? Sure, but I want her to be happy."

So many questions form in my mind. I don't think I could get them all out before Lilly returns. Even if I could, my pride won't let me. I don't want to beg some other man for information about my woman.

"Lilly said she's moving a couple hours south with you?" he asks.

"Yup."

"That's good." His gaze shifts in the direction Lilly disappeared. "You'll be there to watch out for her."

My curiosity overrules my pride. "What kind of doctor are you, anyway, Ted?" Somehow the subject hadn't come up all night.

"Emergency room."

"That's how you met Lilly?"

He hesitates and then nods.

"Was she in an accident?" The more I've thought about it the more unlikely it seems the woman I know could have tried to kill herself. So maybe it was an accident she caused and feels guilty about?

His eyes widen for the briefest second before his face settles into something more indifferent. "Not really."

"Meaning?"

"Come on, Z. You know I can't discuss stuff like that." He's not saying it to be a dick. The guy actually seems stressed he can't share. I'd like to say I respect him for keeping Lilly's confidences, upholding his doctor oath and all that bullshit, but at the moment it's making my life difficult.

"She said she discovered she was pregnant out there."

He leans forward and takes a sip of water and finally meets my eyes. "She loves her son more than anything."

There's a lump in my throat that makes it hard to respond. "I know she does."

Both of us turn and notice Lilly approaching the table. She stops to talk to our waitress and Ted taps my hand. "She'd never give me details and I don't know if she ever discussed it with her therapist...afterward. But something *forced* her to leave here."

For a while I figured that *something* was me, but given everything Lilly's said since she returned, that theory makes no sense.

"But she only came back because her dad was in the hospital."

He snorts and shakes his head. "I doubt it."

"Oh good, neither of you are bleeding." Lilly's cheerful voice interrupts us.

Time's up. If I want more information, I'll have to shake it straight out of the source.

CHAPTER TEN

Z

"Did you have to be so mean to Ted?" Lilly teases on the way home.

"Mean? I thought I was a delight."

She laughs so hard she has to fight to catch her breath. "You're an MC president now, you can't say things like, 'delight.'"

"Babe, I can say anything I want."

More than ever I need to have that conversation with Lilly.

"Wait." Lilly taps my arm. "You missed the turn for Alex's place."

"No, I didn't. Chance is staying with Alex tonight."

"What? When did you—"

"You and I need to talk."

"Z," she protests. "You should've told me."

"But then you would've tried to talk your way out of it."

"No, I wouldn't. I shouldn't impose on my brother—"

I reach over and grab her hand. "It was the most civil conversation we've had."

"Well, I guess that's good," she grumbles and yanks her hand away from me and crosses her arms over her chest. She turns and stares out the window and we both fall silent.

Space and distance. I'll give her those for now. Once we get to the house, I'm going to hit her hard and fast with the questions I know damn well she doesn't want to answer.

For the next few miles, I absorb the silence and prepare myself for the fight ahead of us.

Lilly

I'm going to throw up.

Between Z running back and forth from the downstate club and me preparing for the move, we haven't had a lot of time to sit down and have a heart-to-heart.

Or to dredge up every one of my nightmares from the last few years.

I kind of hoped Z would forget and we could skip this.

Wishful, foolish thinking.

By the time he pulls into the driveway I'm shaking uncontrollably.

"Lilly, we're home."

"Not home anymore," I whisper.

"Anywhere I'm with you is home." He steps out of the car before I can respond and opens my door a few seconds later. "Come on." He holds his hand out and I take it. As I step out of the car, he pulls me against his chest and slides his hand down my back and over my ass. "You look so fucking hot tonight."

I lean up and kiss his cheek, then whisper in his ear. "So do you."

In response, he growls low in his throat. "Don't try to distract me, woman."

"You started it."

"March your ass inside that house."

Maybe it's the lovingly cocky way he says it, but I'm more turned on than annoyed with the command.

Inside the house, I walk directly into the kitchen and flip the burner on under my tea kettle. Z stands in the doorway watching me.

Neither of us seem to know where to take the conversation.

"Do you want some tea?"

"I'm fine." He comes closer and pours a glass of water. "Meet me in the living room when you're done."

I take so long that he finally calls out to me. "Come on, Lilly."

My tea is still too hot to drink, but at least the cup warms my hands, even if my insides are turning to ice.

Sitting next to him, I tuck one foot under me and wait. He sets the tea on the coffee table and takes my hand.

"Tell me about this." He traces his finger down my arm.

"I already told you."

He laughs softly. "Nice try, pretty girl. You didn't tell me a damn thing."

I bristle from the accusation, even though he's right. It annoys me that he insists on worming his way into my personal, private hell.

"There are some things I'd like to keep to myself," I whisper.

His features soften, almost twisting in pain. "Not this, Lilly. I need to know."

"I'm not going to do it again."

"That's not what I'm worried about."

We sit there locked into a battle of wills that I already know I'm going to lose. Because of Chance, I owe Z the truth.

Fear and panic claw at my throat, stealing my words. As if my brain knows I'm about to betray all my secrets and is signaling my body to revolt.

I'm in charge.

Deep breath.

I can do this.

Z's incredibly patient while inside I'm at war. I unburdened myself in California. I had to at the time. But those people didn't care about me. They didn't know me before. I was nothing more than a job.

I don't want to burden Z with this pain.

And just like back then, I'm afraid of what he'll do when he finds out. Afraid of the trouble he'll get himself into because of me.

I'd never forgive myself.

CHAPTER ELEVEN

Z

"We've got all night, Lilly." It's not a threat. I want her to understand that I'm here. Waiting and ready for whatever she has to tell me.

She swallows hard and meets my eyes for a brief second. The pulse at her neck is jumping and she seems to be having trouble breathing.

"Come here." I pull her into my arms. "Easy. Just breathe. Nothing you have to tell me will ever push me away."

She sniffles and nods. After a few seconds, she seems to pull herself together. Resilient and brave, that's how I've always seen Lilly. Strong. That's what I was trying to make her understand by giving her the pendant earlier.

As if she heard me, she reaches up and traces her fingers over the mermaid at her throat.

"After Rock and Hope's wedding...when we said we were going to—"

"Move in together?" I finish for her, because fuck, that was a big step for me and the way things went down afterward still stings.

"Yes." She runs her hands over her legs a few times and blows out a breath. "The next day at work, I got assigned a special project, which meant long hours for me. That was unusual at that time of year because the legislature isn't in session, but I was flattered to get the assignment."

"Why flattered?"

"Because, I think I told you many times. My job consisted of writing policy analysis and proposals that would end up sitting on someone's desk. No matter how qualified I am...or was, I put up with a lot of shit."

"Like what?" I growl.

"I don't want to get into that right now. Let's just say a lot of legislators are old, rich, white men who aren't interested in the opinions of younger, educated females. They're still busy sneaking cigars in their offices and complaining how it's not 'PC' to slap your secretary on the ass anymore."

"Shocking." I don't say it to be dismissive. More like, nothing shocks me anymore. And I've dealt with enough crooked politicians to know most of them are about as advanced as your average cave-dweller.

"Anyway, this was a big project. I wanted to move up at some point and this could've done that for me. I was...flattered that I'd been chosen for it. I thought maybe finally someone noticed more than my big tits for a change."

My stomach tightens with the anticipation of where this conversation is headed.

"I feel so foolish now. I should've recognized what was going on. He wasn't interested in anything I had to contribute. We'd have these long discussions about my research and I thought he valued my opinions, but the whole time..."

Her voice trails off and she glances away.

"Go on."

Her hands ball into fists in her lap and she takes several deep breaths. "Jesus, I don't think I can do this."

"Take your time." I move closer to wrap an arm around her shoulders and she stops me.

"Not right now. Please."

I pull away, even though it kills me.

She stands and paces in front of me. "I said it was long hours, right? That wasn't so unusual when we were in session. Especially around budget time. But in the fall, a lot of people take time off. It can be like a ghost town in our...in those offices."

"Someone give you a hard time?" Even if someone hassled her, it doesn't explain why she'd up and quit. Then move to the other side of the country and keep my kid away from me.

Finally, she stops moving and stands completely still.

Time seems to slow down as she meets my eyes and whispers my worst nightmare.

"Someone raped me. In my office after hours."

"What?" I jump off the couch and reach for her, but she backs away. "Lilly, come here, please?"

"I can't right now."

Okay, this isn't about me. It's about her. Even if it kills me, right now she needs space. I hold up my hands and back up. "Why didn't you tell me?"

"I'm not the kind of woman who runs to a man to solve her problems."

"That's absurd." I'm coming out of my damn skin and stop to rub hands over my cheeks while I process her explanation. "I'm not a man. I'm *your* man." The last syllable sticks on my tongue. "Or I wanted to be your man. That means *I* help you solve your problems."

"How could I tell you something like that? Would you have even believed me?"

"Of course, I would."

"Well, you'd be the first," she mutters.

"What are you talking about?" My blood burns thinking of her going to someone else for help. "Who did you tell?"

Lilly

Being strong helps us survive bad times. Being brave allows us to change our future. Back then I survived by telling myself over and over that I was stronger than one incident. That the rape could only destroy me if I let it. That I could be brave and hold my head up high, even if I was dying inside.

I was wrong. So many things were stolen from me in one night. It took months to calculate the damage and by then, it was a chasm of misery I thought I'd never overcome.

Finally, I stop my furious pacing and drop down on the couch. "Eventually, I had to face that what happened screwed me up more than I wanted to admit. Running to California didn't make the pain go away."

Rage and confusion cloud Z's beautiful eyes. He's shaking with the effort of not losing his shit. "What happened?" he rasps.

I reach down and trace the line on my left arm. "I couldn't take it anymore." Briefly, I glance up and meet his eyes. "Please, don't...I can't go back to that place. To explain where my head was at. I worked so hard...after."

Z swallows hard and gives me a tight nod. "Tell me what you can. Please."

"That's how I found out I was pregnant." I reach over and squeeze his leg. "You're the first person I thought about when they told me..." Even though tears break free and roll down my cheeks, I smile.

Z doesn't return the gesture. His jaw is too tense. Hot fury burns in his eyes. "Go on."

"That's what I meant when I said Chance saved me. I was so scared what I had done, what I put my body through might have hurt him. When the doctors—Ted—assured me he was okay, I was so relieved. I already loved my baby so much." I stare down at my hands in my lap, allowing my hair to fall over my shoulder, providing me with some privacy. "Then I realized..." My throat constricts with shame. "I didn't know if...I couldn't be sure you were the father," I whisper.

"Baby, come here." This time, I allow Z to wrap me up in his arms and pull me closer. He kisses the top of my head. "I wouldn't have cared, Lilly. I just wanted you."

"It mattered to me. I didn't know what to do."

"You should've told me." His anguished voice doesn't make this any easier. "So I could help you."

"How? How could I explain that?"

He pushes me back gently to look me in the eyes. "You should have told me everything."

"How could I? What would you have done?"

"Killed the motherfucker," he says simply.

"See?" I push my way out of his hold and sit back. "I knew that's what your answer would be. What you'd try to do."

He shakes his head and jumps up, pacing in front of me. "Try nothing."

"Are you going to let me finish?"

He stops pacing and stares at me, as if he's surprised there's more to the story.

"The night *it* happened. At the hospital, the police came and spoke to me. I didn't shy away or hide who did it. Sure, in the back of my head, I worried someone would try to cover it up because he was a Senator. But I told myself that was stupid. That this is the real world and he wouldn't get away with what he'd done."

Z stares at me.

"Trust me, I understand now how foolish that was. In hindsight, I think I was in shock."

"Who came?"

"First Empire PD, but then they kicked it up to the State Police."

"Do you remember who?"

That murderous gleam in Z's eyes melts my heart but also scares me to death. "Give it a rest, Z. They listened and took me seriously. At least I thought so at the time."

"What changed?"

"An investigator from the US Attorney's office showed up at my house the next morning."

"What? Why?"

"Do you remember the leader of the Senate, Shane Kelly, the one who was forced to resign after he and a small group of other senators were arrested on federal corruption charges?"

"Yeah, a few were from the city and one was from western New York, right?"

I nod, even though I'm surprised Z remembers that much about it. It seemed to make a big dramatic splash in the news for about a day, then quietly went away. The kind of corruption they'd been accused of was behavior so ingrained in the way business was done in the legislature the arrests and scandal came as a shock. Too many powerful people had a vested interest in making the case go away.

And too many others needed to make sure the charges stuck.

"They had put years of work into this investigation and didn't want my silly little rape to screw up their larger corruption case." The bitterness in my voice surprises me. After all, I've had a few years to work through the injustice. It shouldn't still sting this much.

The outlaw biker lurking beneath Z's charming surface peeks through. "Are you fucking kidding me?"

"No. They strongly suggested I rethink the damage it would do to my career and personal life. Reminded me that my 'past' would be brought up."

"What the fuck does that mean?"

"I was thoroughly vetted when I was hired. I never hid that I used to be a dancer."

"Still not seeing the connection?"

"Danced naked for money equals slut who deserves to be raped. I thought I put that part of my life behind me, but apparently I can never move on from it."

"Jesus Christ. You put yourself through school to—"

"I'm aware. When that threat didn't work, they questioned how much I knew about the corrupt transactions. I had nothing to hide." I reach out and touch his leg. "But the final straw was that they swore all of my current associations would be thoroughly investigated."

"You were worried I'd make you look bad?" he asks.

"God no. I was worried I'd bring trouble to your door. That your club might come under investigation."

"Fuck that, Lilly. My club can handle some government intrusion."

"Let me finish."

I wait until he nods.

"I was afraid if you went after him when he was being so thoroughly watched, *you'd* be the one to end up in prison." My voice breaks. "I didn't want that. No matter how I resisted falling for you at first, I knew how much I already loved you." My hoarse voice dies out and I shake my head, unable to form another word.

"That was my decision to make, Lilly." He kneels in front of me and takes my hands. "I get that I haven't always been forthcoming with information about what I do, but I'm not a stupid man. I don't act impulsively. I also don't let anyone hurt the people I love."

"I was terrified. They wanted me to go back to work as if nothing happened."

"What? How?"

"So I could dig up information about him. Their twisted way to let me "help" take him down so I'd feel justice prevailed or some nonsense. But just thinking of looking at my desk again... The—"

My voice breaks, a startlingly clear image of that night forming in my mind. For a second, I can't speak.

"Lilly?"

"I'm fine," I continue in a calmer voice. "I couldn't do it. I got sick every time I thought about walking through those doors."

"Lilly, a bunch of your friends are lawyers, why didn't you ask one of them for help?"

"I didn't want to put any of my friends in danger. They threatened to arrest *me* if I said anything about the investigation to anyone."

I shake my head and take another deep breath. I'm almost done. I'd survived the darkest memories. "The worst was how terrified I was that he'd get me alone again. I couldn't look at his smug, evil face, knowing what he'd gotten away with." I shrug and shake my head, ignoring the tears now freely raining down my cheeks. "So, I ran."

Z

My damn heart's cracking in two.

This is so much worse than I thought. And yet, in the darkest parts of my mind it's what I'd dreaded the most.

My pride could handle Lilly running because she was scared of me or the club. In my world, those fears make sense. Especially since she's an outsider. More than ever, I wish the club was what chased her away. My love for her can't stand that someone hurt and threatened her.

A fury like I've never known races through my veins. My mind's veering away from logic and towards a punishing murder spree.

"Z," she whispers, breaking through my red fog of anger. "Please. There's nothing you can do."

"Like fuck I can't." My rage pitches toward cold-blooded murdering rampage territory.

"Everyone has their eye on him, in case he tries to flee the country before the trial."

"So?"

"You can't do anything."

"I won't do a thing." The lie rolls right off my tongue. This matter is out of Lilly's hands now. She never has to know. I don't want any of it in her head. But this *will* be handled. My need to fight, to hurt someone, has me clenched tight.

She tilts her head. "Do you think I'm an idiot?"

"You're one of the smartest people I've ever known."

Something about her expression softens. "Then don't lie to me."

"I won't do anything half-cocked. Is that better?"

"No."

"He needs to be punished for this, Lilly." More specifically, he needs to *die*.

"You have enough to handle right now." She raises an eyebrow. Ah, reminding me how my club duties have expanded exponentially lately is a good move on her part. It won't stop me from doing what needs to be done but it's a solid play.

"You're safe with me, Lilly. You know that, right?"

"And I want you to be safe with *me*." She bites her lip. "I can't be the cause of any trouble for you. I've already—"

"Don't." I glance around the living room. A few taped-up boxes are stacked by the dining table. "Is that all you're taking down to the house?"

The change in conversation seems to startle her at first. "You said it's furnished, right?"

"You might want to buy some new sheets and stuff, but yeah."

She chuckles. "I can do that." She glances over at the boxes again. "That's all I need for right now. I told you most of my stuff is still out in California."

"I might be able to sneak away in a couple weeks to go help you pack up and move back."

"Are you sure?"

"Yup."

"Okay. I'd like that." She takes a deep breath and lets it out slowly. "What did you tell my brother? About why Chance needed to stay over?"

"That I wasn't sure how late we'd be." Even though I'm not feeling it at the moment, I give her a cocky smirk to lighten the mood. "I didn't say it was for a fuckfest or anything."

The wise-ass comment has the intended effect. She chuckles softly. "God, I hope not."

Maybe it's stupid, but I'm still curious about her relationship with Ted and her life in California. I'm cautious not to tread on territory that will upset her, though. "What happened…" I'm not sure how to say it. "After?"

She lets out a long sigh and pushes her hair behind her ear. "I was in the hospital for a while. After the way I left my job and dropped everything, I had no insurance so I racked up quite a bit of debt. Ted helped me get a job. Helped me work out something with the hospital. Somehow, we started spending a lot of time together. I felt comfortable around him. He didn't hit on me or want to date me. I figured out why later." She laughs softly.

And there goes my last remaining bits of jealousy over Ted. He helped her at the worst time in her life. It should've been me by her side. But I'm glad she wasn't completely alone. "Guess I shoulda been nicer to the poor guy, huh?"

"I warned you."

"Chance?" As much time as Lilly and I have spent together, I haven't asked a lot of questions about Chance's birth or what he was like as a baby. The pain's still too fresh.

She swallows hard and meets my eyes. "He was a beautiful baby. I mean, I know all mothers think that, but he really was. Calm too. I can't tell you how many times I…"

"What?"

"Wanted to call you. You probably don't believe me. It sounds self-serving, I know. But you were always in my thoughts. That should've been a clue, right?"

Guilt slams into my gut harder than a tire iron. Lilly dealt with so much fucked up stuff. Alone. Had my kid. Shouldered all this guilt.

And what was I doing?

Pouting like a little boy because she left. Fucking anyone and anything in sight to erase her from my memory.

It's an ugly truth I'm not proud of. Something I don't ever want to tell her.

I knew where she was. I'd tracked her ass down because the curiosity killed me. But my pride wouldn't allow me to go to her and beg for answers.

Now, I wish I had.

If I'd known she was pregnant, the circumstances wouldn't have mattered. Besides all I have to do is look at Chance or be in his presence to know he's mine.

"Alex was there when he was born?"

"He was. Ted encouraged me to at least share the news with Alex and he flew out almost as soon as I told him I was pregnant and stayed with me for a while."

"Does he know? Did you tell him about this?" I touch her arms.

"No. God, no."

Thank fuck, because if Alex knew she'd been driven to try and take her life once before and still allowed his parents to treat her so shitty, I'd probably have to kill him too.

"Why not?"

"I was afraid he'd do something stupid." She twists her fingers in her hair. "Or ask me why I was working late, alone with—"

"That's bullshit. Is that the kind of asshole he is?"

Her eyes snap to mine at the venom in my voice, but men who say stupid shit like that piss me off. She opens and closes her mouth and finally shakes her head.

"You've met my parents. You see what they think of me. I told you how they tried to marry me off to someone twice my age. I'll always be the one at fault in their eyes. Alex is supportive but—"

"Go on. Tell me about Chance."

"As he got older, he looked so much like you. But I still wasn't sure... then I was scared because I didn't know how I'd explain what I'd done..."

A couple weeks ago, I would've had a biting response to that. Now, I've got nothing.

"I had another reason."

I lift my head and stare at her beautiful face.

"He came to see me." She wraps her right hand around her left wrist. "Right before he was arrested. I think someone had tipped him off and he wanted to make sure I wasn't going to testify."

"And he went to California to find you?"

"I'm sure he knew where I was all along. I never understood...how *obsessed* he was until it was too late."

Oh yeah, this fucker definitely needs to die.

"Did he hurt you?"

"Not that time. Thankfully, he was arrested when he went back to New York. He's been free on bail since then, so he didn't bother me again."

"Is that when you did this?" I ask, tracing the line on her left arm.

She nods. "Shortly after."

He needs to die painfully.

CHAPTER TWELVE

Z

Alex offered to load up his truck and follow Lilly down to the new house. I plan to meet them there later. First, I need to talk to Rock.

I shouldn't be surprised, but church is letting out when I step into the clubhouse. Makes me feel like shit for missing it.

Rock seems to sense my grim attitude and motions me into the war room. Wrath's less sensitive to my mood and picks me up in a rib-crushing bear hug. "Missed you, fucker. Your whole side of the table is empty. Fucking sucks."

"Christ, without the three of us, what the fuck'd you even talk about?" I ask.

Rock motions for Wrath to shut the door. After we take our seats, Rock sits forward, resting his clasped hands on the table in front of him. "Honestly, we discussed what we're going to do if this situation goes on much longer."

"Jesus, Rock. I'm—"

He holds up his hand, cutting me off. "Not your fault. Teller's stayed on top of his stuff. Sent me his numbers this morning." He snorts and tosses a few pages my way. "Although his cryptic code is a bit hard to crack, I think it's all good news."

I glance at the papers and give up trying to decipher Teller's scribbles and symbols almost immediately. "I think he watched too much *Inspector Gadget* as a kid."

Rock snorts. "Maybe." The laughter fades from his expression. "Murphy's going to come up Wednesday and Thursday to work on a few things if you can spare him."

Makes sense. Not as if Murphy can cover all his Road Captain responsibilities over email. "Yeah, whatever you need." I glance at Wrath. "You doing okay at Furious without him?"

Wrath lifts his massive shoulders, as if he doesn't want to admit not having Murphy around is a hardship. "Jake's covering for him right now."

"You ever consider Jake for a prospect rocker?"

Wrath's shaking his head before I finish the question. "He rides maybe three months out of the year. Besides, his brother will kill him if he gets any more involved with us criminals."

This is news to me. Sully's always been friendly and respectful when I've met him. "Why? Sully's a good guy. He—"

"Exactly," Wrath says, ending the conversation.

"Bronze is still in the area." Our favorite tattoo artist has been a friend of the club for years.

"I think if he had any genuine interest, he would've said so years ago," Rock says.

"True." You either have outlaw blood in your veins or not.

"If you can, I'd like you to take Dex to your next meet with the Demons," Rock says.

"All right," I answer slowly. "Chaser knows him pretty well though."

"He does," Rock agrees. "I want them to get used to seeing his face, though."

"Shit, Rock, you trying to replace me already?" I say it with a smile, like I'm joking, but the mere idea has my stomach clenching. Not that I don't trust Dex. He's vice president material, no doubt. Doesn't mean I'm ready to hand him my VP patch.

"You know that's not what this is about," Rock says.

"Dex isn't as much fun to fuck with as you are," Wrath adds.

I roll my eyes. "Lucky me."

Wrath's phone buzzes and he pulls it out, frowning at the text. "Speaking of Jake."

"You need to go?" Rock asks.

"If you don't need me, yeah."

Three of us stand, but I stay on my side of the table. One grizzly bear hug is enough for today.

"You moving Lilly down this week?" Wrath asks.

"Her brother's helping, but yeah."

"You need anything?"

"No, brother. I got it."

After Wrath's gone, Rock lifts an eyebrow. "Getting along with her brother better now?"

I shrug. "We seem to have called a truce. I still think he's a dick."

"Naturally." Rock tips his head and studies me closer. "You look like you got a lot on your mind."

I drop back into my seat and Rock does likewise. "I finally got some answers from Lilly."

"And?"

After the rage cleared, I considered my options. One of my best opportunities to get at this guy if he's convicted is immediately after the trial. I'll have a narrow window where he'll be at the local Federal facility while he's being processed into the system. After that, it will be tough to track him down.

"I might need help getting access to someone in federal custody in the near future. Stump has a connection—"

"No."

"Rock, I don't need your permission."

He grits his teeth. "Well, I'm sure as fuck not giving you my blessing. That's a big, complicated favor to call in. Risky too, if you get caught."

He's not just talking about my risk. I also run the risk of ruining a long-standing relationship with the Demons if I use Stump's connection and fuck it up. "I don't care."

He sits forward and lowers his voice. "And that right there is why I'm telling you no. You stop caring, that's when shit goes wrong."

"I'll never snitch. Demons will stay clear of any trouble."

Realizing I won't let this drop, Rock blows out a breath. "You're going to have to share more details."

My hands ball into fists. "Senator Kelly —"

"The one who's about to go on trial?"

Great, the publicity surrounding the case isn't exactly going to encourage Rock to help me.

"Lilly worked for him," I continue.

"Jesus Christ." As usual, Rock doesn't need me to paint a full picture.

"He hurt her, Rock. Bad. Feds wouldn't let her do anything that might ruin their case."

"That's why she ran?"

"Short version, yeah."

"Shit," he mutters, shaking his head. He's silent for a few minutes, but I sense his mind flipping through possibilities. Finally, he says, "Let me see what Tony can find out for me."

That's a big favor for Rock to call in. "This needs to be done, Rock. You know that. No matter how hard he might be to get at. I won't let this one go."

"I understand. You need to understand that it needs to be done the right way. The way that doesn't end up with you in prison, missing out on the next twenty-five years of your son's life."

Okay, when he puts it that way, it gives me pause.

"Remember the guard at Slater Correctional?"

"Fuck yeah. I remember the pig." When Rock had been inside a couple years ago, one particular guard had made Rock's life hell by doling out daily beatings, trying to provoke Rock into a fight. The guard was in bed with the Vipers MC and the cowards wanted to take out our president without getting their hands dirty.

Rock wouldn't be tricked into lashing out at a guard while in custody. Then the CO made the fatal mistake of touching Hope on one of her visits to see Rock. That invasive pat-down sealed the guy's fate. As soon as Rock was out of jail, we started planning to end that motherfucker.

"You think I didn't want to take him out right away?" Rock asks.

"This is different. This fuck has gone unpunished for *years*. He's responsible for...a lot of things."

Rock sits back but never takes his eyes off me. "I think I understand what you're saying, Angus. Doesn't mean I'm going to let you risk your freedom for some lowlife. We do this smart."

We.

An injury to one member hurts us all. And we *all* retaliate.

I'm not in this alone.

"Give me whatever information you have and I'll see what Tony can find out."

"Rock, I can track down plenty on my own without involving him."

"I realize that, but he might be able to tell me something the computer can't. In no way do we want this traced back to you."

"Thank you, brother."

"You don't have to thank me. You know where I'll always land in this situation."

Yes, yes, I do. Senator Kelly won't be the first rapist to die at the hands of the Lost Kings MC. Brutal? Maybe. Necessary though, as far as I'm concerned. Haven't lost any sleep over it yet.

"Are you comfortable bringing in the others if we need to?" He motions to the rest of the table. Retaliation at this level really needs to go through a club vote. Since my status is hovering between VP of upstate and prez of downstate, I guess I can choose which charter I want to involve. "There's no one I trust more."

He nods. "You might want to keep your relationship to Lilly a secret for now."

"I'm the only one on the lease for the house downstate."

"Good." He gives me a thoughtful look. "You know if she put your name on Chance's birth certificate?"

Shit, it had never occurred to me to ask. I don't need a piece of paper to tell me Chance is mine. "I don't know."

He shrugs. "Shouldn't matter. She had him in California, right?"

"Yeah."

"Find out. The longer nothing connects the two of you on paper, the better."

"Rock, I'm gonna marry her. Soon. Real soon."

He snorts and one corner of his mouth lifts. "Of course, you are." His smile fades. "But you want this done first, right?"

Damn right I do.

CHAPTER THIRTEEN

Lilly

THE DRIVE DOWN TO THE NEW PLACE ISN'T AWKWARD AT ALL. MOSTLY because my brother is driving in the truck behind me. I needed to take my own car, after all.

Chance decided it would be more fun to ride with Uncle Alex so I have the car to myself, which means I can crank up the stereo to music I want to listen to.

It makes the miles go by fast.

And helps me forget all the horrors I explained to Z the other day.

Who am I kidding? I can't stop thinking about it. The awful feelings it dredged up cling to me like slime. A familiar, heavy, shameful weight presses down on me like a second skin I thought I shed years ago.

Z tenderly took me to bed and curled himself around me all night. Made me breakfast in bed the next day before Chance came home. Basically treated me like expensive glass that might break at any moment.

At first it was sweet.

Until it was annoying.

Then it became alarming. Will that be the new normal for us now? Z thinks I'm a victim and he shouldn't touch me? That I'm broken? I can't deal with him seeing me that way.

As I'm close to my Thruway exit, Z calls.

"How far away are you, pretty girl?"

"About a mile from the exit."

"I'll meet you there so you can follow me to the house."

"Are you sure?"

"Just look for me to the right."

"Okay."

While he said look for him, I should've known Z wouldn't be alone. One of his brothers—Murphy, I think—is with him. They both pull onto the road as I exit the tollbooth.

Keeping an eye on my brother's truck in my rear view, I guide my car into place behind Z's and Murphy's bikes and follow where they lead.

They take us through some winding country roads. Somehow this far downstate, I expected it to be more built up, but there is still some uninterrupted scenery.

Whoops, spoke too soon, he takes a left onto a smaller, newer road. Up and down, we roll over gentle hills until we pass a set of stone pillars. A little further, we come to a gate and small guard building. Z waves something at the box next to the building and the gates swing open. He doesn't move through immediately though, and I realize he's speaking to someone inside the building.

Impressive.

Obviously, I knew Z would find someplace safe and secure for us. I didn't expect this, though. It's a newer housing development that looks more like a nature park dotted with over-sized houses. Most homes are similar in style. What they lack in originality, they make up for in size. Perfectly manicured yards. Intricate stone driveways.

I bet they're going to love having a couple of bikers in the neighborhood.

Instead of being happy for me, my brother seems irritated by the surroundings when he unfolds his long legs from his truck.

"Was Chance good for you?"

"Huh?" He stops scowling at the neighborhood and faces me. "Yeah, he conked out almost as soon as we got on the Thruway."

"Good."

"Daddy!" Chance knocks on the window and before even saying hello to my brother, Z opens the back door to unbuckle Chance.

"Were you good for Uncle Alex?" Z asks, sweeping Chance into his arms.

"He's always good," Alex says.

Z shifts Chance to one arm and holds out his hand to my brother. "Thanks for coming down."

"Yeah, no problem. Fancy area." His gaze lands on Murphy who finally ambles over and nods to my brother. "How're they gonna feel about your hogs rumbling in and out of here at all hours?"

Z shrugs. "Guess we'll find out." He jerks his head toward the house next to the one we pulled up to. "Murphy and Teller will be right next door."

"Hey, Murphy," I call out. "Has Heidi seen the house yet?"

"Not yet. She's coming down tomorrow after school."

Alex shoots me a weird look and I glare at him in return. Obviously, he assumes the worst about Z's friends.

"Z said you didn't have a lot." Murphy points at the truck bed. "Should we start unloading?"

"Yeah." Z pulls a keyring out of his pocket. "Let me open up the place." He clicks a button and one of the garage doors rolls up. Reaching out, he takes my hand and tugs me up the driveway. Chance is eager to get down and explore.

Once we're inside the house, Z sets him down, laughing as Chance races around the sparsely furnished living room, bouncing on the thick carpet.

It takes a while to go through all three levels. We have enough guest rooms for several family members to visit at the same time and a huge playroom for Chance.

"This is my favorite part." Z slides open a glass door and motions for me to follow him.

"Oh my God, the pool is amazing."

"I'm glad you like it." Z snakes his arms around my waist, pulling me against his chest. "Wanna come home and find you sunbathing in a nice, tiny bikini every day."

I snort and slap his arm. "My bikini days are way behind me."

"Like hell they are." He gestures toward the sliding glass doors and the privacy walls beyond. "Besides, who's gonna see?"

When I still don't answer, he gives me Z's version of puppy eyes—a smoldering look that always makes me want to jump him. "Don't you wanna make your man happy?"

"Yes." I glance at the pool again. "Chance doesn't know how to swim."

"I figured." He lifts his chin at the house next door. "We talked about finding someone to give the kids swim lessons."

"Oh, that's a great idea."

"Until then, we'll keep the door locked." He leans down, brushing his lips against my cheek. "But come night time, I plan to be skinny-dipping with my girl."

The low thrum of his voice has me ready to strip down and mount him right now. "Are you sure about that?"

He frowns but doesn't have an opportunity to answer.

"Lilly, which one is your bedroom?" Alex calls out, annoyance vibrating through the words.

Z takes my hand and pulls me into the house. "I should be helping them."

I make sure to lock the door behind us. Chance is busy following Murphy with his stuffed animals. "I helping," he assures me.

"Good job."

When the guys are finished, Z prowls over and kisses my cheek. "I'm sorry, but I need to get back," he explains in a low voice. "You can come over to the clubhouse later."

"Are you sure?" My gaze strays to Chance.

"Yeah, it's a good night for you guys to be there."

"All right."

He turns and shakes Alex's hand, then crouches down to speak to Chance for a few seconds.

"Thank you for your help, Murphy."

"No problem." His lips quirk. "I go where the prez tells me."

"I still appreciate it. I'm excited Heidi's coming down tomorrow. Looking forward to seeing her and Alexa."

"You and me both." His gaze slides toward Z. "This is gettin' old."

He allows me to give him a brief hug before leaving with Z.

"Do you want to grab lunch?" I ask Alex. "That took less time than I expected."

"You didn't have much." Disapproval rolls off him in waves but I don't feel like probing to find out what's bothering him.

"So, what's the story, Lilly? He moved you down here to this...little domestic palace so you can play gangster mistress?"

Apparently, I won't have to ask. "What the hell is that supposed to mean?" I seethe, praying Chance can't overhear us.

"What are you doing? Have you bothered to even look for a job since you've been back, or are you now just a kept woman?"

"That's what you're so concerned about? That I don't have a job?"

"That, among other things. Like, what, are you besties with all his thug buddies now too?"

"Murphy isn't a thug and he's been nothing but kind to me and Chance. His daughter is around Chance's age. Since when are you such a judgmental prick?"

"Oh," he says, finally backing off.

"Yeah, oh. You need to get over this, Alex. I'm tired of you offering opinions on my relationship." I throw my hands in the air. "I can't win with you. If I was working, you'd bitch that Z wasn't taking care of me and Chance properly. I'm not working and you're complaining about that. Make up your mind."

"I'm worried about you being so far away now."

"You didn't worry this much when I was in California."

He rakes his hands through his hair and blows out a breath. "Fine. You're sure you feel safe and this is what you want?"

"Yes."

"Okay. If you change your mind, though, you call me and I'll come get you."

"Alex." I'm desperately striving for patience. "If I change my mind, I'll get in my car and go wherever I damn well please. What do you think Z's going to do, keep me prisoner here?"

"You never know."

A couple hours later, I send Alex home and text Z to let him know I'm on my way to the clubhouse.

The area's still unfamiliar to me and I miss the turn for the clubhouse twice before finally steering us down the right road.

"Daddy!" Chance yelps as I pull into the parking lot.

Z's waiting out front, talking to a brother I don't recognize.

He lifts his head at my arrival and continues his conversation while making his way over to the car.

"Is it okay to park here?" I ask as I step out.

"It's fine. Lilly, do you remember Rooster?"

"I think so." I offer my hand and he gives it a quick shake.

"Things are quiet this afternoon." He taps the back window and waves at Chance.

"Good." Sure, the last party I attended there were people basically fucking on every surface in the clubhouse. Certainly not child-appropriate. I glance at my son, wondering how well the clubhouse is cleaned in between parties.

Z carries Chance into the clubhouse. During the day, when the place isn't swimming in debauchery, it almost looks like the old hotel it used to be. Under the smoky scent clinging to the air, a whiff of chlorine and something musky lingers.

I sneeze and Z raises his eyebrow. "You feel okay?"

"Just dust or something."

To the left, there's a small office. Z sets Chance down inside and explains this is where he spends a lot of time working.

My gaze runs over the small, neat space. Desk covered with papers. Filing cabinets. Another small table in the corner. A couple of broken-in chairs.

"So organized," I tease. The files on his desk seem to be neatly stacked and arranged.

"I'll give Sway that. He's not prone to clutter."

My roaming eyes land on a stack of envelopes and a bronze letter opener.

The air in my lungs stutters and the room spins. I fall back against the door jamb, clutching my chest.

"Lilly? What's wrong?"

"Mommy?" Chance cries. His little hands tug at my pants, pulling me out of the panic threatening to drag me under.

I gasp and struggle for breath. I haven't had an attack like that in… years. Why does it have to happen now?

"Lilly, are you okay?" Z asks again. He places a hand on each of my shoulders, forcing me to meet his concerned eyes.

I sniffle and pat my chest. "Must be allergies or something. Sorry. I'm fine."

He doesn't take his eyes off me for at least a minute. "What do you need?"

I have no idea.

Z

Allergies my ass.

The clubhouse is far from clean. Okay, it's a pigsty at the moment. But Lilly's already spent plenty of time here and never had a reaction like that.

My gaze searches the room, landing on the spot on my desk Lilly had been studying right before she freaked out.

"Just thinking of looking at my desk again—"

She said she'd been attacked in her office. Something on my desk triggered her to panic.

"Mommy, are you otay?" Chance asks.

She smiles and crouches down. "I'm fine, honey. Sometimes Mommy gets sneezy when I'm in a new place."

Bullshit.

Chance seems to have the same reaction. He tilts his head, studying Lilly for a second, before wrapping his little arms around her neck for a hug.

My chest is so full of both fear and love. Fear that I don't know what to do for Lilly. Love for her and for my son.

"I'm fine," she assures Chance one more time before standing again. This time, her gaze, now somewhat defiant, lands on the letter opener. "Pretty old-fashioned tool for a biker?"

I pick up the cool metal and drop it into the pen cup in the corner. The fucking thing is sharper than it looks. Don't need Chance getting ahold of it. "Sway either robbed an office supply store, or Tawny decked this place out for him. He's got all sorts of stuff."

"Hey, pal." Murphy stops in the doorway and leans down to give Chance a high-five. "Hey, Lilly."

Needing a second alone with Lilly, I glance at Murphy, then Chance. "Hey, I'm pretty sure there are Popsicles in the kitchen. Maybe Uncle Murphy will help you find one?"

"Ooo." Chance's eyes widen and he looks up to Murphy hopefully.

Murphy raises an eyebrow at me, but holds out his hand for Chance. "Sure. Let's go see what we can find."

"Subtle," Lilly says after they're gone.

"Shut the door."

Scowling, she closes the door. "It's not exactly the most appropriate time for an afternoon romp in your office."

The corners of my mouth kick up. Can't help it. Even when I'm worried about her, she can make me laugh. Nothing I love more than this beautiful woman with her sharp mind and tongue.

"Tell me what happened." I don't bother addressing her romp comment.

Stronger now, she crosses her arms over her chest and pops her hip to the side. Fuck, she's hot.

"I told you."

"Don't give me that allergy bullshit. I practically fucked you out there not that long ago and the closest thing to a sneeze your body did was coming in my lap."

She drops her arms and lowers her lashes. Hips swaying, she closes the short distance between us and pushes me back against the desk I'm leaning on. "Do you want a repeat?" she asks in a husky voice that has my dick standing at attention, begging, "Yes, please!"

I drop my forehead against hers, staring into her eyes, inhaling her scent. "More than anything. But as you pointed out, not the best time."

I grab her hands, tugging her closer. "Tell me what happened."

"Nothing." She pulls one of her hands free and rubs her fingers over the hollow at the base of her neck. "I'm not sure."

At least she dropped the sneeze excuse. That's progress.

Understanding dawns on me. "Something to do with what we talked about yesterday?"

Her eyes harden and she steps back. "No."

"Lilly, I need to know, so I can help you."

"I'm fine," she insists.

"Please let me help you." I'm practically begging now. And I haven't begged anyone for anything in a long damn time.

"I don't know, okay? Yes, maybe talking about it after so long brought stuff up for me."

"Okay, but what?"

Her hands curl into fists. "I don't know." She backs away and claws at her throat, struggling to breathe again.

"Lilly." Jesus Christ, I didn't mean to push her right into another attack. Not sure if she needs comfort or space, I stand there with my arms curled around her body, but not quite touching.

Finally, she rests her forehead against my chest and I gently rub her back. "I'm sorry," she whispers.

"Why?"

"This isn't me. I've already dealt with this. It's done. I'm fine."

I hug her tighter. *Dealt with it* is probably too optimistic. More like *buried the pain* so she could move forward and care for our son. I'm not a damn doctor, though, and I don't have a fucking clue what to do for her. "Lilly, do you think you need to talk to someone?"

She plants her hands against my chest and pushes me back. "No. Talking about it is what brought this on." She glares at me. "I'm fine."

Maybe she's right. She sure seemed to have her shit together before I forced the truth out of her. I hold up my hands in surrender. "All right. I just want to help you. That's all." I touch her face, grip her chin so she'll look at me. "I love you."

"I love you too. I don't want *that* in your head every time we're together, Z. Please."

"Lilly, you're the strongest woman I know. And I love you more than anything. Absolutely nothing will ever change that."

It's not *her* I see differently. It's the whole sick, fucking world. It's that smug creep I did some research on this morning who's laughing and smiling through his trial like he doesn't have a care in the world. Who knows how many other women he's hurt while the government's been trying to take him down for bribes and kickbacks?

Yeah, I know. For a biker, I have a real simple view of the world. Or maybe I expect too much from people. Certain concepts aren't hard to grasp. Don't hurt women. Don't hurt children. Protect the people you're responsible for. Seems simple to me.

Maybe I've seen too much abuse and savagery over the years. I've never looked the other way. Not with strangers and certainly not with someone I care about.

CHAPTER FOURTEEN

Z

"I NEED TO GO HOME," LILLY WHISPERS.

My stomach clenches. She just got down here and she already wants to go back to her place?

Before I can question her, try to change her mind, Murphy and Chance return. Lilly's whole demeanor changes when she sees Chance. Calm seems to wash over her. She shines a bright smile down at Chance. "Look at your shirt, all orange and sticky."

"I did my best." Murphy shrugs. "Washed his hands and face, but I think the shirt's a goner."

"It's fine." Lilly straightens up and captures Chance's hand. "I need to get home. I want to get our stuff unpacked anyway. Guess I'll start with his clothes." A thin laugh follows her excuses and Murphy cocks his head.

Relief that she meant *our home* blows through me.

"Will you be late?" Lilly asks me.

"I'll try not to be." I'd planned for her to spend the afternoon here, but I can see how badly she needs some space. As long as she's not running away again to get it, I can give her that.

"I don't wanna go," Chance whines and pulls out of Lilly's grasp.

I'm torn. Part of me wants her to leave him here with me. But I also know later tonight the clubhouse will be busier and I sure as fuck don't know any of the girls who hang around here well enough to trust them with my son.

I squat down, so we're eye-level. "I need you to go home and help Mommy unpack all your stuff, okay?"

"But—"

"I bet you can't have all your stuff unpacked and put away before I get home?" Hey, challenging me not to do something has always been the best way to get me to do the opposite. Why would Chance be any different?

"Can too," he counters.

I wiggle my hand back and forth. "I don't know. You brought a lot of stuff."

He backs up and grabs Lilly's hand.

Lilly leans down and whispers in my ear, "He doesn't quite grasp organization yet, Z." Her lips twitch. "But I have a feeling he's going to try hard just to please you."

I stand and pull Lilly closer, searching her unreadable eyes for some answers. "You okay?"

"I'm fine."

"I'll be home as soon as I can."

She gives me a soft kiss on the cheek. "I'll be waiting up for you."

"Everything all right?" Murphy asks after they leave.

I'm still standing in the parking lot, watching the billowing cloud of dust left by her car. "I don't fucking know."

Teller rides up, so Murphy and I stay outside to wait for him. "Was that Lilly leaving?" he asks.

"Yeah."

"Had enough already?"

I don't care for the sarcastic edge to his question. "Watch yourself, little brother."

Because he's a dick, he grins at the warning. Since I need something from him, I ignore it. "You still talk to your cop buddy, Liam?"

Teller rolls his eyes. "He's not my buddy."

I motion for both of them to follow me back inside and into the office.

"What's on your mind, Z?" Teller asks, dropping into one of the chairs and stretching out his legs.

Maybe Murphy's worried about an invasion or something, because he remains standing with his back against the door and his arms folded over his chest.

"Your cop buddy's still with Empire P.D., right?" I ask Teller.

"If I'm buddies with anyone, it's Bree." He flashes a cocky smirk. "Much to Liam's irritation. Why?"

"He patrol any of the courthouses?"

"I don't fuckin' know. Why? Liam's as straight as they come, so if you're looking to get at someone in custody, he's not our guy."

"Right. That's fine. I'd rather avoid him or anyone else I know."

"What's this about?" Murphy asks. "You got a lead on who shot Sway?"

Shit, I haven't given Sway or anyone else a whole lot of thought since Lilly came clean with me. "No. This is...something else."

They both stare at me, but I don't elaborate.

"You close enough to chat up his fiancée?" I ask Teller.

"Bree? If I run into her, sure. I guess. It'd be fuckin' weird if I called her out of the blue, though."

"Heidi can do it," Murphy says.

Teller tips his head back. "Really?"

"Yeah, they've been talking weddings and stuff since they met up at the Furious re-opening."

Teller shrugs. "There you go." He stands. "You still need me? I'm supposed to meet up with Hustler to go over some numbers."

"No, go ahead. Thanks, brother."

Once he's gone, Murphy takes his place in the chair. "What's going on, Z?" His gaze bounces around the room. "Something to do with Lilly?"

Anyone who assumes Murphy's a big, oafish brute, or worse, a big, dumb teddy bear, is fuckin' stupid. He's often quiet but also observant when he wants to be. Perceptive too. It's why he's been such a vital part of the club since he was a teenager.

"There's a trial going on, but it's got a lot of coverage. I only need a minute to send a message, but he's gonna be watched closely."

"Okay. When and where?" he asks without hesitation.

"The Federal Courthouse in downtown Empire."

"Jesus Christ, Z. You're not kidding about it being watched closely. They'll have federal marshals there along with local."

"Still needs to be done."

"All right." He meets my stare head-on. "Whatever you need."

Lilly

I fully intended to wait up for Z, but after chasing Chance around, unpacking more clothes than I thought I had, and getting Chance to bed, I'm exhausted.

Intending to read until Z gets home, I slip into bed.

Sometime later, the bed dips and a slight weight is lifted from my chest. Something *thunks* on the nightstand and I open my eyes to find a shirtless Z stretching over me to click off the light.

"Sorry I'm later than I expected."

"That's okay." He settles down behind me, pulling me against him.

"How'd it go?" he murmurs against my hair.

"Fine. I didn't explore the neighborhood much. Just unpacked our stuff."

He sighs and brushes a kiss against my shoulder.

"Were you worried I wasn't going to unpack?"

"Worried isn't the right word."

At least he's honest.

I'm flirting with falling back to sleep when he kisses my shoulder again. A soft kiss that rekindles my desire. I stretch long and hard, pressing my ass tight against his groin. He groans against my ear. "Can we talk first?"

"About what?"

"The letter opener?" Z asks gently.

Well, that snuffs out every bit of fire that had been building inside me. I should've known Z wasn't finished with this topic.

"I had something else in mind."

"We'll get there."

"Are you sure?"

He pauses and places his hand on my arm, trying to peer down at my face. "What's that mean?"

I turn toward him. "It means you haven't wanted to touch me since I told you about it."

That was hard to say but it feels good to voice it.

I'm aware enough to understand a small part of me needs attention and approval from men to feel good about myself. That I have a compulsion to be reminded that I'm attractive and desirable. Duh, I made my living as a dancer. I also *hate* this about myself, which is why I was determined to get an education and prove I wasn't some shallow shell of a person. I've worked hard to understand I'm more than my physical appearance and that I'm worth more than a man's opinion of me. That I don't exist to please men, visually or otherwise.

But old habits never quite die and I'm feeling needier than ever after sharing my secret with Z. My pride's been shredded and that old desire to feel wanted comes crawling back.

"That's a lie, Lilly and you know it," he says slowly and evenly. "I don't want to hurt you."

"You've never hurt me."

"In here." He taps my forehead. "Or in here." He places his hand over my heart.

How did we ever end up here? When we met, I wanted a good, hard fuck from a bad boy I'd never see again. How the hell did I end up with this sweet, complex, loving man permanently in my life?

He's so much more than I deserve.

If I hadn't resisted him so much in the beginning, resisted admitting we were more than fuck buddies, would I have been spared the horrible nightmare my life became? Would I have spared him the pain of not being there for his son?

My hands curl into fists. I can't stop it. I'm so angry. At myself. At everything. "I had one similar to it on my desk at work," I whisper.

He's so still I can hear the crickets chirping outside.

"That...fucker," I spit out, "gave it to me as present at a holiday party one year."

Z remains quiet while I process the rest of my explanation into words I can actually say out loud.

I swear I still feel the pointy end poking into my neck. Not enough to injure me, unless I moved or screamed. In my peripheral vision, the bronze handle glinted under the harsh fluorescent lights.

All the shame and humiliation crashes over me in a tidal wave I'm afraid I won't survive.

"I'm right here," Z says. "I've got you, Lilly. Tell me."

"He held it to my neck, while he...while..." I can't breathe. My hands claw at my throat and I struggle to sit up. "'Don't worry. You'll enjoy it,' he said." Hot tears burn down my cheeks and I furiously brush them away.

In this moment, I hate Z a little for making me remember all these sick details.

Behind me, Z's tightly coiled body trembles with rage I can feel burning against my back. When he finally speaks, his voice is surprisingly gentle. "It's okay. You don't have to keep going unless you want to."

"I can't," I whisper.

"It's okay. Everything's okay." He wraps his arms around me and pulls me back against the pillows and holds me until I'm almost asleep.

"I want you so much," he whispers. "Don't ever doubt that."

"I don't want you to think I'm broken."

He kisses my head. "Everyone's a little broken, Lilly. Together, we create something stronger and better."

"You really believe that?"

"I do." He's quiet for a few seconds. "I'm sorry I made you talk about it."

"You needed to know. You deserved...answers."

"I never wanted to hurt you to get them."

All my remaining anger blows away. "I know."

"Lilly?" One of his hands slides down my arm and clamps down on my hip. "I really want to make love to you." he rasps.

Damn him. He's going to make me cry again. While he phrased it as a statement, I hear the question in his voice. I don't think Z's ever *asked* in quite that way before. And as much as I adore the big, bossy, biker, I'm-going-to-fuck-you-now attitude he usually approaches me with, this reaches me on a much deeper level. It makes me feel cherished instead of broken.

"I'd really like that," I whisper.

Achingly slow, he slips the strap of my tank top off my shoulder, dropping kisses along the way. He shifts his body over mine and pulls down the other strap. Ravenous, he kisses every exposed inch, catching my nipple between his teeth and tasting with swift lashes of his tongue.

I moan and arch my back, asking for more. While he's consumed with kissing and sucking my breasts, I reach down and shimmy out of my shorts and underwear, kicking them further under the covers.

He groans in appreciation. "Slow down, Siren." He may be trying to slow this down, draw it out, but his hands immediately work between my legs, cupping me. His fingers part my lips and he slowly strokes my clit a few times before pushing a finger inside me.

"Oh," I sigh and roll my hips. So good.

Spearing my fingers in his hair, I drag him up for a kiss. "Please, I need you."

His answer isn't swift enough, so I reach down and shove his shorts down. In case he didn't take the hint, I wrap my fingers around his heavy erection. Satin over steel. I shiver with the anticipation of how good he's going to feel inside me.

He bites his lip and stares down at me.

"That what you want?" he rasps.

"Yes."

"Take it."

I press my hands against his shoulder and push. "I want to ride you."

He quirks an eyebrow. "Yeah?"

"That's what I want."

Keeping his arm around my waist, he rolls to his back. "Show me how you want me."

God, I want him like I've never wanted anything. So much, I can't even put it into thoughts or words.

"Come here." His low command spikes my desire higher.

I straddle his hips and press my hands against his chest, slowly rubbing myself over his cock, but not taking him inside me yet.

He squeezes his eyes shut. "You're so fucking hot."

"Too hot to look at?"

His eyes open. "I see you, Lilly. You're my beautiful goddess above me." His lips twitch. "I *was* trying to worship you."

"Until I decided to play rodeo girl?"

"Until you got greedy." He reaches around me and grips his cock, holding it steady for me to sink down. "Come on."

I roll my hips one more time, loving the way he bites his lip again and groans. His magnificent muscles strain with the effort of holding back.

My legs shake as he slowly pushes inside me.

"Oh, fuck, that's good, Lilly. Just like that." He curls his hands around my hips, gripping me tight.

I take him deeper, watching him battle his need to hold me down and thrust up into me. Rolling my hips, I take a little more, growing slicker and hotter. I close my eyes and relish this feeling I've never gotten anywhere else, take pleasure in how my body responds to him.

"Lilly," he says hoarsely. "I love your fucking pussy."

I can't help laughing and he groans. I take my time riding him, driving us both wild. He touches me everywhere. Possessive caresses up and down my back, over my hips, down my thighs, encouraging and exploring every inch of me.

"I'm close. So close." He's so thick and hard, orgasm isn't far away.

His hands go back to my hips, not guiding or directing. More like he's appreciating every movement.

I gasp and grind into him harder, taking everything. My legs tremble. Heat blooms over my skin. My vision blurs. A low moan pours out of me. The relief takes my breath away.

Under me, he flexes his hips, drawing out the exquisite pleasure until I can't take any more.

"Lilly," he rasps, his voice a warning that he's about to lose control.

I roll my hips slower, run my hands down his chest. "What do you need, Z?" I ask in a playful tone.

"I need to empty my balls in you, woman."

I burst out laughing and he flips me on my back, thrusting back inside so hard, I gasp. His feet dig into the mattress, fucking harder and harder. Pinned underneath him, I lift my legs, wrapping them around his waist.

He growls a savage sound and wraps an arm around one of my thighs holding me tight. All his earlier restraint shattered by his need for release. The power of his body relentlessly pounding into me, his harsh breathing, the way he's so focused on me, all of it has me on the edge again.

My name rips from his throat and he squeezes his eyes shut. His movements slow to a deep grind as he fills me with heat. The sensation triggers me again. Together, we strain and grasp at each other.

His sweaty forehead touches mine.

"I love you," he whispers.

"I love you too."

Instead of pulling away, he wraps me up tighter.

"Z?"

"Hmm?"

I run my hands up and down his back, still enjoying the heavy weight of him over me.

"Am I crushing you?" he asks, opening his eyes. He groans and rolls to the side.

"No, I like it. Every time is better than the last. How is that possible?" I whisper.

His usual devilish smile makes an appearance. "You're my magical, mythical woman. You can turn a man's dick to stone just by looking at it."

"Oh my God." I flop against him and he curls his arm around me. "The stuff that comes out of your mouth."

"You'll never be bored."

I flick my tongue against his nipple and he groans. "Give me a minute to recover."

"Recover in the shower. I'm sweaty and sticky all over."

He glances down. "Never really had sex without a condom before you. Forgot how messy it is." His voice falters on the last few words, as if maybe now isn't the best time to bring up past conquests. I don't want him to think he has to censor himself with me. I crawl up his body and straddle him again. Leaning down, I kiss his chest, swipe my tongue over his neck, and nip his earlobe.

"I like getting all messy with you," I whisper against his ear. "Love feeling your cum inside me for hours after."

He groans and grips my ass. "Fuck woman, what're you trying to do to me?"

"Get you to shower with me."

He grips my ass tighter, kneading and spreading my cheeks. "Love your fucking ass."

"Don't get any ideas. My back door isn't open for business."

He laughs so hard he ends up shaking me off him.

He rolls out of bed and holds out his hand to me. "Come on. Let's clean up and get some sleep. I bet Little Man will be up early. "

"He'll be happy to see you."

"Planning to spend most of the day with you two."

I lean up and kiss him. "Can't wait."

CHAPTER FIFTEEN

Z

MURPHY DOESN'T SCREW AROUND.

Heidi stops by to see me the next day.

"Hi, Uncle Z!" she greets me with a big smile.

"Hey, when'd you get here?" I ask, standing up to give her a hug.

"Just now."

"You even stop to see the house yet?"

"No, Murphy said you needed something." She nods toward the open office door.

I motion her inside. "Where's Alexa?"

"Outside with Murphy." She glances over her shoulder. "She's missed him a lot."

"I promise I won't keep him down here longer than I need to."

A flash of guilt crosses her face. "Sorry. I didn't mean it that way."

"I know you didn't, sweetheart."

"If he's still here when classes are over, we'll just move down for the summer."

"He'd like that. But I know he's pretty anxious to move into that big house he's building for you."

"I swear he added more bedrooms and I'm scared to ask why."

I raise an eyebrow. "We both know why."

She tosses her head back and laughs. "Yeah, probably." Her eyes sparkle and she leans forward. "What about you and Lilly? Chance needs a little brother or sister, don't you think?"

"Hopefully, a brother. He's already got Alexa and Grace to look after."

She claps her hands together and squeezes her eyes shut, something she's done since she was about four years old whenever something made her really happy. "This is so great. They already have a big brother." Her face sobers some. "Sorry. I'm sure it's been rough and I don't really know what happened. I'm just happy they're here now."

I shake my head, not offended at all. It's a weird fucking situation and I'm grateful Heidi has been as welcoming to Lilly and Chance as she has. "Same."

"So," she says, sitting back and adopting a more business-like tone, "I talked to Bree last night."

"Wedding stuff?"

She laughs. "Yeah, lots of that. But I asked her about school, and how on earth she and Liam find time to spend with each other with him working such long shifts."

Damn, Heidi's smart. Instead of placing her firmly in the "little sister" category her whole life, maybe we should've been grooming her to patch-in to the club.

"And she reminded me Liam actually works the afternoon shift. But he's had a lot of overtime lately."

"Working downtown?"

"No, covering shifts for the officers with more seniority who are working downtown, adding extra coverage near the big trial. Sounds like he's been stationed out by the mall and near campus. I didn't ask her directly about the trial or federal building at all." She flashes a devious smile. "Didn't have to."

Perfect. There are plenty of other members of Empire PD who I might know, but it sounds more like they'll be patrolling the surrounding area, not necessarily the courthouse itself. I'll verify that with one or two other contacts before deciding what course to take. "Excellent. Thank you, Heidi."

She shrugs. "Sure, no big deal. I had a coupon to Michaels to share with her anyway. I think she's bought out all the iridescent white ribbon in every craft store from here to New Jersey for these wedding favors she's making."

In some alternate universe, maybe I'd feel bad about asking Heidi to exploit a friendship. But that's not how club life works. For a truly dedicated old lady like Heidi, the club will always come before any relationship with an outsider. Even someone she's known since she was a kid, like Bree.

Being a cop, Liam's smart enough to know the risk of Heidi and Bree's friendship. Had Heidi asked direct questions about the trial and Bree even casually mentioned Heidi's interest to him, he would've suspected we were up to something. Then a few weeks from now, when the poor, disgraced ex-senator comes to a violent and bloody end, someone would've been knocking on the clubhouse door.

Bree's newly-rekindled friendship with a biker's old lady probably annoys the shit out of Liam. Then again, I've met the guy, and while Teller's right, he's a straight shooter—the kind of cop I'd never offer a bribe. When Charlotte was attacked by her uncle, Liam bent the rules and allowed us to straighten things out beforehand instead of tossing Charlotte in jail. Even accepted the phony excuse about why we had video cameras in Charlotte's apartment at face value. So, while the guy's honest, he's also smart and practical.

Believe it or not, I have respect for honest cops. They willingly risk their lives every day for shitty pay and even less appreciation. It's that whole shit pay versus risk of life thing that usually turns them dishonest.

Still, since I plan to murder the ex-senator soon, I don't want even a whiff of a connection between my club and him.

CHAPTER SIXTEEN

Z

"I DON'T THINK I WOULD'VE VOLUNTEERED FOR THIS IF I'D KNOWN I WOULD end up in a suit," Murphy grumbles, tugging at his sleeves.

"Aren't you going to wear one at your wedding? It'll be good practice."

He growls out a few curse words. "I'm not sure what you're going for, but we look more like mafia hitmen than politicians or lawyers." He flashes his hands, covered in lots of ink, just like mine.

"We'll blend in a lot better than we will in jeans and cuts. Quit your bitchin'."

Outside, we run into Hope.

"Oh my. Where are you two off to?" she asks, approaching slowly.

"Just a little side hustle," Murphy quips.

"Oh." Her gaze swings my way. "I thought you might be sneaking off to marry Lilly."

Her assumption both surprises and intrigues me. "You think Lilly would want that?"

She shrugs. "I don't know. She's pretty adventurous." She turns her stern mother-hen stare on Murphy. "Don't get any ideas. *Your* wedding's happening here."

Murphy smirks. "Yes, Mom."

She fusses with the lapels on his suit, which Murphy tolerates a lot better than when I did it a few minutes ago. I'm about to toss out an additional mom joke when she starts doing the same thing to me.

"All right. That's enough of that." I brush off her hands and she grins up at me.

"Well, good luck with…whatever you're doing." Her face turns more serious and she squeezes my arm. "Be careful."

Something she usually tells us when she senses we're up to no good.

"I'll do my best."

All my planning and worrying were really for nothing. We follow a small crowd of people underneath the eight-foot marble eagle resting over the entrance. The heavy, leather briefcase I'm carrying is the final, and most annoying, detail of my schmuck-in-a-suit costume. The guards open it and briefly flick through the contents before passing it through the scanner.

Once Murphy and I pass through the metal detectors downstairs and flash some—fake—identifications to the already-bored guards, we're pretty much free to roam the courthouse. It's five stories of modern but classic styling in the shape of a rectangle with lots of marble and giant columns.

Plenty of police, marshals, or guards are stationed around the place. But we walk with purpose, don't linger, and no one really gives us a second glance.

"Not feeling reassured about our government right now," Murphy mutters as we push the huge, wooden doors to Courtroom B open and scan the room.

"Were you ever?"

"Nah, I guess not. Just surprised we got in so easily."

"Why? We're nothing more than concerned taxpayers here to watch a public trial."

He rolls his eyes at my sarcasm and lifts his chin toward an empty row up front.

Sure, why not.

Bad idea. Because as soon as that piece of scum takes his seat at the defense table, practically right in front of us, I move to stand up. To beat him to death with my bare hands? I'm not sure. Only a thick wooden railing that looks straight out of the 1930's stands between me and him.

Murphy grabs my arm, yanking me back down into my seat. "What the fuck, bro? Calm yourself."

"I'm fine."

The judge enters a few minutes later and, like dutiful citizens, we stand for his introduction to the courtroom.

The trial is boring. We sit through several long, tedious, procedural speeches for pieces of evidence the prosecutor wants to introduce.

"Starting to understand why Hope hated being a lawyer so much," Murphy whispers to me.

What the prosecutor keeps describing, politicians diverting public funds to their friends and taking a percentage on the back-end, doesn't sound much different from how I assumed the government works anyway. Also sounds pretty similar to some of the club's business dealings. No big shock there either.

It doesn't seem like much has been accomplished by the time they break for lunch. No wonder the trial has been scheduled to take at least a month.

After Kelly and his two lawyers walk past us, I nudge Murphy. We end up following behind them to the cafeteria downstairs. It doesn't seem wise to get too close, so I can't hear anything that's being said at their table.

Murphy watches me in silence while he eats a hockey puck-sized hamburger. My tray sits in front of me, untouched. Spilling blood is the only nourishment I need.

"What's the plan?" Murphy asks.

"I'm not sure yet."

This probably seems like a waste of our time, but Murphy goes with it, sitting back to check his phone.

My patience is rewarded a few minutes later when the two lawyers check their watches and stand up. They say a few words to their client before walking away.

Finally. The fucker's alone.

Murphy stands with me and casually picks up our trays. He takes them over to the garbage cans while keeping his eye on the senator. Good to know we're in sync on this one.

We fall in step behind our mark and follow him out of the cafeteria. Right before the elevator, he ducks through a door to the right.

Is he trying to make a break for it?

No, he's stepped into the men's room.

Perfect. The opportunity I've been waiting for.

"I'll stay out here. Make sure no one else comes in," Murphy says.

I couldn't find a way to casually ask Lilly what happened to all the shit from her office. The letter opener she told me about is probably long gone. But obviously the one in Sway's office is similar enough to drive home the point I want to make. That's why I grabbed it last night and stuck it in the briefcase, figuring the officers wouldn't think much of it if it was thrown in with a bunch of other office-y junk. And if they had confiscated it, I would have rolled with Plan B.

Luckily, I was right and they didn't look at it twice.

Now, it's nestled inside my breast pocket.

No, I'm not stupid enough to kill the guy in the middle of the day in a crowded federal courthouse. I'd never put my or Murphy's freedom at risk by being that reckless.

I *do* plan to have a chat with the fucker.

He's washing his hands at the sink and doesn't even bother to look up when I enter. It's nice that he's so carefree and unafraid. Guess no one's ever terrorized him in his whole miserable life.

That's about to change.

I've obsessed over this for days, but I still allow things to happen organically. More fun for me that way. He glances up and scowls. I guess I look a little menacing in the small space. I widen my stance to increase the threat.

Then I strike.

In a quick movement, I grab him and shove him into one of the bathroom stalls. The space is too small for the door to close behind us, but that's fine. I don't need it to.

With one hand, I press his face against the cool tile wall and use my free hand to jam the letter opener into the side of his neck. Not enough to make him bleed or leave a mark that will invite questions, but enough for him to feel the threat.

"Who are you?" he asks, frantically thrashing under me. I allow the weight of my body to sink into him and he squirms. "What? What are you doing?"

"Don't worry," I whisper against his ear. "You'll enjoy it."

He struggles even harder. "No. Oh my God. Get *off* me!"

"What's wrong? Don't like it when someone bigger forces himself on you?"

"Stop, please. Please don't," he begs.

"Tell me, Senator, do *you* stop when someone begs you to?"

He goes completely still. "What do you want?"

"I want justice for the *actual* crimes you've committed."

"I'm on fucking trial!" He sounds so outraged at the indignity of it, I want jam the letter opener in his neck all the way.

No. Lilly and Chance need me. My club needs me. I hang onto my desire to make him bleed by a thin thread. I'm stronger than my base instincts.

"We both know that quid pro quo bullshit is nothing. You pissed off someone higher up and they're gettin' even. This whole trial's a joke. Think hard, Shane. Who else have you hurt?"

"No one!"

I take the letter opener and wave it in front of his eyes. But fuck, who knows how many women he's violated over his entire career? I highly doubt Lilly was the first. The letter opener might mean nothing to him.

After a beat of silence, he asks in a strangled whisper, "Are you her brother?"

Ahh, maybe he remembers after all. "Nope."

"Oh, God."

"Not him either."

"I didn't—"

I use the hand pressing into his skull to choke off his words. "We're *way* past cheap denials, Senator. We both know what you did."

Outside, raised voices infiltrate the heavy wood door. Fuck. *Time's up.*

Kelly takes a deep breath like he's about to scream for help and I grip his throat tighter. "I wouldn't if I were you."

He closes his eyes.

"I'm not killing you today, Senator. Probably not tomorrow either. I plan to enjoy the trial. You'll see me again, though. Don't worry."

"They'll put me in protective custody!"

What a pathetic plea.

I step back and spin him around so fast he loses his footing and lands hard on the open toilet. Leaning over, I slap his cheek a few times. "That's cute you think it matters. It won't matter. Now that I know who you are and what you've done, there won't be a place anyone can put you that I won't find you."

CHAPTER SEVENTEEN

Z

"Glad you're finally back, Prez," Shadow calls out.

Is that disrespect I sense in his snide tone? He's such a jerk in general, it's hard to tell if this is his normal or if he has an issue with me.

"Miss me, bro?" I sneer.

"We may have a problem, Prez," Rooster says.

Now Rooster, I've been able to depend on. I trust his judgment. Still don't care for the way he's standing around uneasily staring between Shadow and me. "Don't stand there with your mouth open. If we have a problem, get everyone to the table."

"Panic and Eazy are on the road," Shadow reminds me.

Fuck, if something's going down, I'd really like to have everyone here.

"That's fine." They're on a planned run. Nothing I can do about it at the moment.

While Shadow stalks through the clubhouse calling brothers to the table, Rooster jerks his head toward the office and I follow him inside.

"What's going on?"

"He says he got word that Vipers are meeting with DeLova on our turf. Tonight."

"Bullshit."

"DeLova's not thrilled we're no longer collecting money for him." Rooster shrugs. "So anything's possible."

Shit. That's a call I made to try and distance us from the mafia. "You don't seem a hundred percent."

"DeLova's not dumb. I can't see him getting close with an MC that has the reputation the Vipers have. Especially when he knows the history between our clubs. He'd kick that action back to his son-in-law or some of his lower guys before going to the Vipers."

"Where are you at tracking down that black caddy?"

"Fuck, Z. You got any idea how many black caddies people rent every month? It's taking forever to comb through them all."

"This is a brother's life we're talking about. I don't give a fuck how long it takes."

He steps back. "I'm tracking them down as fast as I can. That's what I was working on when Shadow started in with this Vipers nonsense."

I let that sink in for a second. "He know what you're working on?"

"Of course. He's been helping me go through them when he has time."

My gut screams Shadow shouldn't be anywhere near that task. "Have Jigsaw and Huck help you. Tell Shadow it was a dead end."

Rooster stares at me.

I cock my head. "Did I stutter?"

"No, Prez. I got you." He hesitates and glances away. "I'll recheck the ones he went through."

"Good."

Murphy knocks and pushes the door open. "What's going on?"

"I'm gonna go talk to Jiggy," Rooster says, brushing past Murphy as he backs out the door.

Murphy watches him go, then shuts the door.

"Teller with you?" I ask.

He swivels his head from side to side, like he's searching for an invisible Teller. "We're not attached at the hip you know," he says once he's finished the theatrics.

"Since when?"

Shaking his head, he pulls out his phone and sends a text to, I assume, Teller.

"What's got you so cranky?" Murphy asks. "Thought you'd feel better after your chat with the politician."

"Better. Fuck no." All I felt was rage that I couldn't gut him on the spot.

I motion Murphy closer. "Shadow insists DeLova is meeting with the Vipers tonight."

"Jesus. What's his hard-on for the Vipers about?"

"I don't know, but if I ignore it, and it is happening, I look ineffective. We go poking around where we don't belong, I'm going to look incompetent."

"Fuck me," Murphy groans. "Let's grab some brothers we trust and check it out."

"We're all sitting down at the table. I'm gonna let Shadow take the lead. Explain what information he has to all the brothers."

"So, it's his ass if this goes wrong."

"Right."

"We're still checking it out though, right?"

"I don't think I have a choice."

"What's the emergency?" Teller asks, pushing into the room and closing the door behind him.

"You fucking kidding me?" he bitches after I explain the situation.

"Do I look like I'm in a joking mood?"

"He's really crabby," Murphy says with a straight face.

I give him a quick shove, knocking him into the desk, and he laughs. "Lighten up, Prez. We've got your back either way."

"Yeah, I feel the love."

"Who else do you trust to go with us?" Teller asks.

"Steer, Jigsaw, Hustler, and Rooster. I don't trust Shadow, but he's definitely going so I can kick his ass when nothing comes of it."

"Good call," Murphy says.

I nod for Teller to open the door. "Let's go before everyone thinks you're jerking me off in here."

Teller rolls his eyes. "You really are crabby."

"I've got enough to worry about without this asshole stirring up trouble for no reason."

"Why not just call DeLova?" Teller suggests.

"And say what? 'Hey, bro. You bitter we won't collect your debts anymore? Going behind my back to the Vipers?' I don't think he'll be real receptive to that sort of accusation."

"It might make things worse," Murphy agrees. "Or give him ideas."

"Exactly."

"They're ready for you, Prez," Rooster says.

"Let's hear what Shadow has to say."

The guys follow me inside and I take my place at the head of the table. I wait until everyone's seated and then nod to Shadow. "All right, VP. Let's hear it."

By the way he jerks his head back, I don't think he expected me to give him the floor. But fuck that. When this goes to shit, he can be on the hook. And if by some miracle he's actually right, I have no problem giving him credit.

Shadow stands and clears his throat. He jams his hands in his pockets and stares at the table for a few seconds before speaking. "You cuttin' off DeLova was a bad move, Z. He's pissed and he's going to the Vipers to pick up the slack."

"That's ridiculous," Steer blurts out. "DeLova hates the Vipers more than we do."

Shadow stares at our SAA and flexes his jaw. Guess he wasn't planning to be questioned so early. I keep quiet and give Shadow all the time he needs to hang himself.

"He might not want to do business with them, but we didn't leave him a choice."

"His son-in-law practically runs the Devil Demons and he's got more than enough minions," Steer points out. "Our relationship was always supposed to be temporary, anyway."

Maybe Shadow wasn't aware of that fact because he frowns at Steer. "It brought in money."

"It's dirty business," Rooster says. "It's beneath us to be DeLova's bitches."

"It sure as fuck wasn't bringing in enough money to justify the headache," Hustler adds.

Well, all right then.

Murphy dips his chin at me and flashes a discrete thumbs up.

"What are you asking the club to do, Shadow?" My tone leaves no room for weaseling around.

"Malone's bowling alley." He points at Murphy and then me. "You two been there, right?"

"Yeah," I answer slowly. "We did a pick-up for DeLova not that long ago."

"Well, Malone's up to his neck again. He's renting out the place for a Viper/DeLova meet to work off some debt."

My immediate reaction is *bullshit*. Malone's too much of a pussy to be that stupid. Then again, desperate men do dumb things all the time.

Maybe he feels DeLova can protect him if we find out.

"Vipers are coming all the way from Jersey to meet DeLova at some dumpy bowling alley in the middle of nowhere?" Jigsaw asks, not bothering to hide his disbelief. "They're so eager for DeLova's business, why aren't they rolling out the red carpet for the old dude?"

"How the fuck should he know?" Smoke rumbles.

Shadow jerks his shoulders and throws his hands in the air. "I ain't exactly privy to what's going on in their minds."

"When?" I ask.

"Tonight."

"And you're just telling us now?"

"I just found out," Shadow says.

"From who? How reliable is this?"

Shadow smirks and runs his hand over his chest. "I'm friendly with one of the waitresses there. She let me know."

"You trust her?" I ask.

"Enough to let her suck my dick."

"Great, that's helpful."

"I trust her. She ain't dumb. Knows what'll happen if she fuckin' lies to me. Also knows Vipers got no business in our territory. Says it's not the first time they've been to Malone's, either."

"But she just told you now?" Teller asks.

"We've gotten closer," Shadow answers with a lazy smirk I'd really like to punch right off his face.

I tap my finger on the table a few times while I think it over, then look down the table at the men I'm in charge of. "I want to take a small crew down there tonight. *Only* to check it out. No cowboy shit. Stay out of the way and observe. Am I clear?"

"I'll go," Rooster volunteers.

I nod at him. "Shadow—"

"I should stay here so she doesn't accidentally tip them off or something," he interrupts.

Not fucking likely, asshole.

"No. This is your show, brother. You're going." My tone leaves no room for discussion. I move on down the table. "Steer, Jigsaw, Hustler."

"You got it," Jigsaw says. The other two just nod.

"Everyone else, I want to stay here at the clubhouse. No partying. Everyone remains alert, in case this is a trap and someone comes to fuck with the clubhouse. Or in case I need you to come back us up. Is that clear?"

"You got it, Prez," Suds says. Not that he's a coward, but I think he's relieved not to be heading into the action.

"We'll bring some weapons upstairs," Smoke says.

"Easy on the guns, old man," I warn. The last thing we need is that trigger-happy motherfucker surrounding himself with an arsenal tonight. The other brothers laugh and rib Smoke, something I'm sure pisses him off.

Confident the brothers who are staying behind can handle things, I end the meeting.

"Let's meet back here in an hour," Shadow suggests.

Curious about how he plans to spend that time, but unwilling to ask, I nod.

Smoke lingers a little too long for my liking, but I ignore him and finally, he slinks off.

"How do you want to handle this, Z?" Steer asks.

"You comfortable riding in?"

"Yeah, got no reason not to."

"You and Shadow take the lead." I nod to Teller and Murphy. "I'm taking them in my truck." I motion for Grip to join us. "You follow behind in the van, just in case. Jigsaw, Rooster, I want you in the van with Grip."

They both give me an odd look, but don't question me. "I think nine Harleys rumbling up might tip our hand," I explain. "This adventure isn't about being seen."

"Gotcha," Jigsaw says.

"The two of you out for a ride isn't a big deal, right?" I roll my eyes at Steer. "Apparently, Shadow hangs out there all the time picking up waitresses."

He frowns. "News to me. But I ain't exactly in charge of his dick, ya know?"

"Christ, who'd *want* that job?" Rooster jokes.

I shouldn't let my irritation with Shadow bleed into my interactions with the other brothers. If Shadow's right, then the club's about to have a serious issue.

"We all watch each other's backs."

Everyone agrees and then breaks to get ready for the night ahead. Murphy and Teller follow me down to my room.

"Are you sure about this, Z? It stinks," Teller says as soon as we shut the door behind us. Even though I appreciate him not questioning me in front of everyone, I'm not in the mood.

"It's bullshit. But I can't afford to ignore it."

"Z's right," Murphy adds. "You're in a shitty spot all around. If Vipers show up tonight, we're fucked. If they don't, then you've got to deal with Shadow."

"I'm aware."

"I still think you should call Chaser and maybe feel him out," Teller says.

"Let's check this out tonight first. If nothing comes of it, I'll call Chaser." I turn, staring out the window at the back parking lot and the shed out back. "If it *is* happening, then Chaser and I need to have a whole different discussion."

CHAPTER EIGHTEEN

Z

"Tell Grip to stop right before the roadway to Malone's. Have him pull the van to the edge of the woods," I order Murphy.

"You got it."

I do the same, slowly steering my truck off the shoulder and down a steep slope of grass.

"Maybe back it in?" Teller suggests.

"Good call," I grunt, shifting the truck into reverse.

It's dark and quiet as we slip out of the truck and walk over to meet the guys in the van. Steer and Shadow should already be in Malone's parking lot.

"Grip, stay here and stay alert. No fucking around on your phone."

"Got it, Prez."

My phone buzzes with a text from Steer. *Nothing.*

I answer: *On our way.*

I'd taken a look at an aerial map before we left the clubhouse and call up the same map on my phone now. "Jiggy, Rooster, take this corner closest to the dumpster. Hustler, take the far left corner. You should meet up with Steer there."

Murphy raises an eyebrow, waiting for more instructions. "Stick with me."

We cut through the woods and emerge at the bottom of Malone's parking lot. Music thumps through the air, but the parking lot only has a few scattered cars and two bikes.

"Not that busy," Rooster whispers.

"No other bikes besides our guys either," Jigsaw says.

"They could be around back." I point in the direction of the cracked asphalt that wraps around the side of the building.

I check my phone but nothing more from Steer. Nothing at all from Shadow.

This reeks of a set-up.

"Go get into your positions." I nod toward the building. Hustler, Jigsaw, and Rooster take off.

Murphy, Teller, and I approach the low, concrete wall surrounding the dumpster.

"This is bullshit," Murphy mutters.

"Tell me about it."

We stop at the wall and the three of us survey the parking lot.

"DeLova would roll up with an entourage ten deep coming into our territory to meet another MC," Murphy says.

"At least. Jesus Christ, he comes in a damn caravan to his own son-in-law's clubhouse."

Teller shifts and checks his phone. "We could be early. Not like Shadow had lots of useful details."

My phone vibrates and I check the incoming text.

Hustler: *I don't see either of them anywhere.*

Fucking great.

I text Jigsaw and Rooster, but neither of them has seen Shadow or Steer either.

Tension curls in my stomach. What if Steer and Shadow are working together and lured us out here? What if Shadow took Steer out and he's waiting to nab the rest of us?

It's never good when you're questioning your brothers' loyalty.

The rumble and whine of multiple bikes has us ducking back behind the wall.

"That ain't Vipers, unless they're lettin' members run rice burners now," Murphy mutters.

Teller snorts and shakes his head. "They could be recruiting anyone."

The bikes pull up to the left of the building. Sticking to the shadows, I take a chance and step out to see who's arrived. "None of them are wearing colors."

"They're cowards." Teller brushes up against my side. "They want to do business on our turf, they might not bother wearing colors."

"True. Still don't see a single vehicle here Emperor DeLova would sit his dainty ass in," I say.

My phone vibrates and I step back behind the wall to check the message.

Rooster: *Who rode up?*

Me: *Not sure. No colors.*

My phone vibrates again.

Steer: *Shadow went inside.*

"*Godfuckingdammit!* I told that motherfucker to stay outside."

I warn the rest of them to stay put.

A few minutes later, a girl runs out the front door, gets into a red sedan, and speeds off. "That's not ominous or anything," Teller says, watching the car until it disappears around the bend.

"I can't see shit," Murphy says in a low voice.

"Me either."

My phone goes off again.

Shadow: *They're not here yet.*

Me: *Get your ass outside.*

Shadow: ??? *I am.*

Who's lying? Steer or Shadow? I don't want to let my dislike and distrust of Shadow cloud my judgment. But I have no reason not to believe Steer.

Sensing my dilemma, Teller touches my shoulder. "I'll go check."

"Don't."

He lifts his chin. "Rooster and Jigsaw should be right up there. If I don't see anyone, I'll come right back."

Murphy scowls at Teller as he creeps along the side of the building.

"Let's go." I jerk my chin toward the direction Teller just went. Hiding out behind the fucking dumpster all night doesn't exactly make me a good president or brother.

Teller grins at me when we reach his side. "Jesus, Dad. I wasn't gone long."

"Don't start that Dad shit with me like you two do to Rock."

"I didn't say a word." Murphy smirks at me. "Dad."

"Asshole." I search the area behind the bowling area. A large field of grass leading into a more heavily wooded area. Plenty of places to hide.

"Come to join our party?" Jigsaw asks.

"Some party," I answer without taking my eyes off the tree line.

"The place is dead inside," Rooster says.

There's a small shed a few feet away. I motion the guys to move over to it so there's something between the woods and us. "You went in?"

"No." He points toward the open windows in the back. "This place is noisy as fuck when the lanes are open and in use."

He's right. Other than the steady beat of music, there are no other sounds.

A metallic *bang* inside the building draws our attention toward the back door.

Finally, a text from Steer shows up.

Steer: *Hustler's with me. I still don't see Shadow.*

I give him our location and wait for them to meet us.

"They lost sight of Shadow." I sweep the area again, but nothing stands out. "He said he was out here."

All of our phones buzz.

Shadow: *I'm down. Right inside back door.*

Fuck me.

Me: *We're coming.*

I turn to Rooster and Jigsaw. "Tell Grip to get ready. Stay here and watch our backs." Teller and Murphy follow me to the building. Halfway there, we run into Steer and Hustler. "What the fuck?" I keep my voice low, but my irritation comes through clearly. "How'd you lose sight of Shadow?"

Not used to being questioned, Steer glares at me before answering. "Said he heard something and went to check on it."

I send Hustler back to the others and motion for Steer to follow us inside.

Before touching anything, I slip on my black leather gloves. The cheap screen door creaks as I pull it open. This place really is a dump.

The stench of gasoline sears my nostrils when we step inside.

It takes a second to locate Shadow's crumpled form in a heap on the floor. Steer rushes over and helps him up.

"You all right, brother?" I ask.

He rubs the back of his head. "Two guys jumped me."

"You should've stayed put." I jerk my head toward the door. "Get him outside."

"No way, Prez," Shadow reaches out, grabbing at my cut. "I ain't leaving until I get the motherfucker who whacked me."

Murphy creeps toward the door leading into the main part of the bowling alley. "How many?" he asks Shadow.

"Don't know. Two? Three?"

Teller eases over to where we found Shadow, crouching down to examine the spot. To our left, there's a whoosh and roar.

Suddenly, that gasoline scent takes on a whole different level of importance.

"Get him out of here!" I slap Steer on the back and he pulls Shadow to the door.

Flames climb the wall to my left and spread out over the ceiling. My gaze lands on a stack of red gas cans bundled together in the corner like a do-it-yourself nuke.

"The building's gonna blow." I wrap my hand around Murphy's bicep and yank him toward the open door. "Teller. Move it. Now!"

Confident they're both behind me, I haul ass out the door and keep on going. Murphy's arm brushes against mine and I turn slightly, surprised Teller isn't right next to him. "Teller?"

"He's coming."

Something a lot louder than the crackling flames whizzes by.

"Who's shooting?" I shout, pulling my own piece. If one of my guys started flinging bullets, I swear to fuck, I'll shoot 'em myself.

Murphy whips around. "Shit!"

My gaze flies in the direction he's pointed and we're both pounding over the grass before I process the scene in front of me.

More bullets soar over us and I crouch low, firing in the direction I think they're coming from.

"Jesus." Murphy drops down, sliding over the grass on his knees to get to Teller's side. "T, you all right?"

Teller groans and pushes himself up with one arm. "I'm alive." He cranes his neck. "But I fucked up my bad leg."

"Come on." Murphy wraps one arm around Teller while I keep an eye on the space behind them.

"Fuck," Murphy groans. "How can your scrawny ass be so heavy?"

Teller's feeling well enough to poke Murphy in the side. "Muscle weighs more than fat. Shouldn't you of all people know that?"

"Shut your mouths and keep moving!" I snap.

Murphy glances at me. "Are we clear?"

"I don't know. Let's get him to the truck. Cut through the woods. I've got your back."

The situation with the building isn't getting any less intense. It's a roaring inferno now. Orange flames lick the dark sky, lighting up the surrounding area. Metal creaks and groans.

More bullets *thwack* into the trees as we race by them.

Steer reaches us and helps Murphy carry Teller. I drop down and jam a new magazine into my gun, not that it's going to do me much good when I can't even see who I'm shooting at. But we can only dodge the bullets for so long before one ends up hitting something vital. Teller's already taken a hit, I won't have any more of my brothers get hurt.

I scan the area for anything out of the ordinary. Any movement.

Nothing.

The gunfire has stopped as well.

Maybe they're done and took off. Maybe they're reloading. I don't plan to stick around to find out.

Turning, I jump up and race over the uneven ground until I catch Steer.

"Where's everyone else?"

"Waiting for us," he answers over his shoulder.

At our vehicles, the guys are tense and waiting.

Once I'm sure Murphy has Teller safely inside my truck, I slam the back door and turn to the rest of the guys. "Take it slow. Cops and fire department are probably on their way. Don't give anyone a reason to pull us over." My gaze strays to Shadow. "Are you okay to ride?"

"Yeah, I'm fine." He scowls toward the fire. "No one came out of the building."

"Two cars whizzed by right before I saw the first flames," Grip says.

"Any bikes?"

"Not that I saw. And I heard the pack that went in not long after you guys left."

"Let's get out of here."

"What the fuck, Prez?" Rooster says once we're in my truck.

I squint out the windshield, watching Shadow for signs he's not okay to ride. We need to get clear of this place now. "Shadow all right, you think?"

"He's gonna wish he was dead," Murphy growls from behind me. "I'm gonna gut him for getting Teller shot."

I glance sideways at Rooster. "Easy, brother," I warn Murphy.

"I'm with the ginger." Rooster shakes his head. "This whole night is bullshit."

I glance into the back of the van. "He all right?"

"He's bleeding a lot. Teller's always gotta be a showoff." The tension in Murphy's voice betrays the joke.

Jigsaw pokes his head out from behind Rooster's seat. "Already sent Doc a text. He should meet us at the clubhouse."

"Thanks, brother," Teller groans.

"I knew this was a bad idea," Rooster grumbles.

"Anyone even see a fuckin' Viper?" Jigsaw asks. "Because I sure didn't see shit. But someone wanted us dead."

"Shadow was already near the wood line when the bullets started flying," Murphy says grudgingly. "It wasn't him."

"Doesn't mean the fucker didn't light the fuse," Jigsaw says. "Create a little chaos."

"What's he got against me?" Teller says.

"He was probably aiming for Murphy." I glance back and lightly punch Murphy's shoulder. Not in the mood for jokes, he grunts and takes the hit without responding.

He and Teller have been friends their whole lives, even before the club. As much as they love busting each other's nuts, they're closer than brothers. The crash that almost killed Teller a couple years ago had rocked Murphy hard.

Forget Murphy. How am I gonna explain to Rock that I got his son shot?

Worse, what the hell did we stumble into tonight?

CHAPTER NINETEEN

Z

OUR CLUBHOUSE IS LIT UP AND THE PARKING LOT IS FULL WHEN WE PULL IN.

"I'm fine," Teller bitches when Steer and Murphy try to pull him out.

Shadow's inside being looked at by the doctor when I walk inside.

"His bump can wait, Doc. We got a bullet wound."

"You guys love to keep things exciting for me, don't you?" Doc mutters.

"Stick with Teller," I say to Murphy, even though it's obvious he's not going anywhere.

"Everyone else in the chapel. Now." I point to Shadow. "You too."

"What the fuck was that clusterfuck?" I roar as soon as everyone's seated.

"Prez, they were coming. I know it," Shadow insists, sounding a lot less sure than he did when he was convincing me earlier.

"Well, whoever was inside is dead now," Jigsaw says. "No one could've survived that blast."

"Not like there wasn't acres of woods surrounding the place anyone could've disappeared into," Shadow mutters.

"How'd the girl know to run?" Rooster asks.

"What girl?" Shadow asks.

"Some chick took off right around the time we lost contact with you."

"My girl wasn't working tonight."

Wait a minute. "Earlier you made it sound like she was there?"

"I got the nights mixed up," Shadow says without looking at me.

"Who else knew we'd be up there?"

"No one," Shadow insists.

"DeLova never showed." Steer crosses his arms over his chest and glares at Shadow. "No Vipers showed."

"There were bikers there," Shadow counters.

"None were wearing colors, bro."

"Did they get out?" Steer asks.

"I don't know." I glance at Shadow. "I was too busy ducking bullets."

We go round and round for a while, but Shadow can't remember anything and he's got no explanation for what went down. The fact that he actually seems remorseful and he's got a pretty solid crack to the back of his skull are about the only things stopping me from choking him.

"Go see the doc when he's done with Teller," I say, jerking my head toward the door.

Shadow stands and looks around the table. "It was a good tip. Either someone played me or they spotted us and didn't come."

"Sure, bro," Jigsaw says.

After Shadow's gone, the other guys glance at me. Everyone's on edge and it's my job to calm them down so they don't do anything stupid. No matter my feelings about Shadow, the brotherhood needs to stay tight.

"We had to act on our VP's information," I say slowly. "I'll call Chaser tomorrow and feel him out." I nod at Steer. "You still got your connections?"

"Yeah."

"See what you can find out." I tick off each item on my fingers. "Who was inside the building. Possible suspects. Known associates. Whatever you can."

"You got it, Prez."

I release everyone from the table and Steer approaches me slowly. "That was a shitshow."

"What the fuck you want me to say?" I growl.

He holds up his hands. "I'm not blaming you, Z. You took the only action you could. Everyone made it out okay." One corner of his mouth kicks up. "We all needed a little excitement."

"I would've been fine not getting shot at tonight."

"Yeah, that was dicey." He shrugs. "Guess Malone won't be a problem for DeLova now."

"Yeah, funny how that worked out."

"He's gonna be pissed if Malone went up in flames before his debts got paid."

"No kidding. Not our problem, though."

"Nope." He claps me on the shoulder and heads out. I follow behind him and run into Doc in the hallway.

"How's Teller?"

"Fine. Bullet didn't hit anything major. Had to dig it out, which he didn't appreciate."

"I bet."

"He needs to rest. Don't let him do any activities that will disrupt the stitches."

"I'll do my best, Doc."

"Make sure he takes the antibiotics I gave him."

"Got it."

"Don't let him drink, either."

Teller's not a big drinker so that shouldn't be an issue.

"No strenuous activity."

"I'll warn his old lady."

Doc shakes my hand.

"Thanks again, Doc," I shake his hand and point him in Shadow's direction. "Make sure he didn't suffer any more brain damage than he already has."

I swear Doc rolls his eyes. "I'll do my best."

I continue down the hallway and knock on Teller's door. "Hear you were showing off your ass."

"Fuck you. You should see the size of the hole he dug in my thigh."

Murphy grins, ignoring Teller's bitching. "He's weirdly proud of his ass."

The smile slides off my face as I approach. Teller's whiter than the damn bedsheets. "Seriously, bro. You all right?"

"I'll be peachy once these painkillers kick in. The fucking stitches hurt more than the damn bullet did."

"Shit. Either of you call Rock?"

"I did." Murphy nods. "I don't think he found Teller's screaming in the background all that comforting."

Fucking great.

As expected, two hours later, Rock shows up. I know it's him by the way he thunders down the hallway. Teller's asleep but won't be for long.

"Jesus Christ, is he all right?" Rock storms into the room, looking like the raging, overprotective papa bear we're always teasing him about being times a thousand.

"Doc says he'll be okay. As long as he follows directions."

"Thank fuck."

Murphy raises his hand. "Uh, I'm fine too, Prez. In case you were worried about the rest of us."

Rock relaxes his stance and shrugs. "Of course, I'm worried about you. Don't be an asshole." He lifts his chin at Teller. "You all right, knucklehead?"

Teller blinks and gives Rock a serene smile. "Yup, just added a few more scars to my already fucked-up leg."

"Ladies love the battle scars," I assure him.

"Um, no we don't," Charlotte says from behind me.

I open the door wider. "Hey, sweetheart," I say. "Glad you're here."

She reaches out and squeezes my hands. "Is everyone else all right?" she asks in a low voice.

"Yeah. Thanks for coming down."

Teller holds out his hand, motioning Charlotte closer. "What are you doing here?"

"I drove down behind Rock," she explains.

"I said *don't* mention it to Charlotte." Teller glares at Rock who shrugs.

"You take a bump to the head and forget who gives the orders?" Rock asks.

Charlotte slides around Murphy and takes Teller's hand. She's a damn miracle worker because his bitching dies down as soon as she snuggles up next to him.

Rock jerks his head toward the door. "I'll check on you later. Get some rest, knucklehead."

Murphy follows Rock and I into the hallway and over to my room.

"What the fuck happened?" Rock asks in a low, controlled voice as soon as I shut the door.

I explain what went down.

"Why the fuck are we always getting shot at down here?"

"Been shot at plenty of times in our own territory, Prez," Murphy points out.

Rock shoots a glare at him, then me. "You trust Shadow?"

"Nope. He kind of had me in a tough spot though."

"Yeah," Rock finally agrees. He gives me a once-over. "You okay?"

"Not really. Don't like getting my brothers shot."

"Rather take the hit yourself, right?"

"Kinda."

"Aw, I'm touched, Dads," Murphy snarks.

Rock laughs and shakes his head. "Anyone tell Heidi yet?"

"No," Murphy says. "She's got an early morning class. Teller didn't want her to know. He'll talk to her this weekend."

"Good luck with that." Rock snorts.

"You staying over?" I ask.

"If you've got room, yeah. I'd like to visit Sway with you in the morning."

I chuckle, not surprised at all that Rock correctly guessed where I planned to head first thing tomorrow morning.

CHAPTER TWENTY

Z

Sitting with Sway's gotten to be a regular occurrence when I'm not busy doing a million other things to keep his charter afloat. Today will be a little different.

"You don't have to keep coming down, brother," Sway says as soon as he sees Rock.

Rock actually smiles. "Sure, I do. Gotta make sure you're not trying to keep my VP."

Sway chuckles, then abruptly stops when he takes a closer look at our tense faces. "What's going on?"

I shut the hospital door, wishing it had a lock. "Ran into some trouble last night." After a sweep of the room, I give him the abbreviated version of events.

"Jesus Christ. Malone go up with the place?"

"We're not sure. Didn't exactly stick around and wait for the cops to get there."

"Yeah, okay." He stares off into space for a few seconds. "I knew Shadow had a piece he was seeing there. That's why he usually took that assignment."

Well, at least Shadow might not have made up the whole thing. "Is it possible she's working with the Vipers?"

"Don't know. Never met her." He clenches his fists. "Feeling fucking useless here."

Rock and I share a look. There's no point stressing Sway out in his condition. As a courtesy, I needed to let him know what was going on, but he can't help us right now.

"The guys are digging into it today," I assure him. "What's new with you? Terrorize any more nurses?"

"Nah." He chuckles, which turns into a cough.

"How's the baby?" Sway lifts his chin at Rock when he settles back against the pillows.

The question seems to surprise Rock almost as much as me and he takes a beat to answer. "She's good. Hope and I talked about bringing her to visit..."

"Nah." Sway waves the suggestion away. "This ain't no place for a baby. Fuck only knows what she'd catch."

"Yeah, that was our thought. But Hope sends her regards to you, Sway."

"Appreciate it." His gaze slides to me. "What about you? Someone said you got an ol' lady and kid. When'd that happen?"

Surprised he gives a shit. "It's complicated. She's moving down here with me, so I'll bring 'em by soon."

"That'd be nice." He closes his eyes and puts his head back. "Missed a lot when mine were little. Let Tawny do it all on her own. Wish I hadn't," he mutters.

Rock and I share a *what the fuck* look. Sway's never been one to venture into the deep end of conversation.

"They turned out good, Sway. Janice has been here every day—"

A faint smile ghosts his lips. "She's the best parts of both of us." He cracks open one eye. "You make sure none of the brothers are sniffing after her."

I hold my hands in the air. "I'll do my best, brother."

"Danny's been keepin' an eye on her," Rock says.

"Shocked he's here at all. I was a real shit to him when he decided not to patch-in."

Again, Rock and I are too dumbstruck to respond.

"You're feeling awfully reflective today," Rock finally says.

Sway huffs out a laugh. "A bullet to the head'll do that to a man."

"Suppose so."

Sway's sort of in and out of it after that. I'm thinking of asking Rock if he wants to follow me back to the clubhouse when the door swings open.

Christ, I wish we hadn't stuck around for so long.

"Z?" Shock colors Stella's voice and I force myself not to groan. I'd heard she'd been to visit Sway a few times. Luckily, I'd managed to avoid her.

Guess my luck ran out.

I shoot Rock a *don't you dare leave* look. Thankfully, instead of laughing at the absurd situation, he nods and sits back. "Hey, Stella," he greets.

"Is it…is it okay? Steer said I could pop in and visit."

"I ain't dead yet, sweetheart." Sway motions her closer without opening his eyes.

Wearing jeans and an oversized flannel shirt, she looks more like a college student than an adult film star. She takes Sway's hand and stares down at him in an affectionate way that's honestly kind of creepy since Sway's daughter is only a few years younger than Stella.

"They still don't know who did this to him?" She glances up, her gaze swinging between Rock and me.

I shake my head. "We're doing everything we can to find whoever did it."

Sway chuckles. "List's gotta be a mile long."

"It was club-related, though?" Stella asks, drilling me with cold, accusatory eyes.

Without flinching or blinking, I meet her stare. "You got some information we should know about?"

"No. I…nothing." She thrusts her chin up. "I want to make sure he's safe now."

Oh, please.

"That's why we got brothers here taking shifts twenty-four hours a day," Rock answers.

"What if it *was* a brother?" she insists.

Rock stands but doesn't move any closer to her. "That's a serious accusation. You got a good reason for saying it?"

He didn't raise his voice, but Rock's size alone is enough to intimidate anyone. Stella wisely backs up a few inches. I stand and Sway opens his eyes.

"Easy," Sway says to both of us. "She don't know any better."

I understand what makes Stella tick well enough to know a comment like that would normally piss her off, but she shrugs. "I thought maybe that was why you brought Z down here instead of promoting Shadow."

She jerks her chin at my cut. "On the other hand, it looks like Sway getting shot earned you a promotion."

Little bitch.

"Hey." Sway jerks her hand to get her attention. "Watch that mouth of yours. Z's doing what he was asked to do. It's not your concern."

Christ if she really thinks I had something to do with Sway's shooting, she never knew me at all. Unless she's hopeful I'm here because I want her back. Both options make me want to vomit. "Why I'm here isn't any of your business."

"Give us a minute," Sway says.

I stare Stella down until she looks away. "Yeah, all right. I'll check in on you later, Sway."

Outside the room, Rock turns and glares at me. "The fuck is wrong with her?"

"We haven't talked in weeks."

"Watch your back. Especially if she's visiting the clubhouse."

"Christ, I hope she's not gonna be over there. That's the last damn thing I need."

"Well, Prez," his voice drips with sarcasm, "that's *your* call to make, now isn't it?"

Banning Stella from the clubhouse probably won't help the business relationship she has with the club. But it's a tempting thought. "Well, gee." I widen my eyes and pat my chest. "What do ya know? You're right."

He cracks a hint of a smile. "Fuckface."

"You love my fuckface."

"I do. That's why I don't want anyone talking shit about you."

"Appreciate that." I glance at the closed door. "I'd like to say she didn't mean anything, but I'm not so sure."

"Come on." He cocks his head toward the waiting room.

Shadow stands and smirks at us. "Stella in there giving him a happy ending?"

Ignoring him, I address the other guys. "Who's staying tonight? We need to sit down and I want to know who we'll be missing."

Two of the younger brothers raise their hands. "We'll stay."

"Keep me informed. I want to know if anyone unusual shows up."

Shadow squints at me. "What's unusual?"

After last night, this clown shouldn't be giving me lip. "Anyone not wearing a LOKI cut. That clear enough for ya?"

He gives me a fake-ass salute and drops down into his chair. "Yeah,

Prez."

Rock remains quiet but sticks by my side through the whole exchange. After a quick goodbye to everyone, we head outside.

"Shadow's attitude seems to have shifted awfully quick," Rock says when we get to our bikes. "Where's all his brotherly concern and cooperation?"

"I can't tell if he's embarrassed about what went down last night or what. Is it too much to hope I can contain his attitude long enough to punt it back to Sway and let it be his problem?"

Rock stops and rests his hand on my shoulder. "Be honest, Angus. You think he's gonna be able to take the gavel again anytime soon?"

"That's always been the plan."

Rock swallows hard and moves in closer. "As much as I don't want to lose you, you're a damn fine president."

"You seem to forget I got your son shot last night," I whisper.

He squeezes his eyes shut and shakes his head. "We both know that's not on you."

"Still not feeling good about it."

"And that's why you're a good president. Always knew you would be." He blows out a breath and looks away for a second. "I don't want you to feel obligated to come back if you'd rather run your own club."

If it wasn't obvious how much Rock's struggling, I'd punch him for suggesting I'd ever want to abandon my family.

"I'm not happy down here, Rock. And I don't know how I feel about wearing the big *P*. How the hell have you done it for so long?"

He ignores my attempt to lighten things up. "Everything's up in the air right now. Once you settle in—"

"You're not hearing me, Rock. I don't *want* to settle in. I'm settled in at *home*. Upstate." Jesus, I'm not a wordsmith. Don't usually have a reason to be. How do I explain without sounding like a lazy fucker? "Upstate is home. I helped build that club with you."

"Yes, you did."

I hold out my hands and turn them over. "You, me, Wrath, Teller, Murphy, Dex, Sparky, we all took down the old one and built up what we have now *together*."

"We did."

"This isn't a lack of ambition talking, Rock. I'm proud of what we've accomplished. That's home to me." *Christ, who am I? Dorothy trying to leave Oz and get back to Kansas?*

He glances around the parking lot. "You have an opportunity to do the same thing here."

"Except for Shadow, I *might* be able to win them over, but it's never gonna be the same. They're listening to me now because they have no choice. And maybe out of respect for Sway. Besides, you think that hardass motherfucker's ever gonna fully retire willingly?"

Rock snorts. "Probably not."

"He'd be a thorn in my ass. Undermining me at every turn. We both know his whole reflective-I-should've-been-there-for-my-kids redemption bullshit has an expiration date."

Now he full-out laughs.

"Besides, you need me there to counterbalance Wrath." I slap his shoulder. "Admit it, you two would've killed each other by now if it wasn't for me."

"You're more than just an intermediary for us. You know that, right?"

"Fuck, yeah." Something awful occurs to me and I try to make light of it. "You're not realizing you like it better without me now, are ya, Prez?"

He pins me with a steely-eyed glare. "Not at all. Your presence is missed. By everyone. But I don't ever want to hold you back, either."

"You're not. Trust me. I'm already feeling shitty enough about leaving you hanging at such an awkward time. I was trying to pick up some stuff so you had time with the baby—"

"Which I appreciate. But club always comes first. You know it and I know it."

"Hope and Grace okay?"

"They're fine."

"Let's try and do a family day or something so you can bring 'em down. I bet Chance would love to see Grace."

Rock finally eases up and laughs. "Don't go trying to set my daughter up already."

"Why not? We can be fathers-in-law together. Maybe go fishing when we're old. It'll be great."

He grins and shoves me sideways. "I don't know about that. Heidi keeps joking about Alexa and Grace taking over the MC one day."

I burst out laughing. "Hell, maybe they'll do an even better job than us." I pin him with a sharp stare. "We done with the spread-your-wings-and-fly-away-little-birdie pep talk?"

"For now. We both know it might not be up to us."

That's what worries me.

CHAPTER TWENTY-ONE

Z

ROCK AND I HEAD BACK TO THE CLUBHOUSE TOGETHER.

Not so surprisingly, there's a cop car waiting out front.

"Jesus Christ," I grumble. "What now?"

I take my time backing my bike into its spot. Rock pulls up right in front of the clubhouse and walks over to meet me. "Go easy," he warns.

In Empire, I don't deal with the cops as much as Rock does. From time-to-time, I show my face. Hand over an envelope of cash or whatever. But most of my social skills are directed at maintaining relationships with other MCs.

Some outlaws prefer to be assholes to cops right off the bat. My way of thinking has always been they have a job to do and until it interferes with my club or my life, I leave them to it. Unless they're disrespectful. Then all bets are off.

As far as I know, Sway's relationship with the local cops is civil. Sway was never forthcoming with all the details, but a few years back, the state police had tried to infiltrate the club. They might still be a little bitter that didn't work out and that their informants *disappeared*.

The locals, as far as I know, haven't been a problem. Yet.

"Afternoon, officer," I greet. He's young. Twitchy. Has an attitude, a cocky head tilt, and smugness that rubs me wrong almost immediately.

"Well, two presidents for the price of one. Must be my lucky day."

See, I knew he'd be a douche.

Rock remains silent at my side. This is my club to protect.

"If you're lost," I point toward the road, "the highway's over there. Follow it on out to the big road and keep on going." The tone I use is pretty similar to how I talk to the dogs.

His partner comes around the side of the car. He's older. Slower. Smiling.

"Settle down, Henry." Apparently old and slow plans to play *aw shucks, these new recruits got no respect* cop today. He holds out his hand. "You're new to downstate, right?"

"Temporary."

"Your prez took a bullet to the skull, right?"

Well, at least he's getting right to the point. "You find the person responsible?"

"Not yet. That's not what we're here for today, Mr. Frazier."

Great, they already know my name. Perfect. I keep my face neutral.

"We don't have all day." I roll my hand in front of me in a *hurry up* gesture. "What do you want?"

"You know Malone's bowling alley out on 55?"

"I've been there once or twice over the years. It's a dump."

"It's a pile of rubble," the young cop says.

I raise my eyebrows like I'm waiting for more information.

"Someone burned it down last night. You know anything about that?"

Hah. Nope. I was there and I still have no fucking idea what happened. "No, sir. You sure it was intentional? The place wasn't in the best shape last time I was there. Was anyone hurt?"

"When were you there last?" the older cop asks.

"A couple months ago, maybe?" The night Murphy and I shook down the owner for some cash he owed the mafia. Just a regular Saturday night of fun.

"Any of your bros been there more recently?"

I glance at Rock, who shakes his head. "You'd have to ask them."

"Can we come inside?"

Sure, please allow me to make your jobs easier. God only knows what's going on inside the clubhouse at the moment. "You got a warrant?"

"Do we need one just to come in for a chat?

Points to the old guy for giving it a solid try. "I'm fine chatting out here."

"Seems like if you're really an innocent club of Harley lovers, it'd be no big deal to let us inside," young cop says.

"What exactly are you hoping to find? A smoldering bowling ball? I already told you I don't know anything about Malone's. If one of my brothers has some info, I'll be sure to have him call ya."

Realizing I'm not dumb enough to let them in the clubhouse, the cops glance at each other. "Here's my card. Let me know if you hear anything."

I stuff it in my pocket without looking at it. "Will do."

We wait outside until the cops leave. No way am I risking opening the door so their nosey asses can claim they saw fuck-knows-what in plain sight and use it as an excuse to barge in and search the place.

"Interesting they showed up here so fast," Rock comments as we watch the car drive away.

"No kidding."

Inside, the clubhouse is quiet.

"Get rid of the fuzz, Prez?" Rooster grins at me as he strolls out of the office.

"You catch all that?"

"Sure did." He tips his head. "Hey, Rock. Glad you're still here."

"Thanks."

"How was Sway?"

"Not too bad. Still seems tired. Stella stopped by to cheer him up."

Rooster snorts. "I'm sure she did."

"Shadow's still down there. So's Grip and Brew."

"You got a minute, Rock?" Rooster asks. "I wanted your opinion on something."

They both step outside and I make my way down to Teller's room to check on him.

I'm about to push open the door when I hear Charlotte's voice.

"Did you take a hit to the head?"

Teller doesn't laugh. "I'm serious. I don't want you spending too much time around her."

"I understand why the situation bothers you, Marcel, I really do—"

"It's got nothing to do with that."

"Yeah, okay." I can practically hear her eyeroll. "Z's your brother."

Figured they were discussing Lilly and me.

"He's going through a lot with this transition," Charlotte continues, "And he needs your support. I'm sure he's already upset about last night. Don't make things harder on him."

"I'm not. I haven't said a word."

Liar. I struggle to rein in my laughter.

"Good. Don't. If he's forgiven her, then so can you."

See, I knew there was a reason I always liked Charlotte. She's a smart, practical woman. Not afraid to let Teller know when he's acting like an asshole. Which is good, because it happens with annoying frequency.

"Where's your sympathy for me, woman? I took a bullet in the ass."

"Oh, I'm not thrilled with you…"

Their voices lower and I'm pretty sure he's trying to coax her into bed. So, I do what any good president would do—cock-block.

I tap my knuckles against the cheap wood and push the door open all the way.

"Don't wait for an answer or anything," Teller gripes.

"The door was open, dipstick." I shut it behind me with an exaggerated turning of the knob. "Besides, I can't count how many times you've walked in on me unannounced."

Charlotte chuckles. "How are you, Z?"

"Better than your man." I smirk at both of them. "Obviously."

"That gratitude of yours needs work," Teller says. "If I hadn't been behind you, your ass would've been hit."

"Yeah, yeah." I'm busting his balls, but really, I'm fucking furious he got hurt. A president's supposed to be responsible for all his brothers. If anyone should've taken that bullet, it's me. "Anyone bother you today?"

"Just you."

Charlotte smacks his arm, making me laugh.

"I'm asking because cops were here when Rock and I got back."

Charlotte raises an eyebrow. "What did they want?"

"To come inside for a friendly chat."

She rolls her eyes. "Does that ever work for them?"

"Probably. Most citizens feel it's their duty to be as helpful as possible. They're just beaming with pride to let the pigs in."

"While lawyers everywhere scream in frustration," Charlotte says.

"I'm glad you were here because if it escalated, I was going to have you come out and talk to them."

She tilts her head. Surprised, maybe? Hope's only ever had good things to say about Charlotte's lawyering skills. I trust her. "You think we wouldn't have a female lawyer?"

"I didn't say that."

"Charlotte's practice keeps her busy enough," Teller says. "Sway must have a lawyer on retainer."

"I'm sure he does."

"Charlotte is capable of speaking for herself about her law practice," she says to Teller.

Behind me, Rock chuckles. "Ah, like looking back in time."

Charlotte ducks her head and laughs. "Poor Hope."

"Were you guys this nice to Sway?" Teller asks.

"Nicer." I grin at him.

CHAPTER TWENTY-TWO

Lilly

No one shares any details, but I gather enough information to understand Teller was shot.

Now Charlotte's middle-of-the week visit makes more sense.

"I don't even want to ask what you were doing that someone shot at you."

Z shrugs. "We were just as surprised."

"That's informative."

He kisses the tip of my nose. "Wasn't meant to be."

"Z—"

"Lilly, I'll share with you what I can."

But this is club business. He doesn't say it, but it's written in his expression. Hope's briefly mentioned there are some things she doesn't ask questions about. Heidi's much more matter of fact about it. Some things just aren't our business. Their blind trust in their men always seemed odd to me. Now I find myself trusting Z, probably more than I should.

"Just tell me that we're safe. That *you're* safe."

He doesn't hesitate. "Yes. If I thought you were in danger, I'd have you somewhere else."

"Okay."

I'm still turning our conversation over in my head when Charlotte stops by the house.

"Come in. Chance and I were just going to have a snack."

"I'd love to, but I have to get back. This came at the worst time. I have a trial starting tomorrow."

"Oh, wow. Sorry." I wave her inside. "At least let me make you some coffee for the road."

"Thanks."

She follows me into the kitchen and pours a generous amount of cream and sugar into one of the travel mugs I hand her.

"You leave room for coffee?"

She chuckles. "Marcel says the same thing." She hesitates, then meets my eyes. "I hate asking, but would you check on him? Later today. Whenever you have a few minutes? I know Murphy will be back later." She rolls her eyes. "And Marcel swears he's fine, but I'm worried—"

"Of course. I can do that."

"Just ignore him if he's crabby."

I chuckle and squeeze her arm. "I have an older brother, remember? Plenty of experience with cranky males who don't want to admit they need anything."

"That'll come in handy. Thanks, Lilly. I appreciate it."

At the door, she gives me a quick, tight hug. "I'll hopefully be back down Saturday morning. We'll see how my trial goes."

"Good luck."

"Want to go visit Uncle Teller?" I ask Chance after his nap.

"Otay."

"What do you think we can bring him to cheer him up?"

He races over to the coffee table and picks up what's become his new favorite coloring book. Full of monster trucks. "Good choice."

Besides motorcycles, I've noticed quite a few of Z's brothers have an affinity for tricked-out trucks. Teller's is especially impressive. It seems to be a running joke between him and Charlotte that no one except Murphy has ever driven his truck.

If Heidi or Charlotte were home, I'd probably go through the back gate and knock on their patio door, but as far as I know, Teller's home alone, so I cross our front yards and ring the doorbell.

He takes a while to answer and I almost consider calling instead, but finally, he opens the door.

"Lilly? What are you doing here?" He winces as he steps back to open the door wider, but otherwise remains stoic.

"Chance wanted to come say hello and show you his book of monster trucks."

Finally, his harsh expression softens as he glances down. "Hey, buddy. You bring that for me?" He nods to the book in Chance's hand.

"Uh-huh."

"Let me guess," Teller says in a low voice as I walk past him. "Z asked you to come check up on me?"

"No, Charlotte did. She was upset she had to leave."

"Damn," he mutters. "She has a rough enough week without worrying about this BS."

As unfriendly as Teller has been to me at times, I'm charmed by his interest in and support of Charlotte's career. Since he's so sweet to his fiancée, his sister, his niece, and pretty much every other female associated with the club, he can't be all bad.

I figure his issue has more to do with *me*. I get it. Z may have forgiven me, but it'll take a while before his brothers trust me. While Wrath had been the one I was most worried about, I haven't had to deal with him much since moving down here.

Teller stretches out on the couch on his side and pulls the coffee table over at an angle so he can flip through the coloring book with Chance.

"Have you eaten since Charlotte left?" I ask. Somewhere in the back of my head, career-oriented Lilly is rolling her eyes and asking, *Are you really offering to cater to Z's over-muscled, caveman brothers now?*

But I shut that voice down because she's a bit of a snobby bitch.

CHAPTER TWENTY-THREE

Z

THE TENSION IN THE CLUB HASN'T GONE AWAY SINCE THE NIGHT MALONE'S blew up. I don't completely trust Shadow, but I'm trying to keep the club together.

I also want to keep my *family* together. I always swore I wouldn't be one of those bikers who claimed to be a "family man" yet spent all his time at the clubhouse. When it's appropriate, I have Lilly and Chance at the clubhouse with me. When it's not, I try to spend my days at the house and wrap up as much club business as I can at night.

Today, we're having a spur-of-the-moment backyard barbeque at my place. Teller's finally feeling better. Heidi and Charlotte came down to stay for the weekend. Charlotte's brother, Carter, joined them, promising to watch the kids if we wanted to go to the clubhouse tonight.

Sun's out today. Pool's warm. Why not?

"Hey," Murphy says. "They're doing good, right?" He nods at the pool.

Heidi and Lilly are teaching the kids to swim. Really, they're just splashing and kicking water at Teller and Carter, but that's fun too.

"How pissed is Wrath you haven't been at Furious all week?"

"Don't tell him I'm here today." He shrugs and glances over his shoulder. "Jake's trying to put together a self-defense class geared toward the ladies. More intense than the usual 'poke the eyes, scream, and run.'

Heidi and Charlotte are doing it. I know Wrath's having Trin go, which means Hope's taking it too. Think Lilly will be up for it?"

"Yeah, why not." I point the meat tongs in my hand toward the pool. "She's right there, ask her yourself."

"It's kind of hands-on."

"So?"

"Showing them how to get out of choke holds and stuff."

Meaning Jake needs to put *his* hands on the girls to give them instructions.

Would Lilly blow a gasket if she knew Murphy was basically over here asking my permission for her to take a class? Probably.

"You're fine with Heidi doing it?" I ask.

"Yeah, she's comfortable with Jake."

"You *trust* him with Heidi?"

"Oh, fuck yeah. She's a dolphin as far as he's concerned."

I snort at the joke, happy that's getting around.

He glances over his shoulder. "I'm still not sure how much I trust some of the brothers down here. I figure a few extra lessons can't hurt."

I snort and poke at the chicken on the grill in front of me. "Shit, I don't know what I worry about more these days, the club or everywhere else?"

"Well, that too. Fucking hate some of the douchewaffles she has classes with."

"Someone bothering her?"

"Nothing she can't handle." He smirks. "Or so I'm told."

"Meaning, Heidi asked you not to come to school and make a scene?"

"Close."

"She asked and you did it anyway."

"Much closer."

"You found the kid and threatened him until he pissed his pants."

He slaps my shoulder. "There ya go."

"Oh, is Murphy telling you how he terrorized one of my classmates?" Heidi walks up behind Murphy and presses her wet body against his back, hugging him from behind.

"'Terrorized' sounds so extreme." Murphy shrugs. "It was a friendly chat."

"*Suuuuure* it was. I told you I had it covered."

"What happened, Heidi?" I ask.

"Just a guy in my class. At first, he was friendly. We worked on a group project together. I probably mentioned my daughter and hubby a million times." She squeezes Murphy tighter and he rests his hands over hers. "He started making jokes about how I'm too young to be tied down. Stupid shit like that."

"Fucker," I grumble.

"Typical 'bro' behavior," Murphy says. He glances over his shoulder at Heidi. "Finish."

Heidi groans. "It's stupid. He started texting me, asking me to go out." She tips her head back to look at Murphy. "Told him my weekends were busy."

"And?"

"He just kept it up. I finally sent him a stern, 'I'm not interested, stop asking' text and he flipped out. Said I wasn't that hot anyway and I shouldn't be such a stuck-up bitch and give nice guys a chance. Crazy shit."

I zero in on Murphy. "Sounds like he needed a beating, not a chat?"

Murphy shrugs.

"Teller go with you?"

"No, he's been laid up. Took Rav with me."

"Why didn't you tell me? I would've gone with you."

"I think you have enough to handle right now, *Prez*."

"Um," Heidi pokes Murphy's side. "No one needed to go anywhere. I blocked his number and reported his behavior to the school."

"Yeah, I'm sure they'll take care of it." Murphy rolls his eyes. "The way that school handles stuff, *you'll* probably be the one who gets in trouble for hurting his feelings."

Heidi sighs. There's no arguing with Murphy when he's fired up.

"I kind of agree with him, Heidi."

She makes a wide-eyed face at me. "I'm *so* shocked, Uncle Z."

"Smart ass."

Heidi tugs on Murphy's hand. "Come in the pool with us?"

"I'll be right there." He leans over and kisses the top of her head.

"Seriously, Murphy, you should've told me. I don't want some punk messin' with Heidi like that," I say once she leaves.

"I told Rock, so I was covered. Happened when I was home taking care of things. Only saw one of the texts by accident, Z. She probably wouldn't have told me otherwise. Didn't think it was a big deal. But you know how assholes like that are. He could be some nutjob who kept it up."

"Yeah, or a nutjob who comes after her even harder next time."

He works his jaw from side to side. "Yeah, I thought about that too. So fuckin' glad she's almost done in a few weeks."

"Until the next one."

"Fuck, I know." He looks over at Heidi and Alexa again.

"I can only imagine what you two are conspiring about over here," Charlotte says. "Is the chicken ready?" She gives the grill a hopeful look.

"Couple more minutes." I lean in and elbow her. "Murphy tell you about his campus visit?"

"Yup, I one hundred percent approve."

"Ginger power." Murphy gives her a fist-bump and the two of them laugh.

"Poor Teller," I mutter.

"This dude had one screwed-up sense of entitlement," Charlotte continues. "After he asks her out a bunch of times, and it finally sinks in she's not interested, he starts calling her names. Typical baby who isn't used to the universe not revolving around his obnoxious ass."

"Probably couldn't handle a real woman," I mutter.

"Right." She turns her concerned eyes on Murphy. "She needs to be careful. I've heard of plenty of cases where the guy ends up going after the woman who rejected him."

Murphy growls and searches the yard until his gaze lands on Heidi, sitting next to her brother. "How the fuck am I ever supposed to let Alexa go to school or anything, knowing what kind of creeps are out there?"

"Teach her young not to take any shit from anyone," I suggest. "Let the club take her to school on her first day?"

Charlotte grins, then turns more serious. "Teach her not to smile and be nice if someone crosses her boundaries. Don't tell her stupid shit like, 'Jimmy only hits you because he likes you.' No, Jimmy hits girls because he's an asshole."

"What kind of bullshit is that?" I shake my head. "If I liked a girl, I tried to kiss her, not hit her."

"Also boundary crossing, Z," Charlotte says. "But an improvement."

I snort and laugh. "Baby steps."

"Is there a Jimmy we need to hunt down and kill?" Murphy asks.

Charlotte laughs. "Oh my god, no. Well, probably. I did hear lots of ginger jokes when I was a kid. But seriously, I have a case where I just want to strangle the mother for filling her daughter's head with that patriarchal nonsense."

Murphy and I sort of stare at her.

"Yeah, yeah, my life is a study in contradictions." She waves her hand in the air. "You know what I mean. There's a difference between men who lead and men who squash."

I know which one I want to be.

Lilly steps out of the pool with Chance. He seems a bit overwhelmed and not sure where to go first. Finally, he spies me and races over, landing with a wet thump against my leg. I reach down and rub my hand over his wet head. "Have fun?"

"Yeth!" He bounces up on his toes and I angle my leg to keep him away from the grill. "Careful."

Lilly reaches for him, capturing his hand and picking him up. "Oh my god, you're so heavy."

I hand the spatula to Murphy. "Here, I'll take him."

"No, he's fine," she protests, but Chance is already reaching for me.

"Oh, yeah. You're drenched." I glance down at my T-shirt. "I wasn't planning to go in the pool until *much* later."

Murphy scratches his beard. "Is that what those noises are we keep hearing at night?"

Lilly sputters. "I don't know what you're talking about."

He leans over and casually flips a few burgers. "Heidi thought it was dolphins mating, but I don't think we have those around here."

"Dolphins." Lilly snorts. "More like a bear—"

"That's what I said," Murphy interrupts. He waves the spatula in my direction. "Now bears make sense. They're massive, violent, territorial, and," he lowers his voice, "they *eff* a lot. Very noisy too."

Lilly doubles over laughing, which makes Chance laugh even though I don't think he followed a word of that.

"Thanks for the bizarre nature lesson, weirdo." I shift Chance to one arm and snatch the spatula out of Murphy's hand. "Get away from my grill."

He walks off. "Heidi, I solved the mystery of the dolphins we've been hearing," he yells across the yard.

"Asshole," I mutter.

Lilly steps closer and slides her arms around us. "He has a point." She bats her lashes.

I lean down and growl at her, which sets Chance off laughing again. So, I growl at him too before swooping in to kiss both his cheeks. He slaps at his face and wiggles to get down. I set him free and point him in Murphy's direction.

"Are you having fun?" I shrug. "Not very exciting, but—"

She glances around at everyone and leans in to hug me again. "I don't need exciting. This is a perfect day."

I drop my hand to her hip. "You're still okay going to the clubhouse tonight?"

"Sure. Is it a dress-up night, or something more casual?" She tugs at her hair. "Trying to decide if I should go wash it now or just wear it up or something."

"Whatever you want. You always look good to me."

Exasperated with my lack of information, she presses her palm against my chest and stares up at me. "Is anyone important coming?"

"Should just be members. Couple girls. Never know if a few nomads or brothers traveling nearby will stop in."

She bites her lip.

I lean down and whisper against her ear, "Wear some tight jeans that show off your hot ass and a top that puts those gorgeous tits on display. Is that more helpful?"

She glances down. "I don't know if I like everyone staring at my tits."

"Let 'em stare. Everyone in that clubhouse knows you belong to me and I'll gut anyone who touches you."

She pokes me in the side. "Murphy's right. You *are* a bear."

I twist and start plucking chicken legs off the grill, dropping them in a bowl of sauce. "More of a beast." I give her ass a soft slap. "Who finally has his beauty."

CHAPTER TWENTY-FOUR

Lilly

Since Teller's "accident," things have been tense. Z's spent a lot of time out of the house.

One of the old ladies summoned me to the clubhouse and while Z didn't ask, I know it will mean a lot of I try to socialize with some of the other old ladies.

All problems can be solved with a good party. At least that's how Angie explained this weekend's event at the clubhouse.

"As Z's ol' lady, you really should supervise the girls," Angie says.

Supervise what?

At least she offered to shop for the party. I wouldn't even know where to start.

Heidi plans to stay home with Alexa so she can study and invites Chance to stay with them.

"It's just you and me," Charlotte says.

"You're coming?"

"I think Teller needs to be there so I want to go with him."

Once we're at the clubhouse, she offers to restock the bar with boxes of liquor Angie left for me.

A number of club girls have stopped in. How they knew we needed help, I'm not sure. I've noticed word just seems to spread and girls will show up on party nights. Some seem to show up early and genuinely want to help out. Others only show their faces long enough to lay claim on a brother before any other girls get to him. Which is an effort in futility. Most of these bikers don't seem to be the type to be claimed by any one woman.

The kitchen's being taken care of by a group of girls who seem to have arrived together. Angie has them set up in an assembly line, chopping vegetables and marinating steaks to be thrown on the grill later.

Shadow and Jigsaw work their way through the kitchen under the pretense of checking on the food. Well, I think that might be what Jigsaw actually came for since he helps himself to a little of everything.

"You're going to get E-coli," one girl warns him, bumping him out of the way with her hip. He spends some time flirting with her before moving on to the next girl.

Angie moves in closer, "I've got this covered. Just tidy up the rest of the place." She glances over at me. "Uh, I mean have the girls help you."

Unsure why she's so nervous around me, I nod and head to the front room.

Shadow blocks my path out of the kitchen. His rat-like eyes turn even rattier as he scans my body. "You plannin' to dress up tonight?"

It's such an odd, creepy question coming from him, I don't know how to answer.

I glance down at the LOKI T-shirt Z told me to wear to the clubhouse this afternoon and my jeans. "I don't think what I'm wearing is any of your concern."

"Sure, it is. You're with our president."

Fuck off, fucker.

Damn Z and his lecture on how important respect is to bikers. Although, I'd argue Shadow's being pretty damn disrespectful to me, I wonder if the club would see it that way?

"Yo, Shadow," Jigsaw calls. "We gotta go."

"Be looking for you later, don't disappoint."

Fuck yourself right off a cliff.

I force a fake smile and almost jump ten feet in the air when he runs his hand down my back and over my ass.

That definitely can't be acceptable behavior.

I turn to say something, but he's already stalking toward the back door. No one's looking my way so I'm not sure if anyone else saw what he did or not.

Still shaking, I continue into the living room. A group of girls waits for me. *Oh, joy.*

At least I recognize a few. Serena gives me a friendly smile as I approach. "Where do you want us to start?"

"I'm not sure yet."

"What do you need, Lilly?" Bonnie asks.

What *does* the rest of the clubhouse need? Besides a cleaning crew with a tub full of bleach. Or a blow torch.

"I'm not sure. General straightening up, I guess?"

"Condoms," a girl they call Josey says. She seems to be the brashest one. The kind who came early to stake out a man, not marinate some steaks. "The guys prefer easy access to them if they don't want to leave and go find a room. At the one outside Portland, they keep bowls in every room. Z should do that here."

Oh no she didn't mention Z's name. "'Easy access', is that what the guys call you?" I ask sweetly.

"It should be." Her friend, Sasha giggles and digs through her purse. She flings a handful of condoms in Josey's face and they both laugh.

So, basically they're making more of a mess for me to clean up.

I glare at them, then shift my gaze to the condoms scattered on the floor. Sasha kneels down to scoop them up while apologizing.

At least one of them knows I'm not fucking around.

Serena leans into me and says in a low voice, "Josey isn't a regular here. She's not usually helpful when she visits. She hangs out at different charters until someone's old lady kicks her out and then she moves on to the next."

"Fantastic," I mutter. "Just what I need."

Josey eyes me up and down, then shoots a glare at Charlotte over by the bar. "Are *old* ladies leaving after they set up this party?" She crosses her arms over her chest and lowers her voice to a soft purr. "I was hoping to get *reacquainted* with Z now that he's here full-time."

This bitch.

My anger spikes off the chart, but I somehow manage to hang onto my cool and not rip off Josey's head. "Since *I'm* Z's old lady, you better readjust your plans."

She feigns surprise by slapping her palm to her mouth. "Sorry, Lilly," she says, not sounding one bit sorry. "It's just, you know, Z's a *real generous* guy."

Sasha's gaze skitters between Josey and me. "You know how it is," she says in a wobbly voice.

I cut her off before she continues. "No. Enlighten me."

"Well," Josey says, speaking to me as if I'm slow, "usually the old ladies go home where they belong so everyone else can have a good time."

Sasha bobs her head up and down as if her friend just offered me some helpful information.

I'm way too old for this nonsense. "Is that right?"

Josey ignores the deadly calm in my voice. "Yeah, and Z's always been fun to party with. I don't think—"

I step forward, pleased I tower over this tart by quite a bit. "You're not as clever as you think, bitch. I'm aware the 'women who've fucked Z club' isn't an exclusive organization. If you need a commemorative patch to help you reminisce about the good ol' days, I'll order it up."

"Huh?"

See, I knew that was too many words. "Z's mine. That clear enough for you?"

Josey narrows her eyes as if she's considering challenging me. When I don't back down, she shrugs. "A brother comes to me, I ain't turning him down. Not my problem if he's saddled himself with some nag."

I refuse to be drawn into a catfight with this twit. She's not worth the effort.

Next to me, Serena shakes her head. "I told you."

"Oh, shut up, Serena," Josey snaps. "You've fucked almost every brother between here and upstate, but I don't see your skanky ass wearing a patch."

Serena's cheeks turn red and, feeling protective of her, I wrap my arm around her shoulders. "If you're not here to help, then you need to leave." I pin Sasha and Josey with a hard stare so they understand I mean business.

Sasha takes a few steps away from her friend. "I want to help out, Lilly."

"Fuck that. I ain't a damn maid." Josey flails her arms around, narrowly missing scratching Sasha's cheek with her long, dagger-esque nails.

In case she forgot the way out, I point to the door. "Don't let it hit your ass on the way out, sweetheart."

She stomps off in her ridiculous lumberjack-meets-stripper boots and hits the door so hard one of her fake nails snaps and flies into the air, landing on the floor with a sad little clatter.

Shaking my head, I turn to the rest of the girls. "Anyone else have some smartass remarks for me?"

The girls blink and shake their heads. A few murmur "no."

"Questions?" I search their blank faces. No one pipes up. I take Serena aside. "What usually needs to be done before a party?"

"The bar is the most important." She scans the large entry room that's basically set up like a living room. Couches, chairs, a few tables, two big screen televisions, and a ratty, almost threadbare carpet fills the space. This seems to be the central location for most of the parties.

Serena taps her finger against her bottom lip and shifts her gaze. "Josey was being a bitch, but they do usually set out bowls of condoms."

Of course they do.

"No glove, no love, right?" I joke.

Serena stares at me for a second before laughing. "Maybe we can hang that over the door."

I nod to one of the signs hanging above the couch that I never paid much attention to before. A garish black and gold one that reads, *Before you bag her, sheath your dagger!*

Good god, what have I gotten myself into?

I end up writing down a list of tasks for Serena to hand out to the girls. Yes, one of them is "go buy condoms". There better be a petty cash fund around here because I sure as fuck am not paying for that out of my purse.

"Any questions?" I ask the girls.

No one answers.

"Good. Serena has the list of things we need done around here before the party. If you have questions, ask her. If you need an assignment, let her know. If you think of anything we haven't covered, come find me."

Serena stares at me with her big, pretty blue doll eyes. "Are you sure about this, Lilly?"

"I trust you. Unless, you don't want—"

"No, no, it's fine. I got it."

"Thank you." I leave her and make my way over to Charlotte at the bar.

She slow claps and grins at me as I approach. "Very nice. You'll be a boss bitch biker's ol' lady in no time, Lilly."

I give her a love-shove, almost knocking her off her barstool, and she laughs even harder.

"What the fuck?"

She's still laughing and I contemplate shoving her again. She wags her finger at me and sputters out, "Don't be a fool, cover your tool."

"Oh, shut up. Seriously, I don't remember bowls of condoms all over upstate."

"In the champagne room and probably some of the guest rooms upstairs…The bathrooms…Yup, upstate's as dirty as downstate. We're just a whole lot classier."

I snort and tap her glass. "You get into the liquor while you were putting it away?"

"This is seltzer." She lifts her chin. "That mouthy one coming back?"

"God, I hope not." I pick at the napkin in front of me, shredding it into pieces. "How the hell does Hope stand this?"

Charlotte sips her drink and sets it down before answering. "I don't think she does. From what I understand, Trinity's always been in charge of the clubhouse."

"No, I mean the girls that just have to let you know—"

"Oh, the former bunnies. Gotcha. I'm pretty sure Rock banished every single one who gave Hope lip."

"Ugh, that doesn't help. Those two are from out of town anyway."

She glances down and taps her nails against her glass a few times. "Teller's mentioned that Z was out on the road a lot more than most of the guys over the last few years."

I open my mouth to respond, then think better of it. Z's hinted he spent lots of time on the road after I left.

Because of me. Because I left.

Karma just loves finding new and creative ways to bite me in the ass, doesn't it?

CHAPTER TWENTY-FIVE

Lilly

AFTER ANOTHER DAY OF GRILLING, SWIMMING, AND SPENDING THE WHOLE day with the kids, we came to the clubhouse for this party.

It's not busy yet. A few brothers mill around at the bar. A few girls I recognize buzzing around. The music is at a more comfortable level for conversation to flow.

Z pulls me over to the couch in the corner of the room. His usual spot where he can see everyone entering and leaving the entire area.

"You still feeling okay, Teller?" I ask in a low voice when he drops down next to me.

"So far."

The front door opens and slams shut. Shadow strolls in, surveying the clubhouse for a few seconds before his gaze lands on Z.

"Aw, bro," he hollers as he strolls over. "Your girl Stella was visiting Sway again and asking 'bout you."

I narrow my eyes at the one brother who gives me the creeps every time I'm in the same room with him. Unsure how much trouble it would cause, I didn't tell Z about Shadow's creepy comments or how he touched my ass.

Z's arm tightens around my shoulders. "This is my only girl, *brother*. So, I don't know who you're talking about."

Shadow covers his mouth and laughs. "This ain't no girl. This is a woman. Hello, again." He holds out his hand.

I glance at Z. Is this guy for real?

"This is my *old lady*, Shadow. I'm pretty sure you've already met her several times." Z's venom-laced voice should send a shiver down the spine of anyone with a brain. Shadow apparently lacks any useful gray matter between his ears because he shrugs.

Instead of taking his outstretched hand, I wiggle my fingers in hello. "Lilly."

"You do movies too?" he asks.

"Are you fucking dense, bro?" Z sits forward, catching Shadow's attention.

"Our side-business." Rooster leans over the arm of his chair to explain. "We bankroll a few independent movie studios."

"Porn," Shadow clarifies, butting into our conversation. "Some of the filthiest fucking you can imagine."

I roll my eyes. "I doubt that. I have a pretty good imagination."

Z rumbles with laughter and squeezes my leg. I don't bother looking at Shadow to gauge his reaction.

"Is producing porn still lucrative?" I ask, because really, Z's club produces pornos? Why not? Upstate owns a strip club. Producing pornography seems like the next logical business venture.

"Depends on the talent," Shadow says, leering at me again. "MILF porn is huge right now." He shifts his smirky face in Z's direction. "Prez, you're sitting on a gold mine with this one."

Z stands and pushes into Shadow's space. I can't hear exactly what he says to his VP, but it's definitely not friendly.

Not sure if I should be insulted or flattered, I mull over the MILF comment while pulling my top a little higher to cover any exposed cleavage.

"Shadow has that effect on a lot of ladies," Jigsaw whispers to me. "I got a Hefty bag around here somewhere, if you want it."

Appreciating his attempt to lighten things up, I laugh at the offer. "Thanks."

Z succeeds in chasing Shadow away and takes his place next to me again.

Murphy joins us. "What's everyone doing hanging out here?"

"Telling Lilly about our porn studio," Rooster says helpfully.

Murphy perches on the arm of the couch. "Lucky Lilly."

Jigsaw leans forward and taps Teller's knee. "How you feeling, brother?"

"Better."

Murphy nods at Teller, then leans over to nudge Z. "Since we're already talking about it, do we have an issue with Stella visiting Sway this much?"

Z glares at him. "No."

Something about the guys discussing this woman in my presence really seems to irritate Z. I blink and stare down at his hand, absently rubbing my leg. His phone vibrates and he pulls it out, checking the text before sticking it back in his pocket without answering.

The movement reminds me of the girl who kept calling Z when he first moved into my house. The girl I saw him with in the parking lot of Crystal Ball. He said they were over.

Are they?

It hits me that she looked familiar. At the time, I was too jealous to worry about who she was, but now I finally put it together.

"Wait a second. Your ex—"

Z groans. "She's not my ex."

Ignoring his attempt to avoid this subject, I press on. "The girl I saw you with is *Stella.* the porn star, author, and aerial artist? *That* Stella?" Why didn't I figure that out sooner?

By the way he glances to the side, I think Z might actually be embarrassed. Sure, dating a porn star is probably a fun story for his biker brothers. A totally different experience to tell your future wife.

Lucky for Z, I'm not like most women. And I definitely see the irony of the situation.

The rest of the brothers stop and stare, waiting, I think, to see if I'm going to blow up.

Uncontrollable laughter bubbles up inside of me instead and I slap my hand over my mouth in an effort to hold it back.

"Why are you *laughing*?" Z frowns.

When my breathing finally evens out and I think I can talk without bursting into more giggles, I answer, "It makes perfect sense."

Nope, I'm not done laughing.

His jaw ticks as he waits for me to settle down. "How so?"

"Well," I say slowly, drawing out the word to mess with him, "You have a porn-sized dick so of *course* you'd date a porn star."

The expression on his face is too much. I fall back against the couch, laughing until my eyes water.

The guys groan.

"You could've kept that to yourself," Rooster says.

Ignoring everyone else, Z braces his hands against the back of the couch and leans down over me, staring into my eyes. "I thought you'd be mad," he says in a low voice. "Maybe disgusted. I did *not* think you'd find it so funny."

I reach up and press my palms to his cheeks, pulling him down for a kiss. "I'm not mad," I whisper.

"Obviously."

Maybe he's miffed by my outburst? But come on. It's ridiculous. Do I love thinking about Z with some porn star? Not at all. From what I remember, she's gorgeous. Younger than me. Probably cellulite and stretchmark-free. Flexible.

Okay, that's enough.

Whatever she and Z were doing before I moved back to New York wasn't significant. Otherwise, he wouldn't have dropped everything to be with me.

So, no, I'm not going to waste a lot of effort worrying about his ex.

The porn star.

I snort-giggle again and Z brushes his lips against my forehead.

"Guys," Jigsaw says. "We don't need visual proof of Z's giant porn-sized dick. We'll take your word for it."

"Uncomfortable," Rooster sings.

Without taking his eyes off me, Z shows them his middle finger.

"I never." He meets my eyes again. "I didn't make any films with her. You don't have to worry about our kids being embarrassed in school one day or something."

My heart squeezes. Porn star exes or not, this sweet, sweet man is too good to be true sometimes. "It wouldn't matter to me if you did." I lean up and kiss him again. "Are you with me now? Are you and your porn-sized dick one hundred percent mine? That's all I care about."

"You're the only woman I want." His mouth twitches. "I don't know *why* since you enjoy poking fun at me so damn much."

"I don't care about her or anyone else you were with before. As long as you're mine now."

"Now." He kisses my cheek, trailing down my neck. His rough hands skim up my legs. "And forever. Don't forget that part," he murmurs.

"I won't."

"Awww, are they couple goals or what?" Jigsaw shouts.

"If *couple goals* means absolutely nauseating, then yes," Teller says.

Jigsaw snorts. "Look who's talking. The one with the smoking hot redhead who comes down almost every weekend to fawn over him."

Teller glares at him. "Her name is *Charlotte*, dickface. You know what? Never mind. Don't ever look at my old lady again."

"Hey, that's an improvement." Rooster reaches over and slaps Jigsaw on the back. "Usually he calls her 'that chick who's way out of Teller's league.'"

"I call her that too," Murphy adds.

I can't help laughing harder. "Well, from what I hear, Charlotte calls *him* her platinum-tongued sex god."

The guys groan, then howl with laughter while I catch Teller's eye and wink at him. He leans over and gives me a fist-bump.

"Speaking of girls out of your league," Jigsaw turns his mischief-making face on Murphy.

"Don't do it," Teller warns. "His old lady is my baby sister."

Murphy grins and shrugs. "I love her anyway."

"So," I interrupt before they continue picking on each other. "Why are two eligible, single bikers hanging out with a bunch of spoken-for brothers?"

"Good wingmen." Jigsaw nods at Z. "Our prez's pretty boy face lures in the ladies." He shifts his finger in my direction. "Then you can get out your claws and scare them right into my lap."

"I thought I was your wingman?" Rooster says.

"No, you're a distraction. The ladies always want to pet your dumbass beard."

Rooster pats his fluffy cheeks. "My beard is awesome. Ladies love riding it."

Everyone groans.

My gaze swings between Jigsaw and Rooster. "I don't think either of you need help drawing in the ladies."

Z raises an eyebrow at me, but I ignore it.

Jigsaw traces a diagonal line from the top of his forehead to his right eyebrow. "The scar scares 'em away."

I sit forward and study the faint, jagged line he's pointing out. "I wouldn't have noticed if you didn't point it out."

"See, it's like I keep saying. It's your annoying personality that scares women away. Not your ugly face," Rooster says.

"You look like a badass. Girls like that," I assure him.

Jigsaw grins. "I guess I've had plenty want to kiss my booboos better."

"All right. That's enough of that," Z says, standing and taking my hand to pull me up off the couch with him. "My old lady doesn't need to hear this."

"But we do?" Teller says.

Z presses up tight against my back, slipping his arms around my waist and kissing my neck. "I want to do a lot of filthy things to you tonight."

Worried his brothers can hear us, I let out a nervous laugh. "Why?"

"Are you looking for a more complex answer than 'you make my dick hard every time I look at you?'" he whispers against my ear.

The timbre of his voice as he admits the level of control I have over him releases a wave a desire. Every inch of my skin hums with anticipation.

"I thought you were mad about me laughing at your wild love life?"

He snorts. "I can never stay mad at you for long, Siren."

The other guys continue harassing each other and Z eases me closer to the bar so we're alone.

All teasing fades from his expression "I should've said something sooner."

My heart skips. What exactly is he trying to confess? "About what?" I croak.

"Jesus, nothing bad." He leans in and runs his hands up and down my arms. "Yes, I was seeing her for a while."

"Stella?"

His face twists as if he hates hearing the name. "Yes. We were never serious or anything."

"Okay."

"I wasn't lying. When you came back, I ended it with her."

"Why? We weren't really together."

"Come on, Lilly. I warned you I wouldn't let you get away again. Anyway, she was pissed at me."

"So, she had feelings for you?"

His eyes widen and he holds up his hands. "Not that I ever knew of. Trust me."

"So, you had feelings for her?"

"Nothing real." He looks me in the eye. "I know the difference now."

How can he make my heart squeeze at the same time he's telling me about his ex?

"What are you trying to say, Z?"

He jerks his thumb over his shoulder. "Like they said, she works with the club. Her company is more Sway's pet project—"

"And he let you date her?" I ask with wide eyes.

"I'm sure he wasn't thrilled. Can I finish?"

"Please do."

He shakes his head and I have a twinge of guilt for messing with him when he's trying so hard to tell me whatever it is he thinks I need to know. "I've run into her at the hospital when she's visiting Sway. I'll probably have to deal with her at some point while I'm in charge down here."

I shrug. "Okay?"

"Once Sway's out of the hospital, hell, maybe before then, I don't know, it's possible she'll be here for some parties or whatever. I don't want you—"

"Z, I appreciate the warning. But—and don't take this the wrong way—"

"Jesus," he mutters and shakes his head.

I place my hand on his arm to soften my words. I'm really not trying to be a bitch about this. "I'm going to guess that more than a few bunnies who hang out here have enjoyed your company at one time or another?"

He grits his teeth. "It's possible," he concedes.

"Stella was more than just a bunny to you, though?"

"Sort of."

"We've talked about this stuff before. I meant what I said. My own past is plenty colorful."

He narrows his eyes, a spark of possessiveness gleaming in their dark blue depths, but I continue anyway. "I honestly never expected to want to settle down and be with one guy, but you changed that for me."

One corner of his mouth lifts. "Keep going."

Arrogant man. I blow out a breath. "I want you. I understand that you come with all of this." I circle my hand in the air, indicating the club. "The only way I'm going to be pissed about Stella, or any other bedmate of yours, is if it's *not* in the past. My son will not be raised by a weak woman who lets her man humiliate her over and over."

"There's no one but you."

"Good, because you should know I am *not* one of those women who will blame the other woman and start fights over you." I move in closer and brush my hand against his crotch. "I am the kind of woman who will straight-up cut your dick *off* if you ever cheat on me."

I'm kidding, of course. Sort of. I do feel a tad murderous when I think of him with Stella or anyone else, though.

Z stares at me.

I smile up at him.

He stares at me some more.

I pat his cheek. "Good talk, Z. I'm glad we got all this out in the open."

CHAPTER TWENTY-SIX

Lilly

Inside our room, Z strips me of my top and tosses it to the side. "Get those jeans off."

I work them down over my hips slowly and he groans. He'd requested tight jeans before, so I found a pair of skinny jeans I hadn't worn yet. Now I remember why. They're like a damn second skin. I'm trapped and getting them off the rest of the way isn't remotely sexy.

Z pushes me back against the mattress and tugs the material down my legs. "Need some help, Siren?"

"I guess so."

I sit up and he tries pushing me back down. But I slide out of his grasp and off the bed, landing on my knees.

He stares down at me with a smile playing over his lips. "What are you doing down there?"

"Whatever I want."

In a swift move, he slides his hands in front of his groin, shielding himself from me. "I don't know if I want you so close to my dick. You threatened to cut it off a few minutes ago."

I play with the button of his jeans, tugging it out from under his iron grip. "Only if you cheated on me."

"That's not happening."

"Then you're perfectly safe."

He moves his hands and I flick the button loose, and carefully ease his zipper down.

I kneel up and wrap one hand around his monster of a cock. "So damn hard. Impressive." I hold his gaze while I swoop in and circle the head with my tongue.

He hisses in a sharp breath. "I'm always cocked and loaded around you."

I chuckle and flick my tongue over the tip.

"Fuck. Do that again. Jesus, that's amazing."

"Well, I'm no porn star, but—"

"Uh-uh." His serious tone stops my hand mid-stroke. He leans down and presses a finger to my lips. "No jokes about that. Not here. This is just us now."

Z

I swear my legs still won't work right. "You broke me, woman," I tease Lilly as she gets dressed.

She grins over her shoulder.

"Come back here."

"Are you planning to get dressed or do you want to show off your porn-sized dick to everyone tonight?"

I rub my hand over my face and try not to laugh. "Thanks for that. I'll never live it down."

She fake-pouts at me. "Oh, poor Z. The other boys are gonna make fun of you for having a big dick."

"Get over here." I grab her hand and yank her down on top of me.

My fingers tangle in her hair and I drag her down for a long kiss. She pulls away and stares down at me. "Come on. The club needs to see more of their president's face tonight."

"Their president needs his woman."

"You just had me."

"You think I'm an asshole because I'd rather be in here with you than out there running my club?"

"What? No. Christ, Z. You're pretty much running the club twenty-four seven. Of course, you need time to yourself."

I lean up and kiss her again. "Thank you."

She sits up and trails kisses down my chest, over my abs, a little lower, then she stops and kneels next to my legs. "You'll get more of that later."

I groan and roll out of bed, snagging my jeans off the floor. She glides over to the closet and pokes through the few dresses and things she keeps stored here. "You planning to wear something else?"

She shrugs.

"Everyone will think we came down here to fuck."

"Like they don't already know."

Maybe fifteen minutes later, we're heading back to the party. It's definitely gotten louder and rowdier since we left.

Murphy and Teller are over by the bar so I head to them first. Not before noticing Jigsaw and Suds tag-teaming an eager club girl over the pool table.

"Anyone ever actually use that thing for pool?" I ask as I approach the bar.

Hustler overhears my question and shrugs. "That table probably has more STDs than a truck-stop whore."

"Lovely," Lilly murmurs so low only I hear her.

I squeeze her hand and she squeezes back.

"You two look miserable." I lift my chin at Teller, then Murphy. "Why not head home? Things are cool here."

Murphy's actually looking past me and I'm not sure he even heard my question. His jaw locks. "He's such a fucking asshole."

Teller follows his line of sight. "Are you joking? What, are you jealous?"

"Fuck no." He shoves Teller. "Doesn't mean I want him hurting any of the girls here, though."

We all glance over to where Murphy's focused.

"Oh, shit. You're right," Teller mutters.

Yeah, Murphy has a point, all right.

Shadow has one slab-sized hand wrapped around Serena's forearm as he yanks her into the hallway. She digs her heels into the carpet and shakes her head. It only forces him to tug on her harder.

When she curls her fingers around the corner of the wall, hanging on, I set down my beer.

"Ow." Her high whine rides over the noise in the clubhouse. People stare, but no one seems to want to do anything.

In another MC, no one would think twice. An unpatched woman steps inside a clubhouse, she's fair game. Serena's been around here long enough that some of the guys feel entitled to use her as they see fit.

That ends now.

We don't tolerate that bullshit in our clubhouse upstate. We don't look the other way. No matter how precarious my situation is with downstate right now, I'm sure as fuck not standing by and watching *any* woman get hurt.

"Z, what are you—"

Lilly doesn't even get her whole question out before I'm stalking across the room. It's dark and the music's loud enough that the only people who notice me are the ones I shove out of my way.

"Shadow, stop. Please, no." The distress in Serena's voice propels me into action.

"Let her go. Now." My warning's low, but I know he hears me by the way his body tenses.

He doesn't release her.

I knew this wouldn't go down easily. And that's fine. I wrap my arm around Shadow's throat and jerk him backwards into a choke hold until Serena's able to free herself and stagger backwards.

Turning, I lift my chin at Lilly and she reaches for Serena, pulling her away from us.

Things are about to get ugly.

"What the fuck you doing?" he mumbles with the last bit of air in his lungs.

"She said *no*."

"So what?"

Wrong answer.

I spin him and slam his back against the wall. "Did she look eager to you?"

"She always says no." He snorts. "She likes it. Eventually."

I'm not stupid. I'm aware *some* couples enjoy playing that game with each other, but it's pretty obvious that's not the case in this situation.

"Why isn't she standing here defending you then?"

"Huh? Who fucking cares?"

"I care."

He twists and tries to free himself, but my hold on him can't be broken.

"That's what she's here for," he whines like the weak little bitch he is. "Why are you making a big deal about a whore?"

Christ, this motherfucker's worse than I thought. I've run into plenty of guys over the years who think hurting a woman makes him a real man. Thinks it shows the world he's in charge.

A real man would rather cut off his own dick than hurt a woman. *Any woman.*

"That's not how I run things. If she's not interested, find someone else who is."

"Fuck you. She ain't patched by anyone." He choke-laughs. "Ain't ever gonna be patched by anyone."

As if being patched by this asshole would be some prize. "That's not the point."

"You want her, have at her." His gaze skips to the space behind me. "You already got a hot—"

I cut him off by pressing my forearm against his windpipe even harder. "Don't speak about my woman. Don't even look at her."

"You got...no right...to interfere." He gasps out each syllable.

"No?" I tilt my head in Serena's direction. "She's under this club's protection. I'm the president. That gives me the right. End of discussion."

By now, we've attracted a bit of attention. A couple guys form a half-circle around us. Lilly slowly backs up, taking Serena with her, and Teller moves them away from the scene.

"No means no." I raise my voice to make sure I'm heard by the other brothers. "Anyone who has a problem with that can leave their cut on the way out the door."

Rooster steps up beside me, arms folded over his chest, and stares Shadow down. "As it should be, Prez." His deep, rumbling voice doesn't invite discussion or disagreement.

Shadow's eyes widen. "What the fuck am I supposed to do? Have a bitch sign a form every time I want my dick sucked?"

I slam his back into the wall. "I expect you to not act like a scumbag."

Again, I raise my voice. "This is a club for grown-ass men. Not a hideout for weak little boys. Real men do *not* hurt women. Period. Am I clear?"

"With all due respect, Prez, she's a clubwhore."

Scowling, I search the crowd for who uttered that bullshit. A younger brother, Tiny, I think, backs away under my glare.

"She's a friend of this club. No one under our protection loses the right to say *no* because they walk in our front door." I look around the room. "If anyone has trouble grasping that simple concept, you're not fit to wear Lost Kings colors. Leave your cut on my desk and get out. *Now."*

Jigsaw steps slightly away from the other brothers, the girl he was with earlier clinging to his arm behind him. "This shouldn't even need to be said." He glares at Tiny. "Why you looking so shocked, bro? You want to behave that way, go join the Vipers or a dozen other shitty MCs."

Tiny shrugs and glances away. "Sorry, Prez," he mutters.

Murmurs of agreement spread through the crowd, but I also note scowls on a few brothers' faces. Maybe this wasn't the best time for this demonstration, but fuck it. Waiting for a more convenient time, when I know a girl's being taken advantage of, makes me as guilty as the rest of them.

I shove Shadow once more. "Don't make me have this talk with you again."

"Sure, Prez. Whatever you say goes."

Why don't I feel convinced?

CHAPTER TWENTY-SEVEN

Lilly

"I'm sorry. I'm so sorry," Serena keeps whispering as I take her down the hall.

"Shh." I push the door to one of the quieter lounges open. It appears to be empty and I close the door behind us. "Are you okay?"

"I'm fine. Z didn't have to do that for me. Shadow's only going to be more pissed and take it out on me later."

I don't bother asking why she keeps coming to the clubhouse or any of the dozens of other shitty questions I've had thrown at me in the past. Instead, I put my arm around her and offer support. "Did you want to be with Shadow?"

"No." She shakes her head. "He's never really concerned with my wants. I mean, sometimes he can be nice. But that seems to be less and less often lately."

He's never struck me as *nice* before, but I nod and ask if she wants something to drink instead.

"Please." She rubs her arm where a dark bruise is already forming. It matches one around her neck that's visible when she pulls her hair back.

This life...*club life* is so complicated.

Teller opens the door and shuts it behind him. "Everything all right? You want Charlotte and me to give you a ride home, Serena?"

"Will she mind?"

"Not at all."

"Okay." She stands and brushes off her jeans with shaky hands. Without warning, she pitches forward and hugs me tight. "Thank you, Lilly."

"Sure." I squeeze her back. "Thank you for all your help this week."

The door opens again and Charlotte smiles brightly. "Are we staying or going?"

"I'm going," Serena says.

Teller frowns. "You don't *have* to. No one's kicking you out."

"Oh." Serena stops and stares at him, then me. "It's probably better…I can help you clean up tomorrow, Lilly."

"Whatever you want. You have my number. Text me if you want to come over." *So I can make sure Shadow's nowhere around.* But I don't say that. I'm not sure what Z's going to do and I understand what an awkward situation this is for him.

"I will."

Teller motions me forward and leans down. "Z doesn't want you anywhere by yourself tonight. Let me take you to him before we go."

"Okay."

Charlotte and Serena wait by a side door while Teller and I return to the main room. Things are calmer now. Everyone's gone back to having a good time. Shadow's nowhere to be seen. Z's in the middle of the room, surrounded by brothers and he lifts his hand when he sees me, calling me over. Teller pats my back. "Tell him I'll be back as soon as I drop Serena off."

"Will do."

I blow out a breath and try to appear as confident and unruffled as possible as I make my way to Z. Weakness won't cut it tonight.

I force my lips into a calm smile as I approach Z and take his hand. Instead of sitting next to him, I plant my ass firmly in his lap and he slips his arms around my waist without stopping his conversation.

Tension lingers in the air, but there's also a feeling of relief.

The party's almost gone back to normal when Shadow storms through the room.

The look he throws our way sends ice spiraling down my spine.

CHAPTER TWENTY-EIGHT

Lilly

NORMALLY, I'D SPEND THE HOUR-LONG DRIVE TO EMPIRE THINKING OVER everything going on in my life. Today, I find singing along to the radio with Chance more entertaining.

My GPS guides me to Furious Fitness and I'm a little surprised to see Hope made it here before me. She and Trinity are hanging out in the parking lot talking.

"I'm so happy you're here!" Hope shouts as she jump-tackle-hugs me.

I can't help laughing. "Are you okay?"

"I'm happy to see you."

I wait while she pulls Grace out of the car. Chance sways back and forth, trying to get a peek at her.

Grace lets out a hearty scream at being woken up.

"I'm sorry, baby," Hope coos to her.

"Oh, boy. I don't miss the screaming months," I say.

"She's actually not that bad," Hope says. "Just doesn't like being woken up. Like me."

Trinity holds her arms out. "Let me see her. Hey, Gracie."

Mara pulls in next to my car and joins us. "Why are you all out here? Are we ditching the exercise thing to get drinks? Because there's a really nice bar like two miles down the road."

Trinity laughs and shakes her head. "It'll be fun, I promise."

Mara fusses over Grace and bends down to say hi to Chance. Finally, we're ready to go inside.

Mara bumps Hope with her shoulder. "You just had to mention this to Damon, didn't you? He's so worried about me since I've been working longer hours."

Hope slings her arms around Mara's shoulders and guides her inside.

If I'm honest with myself, I should have done something like this years ago.

"Hi ladies," Wrath greets us at the front door. All polite and professional. I mean, he's still a scary-ass, tattooed giant, but in this setting, he doesn't seem as intimidating. Almost approachable. I suppose terrifying his customers would be bad for business.

After greeting Trinity with a searing kiss, he messes with Hope, ruffling her hair in a familiar way, like she's a five-year-old. She slaps his hands away and he laughs. It's an odd sort of brother-sisterly scene. Unexpected, because of how mean she used to say he was when she first started dating Rock.

Wrath holds his arms out for Grace. "You here to test out the new baby daycare room your uncle Murphy talked me into?" he asks, holding her up over his head.

Hope snickers into her hand. "Murphy's brilliant," she mutters.

"That's a great idea, Mr. Wrath." Mara gives him a sly smile. "Every mom in our neighborhood complains they can't go to the gym because they have no one to watch the kids."

"I heard all about it." He rolls his eyes. "Murphy hammered me when we were re-building. Problem is, I don't want to hire some random college kid to watch the kids. It's been a real pain finding someone qualified." He turns and searches the room. "Murphy swears it will pay off eventually."

"Yeah, when he needs childcare for the baseball team of kids he plans to have," Trinity says under her breath and grins.

"Come on, let me show you around." Wrath grins down at Hope. "I know *you're* intimately acquainted with the locker room, but I'm going to give your friends a tour."

Hope's cheeks turn red and she smack's Wrath's arm.

Ignoring her, he hefts Grace up and kisses her cheek. "Did your mom tell you how you were almost born here?" His gaze lands on Chance and he lifts his chin. "You hiding out, little man? You remember me, don't ya?"

Chance looks up at me before answering, "Yes."

He holds out his hand to Chance. "Come on. You and Gracie can have a front row seat for the tour."

Eager to get near Grace, my son scampers forward to accept the invitation.

"Swoon," Mara sings, rolling her puppy eyes Trinity's way.

After the quick tour, Wrath leaves us in one of the larger classrooms covered with thick, squishy gym mats. Heidi and Charlotte pop in a few minutes later. We're busy talking and catching up when a man joins us.

"Hi, Jake," Heidi calls out to the dark-haired stranger.

"All right, ladies. Settle down." Jake paces at the front of the classroom for a few beats, then stops and gives us a smile that probably drops panties for him every day of the week.

"Wait, why isn't Wrath teaching us?" I ask.

"Because he'll end up groping Trinity and we'll have to watch. It's better this way," Hope says.

"Shut up." Trinity laughs and shoves Hope. "One time."

"Every time," Hope mutters under her breath.

I flick my gaze toward Jake, who's watching us with an amused expression. He has player written all over him, but if Wrath trusts him with Trinity, then I guess the rest of us are safe.

"Thanks for letting me try this class out on you, ladies. We're going to work on escaping from various kinds of choke holds. If someone is choking you against your will—"

Mara giggles.

Jake zeroes in on her. "Ah, I see who the troublemaker is today. I figured it would be Heidi."

Heidi laughs and shakes her head. "Nope, I'm all ears."

"If someone's choking you," he continues after he has our full attention, "it doesn't take long to knock you unconscious. After that..."

Right. He doesn't need to finish.

"I want you to fight back." He slams his fist into his open palm. "Do whatever you have to, get free and find help."

"How are we realistically supposed to get away from someone, say your size?" Hope asks.

"Size isn't the only thing that matters. And this is self-defense, so it doesn't have to be pretty. Whatever you need to do to get away."

"Fair enough."

"I'm not going to go easy on you." Jake seems to shed his fun, flirty guy exterior and gets down to business. "I don't believe that benefits anyone. It's a waste of both of our time."

"Oh, shit," Mara mutters. She pokes Hope. "What'd you get me into?"

Jake curls his finger and calls Trinity up front. "I've worked with Trinity before, so she knows what to expect." He jerks his head to the side and searches what he can see of the gym beyond this room. "And I think Wrath went out so he won't kill me."

Trinity chuckles. "Bring it on, Wallace."

"So, we'll start with something simple, a forward two-armed choke hold." Jake strikes fast, wrapping his hands around Trinity's neck. Instinctively, she grabs his forearms.

"Now, Trinity's a strong girl, right?" He releases her neck for a second and pats her triceps. That has to be a joke. His arms are the size of her head, muscles flex and bulge just standing there. He gives her a subtle nod as he places his hand back around her neck.

She immediately grabs at his arms, trying to pull them away. Exactly what I wanted to do the minute he touched her.

"This is your normal response," Jake says. "Your first instinct—pull the attacker's arms away, claw at them, pry them off." He pauses. "She's never going to overpower me this way. Nothing against, Trin, but she can't do it in time."

"Kick him in the balls!" Heidi shouts.

Jake squeezes his eyes shut and shakes with laughter. "She beat me to the next part." He straightens up and is all business again. "Now, you're probably thinking she should knee me in the groin, right?" He gives Trinity a warning look that makes us laugh.

She grins at him. "I won't this time."

I didn't realize how fast my heart was racing until Trinity smiled and spoke. He's not actually hurting her.

"You can try that," he says. "But you're already at a disadvantage. If you miss, you might end up getting hurt worse."

Something similar had actually happened to me when I was a dancer. The long-forgotten memory makes me shiver. Back then, I shook it off. Figured working as a stripper, what did I expect to happen to me?

"Instead," Jake's strong voice pulls me back into the lesson, "there are two things you can try. I prefer one over the other, but both can be effective and are targeting the same weakness."

He nods at Trinity again. "Instead of trying to pull him off from the outside, pull your arms underneath and explode outward."

Trinity does it so fast it's hard to see and Jake has her repeat the move.

He has her do it a third time, but this time, he captures her wrist as she tries to escape.

"Now she has a new problem," he says. "I'll get to that in a minute."

He releases her and resumes the choke hold. Trinity tightens her body in a slightly different way. Bringing her elbows in to her side, she makes a swift duck and spin move to free herself. Jake grabs for her, but she's already at the edge of the mat.

"See?" He motions Trinity back to the front of the room. "I won't choke you again," he promises.

"Liar." Trinity stands in front of him with her hands on her hips. "Make sure you duck low enough, so you don't hit his arm," she says, explaining why that move worked. "You're using the weight of your body against his thumbs to break the hold."

As she finishes, Jake comes up behind her and hooks his arm around her neck, dragging her backwards. "This one's a little more complicated," he says.

"Jesus, this is hard to watch," I mumble.

Mara places her hand on my shoulder. "Are you all right?"

"I'm fine."

Jake wasn't kidding about it being more complicated. Trinity needs several tries and a lot more effort to unravel herself from the hold. Jake explains the shoulder slip, the mechanics of why it works, and then has us try it on each other.

"I'm too short to play anything but victim," Mara whines.

"I wish Aubrey could've come today," Jake says. "She'd be perfect."

"I knew you had to have a girlfriend," Mara says.

"Nooooo, she's my brother's girl." Jake holds up his hands. "But she's about your size, maybe a little shorter."

"Damn," Mara mutters.

"You can try a stepladder," I offer.

Mara glares at me. "Not funny. All right, come get me."

Scared I'll hurt her, I don't hold on too tight at first. Jake shows me a better way to place my arms and we try it again.

"Come on, Lilly. Don't wuss out on me," Mara coaxes.

I squeeze tighter until she gasps, but she still works her way out of the hold rather fast.

Heidi volunteers to kneel down for Mara so she can finally get to play attacker.

"Good job, ladies. It's good to practice different scenarios. Not every situation will be as calm and controlled."

"Nor will we be wearing comfy work-out clothes," Mara points out.

Jake taps his chin and pauses for a minute. "You make a good point. A lot of the stuff you ladies have to wear to work hampers your ability to properly defend yourself. Sully and I were talking about a class to address that, but not a lot of people want to ruin their work clothes. There are some things we can talk about. Like if you wear heels, using them to kick shins or stab into an attacker's foot."

"So violent," Mara jokes.

"It's a brutal world."

It certainly is.

"All right, how about some floor work? This is more…intimate, so I'll let you practice on each other."

I see what he means a few seconds later when Hope lies back on the mat and Trinity straddles her hips.

Jake explains the basic premise and then the moves to ward off the attacker.

"This is only because I love you," Trinity says before wrapping her hands around Hope's neck.

"Jake." Hope huffs, already visibly straining to get out of Trinity's hold. "This feels unevenly matched."

"An attacker isn't always going to be a five-foot-seven, hundred-and-thirty-pound woman, Hope."

"Oh, aren't you sweet," she mutters. "I haven't seen a hundred and thirty since college."

"Stop yapping and start moving," Trinity squeezes her legs tighter against Hope's hips. "You don't want the guys to show up to find me still pinning you down."

"Why?" she gasps. "They'd probably love the show."

"Triceps, Hope," Jake reminds her. "Hug your elbows in. There you go. Hips up."

Mara leans closer to me. "I consider this foreplay in my house."

I burst out laughing. "Of course, you do."

"Same, girl, same," Charlotte says.

Heidi rolls her eyes. "Gross."

Hope grunts and twists. Even though I know they're both friends, their struggle is hard to watch.

In a burst of concentrated effort, Hope configures her legs just right.

She gets enough leverage to flip Trinity onto her back and rolls on top of her. "Finally." She thrusts her fists up in the air. "Phew!"

Trinity reaches up and tickles her fingers over Hope's ribs, making her laugh, and roll off her and onto the mat.

"See?" Trinity jumps up and holds out her hand to help Hope off the floor. "Doesn't that feel better than if I just let you win?"

"Shut up," Hope mutters. "Dammit, you're strong." She hugs Trinity once she's standing and Trinity says something against her ear that makes Hope laugh.

The realization that I'm a little envious of how close they are slaps me in the face.

Heidi and Charlotte come down together on the weekends, so they're pretty tight. I don't get to spend a lot of time with them. Serena hasn't returned to the clubhouse since the incident with Shadow. I haven't managed to befriend any of the old ladies at the downstate club yet.

"Who's next?" Jake asks.

Without thinking about it, I take a step back. No way am I letting anyone, even my friends, pin me down like that.

"We'll go." Heidi grabs Charlotte's hand and tugs her up front.

"Wait, what?" Charlotte says.

Jake squats down next to them. "Heidi knows how to get out of this one—"

"Naturally." Charlotte rolls her eyes. "So, I get to have my ass kicked by my boyfriend's little sister. Fabulous."

"It's not a competition, ladies."

It takes Charlotte a few tries, but she manages to flip Heidi over.

"Who's left?" Jake eyes Mara and me.

I shake my head and back away slightly. Much to my embarrassment, Jake seems to recognize my reluctance and smoothly pairs Heidi and Mara together instead.

There's a light brush against my arm. "You okay, Lilly?" Trinity asks softly.

"It's a lot to take in. A different...mindset than how I grew up, I guess."

She stares at me for a minute like she wants to choose her words carefully. "There was a time in my life where it seemed smarter to be passive so I wouldn't get hurt even more than..." She sighs. "You can convince yourself of all sorts of lies when your options are limited. "

I swallow hard and tears prick my eyes. I'm painfully familiar with those emotions.

Her expression hardens. "Now, I'd rather die fighting."

I blink and stare.

"I think we'll call it good, ladies," Jake says. "We're running over our time."

Hope wanders over and curls her arm around my shoulders. "Have fun?"

"Sort of."

A sweet baby's screams pierce the air. "Oh no. That's mine." Hope's easy, breezy attitude switches off and she runs out of the room.

"She lasted a whole hour," Heidi says. "Not bad."

Hope returns with Grace, Alexa, and Chance. Instead of the normal leg-hug I'd normally get, he follows Hope over to the corner where she sits down with Grace and pats the space next to her for him to join her. Alexa sort of side-eyes him as if she's not sure she likes the addition to the party.

"What did you think, ladies?" Jake asks us. "This is a class I want to do for our YouTube channel and maybe offer here. It's a little more intense than some others."

"It makes you think," I answer.

He raises an eyebrow. "That's good. I want you to always be aware and thinking through different scenarios."

"So, Jake, either the guys really trust you, or you're incredibly brave to train a bunch of bikers' old ladies," Charlotte says. "Which is it?"

He huffs a laugh and runs his palm over his stubbly cheek. "Both, I hope. Wrath and I have been business partners for years."

"Wrath's trained me before," Trinity adds. "But he's...very demanding."

Jake chuckles. "Yeah, it's hard to train your girlfriend or partner, you know? Either you're too hard on them because you want them to do well or you're too soft because you can't stand hurting them."

"Wrath's definitely the first one." Trinity laughs.

"You don't say," Jake deadpans. A little more seriously, he adds, "But also, if your partner has any kind of abuse or trauma history, the last thing you want to do is play attacker."

"Ah, I see your point."

"Any real man knows it's not about some guy touching 'his woman.' It's about the person he cares about learning some skills to defend herself."

That puts the whole afternoon into perspective.

"That explains why none of the guys showed up," Charlotte says.

Jake laughs, "Yeah, pretty much."

When he moves away to answer some questions from Mara, I turn to Charlotte. "I'm starting to feel like the guys all got together and set this up."

"I'm sure they did," Charlotte agrees.

Heidi raises her hand. "Oh, I can confirm they did."

Trinity faces me with a much more serious attitude. "They both grew up around MCs. So did I. We understand the life."

I've never pried into Trinity's past before. I've just always been drawn to her nice-but-no-bullshit attitude. Her realness. Now I'm curious, but afraid to probe too much.

"You and Hope didn't. This life can be rough on women." She glances over at Hope and the kids. "I can safely say our men would kill to protect us, no matter what."

Such a powerful statement said in such an easy manner. I've never had anyone I trusted with my life the way I trust Z. Or believed anyone cared about me with that kind of intensity.

"But we also live in the real world. There are more than just threats from other MCs. All you have to do is look around and see it's not always safe everywhere."

How true that is.

"We also have to live our lives, go to work, go out. They just want us to be able to protect ourselves as much as possible. So, cavemen or not, they'll put our safety above all." She lowers her voice and holds her arms out in an imitation of a caveman, "'No man touch my woman.'"

"Now," Heidi says, "if Jake put his hands on any of us like that outside the gym—"

"You'd find me floating face down in the Hudson River," Jake says over his shoulder.

Heidi chuckles.

"Or never find you at all," Trinity says under her breath.

While Charlotte and Heidi sort of drift away to talk wedding stuff, I stick with Trinity.

"Trin, can I ask you something?"

"Sure, anything, Lilly." She bends over to slip her sneakers on. "What's on your mind?"

"Does that..." I can't seem to find the right word. "That hypervigilance to protect us... How does that work with other members of the club?"

She frowns at me. "You mean, one of the brothers? Our brothers? LOKI?"

"Yes."

"Did someone bother you downstate?"

"Why do you assume I mean downstate?"

She narrows her eyes. "For one, you've been spending most of your time there. Two, property patch or not, no one upstate would ever go near another brother's girl intentionally. It just wouldn't happen."

"Okay, so yes, hypothetically—"

"Jesus, you sound like Hope."

"What would happen?"

"If a member disrespected another member's old lady? He'd probably get his ass kicked." She touches my arm. "Be honest, are you worried about someone?"

The last thing I want to do is get a reputation for starting trouble within the club. I have no doubt if I say something to Trinity, she'll tell Wrath.

"I was just curious."

She stares at me for a few extra beats.

"Shadow creeps me out a little," I finally admit.

"I knew it." Her expression twists into something almost murderous. "He is a creep."

"It's just a few things he's said. Coming from anyone else, they might be compliments."

"But you felt like you needed a hot shower after talking to him?"

"Basically."

She tilts her head. "I'm surprised he'd try that with you. I imagine Z's made it clear you're together."

"Practically rubs himself all over me every time we're at the clubhouse. And he had words with Shadow last time it happened."

"Hopefully he learned his lesson."

"Not really. They got into it over one of the club girls last week."

Trinity raises an eyebrow. "Really? How'd that go down?"

I give her brief outline of the night. She smiles and shakes her head. "Gotta love Z. How's the club been since that?"

"Fine. Everyone went back to normal. I haven't been there much since."

"What's wrong?" Charlotte asks as she and Heidi approach.

I glance around, but we're far enough away from everyone else that no one should overhear me. "Nothing, I just had some questions for Trinity."

She drills Charlotte and Heidi with a harsh stare. "Shadow bother either of you when you've been down there?"

Fuck my life. Why didn't I keep my mouth shut?

"I've only seen him once or twice," Heidi says. "I've mostly been staying at the house when I'm down there. But I heard what went down with Serena."

"That asshole. Not only is he an asshole to the girls," Charlotte's voice is little more than a harsh whisper, "No one said it directly, but based on stuff I've overheard, I'm pretty sure he's responsible for Teller getting shot."

Trinity raises an eyebrow.

"What?" Charlotte shrugs. "Isn't that the whole reason we're down there? To protect Z and pay attention? Let him know if anyone's going to threaten or challenge him while Sway's out?"

I'm not sure if she means "we" as in members from upstate or if she literally means "we" as in Teller, Charlotte, Murphy, and Heidi. Either way, I love them for having Z's back.

"Of course," Trinity answers. "Just be careful." Her gaze shifts my way. "Who you talk about it with."

I'm not offended by Trinity's warning to Charlotte. There's always the chance I accidentally say the wrong thing to the wrong person at the wrong time. You know, like this moment right here.

"It sounds like Z handled it. Hopefully that's the end of it and everyone falls in line." She sighs and focuses on me. "You're bound to overhear stuff hanging around the clubhouse or even from Z himself. Don't ever repeat any of it to a brother and be careful which old ladies you share anything with down there." She nods to Charlotte and Heidi. "You can tell us anything. And of course, you can tell Hope. But anyone else, be careful."

"We try to watch out for her," Heidi says. "When we're there."

My gaze swings to Heidi.

"Tawny's still gone and only Angie still comes around." Heidi's nose wrinkles. "It's mostly club girls."

"Yeah, definitely watch what you share with them," Trinity warns. "You don't have to be cruel to them, like Tawny was, but watch your back. A lot of them would kill to be in your place."

"Good to know," I mutter.

What about Z? Would any of the brothers kill to be in his place? Would Shadow?

CHAPTER TWENTY-NINE

Lilly

Z assures me Shadow's been on his best behavior since the Serena incident. Even so I'm a little hesitant to attend tonight's party.

I love him and I trust him, but I'm not convinced Shadow is no longer a problem.

The club's loud, the brothers rowdier than usual. More girls than ever seem to fill the place. Maybe news spread throughout the club girl grapevine that Z had cracked the whip and they could come here to party without the threat of being roughed up.

Z's alternated between sliding his hand over my ass and discussing an upcoming road trip to Texas with one of the brothers all night, so I'm not worried about the extra muffler bunnies.

When he takes a break, I lean in. "I want to call and say good night to Chance."

"I'll come with you." The deep rumble of his voice suggests he's interested in more than a quick phone call to our son.

As if on cue, Hustler slams his beer down next to Z's. "A word, Prez?"

Laughing, I lean in and kiss Z's cheek. "I'll be right back."

The hallways are full of the usual noises. A few doors are open and I may or may not take a peek inside as I walk past them.

Our hallway is quieter. Normally, I prefer that when we're trying to sleep. Tonight, it gives me the creeps for some reason.

My skin prickles and I hurry to open the door, locking it behind me.

Heidi answers right away and we talk for a few seconds before she calls Chance to the phone.

He only has a few short answers for me before giving the phone back to Heidi.

"Thanks again, Heidi."

"No problem. How are things there?"

"Pretty chill, actually."

"Good."

We talk for a few more minutes and I say good night to Chance one more time before hanging up.

I stop in the bathroom, fix my lipstick, and run a brush through my hair. My slippers are calling my name. The five-inch platform heels are killing my toes. But they look much better with this dress than slippers will.

Chuckling to myself, I close the door to our room and lock it like Z asked.

The hallway is still quiet, the sounds from the party slightly muffled by the distance.

As I turn the corner, I bump into Shadow.

Was he waiting there?

Z already explained he couldn't get rid of Shadow without cause. He needed more than manhandling a club girl who isn't claimed by anyone.

Something about that really pissed me off.

Maybe *I* can help give Z the reason he needs.

Let's face it, at best, Shadow's a rapist-in-training. At worst, he's going to end up getting Z or one of the other brothers killed.

With that in mind, I work my lips into a seductive smile and cock my hip.

"Hey, sweetness," he greets me, his gaze roaming over every inch of me.

"Hey." My legs tremble, but I force myself smile up at him. "How are you? Haven't seen you in a bit." I use my low, velvety voice. The faker-than-fuck one I used once upon a time to convince men they just *had* to have a lap dance or buy me a bottle of champagne. My seducing-men-who-disgust-me skills are rusty, but seem to work on Shadow.

Nothing about my sudden interest trips an alarm in his brain? He really is dumb. Or he just assumes every woman he meets is a whore who can't resist his dick.

He's blocking my way and the urge to push past him and flat-out run seizes me. I will myself to stand still. I'd rather not have our bodies touch.

Z's made it clear several times that I'm with him. Shadow's the VP. After the last warning Z gave him, he'd have to be out of his mind to touch me, right?

Life has taught me to always be on-guard because no matter what, too many men are waiting for their chance to degrade and take advantage of you.

Shadow's predatory gaze sweeps over me in a way that sets alarm bells clanging inside my skull.

"This is nice." He slides his fingers over my collarbones, left exposed by the wide scoop neck of my dress. "You're a beautiful woman, Lilly."

"Thank you." Somehow, I'm not reassured by his compliment. "If you're looking for Z, I'm on my way to him."

"Nah, I'll talk to the prez later." He leans against the wall, caging me in, preventing me from running toward the party. I could probably sprint back to our room, but I'm too scared he'll follow or push his way inside and...

I force myself to meet his stare. "What's wrong, Shadow? Tired of little girls? You need a real woman?"

His eyes widen at first, then his expression slides into a laid-back smirk. "You know where I can find one?"

I jerk my head toward the living room. "Out there."

"But *you're* right here."

"And I'm with Z." I'm done. I was an idiot to try and engage him. I slip around him and quicken my steps.

Maybe I've grown complacent. Secure in my position as Z's old lady. Too confident none of the brothers—even creepy Shadow—would ever lay a hand on me.

Shadow's grip around my bicep startles me. I'm airborne for a second and then my back thumps against the wall, knocking the air from my lungs.

Holy shit.

As I stare down at his hand on my arm, icy tendrils of fear wrap around my throat.

He leans into me, using the solid weight of his upper body to nail me to the wall. "Your old man went a step too far," he snarls. "Bitches should *never* come before brothers."

"Then talk to him about it." My confident mask slips. I struggle to free myself, but he's too heavy. He slaps his hand against the wall next to my face.

"Where you going? I ain't done talking to you."

Fear makes the hallway blur around the edges, but I answer loud and firm, "I'm done talking to you."

"Don't act so high and mighty, girl. You may have cut off Z's nuts but you're still a whore desperately trying to prove you're more than a dick motel."

Charming.

I stop struggling and laugh. "How old are you, Shadow?"

"Huh?"

"How old are you? Running around calling women who aren't interested in you dick motels? Sounds like fifteen, sixteen years old?"

He grabs my hand and yanks it toward his crotch. "No, baby. I'm all man."

I pull away but he has an iron grip. "I'm sure you are."

"You want to find out?"

Still stunned, I take a few seconds to respond. "Get your hands off me." I issue the warning in a much more calm, confident tone than my racing heart suggests.

My mind's still swimming with disbelief.

This isn't supposed to happen here.

This can't be happening again.

Not again.

Never again.

Too terrified and ashamed to protect myself, I've frozen until it was too late. Fear freezes me in place. Memories of that horrible incident and all the awful moments that followed threaten to drown me, leaving me weak and useless again.

The world comes rushing back. I'm in danger. And I'd rather fight like hell than do nothing. I slap my hands against his shoulders, attempting to push him away. "Get off me."

Obviously, he's not used to girls fighting back because I succeed in shoving him away enough to slip out of his grasp.

Party. I need to run in the direction of other people. Maybe he's just screwing around. Trying to scare me.

I'm not sticking around to find out if he wants to have a hostile chat or laugh in my face.

I'm jerked to a stop and yanked backwards, almost falling out of my heels. My back thumps into the wall again. A soft *oof* bursts past my lips. My head hits the wall with a painful thud. Stars burst behind my eyelids.

Hostile it is.

"Let go before I scream."

He wraps his fingers around my neck and squeezes enough to terrify me into silence. "Go ahead." He leans in and I almost puke when his lips brush against my ear. "The louder you scream, the harder I get."

Big shock there.

Maybe the sheer terror makes me reckless, but I snort with laughter. "It's not about how hard your dick is, it's about terrorizing and using your strength to hurt someone."

He pulls back and frowns. "Huh?"

Logic and reason are wasted on this dumbass, Lilly. Kick him in the nuts.

I can't work enough leverage to kick him, but I bring my knee up and narrowly miss smashing it into his crotch. He avoids the strike. Probably has a lot of practice avoiding kicks to the dick.

He grins, gloating that I missed.

Jake warned us about that, didn't he? I should've taken a few more classes.

Shadow's not squeezing hard enough to cut off my air. Yet.

The thumb is the weak spot.

Which way is his thumb?

Remembering Jake's instructions, I push past my terror to jerk, twist, and duck, escaping Shadow's hand.

"Hey!" someone yells from the end of the hall.

Nope. Not sticking around to assess whether they're friendly or not.

I want to touch Shadow's junk about as much as I want to swim in a pool of sharks. But I'm still sort of crouched down when he reaches for me again.

I pull my arms in, forming a fist with both hands, kind of like spiking a volleyball. I thrust up as hard as I can, aiming for his crotch.

Gotcha that time, fucker.

He screams and doubles over, backing away from me.

"Bitch!"

I scoop one of my shoes off the floor and whack him in the side of the head with it. They're a solid pair with a hefty one-inch platform. It makes a satisfying *thwack* when it collides with his skull.

"What the hell?" someone else yells. Footsteps pound over the carpet. Great. I don't trust anyone now. What if they all gang up on me and drag me into one of the empty rooms? Z won't know what's happening until it's too late.

I turn and run and make it about five steps before colliding with Murphy. He automatically wraps his arms around me and I finally feel safe. He's bigger and bulkier than Shadow. Plus, I trust him.

He tips my chin back, staring at my neck for a second. Lifting his head, he glares at whoever's behind me. "Who touched you, Lilly?" His grave tone suggests someone's about to die.

Too scared to say much, I whisper, "Shadow."

Murphy growls. His gaze zips past me. "Don't you fucking move, motherfucker!" he shouts. The rumble of his voice even louder with my face pressed against his chest. The soft, cuddly biker who builds swing sets for his baby daughter and makes bear sex jokes at family barbeques is *gone*, replaced by a threatening mountain of a man who's ready to murder.

I'm a huge fan of *this* scary-ass, violent version of Murphy at the moment.

"What's going on?" Teller asks somewhere behind us.

"Get Z. Now," Murphy says in a loud, even voice.

Keeping an arm around my shoulders, Murphy shifts me to his left. Freeing up his right hand, in case Shadow comes at us, I guess. I hang onto him like he's the best damn life raft in an ocean full of deadly jellyfish.

More voices reach me. Whoever shouted at the end of the hall joins us. "I saw part of it," someone says.

"What's going on?" Z asks.

I wriggle out of Murphy's grip and fly at Z, almost knocking him over.

He wraps his arms around me and frowns. "What happened?" His gaze darts from my face to Murphy and then past Murphy. I bury my face against his chest. "Someone want to explain?"

"Hold him," Murphy orders.

"Get the fuck off me!" Shadow yells.

Z's body vibrates and his hold on me tightens. "What. The. Fuck. Happened?"

I can't form any words and risk glancing up at Z. He's focused on something behind me. His entire body pulsing with barely-controlled rage. "Start talking," he says through clenched teeth. "Now."

Shadow lets out a high, strained laugh. "Your girl was all hot for my dick until Stitch walked up on us."

Stitch? Which one is he? The prospect? Great. I bet there's some rule about his word not being as good as a full-patched brother or some shit.

"That's not what it looked like to me, Prez."

"Rooster?" Z lifts his chin.

Oh, thank God.

He'll believe me, right?

CHAPTER THIRTY

Z

THE GUYS WHO DON'T KNOW ME MIGHT THINK I HAVEN'T ASKED LILLY directly what happened because her story doesn't count as much as a brother's.

They're wrong.

Something bad happened to her.

Something that should never happen in my clubhouse.

The only question burning in my mind is how many people do I need to kill?

The scene I walked up on made it clear.

Murphy with his arms protectively around my woman, looking like he was about to murder anyone who came near her. Lilly, barefoot and clinging to him like he just saved her damn life. The way she's trembling all over.

Those few observations told me all I need to know about what I walked up on.

Shadow's in for a vicious beating, one way or another. Simple as that. Hitting on a member's old lady is grounds for a beat down in our world. Hurting one? I'm within my rights to gut the motherfucker.

Do I want the backing of the brothers' in the downstate charter before it goes down? Yeah, it'd be nice. It's not necessary as far as I'm concerned. Let 'em try to strip my patch.

Rooster crosses his arms over his chest and widens his stance, blocking Shadow's only option for escape.

"Looked like she was trying to get away from him, which is why I yelled out instead of pulling up a chair to watch."

I'm not in the mood for his jokes. I grunt at him and turn my gaze on Stitch.

Stitch may only be a prospect, but he speaks up and shows no fear. "She punched him in the balls, Prez. Unless that's his fucked-up version of foreplay, it looked to me like he attacked her."

"Fuck you, prospect," Shadow spits. "She ain't patched."

"That's the excuse you're going with?" Rooster shakes his head. "You *do* remember her being introduced to everyone in this clubhouse as his old lady, right?"

"Nah, Shadow here thought he'd get even with me for telling him he can't do whatever the fuck he wants to the girls around here, didn't ya, bro?" I ask.

The corner of his mouth curls up.

"Too much of a coward to come at me directly, right?" I shift Lilly to the side and behind me a second before Shadow launches himself at my midsection.

The hit to the gut drives me back a few feet.

From the corner of my eye, I see Teller hustling Lilly away.

Now it's on.

I shove Shadow back and take up a better stance.

His fist comes flying at me and I easily duck it.

"Get him, brother," Murphy says from behind me, his signal that he has my back and no one will interfere.

Confident this won't take long, I throw some of my own punches. A sweet burn rips through my knuckles as I collide with Shadow's cheek.

Something crunches under my fist, but I don't take a second to enjoy it.

I weave in closer and take two more shots. One to his face. One to the chest.

Shadow's a bit smaller than me, but mostly muscle and a strong motherfucker. I don't buy it when he stays down.

A few seconds later, he comes at me, attempting to slam his skull into my chin. I avoid that hit, but the momentum takes both of us to the floor.

Shadow lands a shot to my jaw and my head bounces off the rough carpet.

That's enough of that.

Adrenaline rockets through my veins. Wrapping my legs around his torso, I twist and flip us where I can pound the ever-loving shit out of him.

I might not have visited Wrath at the new and improved Furious Fitness for lessons recently, but years of that big bastard tossing me around the ring in the name of "training" doesn't fade overnight.

Blood sprays from his mouth and nose, coating my chin and dripping down the front of my shirt. Still, I don't slow down.

No, I'm just gettin' started.

No one touches my girl.

Shadow twists to the left.

Yeah, I'd duck these shots too.

A flash of silver reveals he wasn't attempting an evasive maneuver. Someone yells out and footsteps thunder closer to us.

A line of fire sizzles over my thigh and while I'm processing the pain, he manages to roll us over.

He pulled a knife on me! A brother. His president.

Even though I'm on my back, I'm acutely aware of every movement. I block out the pain from the slash to my leg because I'm also aware that if he manages to take me out, Lilly and my brothers are in danger.

He jabs forward.

I catch Shadow's hand an inch before he sinks the blade into my chest.

Hanging onto his knife hand for dear life, I seize a hold of his wrist and angle the sharp steel away from my ribcage.

Unfortunately for Shadow, I twist his wrist until the tip of the knife pointed at his liver. The fucker keeps coming at me, all of his weight bearing down.

His wide, surprised eyes when the knife pierces his skin aren't as satisfying as you'd think. My brain's running on pure survival instinct as I shove harder.

He grunts but keeps coming.

Or the momentum carries him forward.

Either way, he ends up impaling himself on his own damn knife.

CHAPTER THIRTY-ONE

Z

WARM, SLICK BLOOD GUSHES OVER MY HAND. STEER ENDS UP PULLING Shadow off me, throwing him to the floor.

"What the fuck are you doing?" he roars.

Shadow rolls to the side, clutching his side while blood seeps through his shirt.

Exhausted, I lay on the floor, staring at the ceiling for a few breaths. Blood and sweat drip off my forehead and into my hair.

That escalated quickly.

The sounds of the clubhouse come rushing over me. I tip my head back, trying to pick Lilly, Murphy, or Teller out of the crowd, but all I see are a bunch of dirty boots and jean-covered legs.

I groan and sit up.

Rooster offers me his hand and pulls me off the floor. "You all right, brother?" he asks quietly.

"Better than he is." I nod at Shadow.

Steer turns and stares at me. "Your call, Prez."

I take in the shocked looks on the faces around me.

In some clubs, this is probably no big deal. Too many men with no respect for brotherhood who think they're top dog in one club. A fight like this could be just another regular Friday night.

Not my club. We'll spar with each other for fun and profit occasionally. Or to blow off steam. Hand out a beating when a brother's earned it.

But pull a weapon on a brother?

Never.

Not since Rock, Wrath, and I took over the upstate charter years ago.

I need to make an example of Shadow. Every brother in this charter needs to understand challenging me or disrespecting me will result in harsh punishment. I also need to do it with a level head and with the support of the rest of the brothers so this doesn't happen again.

I could pull a gun and blow a hole in Shadow's skull—which honestly is my preference at the moment. While that might make everyone fear me, it won't necessarily make them respect me. It'll only be a matter of time before someone steps out of line again.

"Call the doc to patch him up." I give Shadow's injury a more serious inspection. "If he lives, we'll vote on him immediately."

"Prez, everyone saw him pull the knife," Hustler says.

"Yeah, but Z jumped him."

I turn, seeking the brother who uttered that bullshit.

My gaze lands on Smoke.

Figures.

"He touched my ol' lady." I growl out the words and consider punching Smoke.

"Women don't come before brothers. You can't strip his patch—"

"Are you drunk, old man?" Rooster says. He points two fingers at his eyes. "I saw him attack Z's woman. That's grounds for a beating every day of the damn week."

"As our VP, Shadow knows better." Steer nudges Shadow's lifeless body with the toe of his boot. "Or he should."

Lilly

I know better than to get involved or try to stop the fight, but I can't stand seeing Z get hurt.

Well, he's the one doing the hurting. So, I guess I don't like him in danger of being hurt.

I can't look away though. It doesn't seem right.

"He's got this," Teller assures me with complete calm.

"I see that."

"It's about time someone checked that asshole," Lala mutters next to me. She sneaks a quick look at Teller, like she's afraid she's going to get in trouble for saying something against a brother.

Teller doesn't acknowledge the comment. Instead, he draws me closer and leans down. "You all right?"

"I'm fine." I hold up a hand and realize I'm still shaking. "Well, maybe a little freaked."

He nods. "I'm glad Charlotte's not here tonight."

"Yeah, kinda wish I'd stayed home too," I mutter. The guys close in a circle around Z and Shadow until we can't see them.

I push forward and Teller pulls me back. "I'm taking you home."

"I'll take her," the kid everyone calls "Prospect" offers.

"No, she's with me," Teller insists. He nods to the club girls huddled together by the bar. "Get the van and take them home or wherever, but they need to go."

"You got it."

"Teller, I can't leave. I have to know—"

"Lilly, don't argue with me." Teller's calm, grave tone completely freaks me out, but he seizes my arm and pulls me toward the front door. "Where's your car?"

The shouting from the fight gets louder and I make another attempt to free myself from Teller's grasp. "We can't leave him!"

"Murphy's got his back. Trust me, Z will be pissed if I don't get you home."

Arguing with him seems pointless. He's got an iron grip and isn't afraid to use it. Plus, down where I don't want to acknowledge it, I know he's right and the last thing I want to do is make Z's life difficult.

"Z knows how to handle himself, Lilly," Teller says once we're on the road.

"What's going to happen?" I ask.

"To Shadow? For touching you? That beating, for starters. Anything more than that, you don't need to know."

I'd be offended or argue that it is my business, but I already understand how the club operates. If Z wants to tell me, he will. It's not fair to press Teller for information he's not allowed to share.

"I need to see Chance," I whisper.

"He's probably asleep."

"I know. But I need to see him."

"Okay," Teller agrees.

Heidi answers the door in her pajamas and yawns. "What's going on? Why are you back so early?"

She glances past us and seems to wake right up. "Where's Blake?"

"At the clubhouse." Teller leans down and kisses his sister's cheek. "Kids okay?"

"Everyone's fine. They went to bed a while ago." Her gaze swings between us. "Right after you called, Lilly. What's going on?"

"Nothing, I just wanted to check on Chance."

Heidi stares me down for a few seconds. "Go ahead."

They share a few tense words while I rush upstairs.

Z

"That was some fucked-up shit, brother." Murphy squeezes my shoulder. "You okay?"

"Where's Lilly?"

"Teller took her home as soon as it went down." He glances over his shoulder. "Prospect offered to take her, but given the situation, we weren't comfortable with that."

"Thank you." At least I know they always have my back.

He pulls out his phone and taps out a text. "Lettin' him know you're okay, so she's not freaking out."

"I'll call her in a bit. Tell him to get his ass back here."

"You got it."

"It's gonna be a long night."

The club's doctor shows up. There's one thing we're missing upstate— a crooked doctor who shows up to clean up our non-reportable injuries.

Steer and Jigsaw moved Shadow into a side room up front with a cot and some medical supplies, the club's unofficial exam room. I've been in it once or twice myself in the past.

"Z." Rooster touches my shoulder. "You need to have your leg looked at."

Funny, with all the adrenaline from the fight I forgot all about the long cut. I glance down. Blood soaks my jeans on either side of where Shadow sliced.

"Fuck." Now it hurts. "Make sure that asshole's gonna live first, then send Doc down to my room."

"Z," he protests.

"I'm fine."

"I got him, Rooster," Murphy says. He butts his big head under my arm and has me lean on him until we get to my room.

"I'm fine."

"You look like you're gonna pass out."

"Fuck you."

"You kiss your baby momma with that mouth?"

I chuckle as he pushes open my door and helps me into the room. "Every inch of her."

While I drop into a chair, Murphy searches the bedroom before moving on to the bathroom.

"You could at least shut the door." I shout.

"Why? You've seen my dick before."

"Which is why I'm asking you to shut the door."

"I'm not taking a piss, dumbass. I'm looking for something."

"What the fuck for?"

"Something to clean that with. You want your leg to get infected and fall off? You can't ride then."

"When did you get so annoying?"

"I can only find some tiny finger Band-Aids."

"Sorry, wasn't planning to get sliced up tonight."

He stops in the bathroom doorway, shaking a small green bottle at me. "Seriously, Z? Mint-flavored lube? I expect better from you."

I rumble with laughter, which eases the pain in my leg a bit. "That's not mine, you dick. It was in the room when I took it."

He flips the bottle over. "Guess that explains the late-nineties expiration date."

"Why don't you give it a taste test? See if it still works."

He flips me a middle finger and tosses the bottle in the trashcan.

"Go wash your hands after touching that, ya perv."

He returns and throws a towel to me. "Put some pressure on that before you bleed to death."

"Yeah, yeah," I grumble, wadding up the towel and pressing it down over the cut. "Motherfucker."

As he's finishing his search for who-the-hell-knows what, someone knocks on the door. "You think you can get that for me, princess?" I yell.

Before Murphy can get to the door, it opens and Teller slips in.

"You could wait until I say come in."

"I thought you did." His scowl deepens. "Are you really busting my balls right now?"

"When would be a better time?"

"The adrenaline drop is making him cranky," Murphy explains. "You bring some food like I asked? He's lost a lot of blood."

Teller pulls a Snickers bar out of his cut and tosses it to me.

"I said food, not candy," Murphy says.

"My healthy food options were kind of limited at this hour," Teller says as he flings another Snickers bar at Murphy's head. He tosses me a granola bar next. "Best I could find."

"This'll do. Is Lilly okay?"

Teller shrugs and takes the chair across from me. "She was scared, but she didn't argue with me when I told her it was time to go. Once I told her you were okay, she calmed down. Didn't give me any grief about not coming back with me. Warned her it might be a late night."

"Thanks."

He sits back and blows out a breath. "First time I've been happy Charlotte couldn't make it down."

"No kidding."

"What are you going to do?" Teller asks.

Murphy growls and makes a slashing motion with his hand. "Gut that motherfucker."

"He's gotta go," I agree. "But this can't look like upstate coming in to clean house. I already probably overstepped by getting between him and Serena."

"Fuck him," Teller says. "This club isn't about that. You had every right."

"He's right," Murphy agrees. "The only ones complaining about it were Shadow and Smoke."

Teller sits forward. "Smoke needs to go too."

"One execution at a time, brother."

"How long is Doc gonna take?" Murphy grumbles, glancing at the door. "Get your pants off and let's clean that up."

"Why you tryin' to get me naked, bro?"

"For fuck's sake." Teller rolls his eyes. "I think he's trying to save you from getting an infection."

"You two have no sense of humor."

Murphy flips me off. "Watching one of your best friends almost get stabbed in the chest tends to kill a sense of humor."

"He didn't almost stab me."

"You've seen your leg, right?" Teller asks.

"Let's take a look." I stand and unbutton my pants.

"Should I grab that mint lube?" Murphy jokes.

"Only if you're planning to blow me."

Someone else knocks and Murphy answers, opening the door wider to allow the doctor in.

Teller pushes himself out of his chair and stops in front of me. "I'll go assess the mood out there."

"Thanks."

Murphy raises his eyebrows at me, silently asking if I want him to stay or go. "Go ahead. When I'm done here, we're all sitting down at the table."

"We'll pass that around," Teller promises.

"It's been a while, Z," the doc says. He sets his bag on the table. "Let me wash up. I'll be right back."

While the doc isn't one of my favorite people, he's actually good at what he does. He's in the bathroom for a while, vigorously scrubbing up. When he returns, he pulls several pristine white towels out of his bag along with an unopened sleeve of tools.

"You're lucky this wasn't deeper."

"So, it's not as bad as it looks?"

"Nah, you can lose up to a pint of blood without any severe effects."

"I'll keep that in mind for next time."

After cleaning up the cut, he declares it's worse than he thought and says he needs to stitch it up.

"I don't care what it looks like, doc. Just make sure my leg doesn't fall off." Fucking Murphy with his stupid jokes.

When the doc finishes, he pulls out two amber prescription bottles. "Painkiller. Please don't drink alcohol while taking these."

"Yeah, okay." I motion for him to hand over the bottle. "What else?"

"Antibiotics." He smirks at me. "To keep your leg from falling off."

I snatch the bottles out of his hand. "See Hustler on your way out. He'll get you paid."

"Call me if it shows any signs of infection or you have any questions."

"I will. Thanks, doc."

After he leaves, I grab my cell phone and stretch out on the bed.

Lilly answers on the first ring.

"Z! Are you okay?"

"I'm fine, but I'm going to be here the rest of the night."

She sighs. "I figured as much."

"Are you all right?"

She coughs, making me wish I was there to check her over, assess whatever damage Shadow did. "Yes."

"Tell me what happened. From the beginning. Just don't use any names."

Her soft laughter comes through the phone, then abruptly stops. Probably about the time she realized I wasn't joking.

By the time, she finishes, I'm burning with rage.

CHAPTER THIRTY-TWO

Z

Freshly stitched, bandaged, dressed in clean pants, and buzzing from a painkiller-antibiotic cocktail, I make my way down to the chapel.

The main room's brightly lit, but mostly empty.

Except for a few faces I wasn't expecting to see tonight.

Murphy lifts his chin when he sees me. "Why didn't you call us? I would've come—"

"I'm fine."

Teller nods to Rock, Wrath, and Dex. "Look who showed up."

My throat tightens. "What are you doing here? It's the middle of the fuckin' night."

Wrath grins. "Rock and I had a bet going, which one of you'd get stabbed first, and I won."

"Dick." I hold out my hand and he pulls me in, gently—well, gentle for Wrath—slapping my back.

"You really thought Z would get stabbed before Teller?" Murphy scratches his beard. "My money definitely woulda been on Teller. I've been itching to stab him for years."

"I think nailing his sister hurts more," Dex says.

Teller ignores them and glares at Rock. "Really?"

Rock shrugs. "You love runnin' that mouth of yours."

After we're finished busting on each other, Rock squeezes my shoulder. "You all right?"

"I'll live."

"Lilly okay?"

"I just talked to her. She's fine."

"I'm so sorry, brother. I never..." He shakes his head. "This should never happen in our clubhouses."

It shouldn't. But if I think about it, this kind of trouble's been brewing down here for years. Sway's always run his club a little rougher than we run ours. Looser.

Now he's got a bullet in the head and I've been sliced open by a brother.

Obviously, something needs to change.

"This was bound to happen," Murphy says, echoing my thoughts. "Remember the first time we brought Hope down here and some hang-around tried to grab her?"

Rock's jaw tightens. "Yeah."

"You pounded the shit out of him, and that was the end of it," I remind Murphy. "The fucker didn't pull a fucking knife on you. And Shadow did more than grab Lilly's ass."

Murphy rolls his eyes. "That's what I'm trying to say. I'm not surprised it's escalated to this point."

Wrath's silent but watching me with an intent expression.

I blow out a breath, not really in the mood for him to mock me right now. "What?"

"How do you plan to handle it, Prez?" he asks with absolutely no hint of sarcasm to the question.

"You know what has to happen. I can't let this slide or I might as well call Priest now and tell him I'm heading home."

Rock nods. "You've definitely been tangled into a knot here, but I have faith you'll straighten it out."

"Thanks, Rock."

Rooster steps out of the office and nods at us. "Everyone's waiting in the chapel, Prez."

Rock shoots a smile my way, like he's proud to hear someone else referring to me as *Prez*.

Steer steps out of the chapel and closes the door behind him. He shakes hands with Rock, Wrath, and Dex while thanking them for coming down.

At least that's a good sign.

When I first started hanging around the club, Sway was a member upstate. A few years later, after some deaths and incarcerations, Rock, Wrath, and I not-so-gently helped the old president retire. Sway made the wise choice to break ties. With the blessing of National and a few other brothers, he founded the downstate charter.

That's the nice, neat version, the full version's a little bloodier. Basically, we're brothers, but there's always an ounce of animosity between our two charters that runs deep. Old wounds that healed but still ache under certain conditions.

Key members of my club showing up could either be interpreted as support or an invasion.

Thankfully, everyone seems to welcome the upstate members tonight.

Rooster and I are eventually left alone outside the chapel.

"How's Shadow?" I hope to fuck the prick didn't die while the doc was fixing me up. I want to be the one to end that motherfucker.

"Alive." He cocks his head. "I'm behind you, Z. No games. No angles. What went down was wrong and I have your back."

I hold out my hand and he shakes it quickly. "Appreciate that, Rooster. You've been a true brother since I've been down here." I glance toward the hallway. "And I don't know what would've happened if you hadn't walked up on them tonight."

"Guess it's a good thing I was coming out to look for another girl for my three-way."

Laughing, I shake my head. "You could've kept that to yourself. Makes it less heroic now."

The playful smile slides off his face. "I'm nobody's hero, brother."

I'm pretty sure Lilly disagrees, but I nod and thank him again before going inside.

The somber tone of the room washes over me as I step over the threshold.

I take my place at the head of the table and look around the room. There's no need to bang the gavel or even raise my voice. I have everyone's attention.

"I've spent more than twenty years wearing our skull and crown on my back. This club is a brotherhood. Our brotherhood. Our family. We always have each other's backs. That's how this works. Otherwise, we might as well be any other band of assholes wearing leather and riding a hog."

"Amen, brother," someone says. Murmurs of agreement fill the room, but I don't stop to acknowledge the comment.

"The Lost Kings' patch means everything to me. My brothers and this club mean everything to me. Doesn't matter if it's Upstate, Downstate, Mississippi, Washington, we're all brothers bound by a common thread. It might not always feel that way. Priest coming down here and imposing his will prickles against everything we are. Some days our trust in the brotherhood can be tested."

Now the guys are looking at each other. As if I'm about to scold them.

"Our common desire to live outside of the rules of *regular* society doesn't mean we're savages without honor. The code we live by might be skewed by society's standards, but it's our guiding compass."

Now I have everyone's attention.

No one moves or speaks.

"Honor, loyalty, respect. Those words might not mean much to others anymore, but they are values this club lives by."

And Shadow broke all three of them tonight. I don't need to say it. If they're listening, they'll get there all on their own.

"Those patches some of us wear 'Brother's Keeper' and 'Respect Few, Fear None' aren't empty sayings." I slap my palm over my own patches. "We've shed blood. Done hard time. Protected our brothers to earn those patches."

A few brothers quietly brush their hands over their own cuts. Younger brothers glance at the patches on other members' vests. Patches they've probably seen a thousand times, but never given a lot of thought. We don't make a big show of handing out those patches. Bloodshed, incarceration, and sacrifice are what we do to protect what's ours. Things we acknowledge but don't necessarily celebrate.

"Lost Kings protect what's theirs. From the law. From outsiders. From everything. Always. Without question. It's what we do to survive. And we always protect each other."

My gaze strays to Wrath and he gives me a subtle nod.

"None of us are perfect. Sometimes we make mistakes. We depend on our brothers to show us mercy, kick our asses, or carry our burdens until we get back on our feet. We may not always like one another, but we're always loyal."

Almost everyone laughs.

"No matter how outside the law we live, there are consequences when you betray a brother. Our life and the code we live by demands it. The vows we took to be given the honor of wearing the patch requires our loyalty."

Now, it's time to go for the kill.

"Tonight, Shadow betrayed this brotherhood. Twice."

I pause to let that sink in.

"First, he betrayed the most basic law Lost Kings have—he put his hands on my old lady without my permission."

Did I just reduce the woman I love to a piece of property to prove a point to my brothers? Damn right I did. I love Lilly and have endless respect for her, but none of that matters tonight at this table.

"We're not talking about a pinch on the ass or some flirting—which would be enough grounds for punishment." I stare at each one of them before continuing. "He slammed her into the wall. Choked her." My voice vibrates with rage. "He terrorized her someplace she should *never* be afraid—inside our clubhouse."

"No way, brother. Shouldn't happen here." Jigsaw's calm but stern voice reaches me from the end of the table. "Our families are always safe and under our protection in this clubhouse."

Murmurs of agreement go around the table. This is the support I need. This isn't only about me. It's about all of us.

Fuck, is that killing me too. What I really want to do is march out the door and put a bullet between Shadow's eyes.

"This isn't who we are," Steer says quietly from his seat. "We're better than this."

Rooster glances at Steer and then Smoke before raising his hand and standing. "Let's not forget Shadow also pulled a weapon on a brother. On our *president* during a righteous beatdown." He glances around at everyone. "Fighting dirty. Using a weapon against a brother. It's cowardly. It spits in the face of honor, loyalty, and brotherhood."

A few brothers actually clap when Rooster sits down. Not expecting such a passionate speech from him, I nod my appreciation and ask if anyone else has anything to add.

While they seem surprised I asked, no one volunteers to speak.

"Let's take the first vote." I slap the gavel against the table. "Stripping Shadow's patch?"

Even though Rock, Wrath, Murphy, Teller, and Dex are here to show their support, they're not members of *this* charter so they abstain from the vote.

They'll sit out the next vote, too. I want there to be no mistake. No questioning me later about this decision.

The vote is unanimous in favor of stripping Shadow's patch.

The next vote might be more complicated, but it also has to be unanimous. To keep the club strong, it's worth the risk.

And no, Shadow won't be granted an opportunity to defend himself. That's not how this works.

I've done enough preaching at them. Once I get the vote to strip his patch, I go right for the next one.

"All those in favor of putting our ex-brother to ground?" I wait and glance around the room. "Take your time to speak now before we take the vote."

Jigsaw raises his hand. "Brother, for what he did, you're within your rights..."

"I know." I allow my gaze to travel to each brother, meeting their stares head-on. "Each one of us understands the code. We also know I haven't been your president for long. Further, you didn't *vote* me in. I was brought in under unusual circumstances by Priest. Because of that, this decision needs to be a club vote. I'll abide by whatever the club decides." The corner of my mouth lifts. "Although, I reserve the right to kick Shadow's ass again either way."

Brothers glance at each other and low murmurs go around the table. Obviously, this wasn't expected.

Murphy crosses his arms over his chest and sits back, giving me a slight nod. Wrath and Teller are more tense, watching the room for any signs of anarchy. Rock's eyes are on Smoke, which makes sense. Not long ago we were visiting when Smoke brandished a gun around the clubhouse and I had to tackle his drunk ass to the ground and wrestle the pistol out of his hands before he shot someone.

Killing a full-patched brother, a former officer, is about as serious as it gets in our world. Emotions are sure to be all over the place.

Steer finally signals that it's time to take the vote. Next to Sway, he probably has the most time in this club, so his "yes" vote carries a lot of weight.

Each brother's yes is slow and deliberate. We may be a brotherhood full of outlaws, but no one takes killing someone they've shared a patch with lightly.

My gaze lands on Rooster. Instead of a yes or no, he holds up his hand, halting the vote. After all his earlier comments, he's not who I expected to vote this down.

I hide my irritation and nod, giving him the floor to speak. Rooster's got brass ones and doesn't shrink under the scrutiny.

He stands and looks around the table. "I wasn't going to bring this up until I had more information, but something else needs to be discussed before we continue with this vote."

He swallows hard and looks my way.

"Go on," I encourage. Now I'm curious.

"I've been gathering proof…some records, video, shit like that. I think Shadow was involved with Sway's shooting and I think he set us up to get ambushed the night Malone's burned down."

Well, now I understand why Rooster wasn't ready to bring this to the table until he was one hundred percent sure. Two serious accusations. He could be kicked out of the club if he accused a member of this level of betrayal without proof.

Hustler sits forward. "What do you have?"

"His toll records. His *real* ones. He wasn't using the club-issued EZ Pass. He's been using another one registered to his wife."

"His *who*?" Murphy asks.

"He's got a citizen wife on the outside," Jigsaw explains. "None of us really know her that well."

Figures.

"She's his tie to the Vipers," Rooster says. "Her brother is a prospect."

Jesus Christ, what's Sway been doing at the head of this table for the last few years, napping? "How did none of you know this?"

Steer raises his hand. "Like Jiggy said, half of us have never even met her. Shit, the way he plows through clubwhores, I didn't even realize he had a gal on the outside until Rooster and I dug into him when Sway nominated him for VP."

Yeah, 'cause where a guy sticks his dick is proof he's fit to be an officer. Jesus Christ.

"All right. What's the big deal about his toll records?"

Rooster pulls a folder out from under the table and sifts through a few papers. "He's made a *lot* of trips down to New Jersey over the last few months." He looks around the table. "We all know we don't conduct business in Viper territory. There's no reason for Shadow to make so many trips down there."

Someone whistles. A few *what the fucks* are muttered.

"Maybe it's his old lady?" Smoke suggests.

"Could be," Rooster concedes. "Still," he glances my way and down toward Murphy and Teller. "Any of you let your girls go into Viper territory when they held down Ironworks?"

"Fuck no," Teller says.

Rooster's pained eyes meet mine. "I finally tracked down the person who rented the black Cadillac." He tosses a grainy black and white photo down the table toward me.

It's fuzzy, obviously a still from some security camera that's been enhanced. He's not wearing his colors. I still recognize the cocky set of the shoulders and one of the tattoos on his neck. Shadow.

"Time and date are at the bottom." Rooster says quietly.

It's dated a couple days before Sway was shot.

"How convenient," Smoke sneers.

"Come the fuck on," Steer spits out. He sits forward and motions for me to hand him the photo. "Jesus Christ," he whispers after studying the photo.

"You got any idea how many fucking computers and security systems I had to break into?" Rooster says to Smoke. "He rented it in Jersey figuring we wouldn't look there since he had no business being in their territory."

Steer passes the photo down the table and lifts his chin at Rooster. "You still have the actual video?"

"I got copies of everything. Including the video where his wife confesses what went down to Jigsaw." He shoots a glare at Smoke. "Anyone who wants to examine my evidence is more than welcome to. I printed that out before we sat down but there's lots more."

"All right. That's damning enough." I lift my chin at Rooster. "What do you have on Malone's?"

"Word is he did it for the insurance money so he could pay off DeLova."

"Is it possible Shadow got his wires crossed and thought DeLova was coming?" Hustler asks.

Dumb theory, but I get it. We're all grasping at straws. Struggling to wrap our minds around a brother betraying the club.

"Anything's possible." Rooster shrugs. "My guess is Malone hired Shadow to burn the place down. Maybe when Shadow showed up with more people, it made Malone trigger happy. Or maybe Shadow thought it would be an easy way to get rid of his Z problem."

Fury burns through me. "Y'all need to get your priorities straight.

After what went down with Bull, every single member should've been vetted more thoroughly."

I should rein in my temper. Antagonizing everyone at the table when I'm trying to bring them together isn't the smartest move, but fuck, I'm pissed.

CHAPTER THIRTY-THREE

Lilly

I'M EXHAUSTED, BUT TOO ANXIOUS TO SLEEP AFTER TALKING TO Z. WHILE I told him exactly what Shadow said and did, I left out the parts where I encouraged Shadow's behavior in the beginning of our encounter.

I feel that's something I need to confess in person.

My phone buzzes and I notice a text from Hope.

Instead of answering, I call her back. Obviously, she's up.

"Hey, everything okay?" I say as soon as she answers.

"I was going to ask you that. Rock, Wrath, and Dex just headed down your way."

"Oh. Wow. Okay." Does that mean Z's in trouble? Or is Rock coming down to support Z? Either way, I'm relieved Z will have more people he trusts at the clubhouse.

"Did he say why?"

She chuckles softly. "Only that he thought you might appreciate a phone call. Everything okay?"

I consider my words carefully.

"There was a small *incident.* One of the brothers…I don't know, put his hands on me. In a rather hostile way."

"Jeez." She's quiet. "A full-patch?"

"Yup." I try to laugh it off. "I punched him in the nuts, so it worked out fine."

She doesn't join in on the laughter. "Lilly, I'm so sorry. That shouldn't happen."

"That's what everyone said."

"Poor Z. That's not what he needs right now."

"I'm aware."

"Sorry, I didn't mean it that way."

"I know you didn't, Hope."

"Do you want me to come down tomorrow?"

Do I? She has a baby at home to worry about. If things get uglier down here, I don't want to bring her into unregulated chaos. Although, I suppose if it's really a problem, Rock wouldn't let her come down anyway.

"You don't have to do that, but why don't we make plans to meet up sometime this week? We can meet somewhere halfway if you don't want to drive all the way down here."

"We could meet in Woodstock and have lunch at that fancy Chinese place right outside of the village?" she suggests.

"That sounds good. See if you can get Trinity to join us."

"You sure everything's all right? Is there anything I can do?"

"Honestly, no. Chance is next door at Heidi's. I just talked to Z and he said it's going to be a long night. Teller brought me home."

"That's good. If you need something or you decide you do want me to come down, you know, if this goes on for more than tonight and you want some company, don't be afraid to ask me."

"I won't. Promise."

We hang up and I feel a little better after talking to her.

Less alone.

Z

"All those in favor of halting the vote until we get more information from Shadow?"

This time, the vote goes all the way around the table and it's unanimous.

Shadow's execution at the hands of the club has been granted a stay.

Tension twists through the room, thick and suffocating. "Let's take a break and meet in the bunker in thirty." I slam down the gavel and follow Steer out of the room.

As our SAA, he's the one who gets to hoist Shadow up. Jigsaw helps him drag Shadow to the old storm shelter out back. Well, it started out as a storm shelter. Sway got on a doomsday-prepper kick a few years back and turned it into something more secure.

Where we'll have total privacy.

Rooster brings interested brothers into the office to share what he has on Shadow.

Since I want the motherfucker dead no matter what, I don't need to examine anything.

The rest of the brothers slowly find their way outside. A few men stop to shake my hand or offer words of encouragement and thanks.

When almost everyone else has gone outside, Rock slaps his hand on my shoulder and turns me to face him. "You did good in there, brother." Pride shines in his eyes. "Don't take this the wrong way, but I'm really proud of you."

I flash a quick, tired grin. "Learned from the best."

"Nah, those were thoughtful, powerful words." He pokes me in the chest. "Straight from the heart. Everyone could feel it." He glances around to make sure we're not overheard. "They've needed to hear it for a while. I hope it sinks in."

"I think it did."

"I think so too."

Wrath comes up behind me and hooks his arm around my neck. "Proud of you, Angus," he says against my ear.

"You hit your head sometime tonight?"

He doesn't laugh, but he does release me from the chokehold. "That's some fucked-up shit, Z. I knew there was a reason I never liked him."

"Take a number."

"Rooster's smart," Rock says. "He could've told you what he had in secret. He earned everyone's respect by waiting and building his case before bringing it to the table."

"Yeah, he told me straight-up a couple weeks ago, he was loyal to the club, not any one brother." I glance around at the now mostly empty clubhouse. "You guys don't have to stay for this."

Rock and Wrath share a look. "You have everything handled," Rock says. "If you want us here for any reason, we'll stay."

"No, brother. I appreciate it. But you've got a baby at home. You should be there. It's gonna be a long, dirty night. If you wanna catch a few hours of sleep at the house before heading back or something, let me—"

"Nah. We'll be all right," Wrath says.

Dex walks up and waves his hand. "I'm gonna stick around, if that's all right, Prez?"

"Yeah," Rock says. "I think that's a good idea. "You all right with that, Z?"

"Absolutely."

I'd have no problem with Rock and Wrath staying either. I understand why they think it's better to head out. The upstate president came down here tonight to let everyone in this club know he has my back. Now, he's leaving to show them I can handle this on my own.

Since Dex isn't an officer upstate, it's less of a big deal for him to stick around. Teller and Murphy will definitely be attending since they were part of the Malone fiasco.

Tonight will be bloody.

Tomorrow, I have a feeling I'll need a new VP.

CHAPTER THIRTY-FOUR

Z

It's been a long time since I've attended the execution of a brother.

Our national president keeps hounding us to recruit new numbers. Tonight is why we've always been selective and few men ever earn a full three-piece patch.

A brother going behind the club's back to work against us with a rival club is a huge betrayal. The only thing worse is a brother who snitches to the cops.

Trying to take out our president because of greed or because he couldn't get enough members to rally to his side, that's a whole new level of treachery. Every decision an officer makes is supposed to be for the good of the *whole* club. We may not always like all those choices, but we stand by our brothers.

If an officer isn't doing what's in the best interest of the club, there are plenty of options to remove him, even a stubborn bastard like Sway, without shooting him in the head.

Cowardice. There's no room for it in this club.

Steer corralled everyone into the underground chamber out back. It was renovated with this in mind. I've only seen it once or twice since Sway remodeled.

A steel door in the basement's concrete floor leads to a flight of stairs.

Above us, the filters for the pool hum and churn. Dampness clings to the walls.

To the left, there's a room with an elevated tub and barrels of chemicals. We have a similar room at the upstate clubhouse.

The tunnel's low enough that I have to duck to move through it as do most of my brothers.

The next room is empty. It's too small for this sort of interrogation.

At the end of the tunnel, there's a much larger room with a higher ceiling. All the members of the downstate charter are spread around. Back to the wall, facing the accused.

This gets done with the full knowledge and consent of all the brothers. No secrets. No wondering what went down. No fear that brothers are being executed for no reason. Everyone on the same page.

Shadow's on a metal folding chair in the center of the room. Steer stands behind him. Shadow isn't tied or cuffed to the chair. Nothing silly or dramatic like that. There's no point. Where would he run?

Murphy, Teller, and Dex fall back, mixing in with the rest of the brothers.

"Come to execute me, Prez?" Shadow sneers as I step in front of him.

I glance at Steer. "Get him up."

I was wrong, Shadow's hands are restrained by two zip-ties holding them together. Blood seeps through his shirt and he groans as Steer yanks him out of the chair.

"The club voted to strip your patch," I inform him.

To his credit, Shadow doesn't seem incredibly surprised.

"For touching your bitch? After she all but gave me the green light?"

"We already know that's not how it went down," Rooster says.

Hustler shifts forward. "You still pulled a knife on a brother."

"He was beating the shit out of me for no reason."

"So, you didn't try to choke the mother of my kid?" I ask, already tired of his bullshit.

He shrugs. "She likes it rough, so what?"

"It doesn't really matter how she likes it or what she said to you," Teller says from behind me. "Z made it clear she was his property—"

"She wasn't wearing no patch."

"A technicality, asshole," Jigsaw grumbles. "Everyone knew it."

"Everyone knew she was with our prez," Suds says. "Don't matter if she hiked up her dress and put a *free sample* sign over her cunt." I glare at Suds and he holds his hands up. "Just trying to make a point."

"Putting hands on her went way too far," Smoke says. "Leave it at that."

He's probably trying to distance himself from Shadow at the last minute, but Smoke's condemnation of Shadow's actions—no matter how lukewarm it might be—finally shuts Shadow up.

"Take his cut." I nod to Steer, who holds Shadow while Hustler and Jigsaw strip off Shadow's cut. They hand it to me.

Slowly, I pull my knife out of the sheath resting against my thigh. It's a different knife than I carry every day. This one's for special occasions.

Shadow's eyes widen as I use the heavy, curved blade to slice off his VP patch. Overkill, but it gets the job done.

"Burn it," I order, handing it off to Rooster.

Now that his patch has been taken, Steer throws Shadow back in his seat.

I circle the room once, considering how this should go down.

"While we were at the table, some disturbing information was brought up."

Shadow doesn't seem to care. He sits back. "If you're gonna kick me out, just do it."

"You think we woulda brought you down here if you were only getting kicked out?" Steer rumbles.

The gravity of the situation seems to sink in for Shadow. He squirms in his chair.

"What's wrong, Shadow?" I ask. "Were you thinking, even if you got kicked out of LOKI, you'd run to the Vipers and they'd patch-in your disloyal ass?"

He cocks his head and glares at me but doesn't open his mouth.

"Or were you thinking you'd help the Vipers infiltrate our club and you'd patch them over to us?"

His mouth twitches. Jesus Christ, was that really what he wanted to do?

Steer must have the same reaction. "How many of us were you planning to kill to make that happen?" he rasps out.

"I didn't need to kill anyone," Shadow says. "Sway just needed to stop being a pussy."

Sway's many things, but he's not a coward.

"It wasn't just Sway," Rooster says. "None of us wanted to go after the Vipers. We all voted on it."

"Because you're all scared of National coming down on us."

"You thought patching over some Vipers would get you out from

221

underneath National?" Can he really be that stupid? Priest would've come down even harder on them. "If the Vipers took over this charter—which never would've happened, by the way—Priest would've sent in every damn charter he could. All you would've done is spark off a war."

"You're weak," he spits out. "Pushing DeLova away. Been neglecting the Demons. How long you think that goes on before they take us over? Vipers could handle those two threats."

"Neither of them *are* a threat. Our relationship with Stump's club is solid. Always has been."

Shit, we partied with them right before National. Rode with them for a while too. We've done business since then.

Shadow's full of shit.

Even if the Demons had an issue with downstate, they've been close to upstate for years. They wouldn't go after one of our other charters without serious cause.

It doesn't matter. "We're getting sidetracked. So, you admit you were working with the Vipers MC? A known enemy of this club."

"I'm not admitting anything." He sits back, smug as a child who stuck out his tongue.

"Who shot Sway?" Steer asks.

Shadow's calculating stare slides between Steer and me. Finally, he shrugs. "Don't know. I was inside."

"Are you sure about that?" Rooster pipes up. "I got records showing you renting a black caddy with the same last three digits of the one that tore ass out of here after Sway was shot. Not to mention a few other details."

Shadow's head snaps up. "What records?"

Jigsaw steps forward. He has his own knife out and slaps his open palm. "Myra gave you up."

Shadow's eyes widen for the briefest second, then he snorts and looks down. "Like fuck she did."

"I had to give her some encouragement." Jigsaw closes the distance between them and gently digs the tip of his Bowie knife into Shadow's chin, forcing his head up. "Then she had all sorts of stuff to say."

"You're down here stripping my patch because I felt up your old lady's tits?" Shadow yells at me. "But you gave him permission to carve up my *wife*?"

"No one even knew you had a wife," Steer reminds him.

"Some civilian piece on the outside isn't my concern," Jigsaw says.

I glance over at Jigsaw, not happy about how he may have gotten his information. But I'll have to address it later.

Jigsaw pulls out his phone and hands it to me. A beautiful but terrified brunette stares back. Except for being duct-taped to a chair, she seems unharmed.

Someone off-camera, Jigsaw, I assume asks about the night of the shooting.

"I don't know," she cries.

"Think hard. "

"You don't understand what he'll do to me."

"Trust me, sugar. It won't be an issue."

She's silent. Probably weighing her options. Rat out her husband or get carved up by Jigsaw? If Shadow treats her with the same respect he treats other women, I think she'll choose the first option.

"I didn't do anything," she whispers. "And I didn't know what he had planned."

"What didn't you know?" Jigsaw snaps. "Stop fucking around."

"He wanted me to," she stops and licks her lips, "drive this car he rented to the clubhouse. He was going to give me a signal to peel out." She stares at the camera. "It's best if I don't ask Jimmy questions."

"Get to the night in question," Jigsaw prompts.

"I pulled into the parking lot where he told me to so I'd avoid the cameras. He was outside arguing with the tall, older guy."

Jigsaw must flash a picture to her off-camera. "That him?"

She nods.

"Go on."

"The other guy turned to go inside and Jimmy…"

She sobs and hiccups at the same time.

In a gentler tone, Jigsaw asks, "What did Shadow do?"

"He…he…pulled a gun and shot the older man…in the back of the head." She bursts into tears. "I didn't need a signal. I slammed it in drive and floored it out of there."

"Fucking bitch," Shadow mumbles.

"Actually, she was quite sweet." Jigsaw grins. "Once we got to know each other."

"Motherfucker!" Shadow roars and launches himself at Jigsaw, hitting him head-on in the gut.

"Jesus Christ, sit him down," I say to Steer.

Jigsaw's laughing when Shadow's thrown back into his chair. I glare at him and he settles down.

Steer uses his sledgehammer-sized fists to knock Shadow around a few times. "You shot our president?" he asks between blows.

"Fuck you." He laughs in Steer's face. "You should've helped me take Sway out after that shit with Bull, but you're too loyal to him."

Obviously, they have issues to work out.

"Loyal to the club." Steer punches Shadow in the face, snapping his head to the left. "Not Sway."

"Enough," I order. "Did you shoot Sway?" I ask again.

"He was kissing Priest's ass. Closing off avenues of revenue that clubs have used for decades because he didn't want to get on Priest's bad side."

Hustler shakes his head. "None of us wanted in on the stuff you're talking about. We've voted on it more than once."

Interesting that they've voted on whether or not to go against direct orders from National.

"If Sway had been out, I would've convinced you my way was better," Shadow finally says.

"You assumed you'd move into his spot?" I ask.

"I'm the VP! Of course I assumed that, asshole."

"Power isn't given. It's either taken or earned." I drill him with a hard stare. "And you're not strong enough to do either."

"Fuck you, Z." Shadow spits. "I earned my place."

"Nothing is ever guaranteed," Steers says.

"No shit." Shadow sneers. "Never expected Priest to come up here. Especially since the fucker didn't even die."

I pinch the bridge of my nose and shake my head. "Christ, Shadow, you're dumber than I thought. Priest already hinted at National that he wanted us to take over your charter. Then you fucked up by getting arrested down there. No way was he ever gonna let you be in charge of any charter. You're lucky he didn't strip your VP patch months ago."

Steer glances up at me and frowns. Guess it was news to him that we came close to taking over his club last year.

"None of us wanted to take over downstate. We said we'd support in any way we could, but that's it."

Thankfully, Steer seems satisfied with that answer. "I never would've wanted you as president," Steer says to Shadow. "So, if I ran against you, were you gonna shoot me too?" He jerks his chin at Hustler. "Were you gonna take him out if he said no? Jiggy? Were you gonna shoot all your brothers in the back if you couldn't get your way?"

Shadow has no answer.

I'm done playing with him.

I glance around the room. "I promised the decision to put Shadow to ground was up to the whole club. And it has to be unanimous."

Actually, I'm not sure that's true anymore. After what we've learned tonight, even if someone doesn't vote yes, Shadow can't be allowed to remain breathing. "Let's vote," Steer says. "Yes."

Every brother steps forward and gives their yes without hesitation. Even Smoke.

I'll give Shadow credit. He keeps his chin up and doesn't beg or plead for his life.

This was an insult, an injury, to all of us. To purge the betrayal of the whole club, I allow the brothers to put the boots to Shadow for a while.

But I'm the one who finally slits his throat.

CHAPTER THIRTY-FIVE

Lilly

I FINALLY MANAGED TO FALL ASLEEP. SEVERAL TIMES THROUGH THE NIGHT I wake up and realize Z's still not home.

The rumble of more than one bike briefly wakes me but I'm so out of it, I don't fully awaken.

A few minutes, or maybe even an hour later, something brushes over my ankle. Startled, I jerk my feet up. The covers slowly slide down my body and a firmer grip on my leg pulls me from sleep.

"Z?"

"It's me."

Relief washes over me and I blink myself awake. "Are you okay?"

"Shh, I'm fine. Go back to sleep."

While he says *go back to sleep*, his rough hands skimming their way up my legs only awaken all my pent-up needs and fears.

He skims his lips over my calf and behind my knee. Stops to kiss a spot on my thigh. Every kiss and touch reminds me how precious I am to Z.

I turn over and sit up, almost bumping into him. The barest hint of sunrise bleeds into the room but it's enough to see the look of surprise on Z's face when I strip my tank top off and toss it on the floor.

I run my gaze over his damp hair and skin. "Did you take a shower?"

"Yeah, before I left the clubhouse and then again downstairs. You didn't want me coming to bed covered with what went on tonight."

I turn that over in my head. "What happened?"

"Don't worry about it." He lifts his chin. "Keep going."

I wiggle out of my shorts and loop my arms around his neck, dragging him down to me. His forehead touches mine but he doesn't kiss me. He stares at me for a few seconds. "Are you hurt?"

"No."

"It won't ever happen again." The conviction to his words is clear.

I can only imagine what Z had to do in order to make that promise. I doubt I'll ever see Shadow again.

"I trust you."

He closes his eyes for a second, then kisses my forehead, my eyelids, my cheeks, then lower.

"Where are you going?"

Stubble from his chin scratches over my hip, followed by another soft kiss. "I wanted to wake you up with my face in your pussy."

"I'm awake now."

"I still want to taste your pussy." He tightens his hands around my hips. "I need to taste you, breathe you in, feel that you're safe and mine." The words tumble out of him in a tangle of emotion and dominance. "I hated being away from you for so long after what happened."

I whisper, "I was worried about you."

"Lilly, I will *always* punish anyone who hurts you."

I open my mouth to answer, but gasp instead. He drags his tongue up my needy center, stopping to flick my clit.

"The only words I need to hear from you for the next few hours are 'more', 'right there', and 'holy fuck, I'm coming again'."

I shiver with desire, then chuckle. "What about, 'fuck me harder with your giant cock'?"

"That works too."

He lowers his head and spreads me wide, then presses soft kisses everywhere, slowly working his way up to longer, slow, sensual kisses. The tip of his finger circles my clit, lighting up every nerve ending in my body. I'm writhing and shoving myself against his face when he wraps his lips around my clit and flicks his tongue.

"Z, that's so good." My moans fill the room and he encourages me to make more noise.

After long moments of kissing and licking, he sits up and I finally spy the huge bandage covering his left thigh.

"What happened?"

"Nothing some painkillers won't take care of later." He stretches out next to me and pats his chest. "Come sit on my face."

"What?"

He turns and gives me a cocky smile. "Did you come yet?"

I shake my head. "But—"

"Then I'm not finished. My leg is on fire, though. So, come sit on my face."

"Z."

"Unless you're about to say one of the approved phrases for the night, get your ass up. I'm not fucking around, woman."

Good god, will I ever get over that bossy attitude of his turning me on so much? I hope not.

I scramble onto my knees and kneel beside him. My gaze strays to his injury again. "I don't want to hurt you."

"You won't." He cups my hip with one hand and urges me closer. He slides down and I wriggle my way up until he has me exactly where he wants.

The second his tongue makes contact with my flesh again, my legs shake.

"Put your hands against the wall." His warm breath ghosts over my damp thighs. "Can't have you losing your balance."

"Yeah, I'll smother you."

He slaps my ass, driving me forward where his tongue waits for another long, slow lick. Maddeningly slow. How does he have this much patience and self-control?

I tilt my head back, arching and reaching until I wrap my hand around his cock.

He groans and clutches my hip tighter. "Not yet, pretty girl," he mumbles against me.

I squeeze him a little tighter and slide my hand up and down until he groans again.

"Concentrate, Lilly. You can have my cock after you come."

"That seems unfair."

Careful not to add *kicked in the face* to his injuries for the night, I turn over. He wraps his hands around my waist and drags me where he wants, keeping a tight hold of me. Now I have enough room to play.

Except the second I get my fingers around the smooth steel of his cock, he wraps his lips around my clit and sucks.

"Oh shit!"

"Mmmhmm," he encourages. The sound vibrates against my center.

Fully interested in repaying the favor, I open my mouth and relax my jaw, slowly taking him. He groans and his hips jerk as I close my mouth around him. I pull back, careful not to choke.

His hands skate over my ass, up my back, and grab a handful of my hair, giving it a gentle tug. His other arm stays clamped over my hips, keeping me in place.

All thoughts vanish as we race to see who can pleasure the other one more.

"Ah, fuck, woman." He rips his mouth away. "Get on my dick."

Panting and grinning, I sit up and slide my hand up and down his slick shaft a few times. "Make up your mind. Get on my face. Get on my dick. Which is it?"

His hands clamp down on my hips, holding me in place. "Ride my dick," he grits out. "Now."

Careful not to disturb his injury, I brace myself with my hands on his shins, line myself up and sink down. "Oh," I gasp.

He slaps his hand against my ass twice. "God damn your ass is fucking beautiful. Harder."

I place my hands on the mattress, leaning forward to give him a really good show and ease myself up and down.

"Fuck." His voice strains. "That's good."

Blood thunders through my ears. My nerve endings go wild. "Z, I'm—"

"I feel you. Keep coming." He slaps my ass again, setting me off. "Ride me."

The orgasm barrels down on me and I almost collapse.

I throw my head back and he grabs my hair, gently tugging.

"Turn. Want to see you," he rasps. He groans when I pull myself off and again when I stand over him.

"I don't want to hurt you." I'm staring down at his injury, wondering how I'm going to make this work.

"The only pain I'm feeling is in my balls. Get down here." He grabs at my hand and tugs.

As carefully as possible, I slide down. He grabs my hips and pulls me forward. "There you go. Perfect. Work that pussy."

"I'm doing *all* the work."

"I know. It's fucking awesome." He places his hand at the back of my head and pulls me down for a kiss.

His other hand presses down on my ass while he thrusts up into me. Being so tightly held, so close to him, triggers another orgasm and I scream against his mouth.

"Fuck," he groans. His hand fists in my hair. Good god, how many hands does he have? His arms clamp down around me while his hand pulls my hair, keeping me strung tight while he comes with a roar.

"Oh my god," I keep whispering over and over.

"Nope, just me." He grins and bucks his hips, sending me tumbling to the side.

After reconnecting, reuniting, reassuring each other that we're okay and well, fucking ourselves limp, Z pulls me close. Warm skin on warm skin. He runs his fingers through my hair and kisses my cheek.

"What happened?" I whisper.

"Let's just say, he's somewhere he's never going to bother you or any other woman again."

He doesn't need to tell me more than that. I understand exactly what he means. "Good."

"I always want you to feel safe with me."

"I already do." I sit up and trace his jaw with my fingers. "I don't blame you for what happened."

"I blame myself."

"I can tell."

"I should've known. He's been unpredictable for weeks. But that showdown with Serena was the last straw. I shouldn't have allowed you back at the clubhouse until he was dealt with."

Z's guilt churns in the air between us. I can't let him think this is his fault. "Z, I have to tell you something."

His stomach muscles contract as he lifts his head and quirks an eyebrow. "Why the serious tone, Siren?"

Z

What the fuck is Lilly trying to tell me? She looks so damn nervous...
and guilty.

She bites her lip and looks away. "I goaded him a little."

"Excuse me?"

"He scared me, the way he was waiting in the hallway." Her shoulders
jerk. "But I thought maybe if he hit on me or something...You said if a
brother was disrespectful or hit on an old lady, he could be kicked out. I
figured it would happen anyway, I might as well force it now before he
really hurt you or someone else."

None of what she's saying makes sense. "What exactly did you do?"

"Not much, I flirted back a little." She scowls. "But then I really got
scared, so I tried to walk away. That's when he turned violent."

"Jesus Christ." I spear my fingers through my hair and sit up straight.
"Do you realize what could've happened to you if Rooster hadn't come
around that corner?"

"I know all too well, Z. That's why I did it."

Once my heart stops hammering, I pounce on her, knocking her back
against the mattress. "You're diabolical, woman. You know that?
Dangerous too."

She swallows hard and meets my eyes. "Teller getting shot, the way
Shadow treated the girls, the way he came after me, how he kept on
getting bolder in the ways he challenged you...I was scared it would
escalate."

If only she knew how much deeper Shadow's crimes ran. Still, I don't
want to encourage her to put herself in danger.

"Too late, I realized my plan was absurd and I lost my nerve. By then,
he wasn't letting me leave." She frowns. "If he ever planned to in the first
place."

"He knew you were my old lady. Even if you gave him the green light,
he should've walked away. Attacking you was way over the line."

"I knew as long as I reached you, I'd be safe. I also knew you'd make
sure it never happened again."

"Don't ever do that again." I lean down and kiss her. "And don't ever,
ever tell anyone what you just told me. Not Hope, not Murphy, Heidi," I
pull back and look her in the eye. "No one."

"Okay," she whispers.

"All anyone will ever know is *he* attacked *you*. You fought him off.
Rooster and Stitch saw you fighting him off. End of story. Everything that
happened after has nothing to do with you."

She wraps her arms around my neck and leans up to kiss me. "I swear I'll never tell a soul. I'll never speak of it again."

I don't doubt her.

Who else but me knows how well Lilly can keep a secret?

CHAPTER THIRTY-SIX

Z

WHY CAN'T I STAY IN BED FOR LIKE, OH I DON'T KNOW, ANOTHER YEAR?

Lilly stretches and pushes up against me. Her hair falls over her shoulder, exposing the deep black and blue mark ringing the side of her neck. "Motherfucker." I want to find out where they buried Shadow's remains so I can piss on his grave.

My leg's throbbing like a bitch this morning. I'd rather not take the pain pills the doctor gave me, but I do take the antibiotics.

"I need to run out for a bit," I explain to Lilly after breakfast.

"Okay. Kendall's coming over to give the kids swim lessons."

"Good." I lean over and kiss her temple. "Are you all right?"

"I'm fine."

"I won't be gone long."

"You gonna be good for Mommy?" I ask Chance.

"We're swimming!" he announces, pointing toward the pool.

The good feeling from spending the morning with my family fades as soon as I arrive at the hospital.

It's my obligation to inform Sway that the VP spot is now vacant. I'm not exactly looking forward to the conversation.

Head wound or not, he notices my stiff movements and slight limp as soon as I walk in the door.

"Too much fucking?" he asks. The nurse at his bedside scowls, which only makes Sway laugh. "Christ, I can't wait to get out of here," he says as soon as she leaves.

"They give you any idea when?"

"No, but I can start physical therapy soon."

"Good."

"Do you mean that?"

I stare at him for a second or two. "Yeah, I mean it, Sway. I didn't want...I never wanted this. I was perfectly content where I was."

"Well, I appreciate everything you're doing, Z."

His opinion might change in a minute.

I perform my regular sweep of the room for any listening devices or cameras that might have been planted. Fuck knows the room isn't secure. When I'm satisfied, I clear my throat and move closer to the bed.

"You planning to kiss me?" he asks.

"Don't be a dick." I lean in and keep my voice low. "You're in need of a new VP."

"Aw, fuck," he groans. "That asshole. He talked a good game when he wanted to sell you on something, but..."

Well, at least Sway isn't taking the news too hard.

"What happened?" he asks.

"He's been a problem for a while. First, the bullshit with the Vipers that got Teller shot." I pause, not sure how much Sway will care about this next part. "I had an issue with how he was treating some of the girls. Not a way men who wear our patch should behave."

A dark look crosses his face. Brief, but I catch it.

"What?"

"Serena?"

"Yeah, why?"

"I warned him before to leave her alone." He shakes his head. "Pissed Tawny off because she assumed it meant I was fuckin' her."

"Were you?"

"Not in a long time."

I barely restrain my eyeroll.

"Wasn't just her though. I heard stuff from some of the other girls."

Something like that wouldn't be high on Sway's priority list.

"You learn the most about a man's character by watching how he treats people who can't fight back."

Sway stares at me.

"Men who don't stand up for others aren't fit to wear our patch."

He dips his chin, acknowledging the sentiment, but not necessarily agreeing or disagreeing with it.

"Anyway, that's not the worst of it. After that incident, he decided to go after my old lady."

"Jesus Christ. You fuckin' serious?"

"Dead."

"She okay?"

"She's fine. But he and I got into it."

"As you're allowed to do."

I keep speaking as if he hadn't interrupted. I don't need Sway to assure me I did the right thing.

"Maybe he figured I'd still call a vote to strip his patch and he had nothing to lose, but he pulled a knife on me. Sliced up my leg pretty good."

"What? Shadow?"

"Yup. I can show you the stitches if you need to see 'em, but I gotta pull my pants down and that might look odd if any of the nurses walk in on us."

"Sit down and keep your pants on, ya dick."

I chuckle and ease back into one of the chairs.

"You end him right there?"

"No. I took it to the table. The votes to strip his patch was unanimous. We took the other vote after we…extracted some information from him. That one was unanimous too."

He stares at me for a few seconds. "You didn't have to put it to a vote."

"Yes, I did. They didn't vote me in, Sway. I was forced on them by Priest. I couldn't make that call on my own."

"Shit, brother." He shakes his head. "Go on."

"Rooster's been digging into Shadow. He hadn't brought it to the table yet because he didn't have solid proof, but given what we were voting on, he told us he suspected Shadow was the one who shot you."

"Fuck!" He squeezes his eyes shut.

"Something coming back to you?"

"I don't know. Maybe. What'd he say?"

"He came clean, brother." I tip my chin in his direction. "About the shooting."

Sway struggles to sit up. "*He* shot me?"

"Afraid so. Thought you weren't doing enough to stand up to National and take over more territory."

"Oh, fuck that. I should've sent him to take over New Jersey and let them kill him."

"How'd you ever let him slip under the radar?"

"I had my doubts. Told you that before. I was trying to keep him close. Until I had something more solid to go on." He touches his head. "Maybe too close."

"Well, it's done."

"I hope you made it hurt."

I tilt my head not really answering. "I want Rooster as VP. Going to put it up for a vote today."

"I support that."

I wasn't really asking for Sway's opinion or advice, but it's good to know he agrees.

The door swings open and a fuckin' ghost walks in.

"Sway?" she rasps. Her soft amber eyes meet mine and she shrinks back against the door.

This calmer, less made-up version of Tawny is fuckin' eerie. Without the teased hair, pounds of makeup, tight clothes, and sky-high heels, she looks about twenty years younger than I remember.

"Z," she finally says in the same dramatic, breathy voice I recognize. "You're here with him. Good."

"Where've you been?" I growl.

"Where I told her to be," Sway says.

"What?" My jaw drops. I wasted a lot of time searching for her ass. "How?"

"It's an agreement we made a long time ago. Anyone ever tried to take me out, she was supposed to go somewhere safe and wait for me to contact her."

My eyes are so fucking wide, I probably look like a damn cartoon. "Jesus Christ, Tawny. I thought *you* mighta done it for a while." Fuck, I'll admit it to her face. She'll probably take it as a compliment.

"Nah." She runs the back of her hand over Sway's bristly cheek and stares down at him with an affection I haven't seen on her face in fifteen or more years. "I wouldn't risk ruining this handsome mug. I'd shoot him in the dick, for sure."

I can't help it. After every crazy absurd thing in the last twenty-four hours, I sit back and laugh until my stomach hurts.

CHAPTER THIRTY-SEVEN

Z

I CAN'T DESCRIBE WHAT IT MEANS THAT LILLY DOESN'T HESITATE TO JOIN ME at the clubhouse again. After what went down with Shadow, I wouldn't have blamed her if she told me to go fuck myself when I asked her to attend tonight's party to celebrate Rooster being named our vice president.

Having her on my arm, unafraid to return to the clubhouse sends a powerful message to the rest of the club.

My woman won't be intimidated by anyone or anything.

She has love and respect for the club. All qualities any president's old lady needs to have.

"I'm fine, Z, really. You assured me Shadow isn't here, so I'm not worried."

"I didn't say anything."

"The death grip you have on my hand says plenty."

I ease up, placing my hand on her ass instead, and she chuckles. "Much more subtle, Mr. Frazier."

"Watch your mouth, soon-to-be Mrs. Frazier."

She stares at me for a second, then leans up and softly kisses my cheek without saying a word.

Inside, I'm not sure what the hell we've walked in on. The guys are wild, clearly needing to blow off steam after losing a brother. Even if that brother was a piece of shit, they'd shared a patch with him for a long time.

Here's a painful truth. One of the reasons Rock, Wrath, and I decided early on to keep our club and rules tight upstate. The agony of being betrayed by a brother costs too much. To be forced to take a brother's life stains your soul.

We take the club, its rules, and its consequences for breaking those rules seriously and only admit brothers who will do the same.

"How do you feel about flying out to California soon?" I ask after we stop at the bar and have been handed a couple drinks.

Lilly's sinful lips wrapped around that tiny plastic straw have me thinking of something much more substantial she could wrap those beautiful lips around.

She lifts her gaze, meeting my hungry eyes, and teases her tongue over the end of the straw.

"You're killing me."

"What?" she asks innocently.

"Stop trying to distract me. I asked you a question."

"I'd like that. Are you sure you can be away from the club right now?"

"Things should calm down. A couple days won't hurt."

"I want to bring Chance," she says quickly. "So, he can say goodbye to the old place."

"Was planning on it."

She lets out a relieved breath. "Oh, good." She presses her hand to her chest. "The thought of being away from him, even for a couple of days, was making me freak out a little."

I laugh and pull her closer. "I wouldn't do that."

Lilly

"As my first act of faith in my new VP, I'm thinking of leaving you in charge for a few days." Z raises his bottle and tips it in Rooster's direction.

"Wait, what now?" Rooster feigns shock by clutching his chest.

Chuckling, I shift and tug the edge of my dress down.

"Stop fidgeting," Z breathes against my ear. "You look hot."

"I feel like my ass is hanging out. This dress is shorter than I realized. Or I'm wider than I thought."

He slaps my ass, earning us a bunch of hoots and whip-crack noises from the brothers. "Don't disrespect my old lady," he says to me.

I'm still reeling from the shock of his hand on my ass in front of everyone and how much I liked it.

Since our display is probably the mildest thing that's happened in this clubhouse tonight, the guys lose interest fast. Z takes my hand and leads me to the corner stool. Lala rushes over and sets a drink in front of me.

"Thanks, hun," Z says.

She squares her shoulders and takes a deep breath.

Either Z makes her nervous or she's trying to show off her tits.

"I know you don't care what club girls think, but thank you for um, well, you know." She darts away to help someone at the other end of the bar.

Z stands there, staring after her, and finally shakes his head.

"That was sweet." I brush my hand over his arm. "Took her a minute to screw up the courage."

"Am I that scary?"

"Not to me."

"Nothing to thank me for," he grumbles. "Not wanting to see girls hurt doesn't make me a hero."

"Maybe it does here."

His presidential gaze slides over the crowd. "Maybe the herd needs more thinning," he mutters.

"Z." I rest two fingers on his cheek, slowly turning his head my way. He sweeps his gaze over me, lingering on the plunging neckline of my dress.

"I want to bury my face in your tits."

I throw my head back and laugh.

"Hey," he says more seriously. He runs his fingers through my hair pushing it over my shoulder. "It's good to hear you laugh...after everything."

"You always make me laugh."

His hand drops to my knee, slowly tracing little circles. I shift, spreading my knees, opening myself up for him, and he wedges himself in tight. "What are you doing, Siren?"

"Me? I'm just sitting here having a drink with my man." I pick up the drink, teasing the little straw with my tongue.

He slides his hand up and under my dress, heading straight for what I'm offering. I gasp and briefly close my eyes when he stops and runs his thumb over the hot line between my legs.

"Lilly." His breath is a hot puff of air over my cheek. "You're soaked."

"Am I?"

"You want me to conduct a more thorough inspection?"

Holding back my laughter, I scoot to the edge of the stool, opening my legs wider. "I think you have to."

He leans closer, pressing his forehead to mine. "Look at me."

My gaze searches the room one more time. It's so dark, I don't think anyone even realizes we're over here. Well, except the girls behind the bar, but they're not going to interrupt us.

I meet his burning gaze and my pulse jumps. Under my dress, he slides his finger along the edge of my underwear, slowly working it away from my body.

"Oh," I gasp as soon as his rough fingers make contact with my sensitive skin.

"Just what I suspected," he murmurs. Beard stubble scratches my cheek as he drops kisses along my jaw. "Tilt your hips for me."

I loop my arms around his neck and adjust the way I'm perched on the stool. His body is hard under my palms as I stroke his shoulders.

"That's it," he encourages. "Kiss me."

Hunger stirs inside me. Not only for his body, but his heart and soul too. I sweep my tongue against his lip, and he groans, encouraging me. I open my mouth and he brushes his tongue against mine at the same time he slips a finger inside me.

"Oh," I moan into his mouth from the exquisite intrusion. He doesn't give me much time to adjust before adding a second finger. I moan even louder, biting my lip and squeezing my eyes shut. I dig my fingers into his shoulders as he slowly eases his fingers in and out of me.

"So wet." His mouth kicks into a grin. "Who made your pussy so wet?"

Devilish man. He brushes his thumb over my clit and I can't form an answer. What was the question?

"You," I whisper. "Fuck."

He twists his wrist and pumps his fingers in and out faster. "Think you can come for me like this?"

I open my eyes to search the room again.

"No, keep your eyes on me. No one's paying attention to us." He slides his fingers out and makes a slow trail to my clit, rubbing in maddening circles.

I close my eyes and rest my forehead against his chest. "I'm already close."

"Hmm." For the next few seconds, he's quiet, concentrating on the fire he's building between my legs. I risk looking up into his eyes. He's so focused on *me* it pushes me to the edge.

"I want to fuck you so bad," he whispers.

I hook my ankles together behind his legs, pulling him closer. Inviting him to do whatever he wants.

He groans. "Come for me first."

I'm so close to that blissful edge. My hips rock, my breath stutters, my pulse jumps, heat races over my chest and up my neck. I call out his name, a broken cry, louder than I intended. He slows his movements and drags his fingers out, stopping to readjust my underwear. He tickles and traces little patterns on my inner thighs and strokes me through my underwear, each soft touch bringing me gently back to Earth.

Desire still simmers in his eyes when I look up.

I slide off the stool and take his hand.

As we turn to sneak down the hallway to our room, Hustler stops us.

"That was fucking hot, Prez."

Heat sears my cheeks. Yes, I knew there was a possibility someone might see us, but knowing it *could* happen and knowing it *did* happen are two different things.

Z glares at him. "The fuck is wrong with you?"

He throws his arms wide. "You're at the bar, not invisible."

"I don't care if I'm on your dining room table, avert your eyes, motherfucker."

"Z." I tug on his hand. "We have more pressing concerns at the moment." I graze my fingers over his erection straining the zipper of his jeans in case he doesn't know what concern I'm referring to.

He growls at Hustler one last time before tugging me along. Hustler winks as I go by. Not the creepy, makes-my-skin-crawl wink of a predator. More like a friendly go-fuck-your-man wink.

Z stalks down the hallway so fast, I have trouble keeping up in my heels. Inside our room, he pulls my dress up and over my head, tossing it on the chair.

"Stand by the bed and wait for me," he rasps.

I go to kick off my heels and he stops me. "Leave 'em."

Curious, I move to the bed, running my hand over the comforter. Z unlaces his boots without taking his eyes off me. With a twitch of my hips, I turn and press my palms against the mattress, arch my back and glance over my shoulder.

"How'd you know that's what I wanted?" He clutches the edges of his cut and pulls it wide, drawing attention to his broad chest, sturdy shoulders, and inked arms. He places it over the chair, then drags his T-shirt up.

I lick my lips as he exposes every delicious inch. All his naked chest, hard muscles and beautiful ink. His hands move to his belt and my desire ratchets up another notch. I don't know what it is about his big hands working that thick strap of black leather loose, but it gets me every time.

He flicks the button loose and lowers the zipper. The jeans end up on the floor, kicked to the side. He stalks over, cock in hand.

"What do you want?" he asks.

"You."

"How?"

I twitch my hips. "Do you need me to draw you a map?"

He pops his hand against my ass and squeezes. "Careful what you ask for, Lilly."

Now I can't see him, but I feel his heat against the back of my legs. He slides his hands over my hips and down my thighs, dropping to the floor behind me.

"Z?"

"Shh." He hooks his fingers in my underwear and drags it down my legs. Featherlight kisses and licks along the backs of my legs have me squirming. He pushes his hand between my legs, widening my stance, then replaces his hand with his tongue.

"Oh, fuck. You didn't have to…oh my god…I'm ready. Holy shit."

On a mission, he licks and kisses, spreading my wetness everywhere. Too absorbed in the sensations, I collapse against the mattress, tucking my arms under me.

While he stands back up, he continues to stroke me. My legs are shaking so hard when he finally rubs his cock against my slick center. He grips my hips and fills me in one, solid thrust.

It feels *so* good, I'm clawing at the comforter, balling it up under me. The sounds of our skin slapping together as he pounds into me fills the room.

"Hear how wet you are?" he rasps. "So fucking hot."

He falls over me, pressing against my back. "Slide your fingers down and work your clit."

I grunt an obscene noise as I rush to comply. He lifts his weight off me, pulling away. I think to see if I'm doing as he asked. God, even that drives me crazy with need.

He grips my hip and slows his pace, making me feel every maddening thrust. "Fuck, fuck, Z. I don't ever want you to stop." God, I want him everywhere. I turn to get a glimpse of him over my shoulder.

"Good?"

"Yes. Harder."

He gives me a wicked smile and sucks his thumb into his mouth. I squeeze my eyes shut and concentrate on every movement.

A few thrusts later, he presses the pad of his thumb against my ass. I'd object, but in the heat of the moment it feels really fucking good and I arch my back instead.

"That's it," he encourages. "Open."

Fuck. Pressure. So much. But there's a twinge and it starts to feel...good.

Dark, dirty, and *really fucking good.*

"Oh my god." I swear I have a better vocabulary than that, but at the moment that's the only phrase that rolls off my tongue repeatedly.

I'm so full, ready to explode.

Blood thunders through my veins. Beads of sweat roll off my forehead. My entire body is strung so tight with the need for release. My little moans and soft noises morph into screams as my body convulses with pleasure.

I collapse, but Z continues his punishing thrusts. He works a hand between our bodies to play with my clit until I'm sobbing and shaking, begging him to have mercy on me.

His fingers dig into my hips as he pumps one last time and climaxes with a shout.

He sinks his teeth into my shoulder, gently biting down. "You're going to fucking kill me."

I can't catch my breath long enough to dispute it.

CHAPTER THIRTY-EIGHT

Z

GUILT, REMORSE, SHAME, THEY'RE NOT EMOTIONS I'VE EVER BEEN IN TOUCH with. And I'm not feeling any of them after Shadow's death. If anything, I'm relieved that we cut him out before he did more serious damage to the club or got someone killed. Maybe some small guilt prickles at me for not recognizing he was a problem sooner. But fuck, if Sway didn't see it after years around the guy, how could I?

It's been a while since I visited anyone in prison. Grinder's the only member of the upstate charter who's incarcerated. Since he got moved out of the maximum-security facility he'd been at for years, it's easier to pay him a visit.

The Pine Correctional guards toss a few suspicious looks my way. Eventually they approve my visit and I'm shown into a small room. A few minutes later, Grinder shuffles in, shackled and cuffed. The guard at least frees his hands.

Grinder waits until the guard leaves before speaking. "Zero. It's been a minute. How are you, brother?"

"Not bad. Waiting for you to come home, old man."

"Shouldn't be long now." He coughs. "Least that's what they tell me."

"You all right?" What a stupid question. Of course, he isn't. The man's had almost two decades of his life stolen. For a crime he didn't even commit. I have no doubt he's committed plenty of crimes *since* he's been inside. That's just the nature of what you have to do to stay alive, but he shouldn't have gone to prison in the first place.

"Looking forward to getting out. Probably won't recognize anything."

That's true. The world's changed a lot since he was a free man. "We're all here for you, brother. Club will help with anything you need."

"Not looking for any handouts, Z."

"Wouldn't dream of it. Can't wait for you to come home. That's all."

"Haven't seen Rock in a bit. He okay?"

"Yeah." Rock's twitchy with the information he shares about his personal life. Makes sense in our world. Grinder's Lost Kings MC family, but he's also part of a different world right now. Still, I think knowing about Rock's family will make Grinder happy. "He and his wife just had a baby."

He sits back. "Really? That's good. I'm happy to hear that. How's Teller doing?"

Interesting that was his first question.

"Good."

"He and Murphy were coming pretty regularly to visit."

Shit. I've had those two so busy between helping me out and taking care of their responsibilities upstate, they probably haven't had a minute to spare.

"There's been a few shakeups in the club. I'm actually running downstate while Sway's been in the hospital."

"Downstate?" He gives me a blank look. Downstate didn't exist when Grinder went inside. "Right. Right." He touches his head and grins. "Surprised Sway's still alive. Figured Tawny would've shot him by now."

I almost choke. "Yeah, we all thought so."

"You settle down?"

"Funny you ask. Yeah." I clear my throat and pull out a small picture the guards let me take in. All my other personal shit had to be left in a locker out in the waiting area. "Have a son too."

"Shit." Grinder's eyes shine as he takes the photo. "That's great, Z. Damn, looks just like ya."

"Right? He's a fun little dude. I can't wait for you to meet him."

He nods and hands the photo back slowly. "No matter what, you do whatever you have to do to protect 'em, Z."

The emotion in his voice stops me cold.

While I thought the news might cheer him up, give him stuff to look forward to, now I'm questioning my judgment. Grinder always wanted a family. Hell, he was a surrogate dad to most of us in the early days. Then he got tossed in prison, his wife left him, and all his plans for his life went up in smoke. Bragging about how well everyone's doing seems fucking cruel now.

"It's good to have something to look forward to, Z." As if he knew where my mind went, he gives me a shadow of the shrewd biker smile I remember.

"You got plenty to look forward to, brother." We talk a little longer until the guards tell us time's up.

A heaviness I didn't expect follows me out to the parking lot. Never felt this way after visiting a brother inside. Maybe it's the weight of running my own club. Of wanting to do whatever it takes to keep my brothers out of prison. Or the ache of leaving a brother behind. A brother who's already lost so much.

All the connections we've developed over the years have never been able to help Grinder.

Still bothered, I head North.

Not that Crystal Ball will help, but I stop there first.

The only person that could shake off my black mood today stands against the back wall, arms crossed over his chest, watching the room like he's dying for one of the customers to step out of line so he can kick someone's ass.

"What the fuck you doing here, brother?" I shout, slapping Rock's shoulder.

He growls something foul at me, motions for Blue to take his spot, and jerks his head toward the front door. "The fuck you doing here?" he asks when we're outside.

"Wanted to check on things. Talk to Dex for a minute. Never expected to see you here."

"Dex is out. We're short, so here I am. Wrath's taking over for me when Furious closes."

"Fuck, I better get out of here before he shows up. He's liable to kill me."

He chuckles. "Hope is supposed to stop by and have dinner with me later."

"She mad?"

"Nah." His mouth twitches into a smile. "She knows I'd rather be home, elbows deep in diapers, than dealing with this nonsense."

"Some nights that can be arranged here, Prez."

He slaps my chest. "What's on your mind?"

"How'd you know?"

"You look like you're thinking too hard." He taps the side of my head. "Smoke's billowing out of your ears."

"Har, har. Went to visit Grinder. It left me with a shitty feeling, ya know?"

He's slow in answering. "Yeah, I know exactly what you mean. It's not easy seeing him in there."

Actually, it's probably harder on Rock. He and Grinder went inside together. Rock got out after a few years. Grinder stayed behind. Rock almost never talks about that period of his life.

"Made the mistake of telling him about Chance. Thought it might cheer him up. Knowing there's new blood in the family or whatever, but I think it bummed him out."

He nods slowly. "He held onto the hope that Rosie'd be waiting for him when he got out a lot longer than most would've."

"Fuck. I should've kept my mouth shut."

"Don't be so hard on yourself. Anything would bum him out right now. He's been getting jerked around by the parole board for a couple years."

"Nothing we can do?"

"Glassman's at his wit's end. There's not much we can do to move them along. A charming quirk of the criminal justice system Hope tells me."

"Something we can look into? Maybe crack some skulls?"

"With all our free time?"

"Come on, Rock."

"I've tried. I haven't brought it to the table every time because it's depressing as fuck. But believe me, I've tried. I don't want to make things worse for him, though either."

"I hear you." I cock my head and study him for a minute before asking my next question. "Did he know about you and, you know, your relationship to Teller?"

The question seems to throw Rock. "No." He stops. considers the question more thoroughly. "I don't think so. How could...who the fuck knows? Lately, if I've learned anything, it's that even the impossible is possible."

"Amen to that."

"You didn't tell him, did you?"

"Fuck, no. I wouldn't talk about it with anyone but you, brother. You know that."

"How's everything else downstate?"

"Calmer now. With all the chaos of coming in the way I did, I don't think I realized how fractured the club was with Shadow in the VP seat."

"Yeah? Anyone else gotta go?"

"Smoke put in for a transfer to Florida."

"Good riddance."

"Amen. I'm keeping an eye on Tiny, but I think everyone else is solid. We'll see what happens when Sway comes home."

"God help you." His phone rings and he smiles when he checks to see who it is. The call can only be from Hope. I doubt he looks like that when anyone else calls him. "Hey, baby doll. You almost here? I'm out front with Z."

"You want me to go?" I ask when he hangs up.

"Nah, stick around. She wants to see you."

Not sure I should intrude on their brief window of time together, I nod. A few minutes later, she pulls in and Rock goes over to open her door. The intensity of their affectionate greetings hasn't lessened while I've been away. That's a good sign.

When Rock's finished properly molesting his wife, much to the delight of evening traffic, she turns and beams at me. "Z! What are you doing here?" She hurries over and envelops me in a ruthless hug. "I'm so happy to see you," she mumbles against my cut.

For some reason, Hope, more than anyone else, makes me home sick and I hug her back just as hard. "Miss you, sweetheart."

"Nothing is the same without you."

"Yeah, no one comes barging through our screen door every morning," Rock adds.

"Is it really 'barging in' if I do it every day and you're expecting me?"

"Yes."

"Oh, stop." Hope slaps her hand against Rock's chest. "We miss you."

"Eh." Rock wobbles his hand from side to side.

Ignoring his comment, but keeping her arms around him, she asks me what I'm doing here. "Don't tell me you missed CB so much you had to visit?"

"No. I went to visit Grinder, so I wasn't far. Thought I'd stop in and see how Dex was doing. Never expected to find Rock here."

Her mouth turns down at the mention of Dex's name. "The club's having a rough time lately."

"We'll get through it. We always do."

"How's Lilly? Chance? We're supposed to get together again sometime next week."

"I think she's looking forward to it."

"Good." She pauses. "You said you saw Grinder? How was he?"

To my knowledge, Hope's never met him. Only heard things Rock or one of the brothers has told her. But her love for the club runs deep and extends to all the members.

"Hard to say. Tired, but in good spirits. As good as anyone can be in his situation."

"I hope it's not much longer until he gets out. I know he'll probably need a lot of help getting adjusted..." Her voice trails off and she glances up at Rock.

He squeezes her shoulders. "Club'll help him figure it out."

The front door slams open and Blue sticks his head outside. "Rock, need your help."

Rock growls and I turn to answer Blue's request. "I'll—"

"No, I got it. Stay with Hope for a minute," Rock says, stalking off.

Hope watches him go with anxiety glittering in her eyes.

"I'm sure it's nothing," I try to reassure her.

"Oh, I'm more worried he's so pissed about being here. He'll bite some poor girl's head off."

I roar with laughter. "All this time, and the stuff you worry about still blows my mind."

She grins. "Good."

The door opens again and Blue steps out. He nods to Hope. "He should only be another minute. Sorry, Mrs. North. He said you can wait inside if you want."

She glances at the door and smooths her hands over her sweatshirt. "Uh, no. Thanks. I'm fine out here with Z."

"You okay?" I ask after Blue goes back inside.

"Huh? Yeah, I'm fine." She tips her head back. "It feels good to be outside."

"The sunshine agrees with you. You're prettier than ever."

"Oh, please. I look like I've been put through the spin-cycle." Her gaze shifts to the door again.

"You didn't bring Grace?"

"Nope. She's having some afternoon snuggle time with Auntie Trinity."

Ah, shit. Now I miss Trinity too.

"Rock didn't want to expose her to CB so early." Her lips twist with humor, but I can picture Rock saying something to that effect.

"More like he wanted to show you the backseat of his SUV while you were here."

She giggle-snorts into her hand. "Possibly. Except, I'm pretty sure he has his bike."

"Feel free to use my office. Not like you two haven't defiled it before."

Her cheeks turn pink, which cracks me up even more, and she reaches out to smack my arm. "Ugh, does Lilly realize what she's getting into?"

"That I'm a total deviant? I think it's what she loves about me the most."

Her laughter eases up and she's all seriousness again. "Things are good with you two?"

"Better than ever." It sounds flip, but the words roll off my tongue so easily because they're true. "I'm kind of shocked how well she's taken to all the club stuff."

"I'm not. Lilly's smart and practical. Plus, she's always had a bit of bad girl in her."

"Beauty, brains, and deviance. My dream woman."

A hesitant expression freezes her face. "You've forgiven her?"

"I don't know if *forgive* is the right word. I understand." I jam my hands in my pockets. "I'm not as worried about her leaving again as I was."

"Nothing worth having comes without risking your heart." She grins and squeezes her hands together. "I'm so happy for you. This is perfect."

"We're far from perfect, but I'm damn happy."

"You deserve to be happy, Z. And I can't think of a better man for Lilly."

I like that Hope sees me that way. Settling down with one woman, fatherhood, neither of those things seemed appealing to me before I met Lilly. And honestly, I wasn't sure I was cut out for it.

Sometimes I'm still not.

"I love the club and everything, but I also really love just being home with both of them. I don't know, doing small stuff."

"Chemistry is wonderful, and from what I've heard, you two have it in abundance."

A rumble of laughter explodes out of me. "You could say that."

"But," her expression turns soft and dreamy, "I think the real magic comes from all the beautiful, ordinary moments you share together. That's where the love grows, and where the foundation for a relationship that will go the distance flourishes."

"Christ, woman, you're going to make me tear up here."

"I've had a lot of time to ponder this."

Something in her tone makes me ask, "You miss working?"

"Honestly? Not yet. I haven't had time to. And I don't care how silly any of my lawyer friends think it is, but Grace will only be this little once. I don't want to miss it."

"Anyone who runs their mouth is probably jealous they couldn't spend time with their own kids."

She gives me a thoughtful nod. "Maybe. Everyone's journey is different, you know? I just wish some wouldn't judge so harshly."

"Someone give you shit, Hope? Do I need to kick some ass?" I make a big show of cracking my knuckles. "Because I'll do it."

"No." She laughs. "I'm fine."

Before I give it too much thought, my biggest fear jumps out of my mouth. "I'm worried this happy phase won't last and I'll get bored eventually and do something stupid. I don't want to hurt her."

"Oh, Z," she touches my arm. "I think the fact that you're worried about that is a sign it won't be an issue. You're going to go through ups and downs. It can't be all sunshine and rainbows a hundred percent of the time. Those down times will help you appreciate the rainbows so much more."

"Interesting way to put it."

"If you ever feel that way, then talk to her. From what I've seen, in so many of the cases I handled, communication, or lack of it, was the cause of so much misery. Not talking about things or having a partner you're not comfortable sharing your feelings with and then letting it fester into resentment and hatred causes more damage than anything."

"That makes sense."

"And don't take this the wrong way—"

"Here we go again."

She laughs and continues. "Strong men like you—and I don't just mean physically strong. Strong mind and character—have a hard time admitting they even *have* feelings sometimes. It's okay to be vulnerable with the right person."

"What makes them the right person?"

"That you trust them not to use your fears against you."

What *are* my biggest fears? Lilly leaving again. Not being a good enough father. Making the wrong decisions for the club.

Lilly's reassured me in all three areas lately.

"Besides, you're settling down later in life—"

"Thanks, Hope. Appreciate the reminder."

"I don't mean it in a bad way." She points to herself. "As the oldest 'new mom' at the play groups, I feel I can speak with authority here."

"But I bet you're the prettiest one too."

"Aw, Z, you're so sweet. Seriously though, you've done a lot of living. You already know what's out there. I mean, you must have volumes upon volumes of experience—"

When someone you actually like and respect puts your life in perspective, it's a lot less entertaining. "All right. I get your point."

She grins at me. "You don't have to worry whether you're 'missing out' on something. I don't think you'll be bored. Or if you are, you'll be grateful for it because you know what really matters." She reaches up and taps my chest over my heart.

"We should have you teach a class for prospects, 'there's more to life than fresh pussy' or something."

She rolls her eyes. "Don't deflect because I touched on a vulnerable area, Z. It's beneath you."

"Actually, I think it's exactly my thing."

Another eyeroll. Shit, growing up would've been a lot more entertaining if I'd had a sister instead of the two dumbfuck siblings I ended up with.

"So, you still have no regrets about this?" I nod at the front door to Crystal Ball. "The club, everything?"

"Zero regret, Z. Absolutely."

"Rock doesn't drive you crazy with all his overprotectiveness? I'm kinda shocked he let you drive here on your own today."

She snorts and doesn't disagree. "Oh, he makes me nuts. But I love him and I know it comes from a good place."

"It does," I agree.

"I think you were the first person to point that out to me. Wrath might have tried, but—"

"His message is a little harsher?"

"Just a tad."

The door opens and Rock finally steps back outside. "Jesus Christ, I forgot all the petty bullshit that goes on here."

"What's wrong?"

"My ears are still bleeding. Jasmine stole Pepper—"

"Poppy?"

"Whatever. Someone stole some expensive eyeliner from someone, so someone else flushed another girl's shit down the toilet. Kill me."

Hope giggles into her hands. "I've told you guys, you really need a female manager or something to handle this stuff before it gets out of hand. Someone who will understand their concerns without belittling them, but also lay down the law."

"I laid down the law," Rock says. "I told them to both go the fuck home."

"Jesus, Rock, it's Thursday night," I remind him.

He shrugs. "Willow said Swan's coming down later. She needs the extra money."

"Did you ever think of having Swan manage the girls?" Hope asks.

"I have," I answer. "She's gotten better at sticking up for herself, but I don't think she wants to dance much longer."

"Yeah, she's trying to get her yoga teaching going." Hope shrugs. "Well, I guess the place has been successful this long the way it is. Ignore my advice."

"No, it's good advice, Hope. I've just never found the right person."

Rock finally seems to shake off his annoyance and he slides his arms around Hope, pulling her against him. "What'd you bring for dinner?"

"It's in my car."

"Why don't you two go out for dinner? I'll watch things til you get back."

"You don't have to do that, Z. Don't you need to get—"

Rock cuts off Hope's protest. "Thanks, brother." He plucks Hope's car keys out of her hand and tugs her toward her car. "Be back in an hour," he calls out over his shoulder.

"Bye, Z!"

Laughing, I duck inside.

CHAPTER THIRTY-NINE

Z

SINCE THINGS ARE CALMER DOWNSTATE, NOW THAT I'M NOT LOOKING OVER my shoulder constantly, another trip to Empire shouldn't hurt.

Asking Loco for a favor isn't exactly high on my list of favorite activities. Hell, I'd avoid it for the rest of my life if I could.

Rock gave our favorite eccentric pimp a head's up that I'd be stopping by. Not the smartest idea to roll up on Loco without warning him.

Malik opens the front door to the brothel or whatever you want to call it. Usually one of the girls answer, so that's a sign something's off.

Malik holds out his hand and pulls me in for a quick slap on the back. "How you been, brother?"

Here, I'll call him brother. When he's at our place wearing his prospect cut, then he's only *prospect*.

"Not bad. Not bad. Headed to CB in a few. You're missed, Z. Missed a lot. When you coming back, Z?"

"No clue yet."

"You said, *yet*. So at least that means you're coming back."

"Fuck yeah, I am."

"Zee-roh!" Loco stands to greet me when I walk into his ridiculous office. I can't describe it any better than French whorehouse meets the Pope. Lots of gold, velvet, and three-dimensional wallpaper.

"How you been, Loco?" I let him pull me in for a quick hug and slap on the back too. Loco has relentlessly irritated Rock for years, but I've always found him more entertaining than annoying. Usually. We'll see how today goes.

"Wow." He steps back and drags his dramatic gaze over me from head to toe. "Never thought I'd see the day you'd be wearing a president patch. Crazy times we livin' in."

"Don't I know it."

"How's Rock taking it?"

I shrug, not comfortable discussing my club's dynamics with an outsider. Especially after what's gone down lately.

"Sit, sit." He gestures to one of the blue velvet chairs in front of his gilded desk.

Once I'm seated, he leans in. "How's Sway doing?" He holds up his hands before I have a chance to answer. "I know it's probably club business, but I'm worried about the guy too."

Loco does business with Sway sometimes and his condition isn't exactly a state secret. "He's doing better. Seems stronger every time I visit."

"That's good. Damn, that's gonna be one amazing comeback." He hesitates and frowns. "Where's that leave you?"

"Free to return upstate."

"No shit? Really? After you've had a taste of prez power, you gonna give it up? Just like that?"

"Not interested in power, Loco. Upstate is home."

He nods and strokes his hand over his chin. "I can respect that, Z. You're a rare breed."

"Thanks, I think."

"What brings you by?"

I'm sure he wouldn't mind dragging this social call out the rest of the afternoon. We could play 'have you ever' and dance around the senator's name, but I don't have the time or patience for those games. "You ever send any girls to see Senator Kelly?"

"Whoa." Loco sits back against his chair with a dramatic thump. "You going right for it, huh?"

"I don't have time to waste."

"And I appreciate you not wasting *my* time. Since your club has always been such a good friend to my crew and we work together, I'm not gonna run you around."

"Appreciate that." I'm starting to understand better why Loco irritates Rock so much.

"Yeah, I know the ex-Senator fuck."

Well, all right then.

"His trial's still going."

"I watch the news, Z."

"Figure he's gonna be feeling lonely. Maybe a little anxious since his wife left."

"Yeah."

"Since you're the only game in the area, I need you to let me know if he calls looking for a girl."

It's not a difficult request, but Loco looks away and taps his fingers against the arm of his chair a few times before answering. "Are you planning to intercept the transaction?"

"You mean, go instead of the girl? Possibly."

He stares at me for a few seconds. "You plannin' to have some sort of *personal* chat with him?"

"Maybe not a chat." I can't afford for Kelly to see me again and connect me to Loco. What I'm really after is access to the man's car when no one else will be around. Can't think of a better place than the large, private garage behind Loco's place where the more high-profile clients usually park. I'm not sure I want to let Loco know that I might be planting a bomb in one of his customer's cars.

"I'm gonna be totally straight with you, Z. He roughed up one of my girls. She was scared, so she didn't tell me about it right away." He holds up his hand and shakes his head as if I questioned him. "She was new. Didn't realize I won't tolerate anyone putting hands on my girls." He smirks. "Well, handling them in a way that hasn't been negotiated in advance."

"And?"

"Because she didn't tell me until he'd been arrested, I couldn't do anything about it. But I was planning to have a serious conversation with him if he came back here."

"Planning to have Malik wait for him upstairs instead?"

He grins. "Maybe."

"Will it make you feel better to know I have something in mind to make sure he won't be bothering any of your girls again?"

"I can't have someone that high-profile get roughed up in my house, Z."

"I promise it won't come back to you."

He tilts his head, studying me while he considers my request. "How unfriendly we talking?"

"Brutal."

"He hurt someone in the club? I didn't think he had anything to do with the local crime syndicate. Too good for us lowlifes and all." He rolls his eyes.

"He hurt someone close to me. Like you, I found out about it later than I would've preferred."

"Ahhhh. Shit, I'm sorry, Z. If we'd known, maybe one of us could've—"

"I don't think so, but I appreciate that." I run my hand over my chin while I consider whether I want to ask my next question. "The girl still work for you?"

"Nah, she went back to school. The Green Street Crew scholarship fund is alive and well."

It probably sounds like a self-serving fine line, but to my knowledge, Loco only runs girls who are there voluntarily. It's the only reason our club's looked the other way and allowed his "escort business" to operate in our territory. He treats them well and they bring in top dollar. The same philosophy we use running our strip club so his scholarship joke actually makes me laugh.

"Good to know."

"You know how we do here. I like to be a blip on their radar. The benevolent, kind-hearted gangster who gives 'em a helping hand when they expect to be slapped down."

"Uh, okay. That's not arrogant at all, Loco."

He grins even wider. "Love makes the world go round, brother."

"I'm surprised you and Sparky don't hang out more."

"That high-as-fuck ghost boy is welcome here anytime. You make sure he knows any girl he wants is on the house."

"I'll be sure to tell him." Jesus Christ, a chat with Loco is like visiting the Cheshire cat. "Back to the former Senator. What's his type?"

"He's an interesting one. Tall, curvaceous brunettes are his thing. Usually they want big-titted blondes, but he's very specific in his tastes."

A sick feeling rolls through my stomach. I don't want to press for more details even though I need to.

"What else?"

"Christ, Z. You want gory details? He likes choking 'em til they pass out. Figure he must not want 'em laughing at his tiny dick or something."

My throat's so tight, I can barely speak. It hurts to crack a smile and make a joke right now. "Get your psychology degree in your spare time?"

"Don't need no degree to know how some of these sick fuckers work." His gaze strays to the wall behind me where I'm guessing that loud ticking is coming from. "You want me to call you if I hear from him? Set up a date?"

"Have him come here."

"Oh, trust me, I ain't never sending another one of my girls to his place."

"But he's been here before?"

"Yeah, after he messed up Vanessa. I still didn't know and I let him in." He pounds his fist against the desk. "Fucker."

"He hurt the girl he saw here?"

"Not as bad, but if I'd known that's what he's into, I would've provided him with a different girl. It was a little more than Nikki signed up for."

"She okay?"

"She's still here. I won't set him up with her again though." His eyes shine with murderous intent. "Maybe I will and I'll be waiting for him instead."

"I need him occupied for at least half an hour."

"I'll keep him occupied." He cocks his head. "And if he doesn't call?"

"Then I'll have to figure out another way in."

With Loco on board, I want to sit down with my brothers and discuss how things will go down.

Smoke's bitching all those weeks ago about how we should return to the old ways has stuck with me.

Wrath, Rock, Murphy, and Teller meet me at the war room table.

They don't need a lot of information. I wouldn't be coming to them, asking to murder someone in Kelly's league unless it was bad.

"That's why she left?" Wrath asks.

"Pretty much. The government wanted her to cooperate but she couldn't stand seeing him day after day. Or risk it."

"Fuck." Teller shakes his head and stares down at his hands.

"She didn't want you taking care of it, because of how close he was being watched," Murphy says.

"Right."

"Explains California," Wrath says. He's taken this much more calmly and with a lot less skepticism than I expected.

When I question him, he shrugs. "Why the fuck would she lie about that? She gains nothing by telling you *now*. Assuming *you're* telling the truth and you two were finally going stop fucking around, she blew up her entire life to get away from him. I believe her."

His answer makes me laugh for a solid minute. It's really not what I expected out of Wrath. "Speaking of blowing up shit, how about a nice, old-fashioned car bomb?" I suggest.

Rock raises his eyebrows. "You don't want to gut this fucker personally?"

"I do, but with him under so much scrutiny, I can't take the risk."

"And a *car bomb* will be under the radar?" Murphy shakes his head. "That'll attract a *lot* of attention."

"We can wait until he's inside…" Teller suggests.

"No," Rock answers. "Tony says even if he's convicted, he won't do much time. Even if he does, it'll be in a federal facility."

"You fucking kidding me?" Murphy shakes his head. "Fucking government's more criminal than we are."

"Hell, give the guy a few years. He'll probably get re-elected and do it all over again," Wrath says. "They're all fuckin' crooks."

"Let's save the political discussion for later." Rock taps the table. "Car bombing, huh? LOKI haven't gone that route in a long time."

Meaning no one currently in our club has any bomb-making skills.

"Rooster can do it."

"You want to involve him?" Murphy asks.

"I trusted him enough to make him VP," I remind everyone. "He's had our backs down there. He's cautious too. Didn't bring the Shadow issue up until he had solid proof even though he knew I wasn't happy with Shadow."

"I don't know him as well as you do, Z, but I trust your judgment," Wrath says. "Besides, it's your ass, ultimately."

"Thanks for the reminder."

Wrath runs his fingers over his beard a few times and flashes a sinister smile. "Car bomb's nice. Should scare the piss out of all those corrupt fucks. They'll assume it's related to the trial." He nods at Rock. "Or the lack of justice."

"Right. That was my other thought. He's got so many people gunning for him, there's no reason to look my way. And like you said, it's a method we haven't used in decades."

"You can't do it anywhere someone else is gonna get hurt. That's what got that club in Idaho in so much shit," Teller reminds me.

"I'm aware. Trust me, brother, I don't want any collateral damage. Just this guy." I nudge Rock with my elbow. "Loco had some good insight for me. I think planting the bomb at his place and setting it off at the Senator's home will be the way to go."

"Sounds good." Rock shakes his head. "Even if Loco puts the pieces together once it's done, he's sure as fuck not going to snitch on anyone."

"Loco's crazy, but he's not dumb," Wrath says. "He'll put the pieces together fast."

"Trust me, he's got no love lost for this guy. He'll probably congratulate me."

CHAPTER FORTY

Lilly

THE GUYS HAVE "CLUB BUSINESS" TO ATTEND TO SO I END UP AT HOPE'S house, helping Heidi sort through wedding stuff while the kids play together. Well, really, they play near each other. Alexa showed Chance which toys of hers he was allowed to touch when we got here.

"I like her spunk," I say to Heidi.

"Notice it was the "boy toys" she gave him. I've been giving her all the gender-neutral toys and clothes and—"

"She's a girly-girl?"

Heidi laughs. "Yup. But at least she picked it out for herself. I didn't force it on her."

"What about Murphy?"

She considers the question before shaking her head. "Nah, he buys her all that unicorn stuff because she asks for it. I think he was hoping she'd be more of a tomboy."

"She's so little," Hope says. "I'm sure she'll go through a lot of phases."

Heidi stands and clears the table. While she's at the sink washing dishes, I lean closer to Hope. "Gender neutral toys, huh?"

She leans in too. "Heidi makes me feel about a hundred years old. I didn't realize that was such a big thing until Alexa."

I sit back and chuckle. "I imagine college has exposed her to all sorts of theories that will shake up this place."

Hope laughs uncontrollably. "Oh, god. If only you knew how on point that was. Charlotte and I have done our part as well."

"Two female lawyers? Yeah, I can imagine."

She reaches over and squeezes my hand. "What about you? Are you going to look for another job with the legislature now that you're back?"

Even though she's not asking to be nosy or mean, the question sends a current of revulsion through me. I have to remind myself that she doesn't know why I left. "No. That's the last thing I want to do. What about you? Are you going to start taking on clients again?"

"Gosh, no." She glances over at Grace, happily snoozing in her chair. "I mean, we all know how much I hated being an attorney—"

"From the moment you left law school?"

She laughs. "Around that time."

"You and Sophie both."

Her mouth turns down and she glances away. "How is she, anyway? I realize I haven't asked."

"Honestly? We lost touch too." I don't want to explain that Sophie was the only one I told about what Senator Kelly had done and she not so subtly placed the blame on me. After that, I was done. She was between rehabs at the time, but I still haven't been able to accept that as an excuse. "My brother still talks to her."

A bolt of fear strikes me. Would she tell Alex? Did she already tell him? Until recently, I didn't even know they were still in contact. *Shit.* Then again, she'd treated it like a joke. Maybe she doesn't even remember my tearful phone call.

"Lilly, what's wrong?" Hope asks.

"Nothing, sorry. I was just thinking. Alex said she's been in and out of a few rehabs."

"Jeez, I feel terrible I never realized how serious her drinking problem was." She shrugs. "I chalked it up to her being a little wild in law school. Figured she'd settle down."

The door in the corner opens and Rock steps into the living room.

"Hey, Lilly," he greets.

"I didn't even know you were home."

"He comes in from downstairs a lot," Hope explains.

"Is Z with you?"

"Nope. Not sure what he's up to."

Heidi and I share a look. Z said *club business,* but I suppose Rock might not be privy to whatever Z's up to at the downstate clubhouse. Murphy's helping Z out so he probably doesn't check in with Rock about every little thing.

Club stuff is exhausting. I'm sort of glad it's *not* my business and trust Z to tell me anything important.

"Pop-pop!" Alexa sings when she notices Rock's home. He picks her up to say hello. Still holding Alexa, he drops down on the couch to listen to her and Chance. My son's a little reluctant at first, but Rock encourages him to join them. I'm not sure Alexa appreciates the intrusion. I get the feeling she has a lot of "Pop-pop's" undivided attention.

Hope chuckles. "Murphy started that as a joke, but I think it's sticking."

"Just wait til Grace starts talking," he mutters.

Heidi drops a heavy bag on the table. "Are you sure you want to go over this now, Hope?"

Hope glances over and checks on Grace before answering. "Now before she wakes up would be good."

Something pink and sparkly pokes out of Heidi's bag. Thinking it's a kid's toy, I pull it out.

It's definitely a *toy.* But not the kind I imagined. Teasing the edge of the bag down lower, I peer inside. "Heidi, do you have a giant bag of vibrators?" I whisper.

Hope chokes and laughs. Heidi's cheeks turn red and she reaches over to snatch the bag away. "It was a business venture, you know, to earn extra money for the wedding. Then Trinity sold me out to everyone at family dinner, so now I'm providing the club with," she sneaks a glance at the kids, "*products* for the whole clubhouse."

I fall back against the chair, laughing. Seriously, I don't think I've laughed this hard in weeks. "Oh my god," I squeal. "I can picture your brother's reaction to that."

"Charlotte made me order stuff for *her...*for them." She makes a gagging sound. "Do you have any idea how disturbing that was?" She slides her accusatory gaze Hope's way. "Never mind my favorite aunt and uncle."

Hope's laughing so hard she presses her forehead to the table. "We... we...were...trying...to support your new career path." She bursts into giggles again after getting the sentence out.

"Do you see what I have to deal with?" Heidi grins as she says it so I don't think she's as upset as she wants us to believe. "Ugh, Uncle Sparky asked for like a hundred and fifty," she lowers her voice to a whisper, "cock rings. I don't even want to know."

I catch Hope's eye and wink at her. "Do you have a catalog, Heidi? I'll—"

"No way. Uncle Z and Uncle Dex are the only ones who didn't traumatize me by ordering anything."

"Ravage didn't either," Hope says. "I remember he was quite vocal about his opposition to toys."

"Well, he had a come-to-dildo moment because he ordered stuff." Heidi shudders. "I have nightmares about it."

I choke and sputter on my water and decide to set it down until we finish this discussion.

Hope's laughing so hard, she wakes Grace, who starts laughing when she sees her mom. "Aww, did we wake you, precious? It's your Aunt Heidi's fault."

"Uh, I'd argue it's Aunt Lilly's fault. She poked through my bag."

Something about Heidi casually referring to me as anyone's *Aunt Lilly* sends a warm feeling sliding through my chest. "It's true." I reach over the table for Grace. "Can I hold her for a minute?"

"Sure."

"Ah, you're getting so big, Grace."

She waves her fist in the air and grabs on to my finger.

Now that Grace is awake, Chance tip toes over to us. Alexa follows and they both want to say hello.

"I should probably change her." Hope stands and takes her daughter. Rock ends up following her down the hall.

Heidi reaches over and zips up her bag before picking Alexa up and setting her in her lap. "Did you and Chance have fun? Did you share?"

"Yeth."

Chance gives me this raised eyebrow she's-full-of-shit face that looks so much like Z's, I can't help laughing. I don't think he's mastered sarcasm yet, but it's still funny.

Heidi pulls a couple of folders out and starts flipping through cut out pictures of flowers, cakes, and other assorted wedding stuff. She lays it all out on the table in front of us and studies it for a few minutes before rearranging.

Alexa grabs for one of the photos and Heidi lets her play with it.

"You should almost be done with everything, right?"

"Eh." Heidi shrugs. "I haven't had a lot of time. I don't want to go nuts, but I want everything to be pretty. Casual, but fun. Elegant but a little bit country."

"Uh, okay." I chuckle and peer over at her pictures of centerpieces. My eyes immediately glaze over. Maybe I'm *not* marriage material. The thought of doing all this stuff makes me want to grab Heidi's silver calligraphy pen and stab myself in the eye.

And the idea of inviting my parents? Even my brother who's gotten a little better around Z. How would he behave at a wedding with all of Z's biker brothers around? Good god, they'd probably end up burying him in the backyard somewhere.

Is there a way I can skip straight to the wife part?

CHAPTER FORTY-ONE

Z

AT FIRST, I TRIED NOT TO MAKE TOO MANY CHANGES TO DOWNSTATE. I WAS here to get them through a difficult time, not rearrange the clubhouse. But the longer I'm down here, the less tolerance I have for living in filth.

"Enough of this bullshit of depending on the girls to clean up for us. Hire a damn cleaning crew," I bark at Hustler during our next meeting.

"Bro, we don't like strangers in the clubhouse."

"Yeah, unless they're here to suck your dick and make you a sandwich," I growl. "Grow the fuck up. Find someone who's bonded, have 'em sign an NDA, and watch 'em like a fuckin' hawk while they're here, but this is ridiculous."

Next, Murphy prods me into fixing up one of the empty rooms next to the pool as a gym. After church, he takes me downstairs to show me the room he wants to remodel.

He pats his gut. "I've been working too hard to be losing my gains because I'm sittin' around here all the time."

"Give me a break, you just want to fit into your wedding tux or whatever Heidi's making you wear."

"That too."

I point to the pool. "Get a company in here to clean that up, fix it, do whatever the fuck they need to do. It's disgusting."

"Why are you telling me?"

"Because you're standing here annoying me about a gym. For the immediate future, fitness for this clubhouse is your responsibility. The pool falls under fitness."

"Jesus Christ, like I don't have enough to do." He puts his hands on his hips and ducks his head. "Fine, you know what? I need a favor."

"What kind of favor?"

"I got a fight out in Johnsonville tomorrow. I could use the extra backup."

I'm about to strangle his fucking ass. For still taking on underground fights even though everyone upstate has pretty much told him to stop. And also for springing it on me so last minute. "You fuckin' serious? The president gig isn't exactly leaving me lots of recreational time, you know. And I'm supposed to leave for California soon."

Murphy shrugs. "Have some more of the brothers roll with us. It can be a fun bonding activity for the club."

"Do I look like your summer camp counselor, ya dick? I thought you were done with this shit?"

"I wouldn't ask if I didn't need you there, Z."

Guilt, a powerful motivator for a brother. "Fucker."

He gives me a triumphant grin that makes me want to kick his ass. "Fine." I'm not done making demands, though. "If you promise you'll get the pool and gym sorted out before I get back from Cali."

There, that ought to keep his ass out of trouble.

"You got it."

CHAPTER FORTY-TWO

Z

I should've known this calm streak couldn't last.

The dogs are frolicking in the backyard and we're about to go outside when Lilly's phone rings.

She picks it up and glances at the screen. "It's Mara. I should take it."

"You should invite her to come visit."

She nods and answers the call.

I pick up Chance. "Want to swim?" Silly question. The answer is always yes.

"What?" Lilly's shrill tone has Chance and me turning our heads.

I move closer, hoping to overhear some of their conversation.

"Well, good luck to them. I'm at the house—"

"Don't tell me!" Mara shrieks so loud I can hear her from where I'm standing.

"Let's go pick out your swim trunks," I say to Chance. Aunt Hope and Aunt Trinity went bananas buying stuff for Chance once we settled into the house. The kid has enough clothes to fill an entire mall.

He's settled on a blue pair with bright red lobsters when Lilly finds us.

"They're trying to subpoena me again."

The happiness clinging to me from spending the day with my family evaporates. My obsession with Lilly turns dark and hostile with the need to protect her. To protect our family. "What do they think you know?"

"I have no idea." She bites her lip. "I'm scared. I can't do it, Z. I can't be in the same room with him again."

"Hey," I stand and pull her into my arms, "no one's forcing you to do anything. What did Mara say?"

"To lay low. Dodge the process server as long as I can. Hang out at the house since technically no one knows I'm down here."

"All right. So that's what we'll do."

"I'm worried they'll go to my brother's house or my parents'."

"So what if they do? Fuck 'em. They know you worked at the legislature. They must have heard about the trial. Nothing else should come up."

She drops her gaze to Chance who's playing on the floor with some of his cars. "I don't want him to know about Chance," she whispers.

No need to ask which *him* she's referring to. I brush my knuckles over her cheek. "It's clear to anyone with eyes that he's mine." I swallow hard, afraid I won't like the answer to my next question. "Did you name me as the father on his birth certificate?"

Her scared eyes meet mine. "I did," she whispers. "I wanted it to be true with all my heart, and figured if it wasn't…"

"It doesn't matter. I'm glad you did. And obviously it's true."

She nods, but fear still lingers in her eyes.

"What can I do, Lilly?" Besides, kill Senator Kelly, because I'm *definitely* doing that as soon as possible.

"Nothing right now." The worry fades and she shrugs. "Being holed up in the house with my two favorite men isn't exactly a hardship."

The corners of my mouth twitch. "That's my girl. We're going to get through this and everything will be fine."

After convincing her to put on a red two-piece, that's become my absolute favorite thing ever, I encourage her and Chance to go outside so I can duck into the office upstairs and make a phone call.

Loco doesn't seem as happy to hear from me today.

"Z I'm trying. It's not like I can stick some pop-up ads on his phone, man. What do you want me to do, send him a damn flyer?"

"Don't be a dick." I probably shouldn't be that harsh with Loco. He tends to get bent out of shape easily.

"Stop dogging me then. You're the first call I make if I get what you want."

"Thanks, Loco."

"No problem. I'm always happy when the Kings owe me a favor."

Of course he is.

CHAPTER FORTY-THREE

Z

With Lilly planning a girls' night at the house, I'm confident she'll be safe. She didn't want to tell Charlotte or Heidi about the subpoena, but I still gave them the reminder not to open the door for anyone not wearing our colors while I'm out.

There's shit to take care of at the clubhouse and Murphy's still dragging me to this fight tonight. I can't do anything but wait, which kills me. I'm a man of action. Sitting around waiting for a phone call isn't my style.

While I got the approval from my brothers upstate, Rooster and I have been planning to bomb Senator Kelly all on our own. No reason to risk anyone else getting involved.

"Bro, maybe we should go at it a different way?" Rooster suggests.

"He's got cameras all over that property. I don't know where else we can do it and not be seen."

Murphy knocks on the chapel door and pushes it open. "You ready?"

"Fuck me. We still doing this?"

He just rolls his eyes at me.

"You coming, Rooster?"

"Sure, why not."

Bikers are supposed to be all about freedom from society's rules, doing what we want, when we want, so I won't try to stop Murphy. Unless it starts interfering with club business somehow.

I'll happily hassle the shit out of him though. Right up until he needs to get serious and focus. I may be annoyed with him, but that doesn't mean I want him to get hurt.

Somehow Murphy roped Jigsaw into a match as well, so now it really *is* a club matter. It's almost two hours from the clubhouse. A good, long ride that does little to clear my head.

Wrath's business partner, Jake, is also on tonight's roster. "Thought you retired, Mr. Wallace?"

"Nah, a good fight once in a while does wonders for you."

"Wonders for your *bed*," Murphy jokes. "He can't find a date otherwise."

"What would you know about it?" Jake laughs and shoves Murphy. "You're all wifed-up, pretty ginger."

I bark out a laugh. "Pretty ginger, I'll have to remember that."

Murphy's less amused.

Ravage, Stash, and Birch amble through the crowd to join us.

"Fuck, I didn't expect to see you here." I pull each of them in for a quick handshake and backslap.

"Wouldn't miss this for anything." Rav rubs his hands together and searches the room. "Where the ring bunnies at?"

"Thanks for the support, bro," Murphy says.

Stash slaps Rav's shoulder. "Don't chase the girls away like you do at the clubhouse."

"Are you kidding? I'm God's gift to women," Ravage announces.

"More like God's curse," I mutter, cracking the guys up.

"If anything scared them away, it's all the babies at the clubhouse now," Rav says. "No offense, Z."

"None taken. There's only one baby in the clubhouse—*you*."

"That's cold, bro." He shrugs. "At least Grace is a cute little shit. Except when she's screaming her head off."

Tired of Rav already, I turn to Jake. "You recruiting people for the gym here?" Wrath gave up the underground circuit a couple years ago, and runs a completely legit gym. I can't see him being okay with Jake potentially making Furious look bad if this ring ever gets shut down.

"Nah, some of 'em work out at Sully's place. It's not about that though. Lot of young, heavy betters with more money than brains. You should make out well tonight."

I'm still unimpressed. Upstate is doing fine and my bank account is flush. Although, we've neglected to share most of our glowing financials with anyone outside of upstate, so I still need to keep up the appearance that I'm always looking to score easy cash.

And let's face it, downstate needs all the help it can get. Jigsaw's fight will hopefully bring in some hefty returns for the club.

Really, I don't give a shit if the younger brothers want to make money getting the shit kicked out of them. Their bodies, their decisions. Murphy, who has a family to take care of, annoys me more. Especially, since I know he's keeping this from Heidi.

Yeah, yeah, brothers are supposed to be secretive with their old ladies. Even if I don't like it, I'd never rat him out to Heidi. That's just not how the brotherhood works.

I glance around the building. The kids running this ring call it The Castle. It looks like a fortress from the outside. Used to be a juvenile detention facility. Pretty sure it's the same one Teller spent some time in way back when he was a hang-around for the club.

While Jake mentioned the privileged youth, who hang out here hoping to impress their buddies or make some cash, I also see plenty of shifty-eyed youngsters. The kind who might make decent prospects if mentored correctly.

"You ever consider looking for some prospects while you're here living out your degenerate boxer fantasies?" I ask Murphy.

"Of course, I do." He claps a hand on my shoulder and points me in the direction of two early-twentyish guys working their way through the crowd.

"Remy and Griff run this ring. They're honest and no bullshit. Both excellent fighters. Remy could turn pro if he wanted."

"Do either of them ride?" Can't join the Lost Kings if you don't ride a minimum number of hours a year. Never been an issue for any of us because it's in our blood. Not a lot of young guys have the desire anymore.

"Remy does. A 2014 Night Rod I helped him find."

"Sounds about right." Nice bike with a lot of power, but not the best for long road trips.

Now Murphy's excited. Like most of us, he can talk about bikes forever. "It's pretty wicked. Still mostly stock but he chopped out the rear fender, blacked out all the metal. Kept almost everything else."

"Talk to him about stopping by or hanging around?"

"Yeah, I don't think he has a lot of free time."

"Won't make it as a prospect then." Prospects get all the bitch work and are expected to drop everything when the club needs 'em. Harder and harder to find someone with that level of dedication.

"I'll feel out the situation some more."

Since Jigsaw's new here, he should probably go in one of the first rounds. Apparently, Murphy has some pull here and Griff places him in a later fight.

"Don't embarrass me tonight," Murphy warns Jigsaw without his usual I'm-just-fucking-with-you smile.

Whatever tonight is, it's a big deal. There are more matches than I've usually seen at one of these things. Louder music. More energy than my thirty-eight-year-old ass feels like dealing with.

Christ, this president gig has aged me twenty years.

Finally, Jigsaw's up and he's impressive in the ring.

"He shoulda been called Buzzsaw," I say to Murphy.

"Shit, yeah. I feel kinda bad for giving him a hard time now."

"No, you don't."

One corner of his mouth quirks up. "True." A little more seriously, he adds, "But he's good."

"Your boy's not gonna get too cocky, is he?" Jake asks Murphy in a voice so low, I almost can't hear him.

"Why?"

"Brady's a cop."

"Shit, seriously?" I blurt out.

Jake shrugs.

"What happens here is supposed to stay here. Cop or not, Brady's gotta know that," Murphy says.

Jigsaw, thankfully, isn't a show-off and he doesn't fight dirty. He wins, but it's close.

"Jigsaw!" Rooster roars, throwing his arms up in a victory sign. "Wooo!"

Then it's Murphy's turn. "Make me proud, Gingersnap." He rolls his eyes at the stupid nickname he picked up at another MC's clubhouse we're friendly with.

As annoyed as I am with Murphy for still fighting, he's damn talented. The asshole he's up against, not so much.

"Is Murphy holding back?" I ask Jake.

"Probably. I don't think this guy knows what he's doing."

Before each match, Griff lays out the rules to everyone. Yeah, it's an underground match, but there are a few rules to keep things civil. I actually respect that and wonder how they handle it when people break the rules.

His opponent takes a dirty shot before the next whistle blows, snapping Murphy's head back.

"Motherfucker." My whole body tenses, preparing to fuck this guy up.

"Shit," Jake mumbles. "Here we go."

"You got his back?"

"Fuck yeah, I do."

We wait, watching the match.

"That's how he got Gingersnap," Jake says after Murphy lets loose a punishing blur of shots that take his opponent to the mat.

"Yup."

There's a flurry of activity when the match is called in Murphy's favor. I jostle through the crowd to make sure I'm at Murphy's side when he comes out of the ring.

He grins at me. "See, told you I still had it."

"Never doubted it, brother. Let's go."

Griff walks over and hands Murphy his money for the night. They engage in a tight, pulling-each-other in, slapping-backs kind of handshake, that Murphy normally wouldn't allow from a stranger. Just how often is he coming out here to pick up fights?

The kid surprises me by shaking my hand too. "Thank you so much for allowing Murphy and Jigsaw in our ring tonight."

Huh. Respectful attitude for someone his age. "No problem. Murphy speaks highly of you and your partner."

"Good to hear." He jerks his thumb over his shoulder. "I have to get ready for the next match. Stay as long as you want."

He melts back into the crowd.

"Are he and Remy, like *gay* partners-partners or just partners?" Ravage asks.

"Who gives a shit?" Murphy growls.

"You worry about the stupidest stuff," I add. I nod at the other kid Murphy pointed out earlier. "I'm guessing by the number of bunnies hanging off his jock, they're *business* partners."

Jake overhears the last part of the conversation and laughs. "Griff's hard up for Remy's little sister."

"How 'bout that." I poke Murphy in the chest. "No *wonder* you two get along so well."

"Shut up, dick."

"You speak to Rock like that?"

Murphy shrugs. "He's not a dick like you are."

Jake crosses his arms over his chest, his gaze ping-ponging between us. "Man, this is better than hanging out with Wrath and Murphy."

"Please tell me Wrath kicks his ass more often?"

Jake laughs. "Not that I've seen."

"Hey, Jake." I turn more serious because I should've said this earlier. "Thanks for that class you taught the girls. It, uh, came in handy for Lilly."

"I'm glad to hear it." He frowns. "Well, not if someone messed with her." He pauses and glances away as if he's considering his words carefully. "Some of the floor choke holds, where we get inside the guard," He must feel the heat of my glare because he holds his hands in the air, "I had the girls practice those moves on each other. But seriously, she seemed freaked out. I didn't want to make a big deal, so I had her skip it."

There's that sick feeling rolling through my gut again. More secrets Lilly's keeping. She never mentioned anything at the class bothered her.

Was it normal discomfort from trying something new or is there a more specific reason it bothered her?

And if there's more to it, is it a secret I'm even entitled to?

CHAPTER FORTY-FOUR

Z

THE NEXT DAY I GET THE NEWS I'VE BEEN WAITING FOR.

"I got your man!" someone shouts into the phone when I answer it.

"Who is this?"

"Loco." He almost sounds hurt.

"Sorry, didn't recognize the number." The last thing I want to do is offend him when I think he's calling with the news I really need to hear.

"Your sicko placed an order today. I told him we couldn't accommodate his request until later."

"Sounds good."

Loco won't say more than that over the phone, so I'll have to wait for the details.

It's been a tense couple of days, waiting to see if anyone jumps out and slaps a subpoena in Lilly's hands. She hasn't left the house much.

After tonight, she won't have to worry anymore.

"I'm sorry, Lilly, I have to go."

Her weak smile doesn't do a lot to hide her surprise. Can't blame her, told her this morning I'd be home all day.

"Club business," I offer as an explanation. It's not quite true, but I have a feeling if I confide that I'm off to murder Senator Kelly, she'll try to stop me.

"Is everything okay?"

Instead of answering the question, I lean over and kiss her. "Love you."

Chance is more forgiving of my exit. "Bye, Daddy!" He waves without getting up from the floor where he's playing.

I reach down and pick him up, squeezing him tight to me and kiss the top of his head. "Love you, Chance. Take care of your mom while I'm out, okay?"

"Okay!"

Before straddling my bike, I send Rooster a text, letting him know it's go time.

He's waiting out front with a rather unremarkable black sedan. Nothing to draw anyone's attention. One more bland car to blend in with all the others in Ironworks.

"Got everything?"

"Go bag's in the trunk," he answers. "Let's do it."

Rooster and I ride up in silence most of the way. "I can't believe you have me driving an electric fucking car."

"What?" He shrugs. "It's quiet. And no one would expect you to ever drive one."

"Got that right. It's fucking small." My knees have been crammed into the dashboard for the entire drive.

The senator lives on the outskirts of Empire county. East of our clubhouse. No neighbors for miles. According to the cameras I placed a week ago, he's alone. Wife left him when he first got arrested. Wonder if she ever suspected what a creep he was.

Fucker must be lonely too, if the call he placed to Loco is any indication.

Let me get out my tiny little violin.

I won't allow this piece of shit to break her again. No one's dragging her into court to make her look at that pathetic excuse for a man. Not after everything she's been through and how far she's come. How far *we've* come.

I finally have a chance to do what should've been done before.

We park in front of Loco's building and I call him to let him know I'm there. He says to use the basement entrance, so that's where we go.

Last time I was down here, we beat some members of a rival MC who was trying to push into our territory to within an inch of their lives. Good times.

At least things won't get so messy here today. Rooster's only planting the bomb here. We'll set it off at the Senator's house.

Loco meets us downstairs. "He just got here. His car's in the garage. I'll show you." He gives Rooster a second look. "You ain't blowing up my house, are you?"

"No, Loco," I assure him.

"Let's go. I got Malik outside the door in case he gets rough with Emilia. That happens, he's getting a beating and tossed out. So work quick."

Rooster gives me the side-eye and I shrug. Loco's house, Loco's rules. He's doing us a huge favor. I'm not going to bitch about the conditions he puts on it.

"This is it." He stops in front of the white Mercedes I've trailed a few times over the last couple weeks.

"Beautiful car." Rooster shakes his head. "Give me five minutes." He glances around. "You got cameras?"

"In here? Fuck no," Loco says. "I gotta get back inside. Text me when you're done."

Rooster drops down to the concrete floor and scoots under the car so only his lower half is hanging out. I crouch down and hand him stuff as he asks for it while scanning the front and back doors for signs of anyone coming.

My phone buzzes.

Loco: He's coming out in ten.

Shit. "Ten minutes, Rooster."

"Almost done."

I shoot back a text to Loco.

Maybe if the senator walks out and finds us here, I'll just beat him to death instead. Be a lot less messy. I flip the wrench I'm holding in my hand a few times while I picture sinking it into the guy's skull.

"Done." Rooster slides out from under the car. "Let's roll."

I text Loco that we're finished and he tells us to go around the outside of the building.

We jog through the alleyway and slide into our car. This time, Rooster gets behind the steering wheel.

Loco: He's leaving. Should hit Ferry in five.

"Pull up there." I point ahead to where Ferry street intersects with the street we're on. Rooster hands me the cell phone we'll use to detonate the bomb once the Senator's clear of any people.

I pull the small laptop out of the backpack in the backseat and check the cameras at Kelly's house for any visitors. Nothing but some deer frolicking in the front yard.

The white Mercedes passes in front of us and Rooster puts our car in motion. We have to wait to make the left turn and he gets a little ahead of us, but that's fine. I don't want to be too close anyway.

The asshole makes a few stops along the way. Which is annoying as fuck and stresses me out each time. "You're sure it won't accidentally blow?"

"I'm sure. Chill."

Finally, he's on the road to his house.

The property's secured by a gate, we hang back as far as we can without completely losing sight of him until he pulls into his driveway.

The gate swings shut behind him.

"One more check." Rooster takes the laptop from my hands and scans the video feeds again. "Clear. He's parking in front of the house."

We already went over the procedure a dozen times.

The pressing of the send button feels anti-climatic after all this cloak-and-dagger shit.

The blast is deafening, even from where we're sitting. Black smoke billows up over the trees. Rooster checks the feed. "Oh yeah, he's toast."

There's a second blast.

That one sounds like Lilly's freedom.

CHAPTER FORTY-FIVE

Z

ROCK CALLS EARLY THE NEXT MORNING. I'M SURE IT'S BECAUSE HE HEARD about the bombing. It takes him a while to bring it up though.

"You still coming down for family day?" I ask. We've been trying to bring both clubs together as much as possible. Reinforce that we're not rivals. Reassure everyone that the brotherhood is strong.

"Wouldn't miss it."

"You and Hope still want to stay the weekend?"

"If you'll have us."

"Fuck yeah. Lilly's been looking forward to it."

"See that story about the Senator?" he asks when we're finished discussing club stuff. Secure lines or not he won't get more detailed than that.

"Crazy shit, right?"

He laughs into the phone. "Crazier than you think. Two different political activist groups took credit for the bombing. Getting the corruption out of government is apparently trendy."

Holy shit. I didn't see *that* coming. "That's interesting." At least that will keep the investigators busy looking in the wrong direction for a while.

"Yeah, Hope said legally it's brilliant. If either group ever goes to trial, instant reasonable doubt."

Which I suppose also means if *I* ever go to trial for it, I'll have a defense. Not that I'd use it. I have no problem with what I did. I can't imagine any man or woman who cares about someone sending me to prison.

Nothing but the car bombing and the death of poor, crooked, and disgraced Senator Kelly has been on the news for the last twenty-four hours.

If only the world knew the full truth about what a piece of shit he was.

Luckily, we don't watch the news all that much in the house. Lilly's sort of strict about screen time for Chance. The times when the television is on, it's usually tuned to something kid-appropriate.

After Chance goes to bed, I finally have a moment to ask her about her day.

"Nothing exciting, what with me being confined to the house and all."

I suffer some guilt over that. How exactly can I explain she doesn't have to worry anymore? I kinda figured I wouldn't have to, that Mara would call Lilly to tell her the good news.

"Come here."

I pull her to me so she's straddling my lap and run my hands over her ass. I'm about to suggest Lilly come ride my cock in the hot tub when her phone pings.

She reaches over to grab it and slides out of my lap.

I use the time to check my own messages.

She gasps, pulling my attention to her.

"What?"

"Is this...was this...*you?*" She turns the phone my way and there's a full-screen article about the bombing. Compete with photos of the charred and still-smoking Mercedes.

I shift from laid-back-at-home dad to cold, lethal biker, give her a blank stare and shrug.

"Z?" she demands.

"Could have been anyone. Two separate groups claimed responsibility."

"But, Z—"

I launch myself at her, pushing her back against the couch cushions and press my finger to her lips. "Don't ask questions I can't answer, Lilly. Don't force me to lie to you."

"Z." She wraps her arms around my neck, pulling me down so she can whisper in my ear. "I can't have anything happen to you. I can't lose you."

I pull back and stroke my thumb over her cheek. "If something ever happens to me, you and Chance will always be taken care of."

"I don't *want* to be taken care of." She frowns and struggles to push me off her. "I want *you*. With us. In our lives. Every day."

"And I will be."

"What should I do?"

"Nothing. Trial's over. You won't be testifying. Now or ever."

A tear slides down her cheek.

"He got what was coming to him. Don't shed any tears over that piece of shit."

"I'm not," she protests. "I'm scared for *you*."

"Look at me." I grip her arms and give her a shake. "This is who I am. What I do. The risks I take. You're going to be my wife. You take me as I am."

"Z," she cries, her hands slide into my hair, tears stream down her cheeks as I lock her in my arms.

"You're mine. I protect you, Lilly. Always."

She kisses my chest and nods. "Thank you."

I run my hands over her back. "And I'll punish anyone who hurts you."

CHAPTER FORTY-SIX

Lilly

THE NEXT MORNING, MY PULSE RACES WHEN I REMEMBER WHAT HAPPENED.

The man who ruined my life is *dead*, murdered by the man who turned my life upside down in the best ways possible and gave me everything I never knew I needed.

Z's confession. His massive declaration of his love and commitment. To me. To our family. The risk he took to protect me.

I'm scared because I don't know what I'll do if I lose him. But I have to trust him.

After breakfast, I still can't stop thinking about it. I'm staring out at the pool, not really seeing anything. Ruminating over the last few years.

Z's hands settle on my shoulders "Come on, let's go out for a ride today."

We bring Chance next door and he excitedly runs inside to play with Alexa and Carter. I'm not sure Alexa's as thrilled to lose all of her Uncle Carter's attention, but Heidi assures us it's fine.

"Oh, let me go change," I say as Z heads for the garage.

He sweeps his gaze over my outfit and nods.

I hurry upstairs and dig through my closet. I've been dying to wear these for a while now but between rotten weather and hiding out in the house, we haven't gone riding lately.

"What'cha got there?" he asks.

He's leaning against the door frame, watching me with amusement as I zip up the tall black leather boots I bought specifically for riding with him. "These are okay, right?" I ask.

He walks over and kneels down to inspect them, wrapping one hand around my ankle and resting my foot against his leg. "They're fine." He plays with the triple-wrapped strap and buckle wound around my ankle.

"They're decorative. They come off." I lean down to unbuckle one. "If you're worried about—"

"Yeah, looks sexy as fuck, but I don't want it getting caught in anything."

I take them off and end up wrapping one around my wrist and holding out my arm for him to buckle it. "Even sexier." He motions for me to give him the second one. "I definitely like this."

I blink at him and look down at the scars on my arms, shifting the leather to cover them up. He stops me with a hand over mine.

"That's not what I meant at all."

Before I even realize what he's doing, he hooks his fingers in both straps and yanks my arms over my head. I gasp in surprise as he slides his other hand up my ribcage over my breast, flicking his thumb over my nipple. Trapped, I squirm and dance on my toes.

"*This* is where my mind went," he rasps against my ear.

He releases me and slips his arm around my waist, pulling me closer. "Don't ever be ashamed about anything, Lilly. Those scars are as beautiful as the rest of you."

"They show everyone I'm weak."

He wraps his other arm around me, holding tight like a python. His eyes capture mine as well. "They show everyone you're strong. A *survivor*. And they better not fuck with you."

"Is that what you think?"

"It's what I *know*."

I loop my arms around his neck, pulling him down. "Thank you," I whisper against his lips before kissing him.

His hands slide down, cupping my ass, and he gently squeezes. "Maybe we'll go for a ride later."

"We can't ask Heidi to watch Chance just to come over here and fuck."

"Why not?"

Exasperated, but laughing, I push him back. I glance down at my wrists. The happiness drains out of me. "I thought about covering them with tattoos or something. Full forearm sleeves. I'm not sure I'm brave enough."

He picks up my arm and runs his rough fingers over the inside, tickling me. "What about Wonder Woman style wrist cuffs?"

"I was thinking flowers, but wrist armor might be interesting."

"I know a good artist if you want to talk to him and have him draw up some sketches."

Before it had only been an idea, something I played around with in the back of my mind. But now I'm warming up to it for real. A way of saying goodbye to my past and embracing my new life on many different levels.

"I'll have to think of something."

He holds out his hand. "Let's take that ride."

CHAPTER FORTY-SEVEN

Lilly

Family day is just as Z said it would be. Members bring their wives and kids to the clubhouse. The back of the clubhouse has a large concrete patio, several grills, and lots of tables and chairs scattered around to accommodate everyone.

Chance has been playing with one of Bricks' kids most of the morning. Caleb's older than Chance, but patient. Still, with so many people around, Chance doesn't stray too far from me.

Most of Z's upstate brothers have gravitated toward each other. Others are off in the woods, playing paint ball. Another reason I was glad Chance didn't want to stray too far.

Hope drops down in the chair next to me with Grace in her arms. Chance leans over the chair and watches her sleeping.

"Gonna be a ladies man like his dad," Stash says. "Look how cute."

Z comes up behind me and runs his fingers through my hair. "Rock and I are already making our father-in-law plans."

"No, we're not," Rock answers from the grill. "Knock that shit off."

Z and Hope shake with laughter.

"I don't see a lot of dating in Grace's future," I whisper to Hope.

"Tell me about it."

Alexa toddles over to Murphy who scoops her up. "She won't be alone," Murphy mutters.

"We should get our well water tested." Rav leans back and props his booted feet on the table. "Too many pregnancies lately."

Someone throws and actually hits Rav in the side of the head with a piece of tomato. "Get your feet off the table, dipshit," Wrath orders.

"Every time you say that, you just remind everyone of how dumb you are," Murphy says.

Stash nods vigorously. "You'll never knock a girl up if you think *water* is the way to do it."

"The kids are a little young for the birds and the bees talk, no?" I laugh and jokingly cover Chance's ears, which makes him swat at my hands. Realistically, I know this conversation's going right over his head.

"Actually," Sparky starts to say.

Inwardly, I cringe. Nothing useful ever comes out of a man's mouth after the word "actually."

Sparky flails his hands in the air and jumps out of his chair a few times before continuing. Kind of the way Chance does when he's really excited about something.

"I mean," he continues after he has our attention. "Queen bees mate with up to twenty other dude bees their first time! And the bee dudes, aw man, their dicks explode and fall off when she's had her fill. The dude bees die, and she keeps all their sperm. It's so totally radical."

"Talk about a socialist matriarchy," Heidi mutters, sparking off a fit of giggles for Hope and Charlotte.

No words...I have *no words*. I squeeze my eyes shut and howl with laughter. When I finally open my eyes, through the haze of hysterical laughter-tears, I see conversation around us has come to a halt. All the brothers are staring at Sparky.

"What?" Sparky shrugs and sits back down. "It's different."

"I think what Sparky's trying to say," Dex explains, "is people use 'birds and bees' as a cutesy euphemism for teaching kids about sex and that in the case of *the bees*, it's actually *horrifying* if you apply it to human sex." Dex sits back and nods. "That's great. Thanks for sharing, Professor Pot Plant."

Ignoring him, or maybe he didn't even hear him, Sparky leaps out of his chair again and jumps up, waving his hand in the air. "Boss! Boss! Can we get some beehives?"

Chuckling, Rock raises his glass and tips it in Sparky's direction. "Whatever you want, brother."

"Bro, bees are a lot of work," Teller says not unkindly. "You'd have to actually leave the basement more than once a season."

"What if I keep 'em close to the house?" Sparky asks. He waves his hand in the air. "Like by the basement exit?"

Hope raises her hand. "Uh, have I ever mentioned my deathly fear of bees?"

Sparky gives her sad puppy eyes. "Oh no." His face brightens and I brace myself for whatever he's about to say. "The best cure for apiphobia would be probably be flooding. Lots and lots of exposure to bees, First Lady."

She turns to Rock, who shakes his head.

Besides the wild things that fly out of his mouth, I have the feeling Sparky comes up with and discards a lot of ideas. But the brothers are kind and humor his eccentricities. Okay, *kind* is probably stretching it.

"Thank fuck some of the others went for a ride," Teller mutters. He squeezes Charlotte's hip. "I'm regretting not joining them."

"No honey for you when I get my bees, you fuckwad," Sparky says.

"Everything okay at Crystal Ball?" Z asks Dex.

Dex leans forward. "I miss you, bro. Christ, some of them are a pain in the ass. I caught Annie charging an extra twenty for hand jobs in the back and had to fire her."

"I knew she wouldn't last long," Z says.

"Wait, you actively discourage that?" I ask.

They both stare at me. "We're not running a whorehouse," Dex says. "They get caught hustling for anything more than a lap dance, they're out. We haven't had an issue in a while now."

I shrug. "When I danced, the owners didn't care. Made it unsafe for all of us because customers didn't know what to expect. Which girls to proposition and which ones would kick them in the nuts if they tried."

Stash leans forward, suddenly interested in our conversation again. "I'm guessing you were the second one?"

"Watch yourself," Z warns.

"Yes. Officially they said it wasn't allowed and like an idiot, I believed it."

"That's why Salvatore's went out of business," Z winks at me.

"These fuckers know what to expect in our place," Dex growls.

"I meant, maybe the *girls* don't know you're serious. If she danced someplace before that told her one thing when they hired her but looked the other way…maybe she didn't know."

Dex tilts his head and studies me. "I had no idea you danced."

"Long, long time ago." I glance at Z, hoping he's not annoyed I brought it up.

Dex runs his hand over his chin and flicks his gaze to Z then faces me. "We've kicked around the idea of a manager for the girls for a while now."

Z slips a possessive arm around my shoulders. "Yeah, what's your point?"

"You have experience, plus you're a success story. Went to school and landed a job way outside the life. Be a good role model for them."

My stomach churns. "I hardly think I'm a role model for anyone."

"My old lady has plenty to keep her busy, bro." Z's statement comes out more like a threat.

A threat Dex seems to sense because he backs off and holds up his hands. "No offense. Just a suggestion."

I narrow my eyes and glare at Z, not sure I like him speaking for me. What does he expect? That I'll never work again? I'm not sure I could do that.

Z

Fucking Dex. I love that motherfucker, but I could throat-punch him right now.

The conversation goes on around us but eventually Lilly gets up and goes inside. I follow her to our room and shut the door behind us.

"You all right?"

She spins, long hair flying around her. "What do you expect from me, Z?"

She's pissed. About what, I'm not sure. "What do you mean?"

"The way you shut Dex down when he suggested I work at Crystal Ball. Don't you think that's my decision? Or do you not want me working on your turf?"

Huh? My head's throbbing trying to figure out what's happening here. "No. I thought you…I don't know, I thought you'd be insulted."

She places her hands on her hips. "Why would I be insulted?"

Where did I go wrong? "Uh, because you left that behind to do something more important?" Not that I want to bring up bad stuff for her, but I'm not sure how else to explain my reasoning. "I thought now that the sick fucker was gone and…I don't know…I assumed eventually you'd want to go back to working in government."

"Oh." Her shoulders drop and the anger melts off her face. "Really? You'd be okay with that?"

"If that's what you want to do, yeah. Why?"

She shakes her head. "You don't want me home catering to your every need?" It's almost said in a teasing way, but I sense she genuinely wants to know.

My mouth twitches. "Yeah, if that's what sets your heart on fire, I'm down for it. But I can't see you being happy doing that for the rest of your life."

"I don't know if I could, I mean *he* was an extreme example, but certainly not the only one. Government is full of sexist jerks. Even if the culture is shifting and changing a bit right now…it's so ingrained in everything."

"Then, they need more people like you, don't you think? Help keep that change going."

"Wow." She sighs. "You surprise me all the time, you know that?"

"Why?"

She shakes off the question. "Even though it's trendy to talk about it, that's all it is—*talk*. Men don't give up power easily. Eventually there will be a backlash and I don't know if I want to be there for it when it happens."

"Babe, those kind of men gotta die eventually."

She bursts out laughing. "I really love you."

"I want you to be happy."

"I am happy." She glances down. "Let me get used to being your old lady and all that entails."

"You're already good there."

"Let's worry about our wedding. Then, I'll figure out what kind of career I want to have next."

A streak of possession thunders through my veins. A desire to do anything and everything to make sure she's always safe and happy. And I really like hearing her say our wedding's on her mind. "Anything you want."

CHAPTER FORTY-EIGHT

Z

As family day winds down and darkness creeps over the sky, Lilly yawns. Rock and Hope left hours ago. Wrath and Trinity disappeared to their room. Murphy's still here, helping me keep the guys in check. I'm not sure where Teller disappeared to.

"You ready to head home?" I ask Lilly.

The party will turn rowdier. Hell, it already is. The guys built a huge bonfire. Soon, girls will start arriving by the carload to party with the brothers. Seen this and done it so many times over my life. All I want to do is go home with Lilly and Chance.

With Chance asleep in my arms, I walk them out to the parking lot. "I'm going to finish up here. Talk to Rooster, and then I'll be home," I promise Lilly.

"Ooo, stop," she says.

"What, why?"

She lifts her chin toward the mountains where they sky's slowly fading from purple to pink to orange. "I want to take a picture of you holding Chance asleep like that with the sunset behind you. So adorably perfect."

"It'll probably come out too dark."

"Shush. Stand there and flex those dad muscles." She laughs as she holds her phone out, framing the photo the way she wants. "Damn, you're one fine looking man," she mutters.

I never get tired of her saying that.

"Turn toward me a little," she calls out.

I press my forehead against Chance's hair. "You had to pick now to be all cute, didn't you?" He drools on my shirt in answer.

"Perfect!" Lilly says. "One more."

She uses the flash this time, nearly blinding me in the process.

Gravel crunches and engines roar into the parking lot. Again, I'm blinded, but this time by headlights.

Shielding my eyes and turning Chance away from the glare, I scowl at the intruders. "Who the fuck is that?" I growl.

Lilly's relaxed, happy smile fades as she studies the cars. "Z?" Her feet move faster over the gravel. "What's going on?"

I recognize the officer who steps out of the first car. One of the two who stopped by to hassle us after Malone's burned down. "What can I do for you?" I call out, hoping this is nothing more than another annoying social call.

Something about their demeanor and the fact that *two* cars showed up sends dread spiraling into my gut.

"Angus Frazier?"

Fuck me.

"What's going on?" Murphy calls from the front door. As soon as he realizes it's the cops, he joins me. "What the fuck are they doing here?"

"I don't know."

"Sir, this doesn't concern you, go back inside," the first officer orders.

Not likely. Murphy crosses his arms over his chest and widens his stance, making it clear he's not leaving.

Three other officers step out. All of them with their hands too close to their weapons for my taste. I curl my body around Chance and shift him away from the officers.

"Miss are you the child's mother?" the officer asks.

Lilly glares at him defiantly. "What's going on?" She doesn't bother answering the question.

"Miss, I need you to take the child and step away."

Lilly's visibly trembling when she turns back to me, her scared eyes asking what she should do.

I have to get them out of here.

"Here, take him." I hand Chance over. "I'll handle this."

As soon as Lilly steps away, three of the officers swarm on me. "Get down! Get on the fucking ground!"

When I don't go down fast enough, one of them kicks the back of my right knee, sending me to the ground.

"What the fuck?" My jeans don't do much to stop the gravel from digging into my knees.

"Down! Down on the ground!"

The commotion wakes Chance and it only takes him a few seconds to start screaming. "Daddy! No!"

Fuck, this isn't what I ever wanted for my son.

Or Lilly.

Still kicking and screaming, Chance reaches for me as Lilly opens the car door. "Z, what do I—"

"Go home. Tell Rock what happened. He'll know who to call," I answer as calmly as possible. The last thing I want to do is scare her or Chance any more than they already are.

"Shut up!" one of the cops shouts. "Head down. Arms over your head!"

I watch Lilly wrestle Chance into his car seat, powerless to do a damn thing. Four fucking cops standing around and no one bothers to help her.

Fucking assholes.

"Back off," Murphy snarls.

The cop who'd kicked me slugs Murphy in the gut. "Since you're so worried about your brother, why don't you join us, Mr. O'Callaghan."

Great, they know Murphy too. This can't be good. Are they here for me specifically or the whole damn club?

Murphy takes harder hits for fun. From skilled fighters. He's not intimidated by the rogue cop's punch. He sneers in the cop's face. "For what?"

"Interfering with an officer."

"Easy, Allan," one of the other officers warns.

This is a fucking nightmare. My son's hysterical. Lilly's shaking and unable to move. This whole clusterfuck is blocking her car, so she can't leave.

Fuck, I promised her everything would be okay. How'd they even know about the bombing? A mess like this might send Lilly running right back to California.

I look up and catch Lilly's eye. "It's okay," I mouth to her. "I love you."

"I love you too." She pulls her shoulders back and lightly touches the mermaid around her neck.

Some sort of signal?

"Stronger together," she says just loud enough for me to hear with all the noise around us.

Her way of telling me she's not going anywhere.

Behind us, more brothers come out of the clubhouse.

"Prez?" Rooster calls out.

"Go back inside," I order over my shoulder. "I've got this." Fuck knows I don't need these asshole cops getting trigger happy with my family in the crossfire.

"You heard your *prez*," one of the cops sneers. "Walk away, *bro*."

"Fuck you, pig!" Sparky yells. "Get the fuck off our property."

God bless you, Sparky, but shut the fuck up.

"Is someone planning to tell me what this is about?" I ask.

The first cop shoves a piece of paper in my face. "We have a warrant for your arrest, Mr. Frazier."

Z and Lilly's story continues in
Zero Apologies (Lost Kings MC #14)

ZERO APOLOGIES

Zero and Lilly, Part 3 (Lost Kings MC #14)

One by one, the lies have been unraveled.
I've shed blood to protect Lilly. To protect our family.
I'd do it again and again as long as it means she's safe.
It's time to marry her, cherish her, and spend the rest of our lives together.
We were so close to our happy ending.
Then chaos swept it away.
The road ahead remains unknown.
Loyalty, honor, brotherhood.
Kings forever, forever Kings.
I'll never betray my club.
Even if it means losing everything.

ALSO BY AUTUMN JONES LAKE

Slow Burn (Lost Kings MC #1)
Corrupting Cinderella (Lost Kings MC #2)
Three Kings, One Night (Lost Kings MC #2.5)
Strength from Loyalty (Lost Kings MC #3)
Tattered on my Sleeve (Lost Kings MC #4)
White Heat (Lost Kings MC #5)
Between Embers (Lost Kings MC #5.5)
More Than Miles (Lost Kings MC #6)
White Knuckles (Lost Kings MC #7)
Beyond Reckless (Lost Kings MC #8)
Beyond Reason (Lost Kings MC #9)
One Empire Night (Lost Kings MC #9.5)
After Burn (Lost Kings MC #10)
After Glow (Lost Kings MC #11)
Zero Hour (Lost Kings MC #11.5)
Zero Tolerance (Lost Kings MC #12)
Zero Regret (Lost Kings MC #13)
Zero Apologies (Lost Kings MC #14)
Stand Alones in the LOKI world
Bullets & Bonfires
Warnings & Wildfires
Cards of Love: Knight of Swords